LET ME FLY

—〜—

SABRA WALDFOGEL

2018

Let Me Fly by Sabra Waldfogel

Cover Design: Laura Klynstra/EbookLaunch
Interior Design: Ampersand Book Interiors
Author Photograph: Megan Dobratz

978-0-9913964-0-5—Ebook number
978-0-9913964-1-2—Print book number

Sabra Waldfogel, Publisher
WWW.SABRAWALDFOGEL.COM

Published in Minneapolis, Minnesota

For Joel and Mary, who fed us when we most needed it

TABLE OF CONTENTS

PART 1

—↜—

WAR'S END, 1865

1 | THE BUREAU AGENT

THE WAR WAS over, but it wasn't, Adelaide thought, as she gazed out the window of the carriage. It was still strange to remind her former slave Zeke, pressed into coachman's service, to take the southerly route to Cartersville instead of the familiar few miles north to the county seat. The Union Army had cut its swath through northern Georgia twice—on Sherman's March to the Sea, when the crops were burned in the fields and the sheds, and on Sheridan's path, when the towns were set to the torch. On a warm day, like today, the smell of char and the taste of ash lingered in the air, a ghostly reminder under the tang of pine trees and the perfume of late-blooming magnolia.

Adelaide thought of life before the war with a pang. She said to Rachel, "Do you remember the pony cart, when we were girls?"

"Yes," Rachel said, but her attention was elsewhere.

"You drove me all the way to Cassville. Mr. Stockton teased you about being the new coachman."

Rachel nodded. "Your mother sold that pony," she said. "Sold him because she knew I loved him."

"What was his name?"

"Brownie. Little brown horse for a little brown gal."

Before the war Adelaide and Rachel had been mistress and slave, but the Emancipation Proclamation had forced them into a new connection as half-sisters. The return of Adelaide's husband Henry from the war disturbed their peace, and now Rachel was distant and uneasy with her again. As she was with Rachel.

Adelaide asked, "Do you think there will be coffee in town?"

"Maybe," Rachel said, in the same distracted tone. "If the Union Army brought some." The Federals, in the form of the 138th Infantry Regiment, United States Colored Troops, had encamped in Cass County since Lee's surrender.

Adelaide tried to tease her sister. "If they'll sell it to us." But Rachel didn't respond, and Adelaide again stared out the window. Despite the warmth, the September sun had an autumnal slant. The cotton fields on either side of the road had withered, hard hit by the lack of rain earlier in the season. Instead of the gangs of slaves who used to pick the cotton, lone figures—stooped, their faces covered against the sun—moved slowly amongst the plants, dragging the cotton sacks behind them. No one looked up as the carriage passed. Adelaide knew why. They were white folks, ruined planters who now worked their own land, and they were ashamed.

"Town" had always meant Cassville, the thriving county seat, which boasted a fine brick courthouse, four hotels, two colleges—one for men, the other for women, which Adelaide had attended as a girl—and a newspaper, the *Standard*. Now

Cassville was ruined, the railroad tracks destroyed, the hotels and stores burnt to a cinder, the colleges abandoned. Cass County's business had moved to Cartersville, a smaller and humbler place.

Cartersville's main street, rutted with the red Piedmont mud that never froze, did not boast. On it sat the general store, the lettered sign on its window chipped and fading, and next to it was the cotton brokerage, a ramshackle wooden building where slaves had been sold before the war. Two churches, one Methodist and one Baptist, anchored the other buildings, and across the street from the Methodist church stood the saloon, where an unsteady man lingered on the steps, regarding a dog that slept at his feet.

Freed slaves, dressed in the ragged clothes of their former servitude, packed the sidewalk and spilled into the street. They numbered several dozen. Some were men alone and others women with children, the toddlers clinging to their skirts, the babies in arms fussing and crying. The sight of black people without homes and without work was hardly new in Cass County. Since the Proclamation, freed men and women had left their masters to find families torn apart by slavery, to look for work elsewhere, and to roam the countryside to prove to themselves that they were free to come and go. But they rarely crowded together like this, and Adelaide wondered what had drawn them.

Zeke stopped the carriage before the general store and handed Adelaide out. He hesitated, wondering whether to show Rachel the same courtesy. Rachel said, "It's all right, Zeke, I can manage by myself," and she gathered her skirt to step into the mud.

The general store smelled of dust and cornmeal stored too long. The shelves were nearly empty. Behind the counter stood a stranger, a man thinned and paled by four years of privation. He said to Adelaide, "Haven't seen you here before, ma'am."

Adelaide introduced herself and debated how to introduce Rachel. But Rachel walked to the counter, her head raised and her hand extended, and introduced herself as "Miss Rachel Mannheim."

The storekeeper stared. He said to Adelaide, "You shouldn't let your servant sass like that."

"It isn't sass. She's a free woman, isn't she?" Adelaide said.

The door opened, and a woman entered, wearing a dress and bonnet that had faded with the war. It was Adelaide's friend Aggie, whose husband, Cat, Cassville's only lawyer, had lost his life at the Battle of the Wilderness. Aggie had remarried in a rush to a planter named Everett, whose fifteen slaves had freed themselves the moment they learned of the Proclamation. Now her bright hair had gone mousy with a diet of cornpone, and her pretty hands were red with doing the wash. Like all the planter families of the county, she was glad to gossip that that Sherman and Sheridan had spared Adelaide's place because her husband Henry was a Union man and she herself was too fond of Lincoln's Proclamation.

"Adelaide!" she said. "What brings you to town?"

"We hoped for coffee, now that the blockade's been lifted."

Aggie said, "Nothing to be had, and not a dollar to be had to buy it, either."

"Did you see that crowd down the street? All those—" Adelaide hesitated. The pre-war epithets were mean words, as her friend Sarah liked to say, and doubly mean if your half-sister were listening. "People," she said.

"Didn't you hear? It's the Freedmen's Bureau," Aggie said. "First they sent us a *colored* regiment, and now they set up an agency to encourage those lazy, ignorant, no-good"—she glared at Rachel—"*people* to roam the countryside and turn against us."

Rachel said quietly, "Ma'am, I hear the Bureau helps the freedmen find work, and assures them fair wages, and sets up schools for the children."

Aggie laughed derisively. "Maybe they'll hire you, Adelaide. With that school you run for those children who should be in the fields, picking cotton."

Adelaide flushed. During the war, she had begun to teach the children of her former slaves to read and write. She had never intended to run a school for black children, but the word had spread, and now the children of former slaves came from all over Cass County to attend. She said, "Perhaps they'll be better laborers if they can read a contract."

Aggie shook her head and flounced into the street, a remnant of the belle she had been before the war. Adelaide and Rachel followed her. Adelaide said ruefully, "No coffee, and not much of a welcome, either."

Rachel glanced down the street. "No surprise, is it?"

Two men stood on the rickety steps of the saloon. They were hatless and unshaven, and they wore their disheveled hair even longer than General Lee's or General Forrest's. Their clothes bagged on their thin frames. They descended to the street with an unsteady gait.

They were the Turner boys, Ben Junior and Pierce, sons of the most respected man in the county, Colonel Turner, who had fought in the Mexican War and who had organized Cass

County's Confederate regiment. They had enlisted on the day after the news of Fort Sumter arrived, and they had fought a hard and bloody four-year war.

Ben and Pierce had never been good at applying themselves—they had expected to live a life of plantation leisure—but they had come back unable to settle themselves to anything. The Turner place needed attention, but they didn't farm or try to hire labor to oversee. They didn't go to Atlanta, as so many ruined planter sons did, although they boasted that they'd like to go west. They spent their days in idleness at the saloon.

In a loud voice, Pierce said, "Ben, it's Miss Adelaide. She hasn't come to see us since we came home. Let's go to pay our respects."

"She don't think we're good enough," Ben said. "Do you, Miss Adelaide?" Pierce had always been the meaner of the two. In their childhood, he had often pulled Adelaide's hair as hard as he could and laughed when the tears came.

Adelaide ignored them.

From the direction of the encampment marched a single Union soldier, his rifle slung over his shoulder, his cap at a military angle, his brass buttons brightly polished, a man on Army business. Above the blue coat, his face was the color that slave owners used to call medium brown.

The 138th Infantry had arrived in Cass County just after the war ended, and it remained there to keep the peace. As its soldiers marched through Cartersville, the former slaves greeted them with smiles and cheers. The men and women of the ruined planter class watched, their faces pale with disgust, muttering that "those people" couldn't be soldiers.

When the black Union soldier came within a few feet of Aggie, she stopped in the middle of the sidewalk, where even her diminished skirt filled the narrow path. "Let me pass," she said.

He halted. He put his hand to his cap, half in salute, half in greeting. He said politely, "Begging your pardon, ma'am, but there's room for both of us."

"Get out of my way."

He didn't drop his eyes or lower his voice. "Ma'am, I don't believe I'm in your way."

"Get into the street where you belong and let me pass."

"I have as much right to the sidewalk as anyone," he said.

Aggie's voice rose. "Do you mean to insult me?"

"No insult meant, ma'am," said the soldier.

Aggie raised her voice. "This man is insulting me!"

Adelaide reached for Aggie's sleeve. "Aggie, stop it," she said.

Aggie shook her off. Her voice went shrill. "Insult! Outrage!"

Pierce ran across the street and Ben followed him. Pierce gave the black soldier a rough shove and the man shoved back. Pierce grabbed one of the black soldier's arms and Ben yanked on the other. The soldier tried to pull free. "Let me go."

Both of them dragged the soldier by his arms. Pierce said, "Nigger, into the street with you."

The soldier protested. "Here on Army business! Got as much right to the sidewalk as anyone!"

Pierce cried out, "Insult a white woman, will you? Outrage a white woman?"

The black people outside the Freedmen's Bureau office fell silent, and their faces went dull and dark. Adelaide had seen that look many times, the look of a furious slave who would take his or her revenge. Sometime. Somewhere. But not here, and not now.

The soldier struggled in the Turner brothers' grasp. "Damn you, you dirty Rebs!" he said.

The former slaves watched. Adelaide felt Aggie's scorn, and she felt Rachel's eyes on her, pressing her. She thought, *I can entertain the Union Army, I can teach the children of former slaves to read, and I don't know if I can raise my voice for a black Union soldier who is a stranger.*

She cried out, "Pierce! Stop it!"

Pierce twisted to look at her, and his expression chilled her. *I don't care if I die,* it said, *or if you do.* The war had damaged him more than she knew.

A voice rang out and the waiting crowd parted as the Red Sea parted for Moses. In a voice used to command, the man called, "What's the trouble here?"

He was hatless, his hair black and unruly, his skin white but weather-beaten. He wore an officer's insignia on the sleeve of his blue coat, and he was muscular and broad-shouldered within it. The man had deep-set eyes and a mobile mouth; before the war he must have been quick to smile. Now he looked drawn, as though he had heard plenty of trouble today and expected more.

"What in God's name is this?" he asked.

Pierce kept his hold on the black soldier. "This man insulted a white lady."

Adelaide pulled herself to her full height and said, "He did not. She insisted he walk in the gutter to let her pass, and he refused."

The Union man said, "I'm Captain Lewis Hart of the 138th Infantry, U.S.C.T., recently appointed to the Freedmen's Bureau. Who are all of you?"

Pierce threw Adelaide a venomous look. "Ask her! The nigger teacher, come to town with her nigger sister!"

—✺—

A FEW DAYS later, Adelaide sat alone on the porch, glad of the shade against the September sun, listening to the sound of horses' hooves on the gravel of the driveway. She felt Rachel's absence. Rachel had excused herself about an hour before. "Promised Henry I'd go over the ledgers," she said. Rachel had managed the plantation's business since her emancipation, but the real reason for her unease wasn't the ledgers. It was Henry, and the way he had come between them again.

Adelaide had become accustomed to the sight of strangers. Every ragged Confederate soldier who passed through the county stopped here, hoping for a meal and a place to sleep, and every freed slave did the same. But the two men who approached wore the blue coats of the Union Army.

One of the Union soldiers was Captain Hart, who was very nearly a stranger. The other was not.

He had been newly free when he left, so eager to follow the Union Army that he threatened to run away until his cousin Charlie shamed him into saying a proper goodbye. Adelaide recalled the day he departed, standing tall as he imagined a soldier should, the brass buttons on his new coat polished brightly to gleam in the sun. Now he was truly a soldier, his shoulders back, his expression impassive, his hand resting lightly on the sidearm buckled at his hip.

He was the only Kaltenbach slave who had ever run away, and the only slave that her softhearted husband Henry had ever whipped.

"Freddy," she said.

He drew himself even taller. He said sharply, "Sergeant Frederick Bailey of the 138th Infantry, U. S. Colored Troops."

Adelaide said slowly, "You're greatly changed."

He gave her the kind of appraising look that would have gotten him punished before the war. He replied slowly, "Ma'am, so are you." He turned to Hart. "Shall I introduce you to Mrs. Kaltenbach?"

"We've met, although we weren't properly introduced," Hart said.

"I met two Union officers during General Sherman's invasion of Georgia," Adelaide said. "I don't mind an introduction during an altercation in the street." She asked, "What brings you here, Captain Hart? Is it Army business?"

"No, business of the Freedmen's Bureau."

"What interest does the Bureau have in us?" Adelaide said.

"I've heard that you run a school for the former slaves. I hoped I might see it."

She flushed. "As you heard in Cartersville."

"I hear a kinder report from the freedmen. They all praise you for teaching their children." His eyes rested on her. They were a deep, melancholy brown.

She rose. "When General Sherman's scouts came to us in '64, we entertained them," she said. "They liked what they saw, because after they reported, Sherman himself spared us."

"Why, ma'am?" asked Hart.

"Because of the school."

—⁓—

ADELAIDE LED HART and Bailey to the side yard, where a group of black children, ranging from little ones to nearly grown, clustered under the great live oak. They watched as their teacher, a white girl only a little older than themselves, sketched letters in the hard-packed red dirt with a stick.

"Are there no slates?" Hart asked.

"Not enough," Adelaide said. "And none to get, since the effects of the blockade are still with us."

Hart nodded.

Adelaide asked the young teacher, "Sally, how are they getting on?"

Sally laughed. "I'll let them show you." She laid a gentle hand on the shoulder of a boy who gripped a stick like a slate pencil.

He cried, "Miss Adelaide! Just learned how to write my name!" He carefully formed the letters J-I-M in the dirt. "That's me," he said proudly. "That's my name!"

Hart bent to look. "That's fine, young man." He straightened and addressed the children, who giggled and squirmed with pleasure in his attention. "What about the rest of you?"

"I can write!" "Me too!" "Let me show you!"

Both Hart and Bailey watched as the children took up their sticks to write their names. Hart smiled, and even Bailey's severe expression softened a little. Hart said, "It makes me proud to see this."

He stood close enough that Adelaide could smell a faint whiff of his scent. The odor startled her. It was the same as her husband Henry's, eau de cologne from Germany. She shook off the thought and introduced Hart to the teacher. "This is Miss Sally Hardin, who schools the beginners."

"She looks so young," Hart said.

"I'm fourteen," Sally said. "My mother taught me my letters when I was just a little girl."

"Her mother, Mrs. Sarah Hardin, also teaches," Adelaide said.

"And my brother, Johnny. He's sixteen. He teaches the big boys because they mind him."

"Where is your father?"

Adelaide said swiftly, "He died during the war."

"Was he a soldier?" Hart asked.

"No," Sally said matter-of-factly. "He was a bushwhacker, and the Union Army shot him."

"I'm sorry to hear it," Hart said.

"We aren't. He was rough to all of us. Especially Ma."

"I'm sorrier to hear that."

"Mrs. Hardin is inside the schoolhouse. You'll meet her," Adelaide said, hushing Sally.

"It's new," Hart said, surprised at the sight of the freshly painted boards.

"My people—they were my people before the war—insisted on building it for the children. Before they rebuilt their own houses."

Through the oilpaper windows came the sound of children reading, one at a time. "We share the spellers, too," Adelaide said. Inside, black children of all ages crowded the benches. Some wore clean, whole clothes and shoes, but others were ragged and barefoot. "We serve them midday dinner, all of them." She sighed. "We're the only place in the county that has food to spare."

At the edge of a bench, two little boys, one black, the other white, bent their heads to read from the speller together. "Do you teach white children, too?" Hart asked in surprise.

Adelaide said, "That's my son, Matthew. He won't be separated from his best friend, Ben. They insist on doing everything together."

At the sight of the blue coats, the room fell into a hush. Adelaide said, "Mrs. Hardin, children, Captain Hart of the Freedmen's Bureau has come to visit us."

Sarah nodded politely and turned to her class. "Children, will you sing for them?" Sarah's favorite songs were hymns, and she led the children in one that Adelaide knew she favored, "Nearer, My God, to Thee." Hart listened politely, but his face wore an expression of discomfort. Adelaide wondered if he were an unbeliever. Well, as a Jew, she was an unbeliever, too, at least to the minds of the Baptists and Methodists of Cass County.

Hart applauded when the children finished. *A courteous unbeliever*, Adelaide thought. "A fine performance!" the captain was saying. "Will you sing with me?" he asked, and began the hymn that every Union soldier held dear. They all knew it—every free black child did—and he didn't seem to mind that some of them sang the words to "John Brown's Body" instead of "The Battle Hymn of the Republic."

Freddy—she would have to remind herself to call him Sergeant Bailey—did not alter his severe expression. He'd been fragile and sensitive as a boy. He must have suffered a worse war than Captain Hart, and been toughened by it.

Outside again, Hart said to Adelaide, "You do the Bureau's work."

"I never intended to," she said. "Only to help those who need it."

"We should help you."

"Slates and spellers, Captain Hart," she said.

"At the least," he replied.

She asked both men, "Can I offer you some refreshment?"

"Thank you, Mrs. Kaltenbach, but I'd like to visit my cousin," Sergeant Bailey said.

"Mr. Charles Mannheim?" she asked.

Bailey smiled for the first time. "As he now calls himself. If you don't mind."

"Not at all," Adelaide said. She held out her hand to her former slave, offering him the courtesy of an equal, and he took it.

Adelaide led Hart back to the main house. He hesitated at the door, and touched the *mezuzah* in surprise. He said, "I didn't expect to find a Jewish house in northern Georgia."

Not an unbeliever after all. "You're an Israelite," she said.

"Perhaps there's a synagogue nearby, as well."

"No, not nearby." She thought of Mickve Israel in Savannah. Like the city itself, the synagogue was in bad repair.

"What will you do for the New Year?" he asked.

She thought of the half-truth she had told as a girl, when her friends asked her how she prayed, if she didn't go to Sunday meeting. "We'll pray at home," she said.

"May I join you?" His eyes, which had looked so saddened in Cartersville, were alight.

She felt a warmth that she didn't trust. It disturbed her to feel it, as the earth must be disturbed when the cottonseeds burst and the seedlings broke through the dirt. "Come to us for Sabbath dinner this Friday night."

— ✍ —

ADELAIDE WAS ON her way to the kitchen when she overheard the voices in the study through the open door. She lingered to listen.

She heard Rachel say, "Have we heard from the bank in London? The Bank of England, where their cotton money had been deposited after its run through the blockade and its sale in Liverpool.

"There's no trouble to get the money to a bank in New York," Henry replied. "But they can't send it to a bank in the South, not until we recover from the war."

"Folks want the money we promised them." Even before freedom, everyone on the place knew about the fortune made by running the cotton through the blockade. Once free, the former slaves had insisted on getting paid. Adelaide and Rachel had let them decide whether they wanted wages or a share of the crop, and they had chosen some of each. Rachel kept a careful record of what was owed. Now that the war was over, everyone who had waited for the money wanted to feel it in their hands.

Henry sighed. "I know."

"How is the crop?" Rachel asked.

"Charlie's worried," Henry said. "We haven't had enough rain this year."

"How many bales?" Rachel answered. The crop, always the crop, their first and most enduring connection.

"He always says, 'Won't know until it's ginned and baled.'"

Adelaide could hear Rachel chuckle. "We did all right last year," she said.

"I know, beloved."

Adelaide thought, *I've renounced him. We agreed, in the friendliest way, to a marriage in name only.* She was a different woman from the jealous wife and angry sister who had manipulated her father into threatening to sell Rachel and sending Henry off to war. But at Henry's easy endearment, she felt jealousy rise in her again. Sarah had entreated her to ask God to help her and she had tried. She had struggled against herself in her own unbelieving way, too. The feelings returned like malaria's chill and fever. The symptoms might ebb and flow, but the disease remained.

Please God, she thought, *let him go to Atlanta like he promised, and let her leave with him.*

She stepped into the room, tapping on the door to warn them. "Do I intrude?" she asked. She felt a blush rise to her cheeks and chastened herself for it. Had she really heard the endearment?

Henry turned. "No, not at all. What is it, Adelaide?" He now found it easy to be tender with her.

"The Freedmen's Bureau agent came to visit us. Captain Hart. He wanted to see the school."

"What did he say?" Rachel asked.

"That he hoped the Bureau could help us." She thought of the gleam in Hart's dark eyes. Before either of them could interrupt, she said, "He's an Israelite. I invited him here for Sabbath dinner."

—⌇—

RACHEL NO LONGER helped Adelaide dress. Instead, it was Sarah who fastened the little pearl buttons and smoothed the skirt as Adelaide readied herself for Captain Hart's visit. "You look pretty," Sarah said, taking undiluted pleasure in Adelaide's appearance.

"It fit better before the war." Adelaide twisted to get a view of her backside. She was thinner. "Suited me better, too."

"Do you want me to brush your hair?"

Rachel's task. She still missed Rachel's touch. "No, it's all right, I'll manage by myself."

She brushed the unruly curls and fastened them with hairpins. Her hair looked makeshift. Well, that was right, wasn't it? Everything in their lives was makeshift.

She picked up the wedding ring that she had removed when she began to work in the garden and at the washtub, when she wanted to spare the diamonds and sapphires in their rose-gold setting. Now her hands had swollen and coarsened and the ring no longer fit, no matter how much she forced it. She sighed, smoothed her hair and her skirt once more, and walked resolutely down the stairs to wait for her guest.

—⁓—

CAPTAIN HART STOOD on the steps in the waning evening light of September. He wasn't in uniform, but he was neat in the well-fitted coat that made his shoulders look broader, and he had tried to subdue his hair with pomade. Beside him was Sergeant Bailey, dressed in uniform, armed with his Springfield rifle.

"Welcome, both of you," Adelaide said.

Bailey said politely, "Begging your pardon, ma'am, but I won't be joining you." He had modeled his diction and his accent on the Yankees who commanded him during the war.

She insisted, "You're welcome at our table."

"I didn't come to visit. I came to escort Captain Hart."

"Sergeant Bailey insists on being my guard," the captain explained.

Alarmed, she asked Hart, "Is there trouble?"

He said lightly, "Better to prevent it than to walk into it. Isn't that so, Sergeant Bailey?"

Bailey said, "Yes, sir." To Adelaide, he said, "Excuse me, ma'am."

"As you wish," she said.

—⁓—

ADELAIDE HAD KINDLED a fire in the parlor's hearth and lit candles against the dusk. The low light hid the age in the furniture and the wear in the curtains that had been new before the war. Hart smiled at the sight of the room. "This is the loveliest room I've seen in Cass County," he said. "Perhaps the loveliest room in northern Georgia."

Henry, who stood in the hallway, said, "My wife was awfully persuasive when your fellows came through with General Sherman."

"Captain Hart, this is my husband, who was also a captain in the Confederate Army," Adelaide said.

Henry explained, "I don't claim the distinction. Plain Mr. Kaltenbach is fine with me."

Rachel stepped into the hallway. She had smoothed her hair into a roll at the back of her neck and she wore her best dress, the plaid taffeta she had made just before they had their portraits taken a few months ago. The bright colors—red and yellow together, so pretty against her skin—glowed in the candlelight.

Adelaide said, "Captain Hart, this is Miss Rachel Mannheim." She forced herself to say the rest, which he already knew. Hadn't he heard Pierce Turner's taunt in Cartersville? "My sister."

"How do you do, Miss Mannheim?" Hart asked. He took Rachel's hand as though he were unfazed at offering a courtesy to a woman who used to be a slave.

It still gave Adelaide a pang to see a man treat Rachel with interest.

"Where is your little boy?" Hart asked Adelaide.

Surprised, she answered, "He eats his dinner in the kitchen with Mrs. Hardin and the servants."

"Not with you?" It was Captain Hart's turn to be surprised.

"They dote on him and make such a fuss over him," she said. "Ah, Captain Hart, you're looking askance at me. Do Yankees eat their dinner surrounded by their children?"

"Some of us do," he said, smiling.

"And do you think the less of us Southerners for doing otherwise?"

The smile faded. "I miss my family, Mrs. Kaltenbach," he said. "I wish they were here to surround me."

"We'll have to be a poor substitute," she said. "Come with me," she said, and she guided her guest into the dining room.

She had polished the silver candlesticks and set out the best dishes, the gold-rimmed plates that sparkled when the candles flickered. The Sabbath tablecloth, little used during the war, still looked bright and fresh.

Hart hesitated as he surveyed the room. He sighed. "I've had so few Sabbaths since the war began."

Adelaide lit the candles, and as she murmured the prayer, she covered her eyes as her mother had once done, the only moment of peace in her week. She thought of her mother, dead now, so bitter and unhappy all her life in Cass County, so patently hopeful for Adelaide's marriage into the grand Pereira family of Charleston, so disappointed that her daughter had to marry Henry, because no one else would have her. Adelaide uncovered her eyes and blinked at the flames. She wondered what her mother would have thought of Captain Lewis Hart.

As she sat after the prayer, Adelaide said to him, "During the war Miss Mannheim saved our silver candlesticks from a thief."

Hart asked, "Was he a Union soldier?"

"No. A bushwhacker." She smiled at her husband. "Henry, will you say the blessing over the wine?"

Henry said, "I'll try. I'm rusty." He nodded to Hart. "Like you, I had few Sabbaths during the war."

"We'll forgive you," Hart said, also smiling.

She had meant to give Henry the host's prerogative, but as he stumbled through the prayer he barely remembered, she thought, *It was mean of me, even though I didn't intend it.*

As with so many things in their marriage these days.

She uncovered the *hallah* plate to reveal cornbread. "Our staff of life, today and every day," she said.

Rachel laughed. "On Passover we were ready to bless cornpone as the bread of affliction."

Hart laughed, too. "Surely not!"

Adelaide addressed herself to Hart. "Would you bless our bread?"

Hart nodded. He raised the plate and spoke the blessing in a strong, clear voice. Adelaide thought, *He knows his Hebrew prayers pretty well for an unbeliever.*

Hart was a good guest. He praised the food, his appetite even better than his blessing. He was careful in his conversation, avoiding the subjects of politics and cotton farming, enquiring after their original homes, and after their parents and their children. He was from Cincinnati, he told them, but he was born in Germany. "When did you leave?" Henry asked. "Was it after the Revolution?"

Hart said carefully, "Yes."

"Forty-Eighters." It took very little to make Henry tipsy, and now his face flushed and his eyes glittered. *Why do I carp so?* Adelaide thought. *It's unfair.*

Hart said, "Many are, in Cincinnati." *He's tactful,* Adelaide realized. *Another unfair thought.* She asked, "Captain Hart, what is the family you miss in Ohio? Are you married?"

He smiled. "No wife or child, but my parents live there, as do my brothers and sisters, with plenty of nieces and nephews to spoil. My family has made Hanukkah a festival to rival Christmas. We surround the children with a heap of toys!"

Henry said, "We always have Christmas for the people on the place. A festive meal and a frolic, with music and dancing. Rachel, how will we manage this year, without our best fiddler?"

"His brothers are still in the county," Rachel answered. "They're fine fiddlers, too."

Henry asked Hart, "How is the Bureau faring in its efforts to help the freedmen?"

Their guest sighed, and the light of pleasure dimmed in his face. More sharply than she intended, Adelaide said, "Henry, it's the Sabbath. Let the man rest from his labors."

"No, it's all right, Mrs. Kaltenbach," Hart said. "Every planter in the county has the same question, and few ask it so politely."

Henry said, "We worry daily how the freedmen will find work, and how we'll compensate them."

"That's the nub of it," Hart agreed.

Rachel said, "We have the land, we have the work, we have the laborers, but we don't have the money."

Hart looked surprised to hear a woman, a former slave, voice an opinion formed by her thoughtful reading of the commercial pages of the *Atlanta Weekly Intelligencer*. Nevertheless, he said, "That's the problem throughout the South. No capital."

Rachel said, "We'll have to pay them in shares of the crop. I don't like it much."

"They deserve better. I wish I could give them a substantial sum to help them start their lives in freedom," Henry said.

Adelaide shook her head. "Even if you could, it's not prudent."

Henry said stubbornly, "It's a matter of fairness."

In a moment he would tell Hart about the money they had made in running the cotton through the blockade in '63 and '64, trapped in a London bank as long as the South's economy lay in ruins. If she had no stomach for tale-telling, she had none for a spat, either. She tamped down her irritation and asked, as sweetly as she could manage, if their guest would care for dessert.

Hart laughed. "Mr. Kaltenbach, I'd like to hear your views on the freedmen, and yours as well, Miss Mannheim. But Mrs. Kaltenbach's offer is much more agreeable."

"There's brandy, too," Adelaide said. "From before the war."

Hart laughed again. "Even more agreeable."

— ❧ —

AFTER THE BRANDY was drunk, she saw Hart out, and they stood on the covered porch together in the piney quiet of a late fall night.

"Thank you for the pleasantest evening I've had since I came to Cass County," Hart said. "One of the pleasantest since I left Cincinnati, in fact."

"My husband has the best of intentions," Adelaide said. "Not always the most practical, though."

"We need men like him. To truly change the South and put the war to rest."

He took her hand in his, a gesture a little too intimate for a Sabbath guest, and said to her, "And people like you. You don't realize how courageous you are to run the school."

At his kindness, tears rose to her eyes. She had drunk too much, brandy as well as the claret at dinner. "You're the only one to say so."

"We need your noble effort."

"Thank you."

He pressed her hand. "No, thank you, for a lovely reminder of what the Sabbath should be." He turned, walked down the stairs, and went in search of Sergeant Bailey for the long, dark, dangerous ride back to Cartersville.

She raised her hand to her face. The faintest scent of eau de cologne lingered there, and she pressed her palm to her nose to breathe it in.

2 | Love with Honor

RACHEL LEANED AGAINST the doorframe of her daughter Eliza's room in the house where she had lived since Emancipation. It had been Henry's first house on the Kaltenbach place, before he married Adelaide, and it had been the house where Rachel and Henry confessed and later consummated their love for one another. She watched as Henry put Eliza to bed, the candlelight flickering over his face as he bent down to pull the coverlet to her chin.

"Where's your dolly?" he asked.

Rachel had made Eliza a corncob doll, and it spent every night in the crook of her arm. "Under the covers," Eliza said, laughing. "Read me a story, Daddy."

"What should I read to you, *liebchen*?" he asked her.

"Read about the little girl and the big bad wolf!"

Rachel chided her. "Eliza, honey, are you sure you want such a story before you sleep?"

Eliza said, "If the wolf come here, Daddy shoot him like he shot the Yankees."

As Henry took the book from the shelf, he smiled and said to Rachel, "She has such faith in me."

Eliza and her father had a pure pleasure in one another. Rachel listened as Henry read the familiar words. This was the first story that Adelaide had read to her when they were girls together, and the first story that she had read by herself.

Eliza's eyes began to droop and then to close, and soon she was asleep. Henry shut the book, bent over his sleeping daughter, and kissed her brow. "Sleep well, liebchen," he whispered. Watching him, Rachel softened with a tenderness she rarely felt these days.

But she was sharp with him as they prepared for bed. As she unpinned her hair, she said, "Wish you wouldn't watch."

"But it's so lovely to watch you undo your tresses."

Too sharply, she said, "I ain't Rapunzel in that book of tales you read to Eliza."

"It's beautiful. Like a halo."

She ran her hands through it and let it loose, dense and springy and soft to the touch. Unpinned, it went wild, and she wasn't sure that she would ever love it. She quickly bound it in a scarf and hid it away.

She pulled off her petticoat and took off her chemise. Adelaide, upset to learn that Rachel slept in her chemise—that she slept in her skin on a warm summer night—had given her a nightdress that buttoned to the neck, itchy with lace. It made Rachel think of Adelaide dressed for her wifely duty, and Rachel couldn't wear it. She stuffed it into the bottom drawer of her bureau, out of sight, but it still bothered her. Adelaide haunted her in her own house, in her own bedroom, summoned by a length of lawn and a yard of lace.

Henry was already in bed, and as always with her, he dispensed with his nightshirt. "You keep me warmer than any blanket," he told her, fondly. Now he held out his bare arms to her. "Come to bed, beloved," he said.

She was slow to blow out the candle. When he was gone, she had written to him, alight with love for him. Now that he was home, in her bed every night, she felt a disloyal irritation. When he first returned, she relished that they took their leisure to touch and taste each other again, and she didn't begrudge the effort it took to rouse him. But it had become more and more difficult to bring him to pleasure, and last week, for the first time, he said ruefully, "It's all right, beloved. We'll try again later."

She was weary. She felt like any wife, a woman whose back ached after a day of baking bread, standing at the washtub, and tending to fussing children, for whom the act of love was another chore to be got through so she could sleep.

She pushed the thought away. She blew out the candle and slipped under the covers to embrace him. On a moonless night, their room was profoundly dark, and they had to find each other by touch. She miscalculated and her foot met the shin of his wounded leg. He flinched.

"Are you all right, sugar?" she asked, contritely.

"It's nothing," he said.

She tried to nestle against him. He'd always been a slight man, but his shoulder had once pillowed her. Not tonight. She couldn't find a place to settle that gave comfort.

29

He stroked her hair and turned to kiss her. In the dark, he miscalculated, too, catching the corner of her mouth rather than getting her full on the lips.

She felt the flicker of irritation, and then the flash of guilt. She moved carefully, not wanting any more misses, and kissed him on the lips as passionately as she'd ever kissed him.

Her hands found him, his ticklish ribs—he laughed softly as she touched him there—and the bones of his shoulders and his spine. She kept searching until she found the soft hair on his belly and the flesh below it. He sighed with pleasure. She found the softest part of him, and as she touched him there, he remained soft under her hand.

Now she was worried that it would be like the last time. She asked, "What can I do for you, sugar?"

"Don't fret," he said. His hand lay on her hip. He said, "Sweet and slow. Remember, like our first time together? Sweet and slow."

He touched her, her breast, her belly, and between her legs, but the pleasure was dimmed by the memory and the worry.

"You're fretting," he said gently. "What is it?"

She felt a ghostly itch around her wrists and at her throat. "Nothing," she whispered. "Don't stop."

He started again, and touched her until her breath came in a rush and her back arched. "That's better," he murmured, and he rolled atop her and pressed himself inside her. She breathed out a sigh of relief that was deeper than pleasure. *It's all right,* she thought. *He's all right.* Reassured, she moved her hips to help him, and he caught her rhythm.

But it wasn't. She felt him fading inside her. Weariness washed over her, more profound than a spasm of love. She couldn't bear to think that it would be like last time. She gripped him hard, willing him to rouse as she rolled her hips to encourage it. She moved until her back ached. She moved until she wished for sleep more than she wished for release.

Finally, he swelled inside her and answered the call of her fervor. The spasm came, his cry muffled, not wanting to disturb the sleeping child in the next room. She hadn't come and she didn't care. The relief was deeper than any spasm.

⌐⌐

RACHEL AND ELIZA walked through the pine trees, bound for Sunday meeting. The weather remained unusually warm and summery for fall, and the morning sunlight poured over the cotton fields like butter. The last of the season's bees hummed contentedly as they flew by. The air smelled of the sweetness of ripening apples and harvested clover.

The people on the Mannheim place had started their meeting back in slavery days, when their Jewish master didn't mind how they worshipped. The little pine church was newly whitewashed, and the sun made the oilpaper windows glow. The smell of soap—some of it homemade with ashes and lye, some of it perfumed with rosewater—floated from the crowd. People who sweated all week wanted to smell sweet on the Lord's Day.

The men clustered around the preacher, Judah Benjamin, who wore the suit he kept carefully for meeting. With him stood his sons Asa and Adam, dark-skinned and muscular like all the Benjamins, and talented fiddlers like their absent brother Micah, gone to find his fortune in freedom. Charlie, who now called himself Mannheim, put his hand on Adam's shoulder, and his neighbors Luke Hutchens and Davey Edgefield, formerly slaves on the Kaltenbach place, laughed at something Rachel couldn't hear.

Instead she joined the women. Becky Mannheim, Charlie's wife, greeted her with a polite "how do," but she bent down to hug Eliza and to croon, "Give me a little sugar." Salley Edgefield smiled and turned her attention to the baby clasped in her arms, who tried to pull her kerchief from her head. Salley's sister, Harriet, recently married to Asa, stood with her hands over her belly, cradling the child due in a few months. In their midst was eighteen-year-old Lucy Payne, who attended Adelaide's school. Lucy wore a newly made white dress that turned her skin the color of honey. With a pang, Rachel recognized the fine cotton fabric. It was one of Adelaide's dresses, made over.

Salley put her hand on Lucy's arm. "Miss Lucy, tell Miss Rachel."

"Don't want to spoil the surprise," Lucy said, smiling. Her resemblance to her father was striking. Catullus Payne, her former master, had been Henry's friend and fellow officer, but he had never recognized his slave daughter, even though his features were obvious on her face.

The reverend Judah called to the cheery, gossiping throng, "Come in and settle down, everyone. Got news! Want to tell it before we get underway."

As people settled onto the benches, the hubbub diminished to a whisper. "News." "What news?" "Good news or bad news?"

Judah stood before the congregation. He said, "Adam, Lucy, join me."

Adam caught Lucy by the hand and led her to the pulpit. People began to smile. Adam and Lucy had been courting for months. "Good news," they began to murmur.

"They getting married," Judah said. "My son Adam and Miss Lucy Payne. Tell them!"

Lucy said shyly, "Intend to get married. Wait until harvest done."

Adam, so much taller and broader than Lucy, enfolded her in his ambition to love and cherish and protect his wife in marriage, and she leaned against him, full of hope that they would be together in love forever.

"We have a wedding and a frolic at Christmastime," Adam said.

Judah added, "All of you, come rejoice with us!"

People rose from the benches, clapping their hands and calling out, "Happy day!"

The little church filled with elation. A wedding was always an occasion for joy, but a wedding since freedom was even better, since it was right in the eyes of the law. This wedding, the first since the end of the war, was even greater cause for celebration.

Rachel thought of the day she had explained the Emancipation Proclamation to the people on the Kaltenbach place. "Free to get married," she had told them, and all of them had savored the thought of a marriage that no master could tear asunder, of wedding vows that no longer said, "Until death or distance do us part."

Rachel felt more than a pang. She felt envy so powerful that it made her sick to her stomach. She would never receive the joy of her friends by telling them about her wedding. She would never stand with Henry before the people who knew them and cared about them. She would never face the man of God, neither reverend nor rabbi, to promise love until death. She felt the tears rise in her throat, and she sat through the service and the sermon wretched with the effort of trying to look cheerful.

After the service, she pulled on Eliza's hand, not wanting to linger. When Charlie came up, wanting to fuss over her daughter, he saw the look on Rachel's face. He patted Eliza's cheek. "You go on with your Aunt Becky." To Becky, he said, "I'll be along. Want to say a word to Miss Rachel."

Rachel said, "You can talk to me right here."

Charlie said, "We talk private, you and I." She recognized the voice, the driver's voice, knowing when someone on his field gang was too upset and heartsick to work. "Come along."

They took the familiar path through the trees, and he led her into the little grove where he had conducted plantation business that needed privacy in slavery times. The two of them, she and Charlie, had stood here to talk about selling the cotton through the blockade and managing the newly free just after the Proclamation. She would always associate the smell of pine resin with slavery's secrets.

He said, "You mighty bothered about something."

"Ain't really your business, Charlie." The words came out too angry.

"Saw how ashy you got when Adam and Lucy stand up."

"Why would that trouble me?" Much too angry.

He put his hand on her arm, his calming gesture. "I worry about you. We all do. You and Marse Henry."

If I stay angry, she thought, *I might not cry.* "That really ain't your business."

With sadness, he said, "Rachel, there's nothing but sorrow in it, and it trouble me. It trouble all of us."

"It's my trouble. Whether you disapprove it or not."

"I wish—we all wish—you would find a good man to marry you."

The tears came in a storm not to be stopped, and she covered her face in shame. He enfolded her in his arms. "Oh, sugar," he said, as he had said so long ago, when they loved each other and hoped to spend their lives together.

Regret surged through her like a flood through a dry creek bed. She thought of herself, married to Charlie, happy with him, their children gathered about them. She raised her tearstained face and said, "Should have married you when I had the chance."

He gently let her go and stepped back, out of reach. He was too kind to remind her that she had pushed him away, wanting to hurt herself first before Mordecai Mannheim, master to them both, had the chance to destroy their happiness. He said, "Rachel, you know I love you the way a brother loves a sister, and I always will. But that's over and done."

She turned her face away. "Go on," she said. "Leave me alone."

He turned to walk through the pines, back to his house and his wife and his family, and she wept, unable to stop herself, until her eyes were raw.

— ᔐ —

AFTER HER TALK with Charlie, Rachel was sharp with Henry and sharper if he tried to cajole her. Even though she rued it, she was sharp with Eliza. She was sharpest with Adelaide, and so afraid of what she might say that she couldn't stay in the same room with her sister.

She felt odd wherever she sat in the Kaltenbach house, whether it was in the study with Henry, on the porch with Adelaide, or in the kitchen with Minnie. She was no longer a slave, but she wasn't properly a sister, either. And as much as Henry wished she were his wife, she was not.

One day, she wandered through the breezeway into the kitchen. As she stood in the doorway, her fists on her hips, Minnie looked up from the potato she was peeling and said, "You mighty out of sorts lately. Are you carrying?" Minnie was so small for a grown woman that strangers mistook her for a child, but her eyes were weary and owl-wise in her dark-skinned face.

She and Minnie had been slaves together, housekeeper and cook to Henry and Adelaide when they were Marse and Missus. Minnie had watched Rachel fall in love with Henry and had been midwife to their child. She had never approved of the connection, and she had never changed her mind.

"No. And it ain't your business, even if I was," Rachel said.

"Well, you can set down and stop glowering. I could use a hand."

Rachel sat and picked up a potato to peel. The kitchen was no longer her responsibility, but she felt shamed into helping Minnie. At moments like these, she felt as though slavery had never ended, as though it were a disease she'd suffer from all her life like the ague.

Minnie set down her paring knife. "You met that man from the Freedmen's Bureau, didn't you? Captain Hart?"

"Sat at the Sabbath table when he came for dinner," Rachel said.

"The Bureau. Do it find people?"

Rachel stopped peeling. "Find people?"

"Do you think the Bureau could find my husband?"

Minnie's husband, Kofi, had been sold away before the war to settle their master's gambling debt. Minnie had mourned his loss ever since, and had never even thought to remarry.

Rachel was ashamed to be shrill with Minnie. "Don't know about the Bureau. But there's someone else who might." She set down her own paring knife. "Lieutenant Randolph."

Randolph had been one of the Union scouts who told General Sherman to spare the Kaltenbach place. He had also scouted Rachel's deepest secret from her, her love for Henry, and she suspected that he could find Minnie's husband without any difficulty.

"Do he scout people, too?" Minnie asked.

"I reckon he could."

Minnie's somber face lit with hope. "Would you write to him!"

"Can't promise he'll be successful." She felt a pang at Minnie's faith in Randolph.

"Will you ask him to try?"

It was unfair to hurt Minnie for her own hurt. She pushed the sharpness away and said, "Yes."

—⚬—

THAT NIGHT, RACHEL woke alone in bed. She rose to find Henry before the cold hearth, wrapped in his dressing gown, sitting quietly in the darkness. He seemed forlorn, and her irritation dissolved as she knelt beside him. "What is it, sugar?" she asked, darkness making it easier to be sweet.

"It's almost Yom Kippur. A time for atonement."

"Didn't think there was a synagogue to go to."

"I want to atone for slavery."

"Slavery's over and done. President Lincoln saw to that."

It was too dark to see his face. All she had was the movement of his cheek under her hand, and his voice. "I want to do more," he said.

She thought of all the promises of the Emancipation Proclamation. She whispered, "What?"

"For you. And for everyone I held in bondage. Some restitution. Some recompense."

"Money?"

"It isn't enough," he admitted. "But it's a beginning."

She thought of Adam and Lucy, free to marry, and the happiness of everyone who loved them, glad to see it. She took her hand away, and sighed as she rose.

—◆—

THE NEXT MORNING, as she sat in the study with the ledger before her, she stared out the window at the September rain that halted the cotton harvest. When Henry came into the room, last night's sweetness fled and she was sharp again.

"Sit with me," he said, gesturing to the chairs before the hearth. She hadn't laid a fire—it wasn't chill enough—but she suddenly felt a yearning for one.

He said, "I've been thinking about this business of paying people."

"Freedom money," she said.

"I want to do more than that. I want to give all of you a substantial sum of money to start a life in freedom."

"How much?" she asked.

Resolutely, he said, "Five thousand dollars for every adult, and a thousand for every child."

She thought of so much money in her hands, five thousand silver dollars, too great a weight to carry. "That's a powerful sum of money."

"It's nothing against the money we made selling the cotton during the war."

"How do we get it to people?"

"We can give them accounts in their names. In London, or in New York."

"But they'll want it in their hands." She stretched out her own hands, wondering how many silver dollars she could cup there.

He took her hands and cradled them in his own. "That we can't do. Not yet. But we can promise it, and when there's a bank in Georgia again, they can have it for their own."

She felt her anger spike. "Ain't enough to have a paper that says you can have five thousand dollar sometime. People want the money now. They free, they work for it during the war, they want it now."

"I wish I could do that."

She thought of freedom's promises. Free to get paid. Free to marry. She pulled her hands away. "Don't matter if you repent of slavery," she said. "Not if you can't do the things to make it right."

"Oh, Rachel."

Trembling—was it anger, or upset?—she said, "Slavery's over. War's over. But nothing's changed enough to feel different."

"That isn't so."

"Ask Charlie, who want to buy land from you. Ask Luke, who want to work for you for wages. Ask me." She felt the salt in her throat. "Ask me what I want."

He put his arms around her, but it didn't comfort her. *He want me to hush,* she thought. *He don't want to hear it.* She squirmed away. "Not in the house," she said. Reluctantly, he released her.

There was a tap on the door. It was Adelaide, who looked thin and drawn. She had always been wiry, but she had lost flesh since Henry's return. It bothered Rachel to think that Adelaide, like herself, found it hard to eat when feeling burdened her.

"I know I intrude," Adelaide said, "but if you want to give our people a great sum of money, I think you should consult with me, too." She took them both in with a keen glance that made Rachel's cheeks go hot, and she said, "Henry, don't you know it's cruel to make a promise you can't keep?"

—❦—

RACHEL BROODED OVER the problem of getting money into the hands of newly freed people in a land without banks. Whenever she thought of money, she thought of her former master and father Mordecai Mannheim, who had passed his business sense to her. She didn't tell Henry that she planned to talk to Mordecai. Henry still remembered the bitterness of being in

Sabra Waldfogel

debt to Adelaide's father, which had been erased only by their good fortune during the blockade. If she mentioned that she wanted Mordecai's advice, Henry would try to dissuade her. She thought, *Henry ain't my master or my husband. He can't forbid me.* Seeing Mordecai would help Henry, but it would spite him, too. She should be ashamed to enjoy being spiteful, but she wasn't.

She took the familiar path through the pines to the Mannheim place. The old house, the pleasant four-up-and-down of her childhood servitude, had been destroyed by Sheridan's army, and Mordecai now lived in a hastily built one-story house made of pine, smaller than her own, with oilpaper instead of glass for windows. In the side yard, chickens pecked in the dirt, and behind the house were fields, half harvested of their cotton. Rachel wondered who worked the cotton fields and how Mordecai paid his people.

Mordecai's only remaining servant, old Ezra, answered the door. The war had aged Ezra badly, and he moved with the slow, painful gait of rheumatism. "I tell Marse Mannheim you here," he said, as though he were still the majordomo at a grander place.

Mordecai sat before the hearth in a rough-hewn pine chair. He had lost a great deal of flesh during the war   at the worst of it, just after his wife Rosa's death, his skin had fit him as badly as an elephant's—but he was looking a little fatter and redder in the face, more like his pre-war self. He motioned to the only other chair in the room. "Sit down," he said.

She looked around the room, less comfortable and kept less clean than her own, and she thought, *He come down in the world and I come up.*

41

He asked, "What brings you here? You haven't got a charity basket with you." After the first dreadful invasion, when Sherman burned the crops in the field, Adelaide had brought her father and Ezra food to live on, and he remembered that now.

"No, sir," Rachel said. It gave her pleasure to say "sir" like any free person. She would never call a white man "massa" again. "It's a matter of business."

"Business! What business? About selling your crop?"

"No, sir, although we hope to have a good crop to sell this year." She nodded toward the oilpaper window. "You've planted some cotton this year."

"A few acres."

"Who works for you?"

"Some hands who came through after the war. Said they used to live down near Macon." All of Mordecai's slaves had left in 1863 when the news of freedom swept through Cass County, after Henry had written in a frenzy to let Rachel know.

"How do you pay them?" she asked.

"Pay them? Ain't got a dime to pay them. Promised them a share of the crop, less expenses for food and furnish once we harvest the crop." He looked at her with the full force of his pre-war acquisitive eye. "Why? Do you have money to pay your people?"

"We have money," she said. "You know that, sir." Mordecai had introduced her to the captain who ran their cotton through the blockade to Liverpool. "It's in a bank in England, and we can't get our hands on it."

"Not in Georgia."

"Not until there are banks in Georgia again," she said.

"Well, there ain't. Not in Savannah, not in Augusta, not in Macon, and certainly not in Cass County. What's this about? Who wants cash to pay people? Don't you promise shares, like I do?"

She didn't want him to know about the freedom money. "We've promised everyone a share, and we kept the accounts throughout the war. We want to give them their money now."

"Is this some soft-headed scheme of Henry's?"

Despite all her irritation with Henry, she didn't like hearing Mordecai disrespect him. "He wants to help his people out. Give them a start, now that they're free."

Mordecai snorted. "He's as bad as the Bureau. Forty acres and a mule! Now there's a promise made to be broken."

What could she say? Henry couldn't keep his promises any more than the Bureau could. "The banks. Will they come back? Will there be a bank in Savannah again? Or in Macon?"

He shook his head. "Not there. Savannah's done. Atlanta, that's different. If anyplace in Georgia will come back, it will be Atlanta. I'd put my money on it." He glanced at her. "I thought you were going there. You and Henry."

He knew all the Kaltenbach business. Who told him? "Maybe. Haven't decided yet."

"I'll be settling there, once I get the crop in. Start anew. Make some money." He laughed. "Find a bank to put it in, once there is one."

"But not yet. So we can't get our money out of London and put it into people's hands in Cass County?"

"You can't. It ain't possible, in Georgia." He looked at her again with the beady eye she recalled so well from before the war, when he could sell her. "What about you? What's Henry going to do for you?"

"Don't believe that's your business, sir," she said, very sharp.

"Didn't you save his place for him? Don't deny it, I know it were you and not Adelaide. Didn't you factor his crop and make him a fortune? He's in your debt." He chortled at the thought.

"I ain't insisting that he pay it."

"Don't act the fool. You ain't a fool, not about money. He owes you. You decide what you want from him, and you get it."

—☙—

THE DAY OF Yom Kippur eve, Adelaide stood on her doorstep, and with reluctance, Rachel said, "Come in," wondering why she was there.

"Henry isn't the only one who feels like atoning," Adelaide said. As she held out a packet of brown paper, a rich and lovely smell arose from it. "A twist of coffee. And some honey cake to go with it."

Rachel didn't reach for the packet. "Where in the Lord's name did you get coffee?"

"It was a gift from Captain Hart."

Coffee, Rachel thought, *and flour, too, to bake that holiday cake.* Captain Hart must have become more familiar with Adelaide than she realized.

"Rachel, take it. Please. I know how much you've yearned for coffee."

Some promises might be kept. She took the proffered packet, and the cake, too. "Can I offer you some?"

"No, Matt and I have already eaten ourselves sick on it."

Rachel wondered if Henry had tasted the honey cake or not.

Adelaide asked, "May I sit with you? Just for a while?"

"All right." Rachel gestured toward the big pine table, where the top's expanse put a distance between them.

Adelaide looked around Rachel's house. "It's comfortable here," she said. "I wish I felt as comfortable in my own house." Rachel heard her wistfulness. Neither of them felt right in that house.

"Adelaide, what is it? You didn't come to wish me a happy holiday."

"Yom Kippur isn't happy. You know that."

Rachel leaned back in her chair and sighed.

Adelaide fidgeted, tapping her fingers on the table's edge, staring at the scars in the wood. She said, "Rachel, we can't go on like this."

"How do we go on?"

Adelaide met her sister's eyes. "I thought that you and Henry were leaving for Atlanta."

"So did I. But he wants to settle this business of the freedom money first."

"But he can't." She was matter-of-fact.

"Not until there's a bank in Atlanta to put the money in," she said.

"And when will that be? What do we say at the Seder? Next year in Jerusalem?"

"Sooner than that, I hope. But not soon."

Adelaide said, "You know that people are saying the most dreadful things about us."

"Yes, I've been to Cartersville, just like you have."

"Aggie came to see me, to let me know."

"Come to tell you, to hurt your feelings," Rachel said, with some heat. "What was it?"

"That Henry dishonors me with you." Adelaide hesitated.

"And what do she say about me?" Rachel asked.

"It's too mean to repeat."

"Did she call me his nigger whore?" Rachel asked.

Adelaide flinched. "It's a mean word, like Sarah says. And it's not even true."

"It's mean, but it's true enough. We both know it," Rachel said.

Slowly, reluctantly, Adelaide nodded.

Rachel said, "If I left, would it stop?"

"What do you think?"

Rachel felt her head begin to ache. "Go on home," she said. "Give your husband a little honey cake."

Adelaide rose. She shook her head. "When he comes to you, you give it to him," she said, and with a swish of her diminished dress, she walked out the door and down the steps.

Rachel sat unmoving at the table, the smell of honey cake and coffee tormenting her. Both were too precious to throw away. She thought of the freedom money, recalling the imagined weight of the silver in her hands, and suddenly she felt worse than she had for a long time. White men treated their wives with honor, but they paid their whores, whether in Confederate scrip, Union greenback, or silver dollars to cup in their hands.

—⁓—

THAT NIGHT, HENRY came to eat supper with her and Eliza. He brought wine, which he drank with the meal of roasted chicken and sweet potatoes, and they all shared the honey cake, which gave him a wistful look.

"It's just like my mother's," he said. "It takes me home, to my boyhood."

After the meal, he sat before the hearth, where the fire flickered. He gathered Eliza into his lap and she leaned against his chest. Rachel watched as he tightened his arms around his daughter, kissing the top of her head. His tenderness with Eliza brought back the raw feeling in Rachel's throat. Whatever her own connection with Henry, Eliza was his daughter.

When Eliza was abed and fast asleep, Henry said, "Come to bed, beloved."

"Don't want to say this in bed."

He looked at her with surprise. "What is it, beloved?"

She struggled to find the word. Relation? Connection? Circumstance? Shame? "Us."

He reached to stroke her cheek. "I know it isn't easy."

She closed her eyes, feeling the tenderness in his caress. She thought of Charlie's interference, disguised as concern. She thought of Miss Aggie and her meanness. She thought of Captain Hart, who had given her a knowing look at that Sabbath dinner, as though he saw this kind of dishonor every day. "It's too much like it was before the war," she said.

"Rachel, beloved, I promised you that I mean to honor you."

She drew back, shaking her head. She thought of Lucy, free to marry, and Adam, free to honor her before the law as well as before everyone they knew.

Henry reached to touch her, but she felt the tears start and the anger come over her like a fever. She cried out, "If you want to honor me, marry me!"

3 | Oath of Loyalty

THE SUN SLANTED through the oilpaper windows of the schoolhouse, but as Adelaide sat on the scholars' hard bench, she wrapped her shawl close against the morning chill in the unheated room. The children and the teachers were yet to arrive. She was alone.

She watched the oilpaper lighten as the sun rose, and she wished that she could stay here. Live here. Sleep here. Lying on the hard wooden bench, a blanket drawn over her for warmth, would feel easier than living in the house where Rachel was always present, her scent of woodsmoke and sassafras lingering in every room, a reminder of all the trouble with Henry.

Aggie's poisonous words echoed in her head. Adelaide recalled what she had said before the war, when her husband dishonored her with the slave who was Lucy's mother. "If I don't see it, it doesn't bother me." Adelaide understood the words afresh. *Send it away*, she thought. *I can't bear it any longer.*

Later that morning she sent for Henry and waited outside the schoolhouse as he limped slowly toward her. She had never seen the wound on his leg, and she wondered how well his flesh had healed. He smiled as he approached, but she could see the shadows under his eyes. "What is it, Adelaide?"

She kept her voice low. "I wanted to talk private, as Charlie puts it." She gestured toward the nearby pine grove, and she led him there. The pines released their spicy, resinous smell. The dried needles felt spongy underfoot, and the fallen cones crunched when she trod on them. A disturbed squirrel scrabbled up a tree trunk to chitter in agitation.

"What is it, Adelaide? The business of the place, or the school?" He tried to joke. "Don't tell me you want freedom money, too."

If she felt more forgiving—or more flirtatious—she would have put her hand on his arm. "No, not that. It's about us, Henry." She hurried the words. "We can't go on like this."

"It's not for much longer, Adelaide."

"No. No longer."

"I have business here. The tenants. The freedom money."

"You can manage that just as well in Atlanta as you can here." The squirrel scolded again, louder than before.

With regret, he said, "I can't. Not until I resolve this business of how to rent the land and pay our people."

Adelaide looked at her husband and tried to find the man she had liked when he courted her, the man she had willingly married, the man whose child she had borne, in this stranger's face. She stepped back. "If you have any feeling for me, spare me."

"Adelaide," he said, trying to placate her, and when he touched her arm, she shook it off.

"Do you know what our old friends in the county say about us?" Shame shadowed his face. "Don't speak of it."

She said, "Everyone in the county knows that you go to my sister as your wife. Everyone! They talk about it in the saloon in Cartersville. And you want to honor her!"

"I do."

"Then go to Atlanta, and take her with you."

"More than that."

"Don't be a fool, Henry. How?"

"I intend to marry her."

Henry's wartime letters had described the horror of battle, and he had been vivid about the impact of a bullet to the gut. Adelaide felt as though she had been gut-shot. "You're mad."

He grasped her wrist. "We can divorce," he said. "A Jewish divorce is an easy thing."

In a rage, she yanked her hand away. "A Southern divorce is not. Do you really want to go into the courthouse—wherever it is now, Cartersville or Floyd County—to sit in the courtroom, to tell the judge and jury and every spectator for miles around how you've been dishonoring me? To let every newspaper in Georgia tell the story, and spread our shame all over the South? To let every gossip in the former Confederacy lick her lips over our disgrace? That's what you're in for, if you divorce me. Do you want that?"

"No," he said, steely in the face of the damage he wrought. "But we can't go on as we have."

She could be steely, too. "Go to Atlanta. And take Rachel with you. Just go."

"Adelaide, I swear that I never intended to do this to you."

She put her hand over her belly again. Gut wounds were inoperable, she had read. They assured a slow and painful death. "I regret the day I married you," she said. "I should have married William Pereira. I knew what kind of scoundrel he was. And to think I trusted you! Lover to my servant, and father of her child. God help me. God help all of us."

He limped away and she sank to the ground, her head in her hands, until she felt a light hand on her shoulder. "Adelaide," said Sarah, who knelt beside her and brushed her cheek with a light hand. *She knows,* Adelaide thought. *But I can't bear it if she tells me to pray for the strength to forgive him. I can't manage it. I'll always be a disbelieving Israelite and Christian charity is beyond me.*

Sarah said, "Dry your tears, Adelaide. You have a visitor."

Without thinking, Adelaide wiped her face with her sleeve in the gesture she chided Rachel for, telling her that a free woman used a handkerchief. "Who is it?"

"It's Captain Hart."

He had made the hard hour's ride from Cartersville to see her. She would be wrong to send him back without a word. She took a ragged breath. "How do I look?" she asked Sarah.

Sarah laughed, a light and musical laugh that belied all the misery of her own marriage and the circumstances of her husband's death. "No worse than usual," she said, and she helped Adelaide to her feet.

He stood in the front yard, out of breath, his cap askew. He waved his arms and cried, "Good news, Mrs. Kaltenbach. I have good news!"

She put on the lady's polite mask. She even managed a little joke. "Captain Hart, what is it? Are you engaged to be married?"

He laughed but didn't blush. "No, I'm afraid not. It's good news from the Bureau." His face was alight. "It comes from General Tillson himself. The Bureau wants to fund your school, with help from the American Missionary Association. The Association can send you slates and spellers and anything else you need for the classroom. They can send warm clothes, too, if that will help. The Bureau can pay your teachers, the Hardins, and the Army can spare flour and cornmeal to feed your young scholars their midday dinner."

The faint scent of cologne came towards her, and she thought anew of Henry. *It is good news*, she thought, but she couldn't manage to smile or say so.

He reached for her hands and clasped them. She was too startled to pull away. "You look so downcast! I hoped it would cheer you," he said.

She forced herself to sound pleasant. "We'll have to learn the habit of cheer again. It's like peace. We aren't the least bit used to it."

"However I can help," he said, smiling.

Whatever the Bureau's power, she was sure that mending marriages was beyond it. She said, "Captain Hart, I'm very grateful for the Bureau's help, but it's unseemly of you to clasp my hands," and tried to disengage from his grasp.

He let her go gently, his fingers trailing over her roughened skin. "I apologize for being forward," he said, smiling, "but I won't apologize for being glad for you."

—⁓—

A FEW DAYS later, Adelaide sat wearily on the ground beneath the ancient live oak next to the school. The October sun slanted low over the cotton fields, and the breeze held a whiff of winter, the damp and cold that would wither the stalks in the fields after the cotton harvest. She pulled her shawl tightly around her.

Charlie approached her, his gait deliberate. His greeting was courteous. "Miss Adelaide, how are my young'uns doing?" He had dropped the old address of "Missus," but he was still uneasy calling her "Mrs. Kaltenbach." He compromised by using "Miss," as he'd address any grown woman.

She brightened. "Josey is a fine scholar. She could be a teacher herself someday. And Ben! Only four, but he reads already! I'm proud of them."

"So am I, ma'am." He hesitated. "May I speak to you on some business?"

She rose. "Of course, Charlie." It slipped out. It was hard to remember to call him "Mr. Mannheim." "What is it?"

"Do you recall, when Marse Henry get back from the war, that he talk to me about selling some land?"

"I do, Charlie." *He's going roundabout,* she thought. She wondered where he would end up.

"He tell me he want to sell me all of it—a hundred acres, stock, tools, seed—for a dollar. I said no. Ain't fair to him, or to you. Ain't right. I studied it a little and I found out what good cotton land go for. Thought I'd offer him a decent price. Went to talk to him about it."

"What did he say?"

"Wouldn't listen. He talk about how wrong slavery was, and how he want to make it right, and how he wish he could pay us our freedom money, but he can't, since there ain't a bank in Georgia to put it in."

She heard the frustration in Charlie's voice. "I know."

"We all know that a man can't buy anything, for any price, unless he has money or the promise of money to pay for it."

Forty acres and a mule, Adelaide thought. *The Bureau's promise.*

"But I have a notion, Miss Adelaide."

She had heard this before. He had "studied" it, in his words, and had come to a decision. She asked, "Don't it tire you, Charlie? Going roundabout?"

His face flickered, and Adelaide briefly saw the man beneath the servant's mask. "Wouldn't be seemly to say."

I've been a liar all my life, too, she thought. "Just go straight ahead."

"I'll try." His face flickered again. Like slavery's address, it was too deep a habit to relinquish. "I'd dearly love to get a sum of money so I can buy land from Marse Henry. But it has to wait, and the crop can't. If I have to work for a wage and a share for another year, I'll do it. I'd prefer to buy. You know that, ma'am."

"Straight ahead, Charlie."

With the greatest tact, he said, "Ma'am, I believe that when we sell the cotton this year, we don't have to run it to England to sell it there. Won't have to keep the money there. Sell it here for greenbacks. Cash in our hands, to use as we see fit."

She said thoughtfully, "To buy livestock, or provision, or tools." She looked up. Charlie's expression encouraged her. "To pay people."

He nodded and waited for the rest of it. She said, "Your wages and your shares since the Proclamation, or part of them."

He dared to say it. "Cash in my hands."

"To use as you see fit," she said.

"To buy land, maybe."

She nodded, and he said, "Won't sell the cotton for months. Won't have the money until then."

She saw the answer, like one of her own scholars, and she laughed with relief. "Charlie, my father always bought what he needed—land, tools, stock, provision"—*and slaves*, she thought, not wanting to say it to Charlie—"in the fall, and promised to pay when the crop was sold."

"Miss Adelaide, I believe you talk about debt."

She said ruefully, "Isn't every farmer in debt?"

"I ain't easy in my mind about it. But I reckon everyone who grows cotton carries a debt."

She was intent on helping him. "I think you'll find my husband more lenient about debt than my father was."

"Miss Adelaide, I believe you're right." He smiled. "Will you come with me, to speak to him?"

"No, you go by yourself. My husband doesn't think much of my opinion these days."

"That's a shame, ma'am." What was that look? Sympathy? Sadness? Charlie knew more than he would ever tell her. On the matter of her trouble with Henry, and with Rachel, he would not even go roundabout. He would stay silent.

—⁓—

THE NEWS OF Henry's bargain with his former slave traveled the county, but Henry, who didn't drink in the saloon, and

Adelaide, who didn't attend the church, were slow to hear how white and black, planters and former slaves, talked about it. A few weeks after Charlie came to her, Adelaide was surprised to find Colonel Turner at the door of the Kaltenbach plantation.

"Come in," she said, looking at his kindly face, which was lined and creased with the weight of war and the new burden of peace. He had always been sweet to her, asking after what she was reading and praising her for being intelligent. When she was a little girl, she had secretly wished that Benjamin Turner were her father.

"Is Captain Kaltenbach at home?" he asked.

"He's in the study." She led him there, where Rachel sat at the desk and Henry sat in the chair before it. Adelaide saw Turner's eyebrows rise at the sight of a black servant writing in her master's ledger.

Colonel Turner said, "Henry, I have some business to discuss." He turned to Adelaide. "Excuse us."

Henry said pleasantly, "The ladies take part in our business." Turner glanced at Rachel as he sat. He said, "I've heard that you want to sell some land to one of your people."

"That's true," Henry said. "What of it?"

Turner sighed, and the lines in his face seemed to deepen. "There's a lot of strong feeling in the county against it," he said. "From people who lost a great deal in the war. I'm not sure it's the wisest thing to do."

Henry's voice rose. "I held the man in bondage," he said. "It's a small thing to sell him a few acres for him to farm by himself."

"You understand—" And he looked at Adelaide, too. "That planters who lost their slaves—planters who can't get anyone to work a place—"

"What can be the harm in selling our most loyal servant a few acres of his own?" Adelaide said softly. "He stayed with us throughout the war and brought in our crop, much to our advantage. We owe him a debt of gratitude, if nothing else." She put a gentle hand on Colonel Turner's arm. "It's the least we can do to repay him for his loyalty."

Rachel shot her a surprised glance. Adelaide thought, *I can Br'er Rabbit, too. I learned it from you.*

"The war is just over, Henry," Turner said. "Let the ashes cool. Wait a little. Rent the land out for another year, and see how things stand. Then decide."

"I held the man in bondage," Henry repeated. "It's a small recompense to start him in freedom."

"I know it troubles you," Turner said, and his kindness broke through the clouds on his face. "I won't ask you to deny your conscience. Just to wait."

"It can't wait," Henry said stubbornly.

Turner rose. "You know how I feel about keeping the peace," he said, "but not everyone in the county feels the same way."

"Like your boys?" Henry asked.

Turner bent his head in regret.

"I'll do as I see fit," Henry said.

—⁓—

HENRY DREW UP the deed for Charlie and contracts for all of his tenants. The trip to Cartersville—to consult with the Bureau about the contracts, and to ask Captain Hart to witness the deed—became an outing. Luke harnessed the carriage for Adelaide and Rachel, and Charlie hitched his mule to a wagon, Henry on the seat beside him, Asa and Davey in the wagon bed. Asa joked with Davey, and their laughter drifted past, low and musical. Adelaide sat opposite Rachel in the carriage, where the air felt too warm, despite the open windows and the fall chill.

The talk and laughter from the wagon didn't stop—men could chatter, too—and in the silence in the carriage, it was doubly audible. She sought for something to say to Rachel that wouldn't bring a sharp response, or worse yet, silence. Schooled all her life in courtesy, she couldn't find it. She stared out the window.

She tried not to worry about Cartersville. She knew that Aggie gossiped about the Bureau's help, and speculated about her connection with Captain Hart. "Slates and spellers!" she could hear Aggie jeer. "Did they talk about slates and spellers when he visited them on their Sabbath?"

Adelaide thought of Captain Hart's face in the glow of the Sabbath candles as he recited the blessing over the bread. The ritual had erased the burden of the Bureau from his face. She had seen the man he had been before the war, the idealistic young Israelite who believed in freedom. He had fought a war for it, and now he had befriended her, making her a rebel to the other rebels in the South.

She wished she could tell Aggie that the slates and spellers were a matter of business. The rest was charity. Jews knew about that, too.

In Cartersville, the main street was nearly empty, unlike the early days of the Bureau, when the crowd of former slaves spilled from the building and extended down the street. Two white women, both of them strangers, gossiped outside the general store. A yellow hound slept outside the saloon, where horses were tethered. The Turner boys had loved and coddled their horses before the war, but these poor beasts were thin and spavined.

Luke helped both women from the carriage, and the men in the wagon jumped down. Henry was smiling. Adelaide thought, *Will he offer me his arm? Or will he offer it to Rachel?*

He did neither. Still smiling and joking, his former slaves flanked him. Adelaide said to Rachel, "Shall we?" and they trailed after the men to enter the ramshackle wooden building that housed the Bureau.

The room smelled of sweat and unwashed clothes, like her schoolhouse. During the war, Adelaide had gotten used to being dirty herself. She knew how much effort it took to heat enough water to fill a tub.

Everyone in the room, save herself and Henry and Captain Hart, was a former slave.

"Mr. Kaltenbach!" Hart said, smiling. He greeted Adelaide, Rachel, and Charlie, and asked to be introduced to Luke, Asa, and Davey.

Henry said, "I've come with my tenants so you can read their contracts, and I have special business with Mr. Mannheim. But we'll wait our turn."

A murmur went through the room at a white man who would defer to former slaves.

As they waited, Adelaide watched Hart, who listened as a ragged man told him about the planter he rented from, who had promised wages and hadn't paid them. "Hasn't even given us our provision," the man said.

His face grave, Hart said, "That isn't right. I'll visit him to investigate." As the man stood, Hart shook his hand, and the man was so startled he didn't protest.

When their turn came, Hart looked over the contracts with the tenants. "Half the crop, and you'll provide them with livestock, tools, seed, and provision as they need it, and not charge it against the crop. That's generous of you."

"Only fair," Henry murmured.

Hart addressed the three tenants. "Has Mr. Kaltenbach explained the contract to you? Do you understand what you're signing?"

"He read it to us, and let us ask questions, too," Luke said. "I know what I'm signing." Davey and Asa nodded in assent, and all three of them signed, proud that they could write their names.

Henry said, "Mr. Mannheim and I have come to a different agreement. He's buying a parcel of land from me. I've brought the deed and the note. Will you witness them?"

Hart read through it and asked Charlie, "Do you understand what this document says?"

"It says that Mr. Kaltenbach owns the land free and clear, and that he sells it to me, so I own it free and clear. And that I owe him a sum of money that I'll pay when my crop comes in," Charlie said.

Hart nodded. "Can you sign?"

With a smile, Charlie said, "I can manage to write that much," and he picked up the pen to sign his name. He gripped it laboriously, as though a pen demanded the strength of a hoe, and he signed his name with a look of fierce concentration on his face. Henry and Hart added their signatures—Henry in his neat

German script, and Hart in the scrawl of a man who signed his name many times in a day.

Hart handed the deed to Charlie. He said, "I believe you're the first black man in Cass County to own a piece of property. A cause for celebration!" and the small crowd that waited its turn clapped and cheered as though they were at a frolic.

"Where can I find the county clerk?" Henry asked.

"Mr. Humphreys?"

Adelaide asked, "Is he a hill country man?"

"I don't know," Hart said. "I believe he's set up shop in the saloon."

"I'll find him," Henry said.

Charlie said, "We all go with you."

"I'll go, too," Adelaide said quietly.

"Ma'am." It was Charlie again. "It ain't seemly—"

"Some people think it isn't seemly for a black man to buy a parcel of land," Adelaide replied. "Are they right?"

They walked down the street to the saloon, Henry, Adelaide, and Rachel in the midst of the five men. Henry pushed the door open, and they squeezed inside.

A blind obscured the window, and despite the sun, the place was as dark as dusk. It smelled of sawdust and whiskey. A scarred wooden counter ran the length of the room, and against it, two men leaned over their glasses.

Henry asked, "Is Mr. Humphreys here?"

One of the men turned. He was slight and pale, with the bowed legs of a hill man who had grown up eating little more than cornmeal. He said, "I'm Humphreys."

Henry said, "I just sold a parcel of land to this man." He gestured to Charlie, who knew better than to extend his hand. "We have a deed to file."

"You sold your land to a nigger?"

Henry flushed. "I sold my land to Mr. Mannheim."

"Damned if I'll file such a deed," Humphreys said.

Aggravated, Henry said, "Why not? Aren't you the county clerk?"

Humphreys replied, "I should tear that deed up."

"You'll do no such thing." Henry said, his color very high.

Adelaide pushed past her furious husband and said sweetly, "Mr. Humphreys!"

She knew him well. He had been a deserter during the war, whose farm faltered when his wife tried to run it. "How is Miss Mattie?" she asked. "And how are the children?"

Humphreys ducked his head, and Adelaide continued, in her best Lady Bountiful tone. I was glad to be able to help them during the war. And nurse your youngest, when he fell sick."

Humphreys didn't reply. Adelaide said, "Is it true that the courthouse will be built in Cartersville next year? So it can become the county seat?"

"Yes, ma'am." He sounded sullen.

"Then perhaps my husband should hold the deed for safe-keeping." She glanced at Henry. "Until the new courthouse is finished."

She could tell that Humphreys was torn between courtesy to the lady who saved his family from starvation and rage at the man who had given a former slave a better farm than he would ever own. In a strangled tone, he said, "As you like, ma'am."

They left the saloon in silence, but in the street, Adelaide whispered a word to Charlie. "Roundabout."

—◌—

A FEW DAYS later, as Adelaide and Sarah greeted the schoolchildren, Ben and Josey arrived, Charlie and Becky flanking then. Matt ran to Ben, shouting, "Why did your mama and daddy bring you to school today?"

"Hush," Charlie said. He gently shooed the children toward the schoolhouse door.

"Charlie? Becky? What is it?" Adelaide asked.

Charlie waited until Josey and Ben were safely inside. "The Turner brothers come by while Becky and I pick the crop," he said. "Don't do anything, just watch me, like they overseers in slavery times."

"Was there trouble?"

"Well, you know they carry guns, and I don't trust them when they ain't sober. Which they weren't."

"Have you talked to Captain Hart?"

"That they watch me harvest my crop? No."

Becky added, "But we keep the children close for a while."

"It's about the land my husband sold you," Adelaide said.

"So much for going roundabout," Charlie said. "Everyone know."

"Charlie. Becky. If there's any trouble, talk to Captain Hart."

To her astonishment, Charlie laughed. "I reckon trouble come with being free and being black, Miss Adelaide."

— ✑ —

AT HIS NEXT Sabbath visit, Hart regarded the dinner on the table, fried chicken in a crisp crust and sweet potato pudding. "If I didn't live so far away I'd offer to board with you," he said. Adelaide itched with Charlie's news, but instead she asked, "Where do you board?"

"There's a widow who keeps a boardinghouse in Cartersville. A freedwoman. No white person would rent to me. She does her best, but her dinners are nothing like this."

"We may lose our Minnie, who is our cook," Adelaide said. "Henry, did Rachel tell you that Lieutenant Randolph is looking for Minnie's husband?"

"Randolph? The photographer who took our portraits?"

"He's a scout, too."

"A spy or a sharpshooter?" Henry asked.

"Both, if I recall," Adelaide said. "Perhaps we could send him to keep watch over Charlie's place."

"The man you sold land to? Did the Turners threaten him?" Hart asked.

Both Henry and Adelaide glanced at Hart. Adelaide said Henry, "Did he ask you not to mention it to the Bureau?"

"What is this?" Hart asked.

Henry flushed. "About the Turners? Of course he did. He told me he didn't think much of it."

"I'm upset that he would think so. I wish he'd come to me about it," Hart said. He put down his fork. "He should carry his sidearm with him, and the other men on the place should have a some kind of gun. Even if it's only a musket. Mr. Kaltenbach, you should see to it."

Henry said, "I'm your ally in Cass County, Captain Hart. Not your man to command."

"I beg your pardon," Hart said.

Adelaide let her fear overwhelm her. She said sharply, "Captain Hart sees the dangers every day. He's wise to warn us."

"Captain Hart is a stranger here," Henry said.

Uneasy, suddenly the guest and not the agent, Hart said, "I don't mean to cause a quarrel between the two of you."

Before Adelaide could reply, Henry said, "I won't let fear deter me. Not from being fair to my tenants or selling land to Mr. Mannheim, or from dispensing money to help these people live in freedom." He gave Hart a long, appraising gaze. "I mean to swear the oath."

"The Oath of Allegiance?" Hart asked.

"Whatever it's called. The loyalty oath."

Hart said, "I never thought to dissuade a man from showing his loyalty to the Union. But things are hot right now. Think of your people. Wait a while."

"I'm a Union man and I don't mind that the world knows it," Henry said stubbornly.

"Let me make it easy on you. You can swear it at the Bureau."

Henry was insistent. "Who usually administers the oath?"

"The county clerk does, at the courthouse."

"I'll take it from Humphreys in his makeshift courthouse at the saloon."

Hart glanced at Adelaide and she sighed before she dropped her gaze. Her husband's good intentions were nothing but trouble to himself and everyone around him.

— ◡〜 —

HART VISITED THE school to tell Adelaide that the slates and spellers were on their way from Upstate New York. He added that Humphreys would allow Henry to sign the oath in the Methodist church in Cartersville. "Colonel Turner and his wife attend the service at the Methodist church," he said. "I doubt that their sons will start a melee there."

"I hope you're right," Adelaide said.

Henry asked Charlie to accompany him and serve as a witness. Rachel insisted on going, too. Adelaide asked Henry, "Am I welcome to come as well?

He softened. He knew he'd been sharp with her lately. "Of course you are."

— ◡〜 —

THE MORNING THEY left was an achingly beautiful day, mild for November. The sun shone a thin, buttery light over the house, turning its white paint to gold. As she waited for Charlie to hitch up the horse, Adelaide thought of the first time she had ever seen this house, and how disappointed she had been in it.

In Cartersville, Charlie stopped the horse outside the church. It was midweek, and the street was sleepy. Adelaide hoped they would be able to do their business quietly and slip home again.

Before the war she had attended the women's college in Cassville, run by Methodists, and she had often sat in the chapel, where musicales and recitals were held. But she had never set foot in the Methodist church in Cartersville.

The Methodists of Cassville had built a substantial church of red brick, but the Cartersville church was small and plain, its clapboards painted white like an ordinary house, the paint cracked and peeling with neglect. Only the bell tower, rising from the worn red shingles of the roof, proclaimed its purpose as a church.

Henry opened the door. The interior was unadorned, the walls painted white and without ornament of any kind. The pews were a polished dark wood. Through the narrow windows, half the height of the room, streamed a tender, contemplative light. Humphreys stood at the pulpit, where a Bible rested, the one the minister used when he preached, and atop it a smaller book bound in leather. Before the pulpit curved a railing of the same burnished wood as the pews.

Henry walked down the aisle, and the rest of them followed like a wedding procession. He rested his hands on the railing before the pulpit.

Humphreys regarded the supplicants before him. In a less hostile tone than he used in the saloon, he asked, "Who are all these people?"

"Witnesses," Henry said.

The door creaked open and a light footstep sounded on the threshold. Adelaide turned her head. Was that Colonel Turner, sitting quietly in the last pew by the door?

Henry said, "I brought them to make sure you won't tear it up once I sign it."

"I won't do that," Humphreys said, glancing toward the back of the church. He opened the smaller book. "The oath book," he said. "We keep all the signed oaths together."

Henry bent over the ledger. Humphreys proffered a pen, but Henry hesitated.

"May I read it aloud?" Henry asked Humphreys.

"Why?"

Henry gestured towards the crowd behind him. "I want them to hear it."

"Suit yourself."

Henry began, "I do solemnly swear in the presence of Almighty God..."

Adelaide's mind drifted to the last time she had been in a Methodist church, attending the wedding of one of her classmates from the college. The familiar figure of the bride had been lost in a great puff of white satin and a cloud of lace. Dearly beloved, we are gathered here in the sight of God... They were called vows, but weren't they a kind of oath?

Henry read, "That I have not been disenfranchised for participation in any rebellion or civil war against the United States... or been engaged in insurrection or rebellion against the United States... or given aid or comfort to the enemies thereof..."

Startled, Adelaide thought, *No wonder the former Rebs hate this oath so much. It makes a lie of the war they fought and the cause they cared about. Whoever takes it repudiates the Confederacy and his confederacy in it.*

Henry's voice floated to her. She heard the words in snatches, as from a distance. "That I have never taken an oath... to support the Constitution of the United States... and afterwards engaged in insurrection or rebellion against the United States, or given aid or comfort to the enemies thereof..."

Adelaide's mind wandered again to the wedding ceremony from the Book of Common Prayer, to the oaths of loyalty she knew better than the vows she had made to Henry under the *huppah*. To love and to honor, to abide for better or worse, for richer or poorer, in sickness and in health. What had she and Henry sworn when they married according to the Jewish service? She no longer remembered.

"That I will faithfully support the Constitution and obey the laws of the United States, and to the best of my ability, encourage others to do so." Henry rested his hand on the Bible on the pulpit. "So help me, God."

Adelaide thought, *Forsaking all others. Until death do you part.* Henry was getting married again to the United States, a union with the Union.

Henry picked up the pen. His hand shook a little as he signed his name in the oath book. Humphreys extended his hand for the pen, and signed as well.

Adelaide glanced at the back of the church, but the pew was empty. She was sorry to have missed Colonel Turner. She hoped for a word of encouragement from him or a word of blessing, as after the marriage service.

They lingered on the covered porch. "It's done," Henry said.

Adelaide thought, *When Henry and I married, I said that after the service. It's done.* She looked at Rachel, who wanted so badly to marry her husband and to make the vows in a church like this one. Rachel looked ashen. Adelaide thought, *He's broken the oath of loyalty he swore to me. What makes you think he'll keep his promise to you?*

4 | FREE TO MARRY

AFTER HE SWORE the loyalty oath, Henry was more insistent than ever about the freedom money. On a gray day in November, he asked Rachel to write to the Bank of England to inquire about setting up the accounts and transferring them to a bank in the United States.

Rachel lifted her head from the ledger and put down the pen. "Won't they wonder who I am and why I'm writing to them?"

"I'll tell them that I've entrusted you with my business affairs."

She rubbed her temple, feeling the start of a headache, unhappy that everything in their lives was irregular and needed explanation.

He bent over the desk to cover her hand. "It's only for a little longer, beloved."

"Until we marry?" How had freedom been narrowed to this? She was free to come and go, free to earn money, free to sign a contract, but all she could think of was being free to marry.

He took his hand away. "Until we go to Atlanta."

"As we are."

"I've asked Adelaide to think about a divorce."

"Didn't say yes, did she?"

"Rachel." He cupped her chin in his hand, and she was angry at him for beguiling her. "Jews can divorce. Southerners can, too, if they dare to live down the shame."

"She'll never say yes," she said.

— ❧ —

MIDMORNING A FEW days later, Rachel stopped in the kitchen, and Minnie immediately knew why. "Is there news from Lieutenant Randolph?" she asked eagerly.

Rachel nodded.

Minnie asked, "What do he say?"

"Didn't put it in a letter. Just said he'd visit. Expect him today."

Minnie's face went taut with worry. "Today! Must be bad news if he's come to tell me."

"Don't know." Rachel tried to keep the irritation from her voice.

Minnie, who had often scolded Rachel for being distracted in the kitchen, began to pace the floor, too preoccupied to mix a batch of pone or take up a cloth to dry the dishes. She sat at the table and then jumped up. She excused herself—"Got to feed them chickens"—to have a reason to stare into the yard, and came back again. She leaned against the edge of the table, unable to stand still or sit, and wrung her hands. She implored Rachel, "You'll tell me as soon as he come?"

"Yes," Rachel said sharply, and she opened the door that led to the yard, the one Minnie used when she wanted to milk the cows. On the doorstep she waited until she saw them.

One was broad of shoulder and ivory of skin. The other was tall and slender, as graceful as a birch tree, and nearly as dark as Minnie herself.

"Minnie," Rachel called.

Minnie pushed past her and her eyes widened. The figures came closer, and her hand went to her mouth in surprise. Still closer, and the tall man quickened his pace. Minnie ran towards him, screaming out a name: "Kofi!"

Her husband held out his arms and she flew to him. He lifted her up, engulfing her, as she said, sobbing, "I thought I'd never see you again! I thought you were dead!"

"Minnie," he murmured, kissing her tearstained cheeks. "Oh, sugar."

Minnie, usually so composed, so contained, now wept and wept. Her voice barely audible, she said, "You didn't give up on me? You ain't married to anyone else?"

He kissed her mouth to hush her. Kofi Davis, the man sold away to Mississippi in 1858, whom Minnie had mourned ever since, said loud enough for Rachel to hear, "Oh, Minnie. How could I? I was always married to you. Always married to you."

Rachel turned away, too jealous to be glad for Minnie. Lieutenant Randolph plucked at her sleeve. He said quietly, "Let's leave these two alone," and he led her far enough away to talk in a low voice.

She didn't mind the chill or the mist that settled on her skin like a fine rain. She stared somewhere behind Randolph's head, too upset to care about her rudeness in not thanking him for his trouble.

He put his hand on her arm. He had seen into her from the first time they met. Now, he asked her gently, "It isn't the same to be secretly married, is it?"

She raised her head, too distraught to give him anything but the truth. "No, it ain't," she said. "And it's a misery."

— ⌇ —

BY MID-DECEMBER, THE cotton had been picked and ginned and the corn shucked and stored. The growing season was over, and only the school was still busy, crowded by children who could now be spared by their parents to learn their letters. Minnie, who wanted to see Lucy and Adam married, had promised to stay in Georgia for the wedding. As she did every year, she had filled the house with pine wreaths for Christmas. Pine boughs made a swag over the mantel in the study. The air smelled doubly of pine, since the fire on the hearth was pinewood.

Henry said regretfully to Rachel, "It will be hard to see Minnie go."

"She should be with her husband."

"Of course she should." Henry sighed. "But I'll miss her."

Rachel was still too jealous of Minnie's happiness to say anything glad for her. She stared at the ledger, even though there was nothing new to write in it, and bit her lip against the words she wished she could address to Henry.

Henry said, "I want to give everyone something special this Christmas."

Rachel thought of the first year that Henry had been her master, when he gave her the Shakespeare book that caused endless trouble with Adelaide. "What are you considering?"

"The freedom money."

She sighed. "Letter from the bank ain't much of a gift," she repeated. "They want to feel the money in their hands."

"Can't we get some coin?"

"The Bureau," she said slowly. "They have specie, like they have coffee and flour."

Henry grinned. "Ask Captain Hart."

—⁓—

SHE SENT CAPTAIN Hart a note, telling him that she had Bureau business to discuss, and she invited him to midday dinner at her house on Sunday for his trouble. She thought he might be pleased, since he was doubly alone on Sunday, as the Bureau man and as an Israelite.

She wanted to feel the money in her hands, too. God willing, as soon as it was handed over, Henry would feel free to go to Atlanta.

And she had some business of her own with the Bureau. Private business. She sent Eliza to stay with Becky and Charlie.

She had been careful with the meal. She knew Captain Hart wasn't religious, but neither were Adelaide and Henry, and pig meat never graced their table.

He ate with appreciation, telling her, "I never refused anything during the war, but thank you for humoring an Israelite at his dinner."

"I've been around Israelites my whole life. I know what they believe and don't." She was careful with her speech around Captain Hart. She wanted him to hear her education, and her pride in it.

His eyes were very keen, a little too much like Randolph's. He knew more about her than she liked. "What do you make of us?" he asked.

"Some Israelites take their religion to heart. They remember it and ponder it and let it trouble them. And some don't."

They left the table to sit before the hearth, where she lit a fire against the November chill. He settled into his chair, looking so much at ease that she was sorry to trouble him, even if it weren't his Sabbath. "The Bureau business," she said softly.

"Ah, the Bureau, which never allows me to rest. Do you know that people badger me all the time? When I buy a stamp at the general store, and when I go into my boarding house for my dinner?"

"The Bureau's work is like a housewife's work. Never done."

He laughed. "True enough. Tell me about your Bureau business."

She first made Henry's inquiry about the money.

He said, "How much cash are we talking about?"

"Ten dollars for each grown person, that's thirteen, and a dollar for each of the children, four of them. A hundred and thirty-four dollars."

"The Army pays the Bureau," he mused. "If Mr. Kaltenbach can write a draft from the Bank of England to the United States Army, we can find the money."

"Can we get it in coin? They want to feel it in their hands."

His eyes gleamed. "The Army has plenty of coin."

She laughed. "Could the Army handle a draft of nearly seventy thousand dollars? That's all of the freedom money he's promised."

Hart pressed his hands to his temples, miming a headache, and they laughed together.

"I have some other business for you, Captain Hart," she said. "Still Bureau business, but it's too private to bring to the office."

He sat up in his chair. "Now I'm curious, which I rarely am these days. What's this business that's too delicate for the Bureau office, Miss Mannheim?"

"It won't bother you?"

"Miss Mannheim, I spend my days listening to every dodge and cheat and outrage that former slave owners can figure out to use on people who are now free. Believe me, whatever it is, it won't bother me."

"I know that folks who used to be slaves can get married in the eyes of the law now. But I've been wondering something else." She took a deep breath, still worried about his tolerance for the circumstance that he surely knew about. "Can white and black get married in the eyes of the law?"

He knew exactly what she meant, but he replied with tact. "I think so, in places like New York or Ohio. But you're asking me about the South."

"I am."

"That I don't know, but there's a lawyer in Atlanta that the Bureau consults. I'll write to him to inquire. He's a colored man, and he should have no prejudice in the matter."

Rachel raised her eyebrow. "A colored man? A lawyer?"

"His family was free before the war. He comes from Charleston."

In a rush of relief, she said, "Thank you. I was afraid you'd be offended—afraid you'd refuse—"

He said softly, "I have a friend, an Ohio man who attended Oberlin College. He settled in Mississippi and met a colored woman from New York. They fell in love and got married."

"In New York?"

"In Mississippi."

She didn't reply. He said, "As soon as I hear from Mr. Pereira, I'll let you know."

—⌒—

CHRISTMAS DAY DAWNED cold and overcast, the kind of day when the sun never seemed to shed any light, and when the mist in the air made it feel even colder. Rachel, who needed something to keep herself busy in Adelaide's house, kindled a fire in the hearths in the parlor and the study and lit candles against the gloom. The smell of fresh cake wafted from the kitchen, the fruitcake for Christmas and the honey cake that Minnie felt should accompany every festivity in a Jewish house. Rachel had put on her best dress for the occasion, the plaid taffeta that Sarah Hardin had made for her just after the war. Despite its cheery pattern, she felt as weary as a slave who had spent the morning making Christmas dinner.

Henry's notion of giving out a taste of the freedom money felt as heavy to Rachel as a bale of cotton.

The rap at the door was bound to be Captain Hart. Adelaide called, "I'll get it." Rachel lingered in the hallway to overhear whatever he had to say to her sister.

Hart stood at the door, flushed with the cold, carrying a blanketed bundle under his arm.

Adelaide had put on her best dress, too, the blue velvet that had beguiled the Union Army in 1864. She laughed. "I hope you've brought us more than a blanket, Captain Hart."

His eyes twinkling, he said, "Would I do such a thing? To my best sub-agent?"

"Dear me! Captain Hart, when did I become your sub-agent?" Adelaide teased back.

Hart handed her the bundle and greeted Rachel. "Miss Mannheim! Merry Christmas!"

"Thank you, Captain Hart, and I hope you have a day of rest, even if it isn't your holiday."

As he followed Adelaide, he whispered to Rachel, "I have news."

The study, decorated with swags of pine bough and brightened with candles, smelled pleasantly of brandy. Henry raised his half-empty glass. "Would you like some, Hart?" he asked, his eyes bright.

"I would, thank you."

Adelaide set the bundle on the desk and unwrapped it. Inside was a mahogany box the size of a tea caddy, the rich wood inlaid with mother-of-pearl. *Good God*, Rachel thought, *where did he find such a thing in war-ravaged Georgia?* She said, "Awfully fine for a strongbox."

Looking at Adelaide, Hart said, "It's a gift for you and your husband, once your people receive what's within it." He took a little silver key from his pocket and unlocked it.

The coins gleamed in the candlelight. For all her doubt, Rachel felt a sharp stab of desire at the sight of the money. She picked up a gold coin and turned it over in her palm, admiring the eagle on one side, and on the other, the head of a woman in profile. "Lady Liberty," she said.

"What else for freedom money?" Hart asked, lifting his glass. "To freedom, Mr. Kaltenbach."

They heard the sound of the door knocker, muffled and polite, from people who were still tentative about walking in the front door. Adelaide went to admit them, and a burst of cold air accompanied them as Rachel watched from the doorway of the study. She would let Adelaide wait on the guests today.

The tenants stood on the porch: the Hutchenses, the Edgefields, and the Benjamins. "Welcome, all of you," Adelaide said, smiling and pressing their hands as they passed into the house. "Merry Christmas."

Zeke asked, "Is it all right to wish an Israelite a Merry Christmas, Miss Adelaide?"

"Today it is."

Behind them came Charlie and his family. And behind him, hanging back, his face severe under his Army cap, his bearing rigid in his Army coat, was Sergeant Bailey. Rachel had never seen him in civilian dress. She wondered if he slept in his Army shirt.

Sergeant Bailey nodded stiffly when Adelaide wished him "Merry Christmas," and didn't return the pleasantry.

The guests arranged themselves carefully in the room, not wanting to sit without being invited, not wanting to touch the gleaming surfaces of the furniture. Henry said, "Come closer, all of you." They edged toward the desk where the mahogany box reposed.

Sergeant Bailey remained near the door, clearly unwilling to feel welcome.

To the smell of pine and brandy, they added their clean Sunday scent of starched clothes and soap scented with rosewater. They were hushed, as they had been when they waited to hear the Proclamation that set them free.

"All of you have heard that I've promised you money to help you in your freedom," Henry said. "A substantial sum, five thousand dollars for every adult and a thousand for every child."

Nods. Murmurs. If they were in church, they'd talk louder and more freely, calling back to the words of the preacher.

"The money is in a bank in London, and I've set up accounts in each of your names. But we have a difficulty."

"Miss Rachel told me," Zeke said quietly. "No bank to put it in."

"Miss Rachel spoke right. Not in Georgia. So I can't put it in your hands yet, as much as I want to."

"When?" asked Harriet, also quietly.

"Don't know," Rachel said.

They shifted from foot to foot, dropped their eyes. Rachel felt their unease. Now that they were free, they were not as patient as they had once been.

Henry said, "That's why I wanted to give you a gift today. A little money to feel in your hands until I can get you the rest." He gestured toward the mahogany box. "Ten dollars in gold for every adult, and a silver dollar for every child."

Sergeant Bailey raised his voice. "Freedom money!" he said derisively.

"What's the matter, Sergeant Bailey?" Henry asked.

"No amount of money can repay me for what you did to me in slavery."

Rachel recalled that day, as they all did, their faces darkening with the memory.

"I know," Henry said softly.

Bailey strode toward the desk to face his former master. "Is there really money? Or is that a promise, like 'I won't whup' was a promise?"

Henry turned his face away.

"I don't want any money from you, Mr. Kaltenbach. I've been paid by the Army since I mustered in. As a free man gets paid." He gestured toward the mahogany box. "A gold coin! That's a slave's Christmas gift. No better than the dram of rum you gave me when I was your slave."

Rachel recalled all of the gifts that year: the tools, the bonnets, the toys, and her Shakespeare book.

Bailey continued. "I won't take it. None of it. Not the gold coin today, and not the rest, if there's any to give me." He threw a furious glance around the room. "You should all be ashamed of yourselves! Free men and women smiling at Massa for a Christmas gift."

He turned to stride from the room.

Hart followed him into the hallway, where their exchange, conducted at a high volume, was perfectly audible in the study. Hart said, "You're his guest. It's a gift. Be gracious."

Bailey's voice rose to a level better suited to the battlefield than the parlor. "I won't act the slave or the toady just because it's Christmas. Not even to oblige you, Captain Hart."

Charlie excused himself. From the hallway, his voice floated into the study, too. "Freddy, there's a time for anger, but this ain't it."

"When? When is the time for anger?"

"When your enemies come for you. These people ain't your enemies."

"There are scars on my back that say different." His departing tread was heavy and angry, and the door slammed as loudly as a gun's report.

When the two men returned, Hart looked flushed and dismayed, but Charlie spoke in the tone that everyone who had worked for him knew so well. His coaxing tone. He said to the crestfallen group, "It's a gracious thing to give a gift, and just as gracious to take one. Ain't it, Marse Henry?"

"I hope so, Charlie."

Charlie turned to the people he had wheedled in slavery and smiled. "I know so, Marse Henry."

Br'er Rabbit, cajoling Br'er Fox, playacting to get Br'er Fox to throw him into the briar patch. Rachel felt sick at heart. Why had she thought that they were done with it? Pretending that the broken promises didn't matter? Lying to Missus and Massa? Smiling to cover up the fury and the hurt?

Charlie asked, "Marse Henry, may I help Miss Rachel give out the money?"

The people who remained in the room knew what their former driver had asked of them. They began to nod and to smile. Playacting.

"Miss Becky?" Charlie asked. "Will you go first?"

Rachel pulled the coins from the box, holding them high to let them gleam, and gave them to Charlie, who dropped them into his wife's upturned palm.

With conviction, Becky said to Charlie, "And more to come."

They came one by one, and despite all their doubts about the future, they hefted the coins in their palms and admired their beauty. The glint of the gold helped them dream. Salley said, "Five thousand dollar! How much money is that, Harriet?"

Harriet grinned. "Can't even imagine it."

Zeke said to Davey, "What will you do with all that money?"

Davey said, "Think of something." He hugged Harriet tightly. "Buy something big!"

The older children knew to hold the money in their fists, but Salley's baby tried to put it in her mouth instead. Taking the coin away from her, Salley said, laughing, "It's a taste of the rest, but sugar, you ain't supposed to eat it!"

They laughed in relief, and it took away the disquiet that rippled in the wake of Sergeant Bailey's outburst.

Henry offered brandy and Adelaide offered cake, and after everyone had taken a polite glass and a polite taste, the glasses and dishes were carefully set on the sideboard. The guests left, shaking their heads at the thought of how much money they would see, if Georgia ever had a bank to put it in.

Rachel accompanied Charlie into the foyer to watch the guests leave. The cold air that flowed through the open door was a respite after the close heat of the study. She asked, "Do you think he'll be able to keep his promise?"

Charlie said softly, "Someday."

"Someday next year or someday when Our Lord return?"

"Won't say," Charlie said.

She watched him go and remained there until she began to shiver with cold. Just as she turned to go inside, the door opened, and Captain Hart joined her on the porch. He touched her sleeve and spoke to her in a low voice. "I had a letter from the lawyer, Mr. Pereira." She bent close to hear. "It's as I thought. Not legal in Georgia, or anywhere in the South. My friends married in defiance of the law."

— ✒ —

ON THE DAY after Christmas, hours before Lucy and Adam's wedding, Rachel made her way to the Kaltenbach house. The smoky, meaty odor of roasting pig drifted from the backyard, along with the talk and laughter of the men as they tended the fire. She couldn't make out the words, but she was sure they were teasing Adam about becoming a husband.

She let herself in through the unlocked front door. The house still smelled of Christmas, pine and brandy and spiced cake. From the second floor came a sound Rachel had rarely heard in the Kaltenbach house, the laughter of young women. Adelaide had offered her own bedroom for the bride to prepare herself, and Lucy was upstairs, surrounded by her friends. Even though their voices were no more distinct than the men's, Rachel knew they, too, were teasing Lucy about her wedding night.

Uneasy, unsettled, neither servant nor sister today, she drifted through the house. Unable to act as a guest, unable to bring herself to help in the kitchen, she lingered in the breezeway to listen to the women laughing and joking as they worked.

Becky, Jenny, Salley, and Harriet had joined Minnie there, along with Adam's older sister Abby, who was as big, muscular, dark-skinned, and deep-voiced as her brothers. Abby lived in Atlanta, where she had become worldlier than her country family.

Her voice resonated through the open kitchen door. "This Rachel, who call herself Miss Mannheim—who is she?"

Minnie's sharp voice came to her defense. "Used to be Miss Adelaide's maidservant, back in slavery."

"Don't act the least bit like a servant."

"She Miss Adelaide's sister. Miss Adelaide admit to it."

"Is that why she don't work in the house?"

"She do work. Keeps them account books for Marse Henry."

"Her old Massa? Never heard of such a thing."

"More than her Massa," piped up Salley.

How dare you! Rachel thought. *Tell a stranger what should be private.*

The Benjamin sister laughed. "Do that mean what I think?"

"Yes, ma'am," Salley said.

"Ain't she ashamed? Slavery over. Why don't she go away and get properly married to a colored man?"

Becky said, "He's her little girl's daddy and he dotes on his child."

A snort. "He can dote on her from afar. Send money in an envelope to dote on her. Why do she stay here and show her shame?"

Minnie said, "She do talk about going to Atlanta. But he plan to go, too."

Another snort. "Know all about that in Atlanta," said Abby. "Pretend she his housekeeper, won't he? Call her his housekeeper, but she really his doxy. Just like back in slavery!"

"Stop it." Minnie's voice was very sharp. "She have enough trouble without you disrespecting her."

Rachel had told herself the same thing, more than once, but it was painful to hear it from a derisive stranger. She leaned against the wall of the breezeway and closed her eyes. *Don't belong upstairs*, she thought. *Don't belong in the kitchen. And don't belong in the study, not right now.* She slipped back into the house to wait for the wedding.

The parlor was a chapel for the day. The furniture had been cleared from the room, and every chair in the house had been pressed into service to make two rows separated by an aisle. A fire burned against the cold, and candles had been lit against the afternoon dusk.

She sat in the back row near the door, wanting to be as far as possible from the makeshift altar at the front.

People came in, the Benjamins loud and boisterous, arranging themselves in the front rows as the guests of honor. Behind them came Lucy's well-wishers, her friends on the place and the Hardins, who had taught her. The men brought the smell of corn whiskey and heat, which mingled with the starch and rosewater smell of the women, wearing their best dresses for the second day in a row.

Captain Hart entered the room and slid quietly into a seat in the back. Adelaide and Henry came together, Missus and Massa again, to smile at the wedding of one of their people. Adelaide whispered to her, "May we sit with you?"

Rachel nodded. Today it was less painful to be Adelaide's sister than to be whatever she was to Henry. To her surprise, Adelaide took her hand and squeezed it. Her fingers were icy.

Judah Benjamin entered the room, dressed in a reverend's black coat, holding the prayer book, even though he knew this service by heart. As he stood before them, the room quieted.

Bride and groom arrived together, the groom's steps sure on the carpet, the bride's dress rustling as she moved. They paused on the threshold, standing hand in hand, as everyone in the room turned to take them in.

Adam was tailored, barbered, fitted, and starched into a new black suit, and his relations murmured in appreciation to see him looking so fine. But the sight of Lucy struck them silent.

She wore a white dress, as at her engagement, but this dress sparkled with lace and her honey-colored face shimmered above it. She gleamed in the candlelight, her happiness shining around her, as audible as a church bell, as potent as a perfume.

Rachel whispered to Adelaide, "You cut that lace off your own wedding dress!"

Very softly, Adelaide said, "I don't need it."

Someone murmured—was that a deep woman's voice?—"Look at that, a colored girl, getting married just like a lady."

Bride and groom stood before Judah Benjamin, still hand in hand, and bent their heads to hear the words from the book of prayer that now belonged as much to them as to anyone.

The sight of a black woman, a free woman, ready to get married before man and God and the state of Georgia, sent a searing pain through Rachel. Her eyes blurred, and she heard the words of the ceremony faintly, as though her ears were plugged with cotton.

"Dearly beloved, we are gathered here… in holy matrimony… come to be joined…"

Adelaide tightened her grip on Rachel's hand, but Rachel didn't feel it. She scarcely heard the words. "Live together in holy marriage… love and comfort… honor and keep… forsaking all others… until death do you part…"

Adam's voice was pitched low as he assented. "I will." But Lucy's resounded. "I will."

The reverend Judah said, "It's done. You married!" and the room lost all decorum, laughing and crying and shouting, "They married!"

In the pandemonium, Lucy threw back her veil and Adam grabbed her tight to give her a real kiss. The deep voices of the Benjamins rose to sing: "O Happy Day…" They stood and turned to the crowd, clapping their hands as they sang, and the whole room echoed and swelled with the joy of the song.

Numb, deafened, Rachel applauded to add to the noise, and as the new couple made their way down the aisle, she rose to take Adam's hand in congratulation. She pressed her cheek to Lucy's and forced out the words, "Wish you a long and happy life together, the two of you."

When the room emptied and the guests had found their way into the dining room for the wedding meal, Rachel left the house to stand beneath the huge live oak, where she let the cold air flow over her. Her chest felt too small to contain the pain in her heart. A woman secretly married would never wear a white dress trimmed with lace, or stand before the preacher to hear the words about love and honor and fidelity forever, or make the promise of "I will."

She let the cold calm her heated body and heated mind. She thought about the wedding she would never have, and the marriage she would never have, as long as she loved Henry and twined her life with his.

She recalled the hope she felt when she fell in love with him, the hope she kept alive while he was at war. She was in despair now.

She didn't know—how could she?—that his deepest promise to her, to love and cherish and honor her, would be made a mockery by black as well as white, by custom as well as law. He would never marry her because he could not.

The housekeeper's marriage, the secret marriage, the mockery of marriage in being a doxy and not a wife, was no marriage at all. Marriage wasn't all of freedom, but a life without it wasn't the life she longed for.

Her connection with Henry would never be marriage and would never be freedom. When he went to Atlanta, she would not follow him. She would find her freedom without him.

She let the tears slip down her face. The thought of parting with him hurt almost as much as watching Lucy get married, but there was a life of freedom that would take her past the pain of sending Henry away. She would find it someday, but not just yet.

PART 2

—⁓—

RECONSTRUCTION,
1866-1867

5 | The Yankee Schoolmarm

RACHEL RECOGNIZED THE handwriting before she opened the envelope. It had come to her in letters from his battlefields, the terrible litany she had by heart: Seven Pines, Second Manassas, Sharpsburg, Chancellorsville, Gettysburg, The Wilderness. This letter bore an Atlanta postmark.

Dearest Rachel,

I am writing to you rather than coming to see you because I am afraid. I am afraid that you would refuse to see me, and if you did, that you would refuse what I offer you. It is not a gift. It is money that I have owed you since 1864, when you factored the crop for me. We realized half a million dollars when the cotton sold in Liverpool, do you recall? You only asked me for ten percent in commission. This is your payment.

If it offends you to take it for yourself, please take it for Eliza. Think of her future, and her education. Whatever happens between us, I will always be Eliza's father, and I hope with all my heart that you will always be my friend.

Your Henry

The enclosure was a bank draft. It was drawn on the account of Henry Kaltenbach at the Bank of England, payable to the account of Miss Rachel Mannheim at the same, and it was for the sum of fifty thousand dollars.

She held the paper with trembling fingers. This was more than freedom money. It was enough money for every dream she might ever have, and for every hope she might ever cherish for Eliza. It was money to soar on. It was money that would let her fly away.

It was money that would keep her bound to Henry forever.

The afternoon light slanted into the room, gray and damp as fog, but Rachel didn't rise to light a candle against it. She held the paper in her hand and sat unmoving.

A small hand tugged at her sleeve. "Mama?" Eliza asked.

Rachel raised her head. Eliza had just turned four, and she had lost the baby roundness in her cheeks that made her look so much like her mother. Looking at Eliza was a bittersweet thing, because she now resembled her father. "Yes, sugar?"

"Will you read to me?"

"Later. After supper."

"Where's Daddy?" Eliza asked, even though she knew.

"In Atlanta, honey. He went there to attend to his business."

"Will we go there to see him?"

Eliza's face was so eager that it hurt Rachel to answer. "Not right now."

"Will he come home to see us?" Eliza asked, tugging again on her mother's sleeve.

Rachel's eyes filled and she turned her head away. Eliza clambered into her lap and nestled against her chest. Rachel pressed her wet cheek into Eliza's hair. For Eliza's sake, she told a fib. She said softly, "Sometime, sugar."

At the sound of feet on the front steps, she rose to look out the window. They had all been more wary since the Turner brothers had patrolled Charlie's property.

But it was Adelaide, holding a familiar-looking packet in her hand. She raised the brown paper to release the aroma. "I brought you coffee."

"Captain Hart's gift?"

"Yes, even though it's none of your business."

Rachel took the packet. "Don't tell the Turners. They'll raid us for it."

"That isn't much of a joke," Adelaide said, as she came in. "May I sit?"

Rachel gestured to the chair before the fire, and Adelaide made a fuss of arranging her skirt as she sat down. "There's something that's been bothering me since Henry left for Atlanta last month," she said.

Alarm sparked in Rachel. "What is it?"

"The business of the freedom money made me think of it. I'm ashamed I didn't think of it sooner. I want to pay you."

"Pay me?"

"It isn't right that you keep the accounts and don't get paid for it," Adelaide said.

Rachel was silent. She was thinking about the bank draft. She was certain that Henry had neglected to tell his wife about it.

"You act as our business manager. I should pay you, as I've agreed to pay Jenny and Lucy, and as the tenants will be paid when the crop is settled."

"Have you asked Henry about it?"

Adelaide shook her head. "I don't believe I need to," she said, a sad smile on her face. "I believe it's up to me."

Now they both had a secret.

She reached for Rachel's hand. "Will you consider it?"

"If it truly come from you, and he had nothing to do with it—"

Adelaide clasped her hand. "I know he broke your heart," she said. "I can't tell you how sorry I am about it."

At Adelaide's words the tears returned to sting her eyes. Defiantly, she said, "I broke my own heart."

Adelaide said, "He's the kindest man. He has the best of intentions, and he manages to hurt everyone around him because of it."

"Let go my hand," Rachel said huskily. "I believe I need to wipe my face." She shot her sister a glance. "And not with my sleeve!"

After Rachel blew her nose, Adelaide said, "I came for another reason. I have some news about the school."

"Why do you come to me?"

"You'll see. Captain Hart has been in correspondence with the American Missionary Association—remember, they sent us all those spellers? Now they've agreed to send us a teacher. They'll pay her, too."

"A teacher? What is she like?"

"She's a graduate of Oberlin College, with highest honors. And she's been teaching in the South since 1863. Two years in Virginia, not far from the battlefield, and this past year in Georgia, in Bibb County."

"She should suit you just fine."

Adelaide leaned forward. "She's colored."

So that was the reason for all the pussyfooting. "Colored? Oberlin College? A teacher for the American Missionary Association?" Rachel tried to imagine a black woman from Ohio who had gone to college. She could not.

"Oh, she's a paragon, Captain Hart tells me. Her minister recommends her, and so do all the ministers at the AMA." Adelaide said, "I don't mind that she's colored, but Cass County won't like it."

Rachel frowned. "When does she arrive?"

"Next week. She'll be here by midmorning, and I hoped you'd be with me when I meet her."

Rachel looked up. "To welcome her or warn her?"

Adelaide shook her head. "Some of both," she said.

— ✐ —

MISS FRANCES WILLIAMSON was not tall, but she held herself with a dignity that made Rachel stand straighter. She wore a severe traveling dress in gray, and had pulled her hair tightly back, fighting against its natural inclination. The hand she extended in greeting was well-tended, unsullied by labor, but her handclasp was strong. And she was nearly as dark-skinned as Rachel herself.

"Miss Mannheim," she said politely. "I'm so pleased to meet you."

Unable to contain her surprise, Rachel blurted out, "You sound just like a Yankee!"

Miss Williamson laughed. "Well, I am! I hail from Lorain County, next door to Oberlin College, where I was a scholar before I came south to teach for the American Missionary Association."

"Did Captain Hart tell you that he's from Ohio?" Rachel turned to him.

Hart said, "We found that we have acquaintance in common at Oberlin."

Miss Williamson addressed Adelaide now. "I appreciated the courtesy of seeing him at the depot."

"We wanted you to feel welcome, from the beginning," Adelaide said.

"And the safeguard, with Captain Hart and Sergeant Bailey," she said. "Has there been trouble here?"

"Not at the school," Adelaide answered.

"But in the county?"

"If you've been in Bibb County, you know that not everyone is glad of a school for black children," Hart said.

Miss Williamson smiled ruefully. As though she were correcting a schoolboy, she said, "Yes, I know that very well, Captain Hart."

"Captain Hart, Miss Williamson has just got here," Adelaide said. "Surely you don't want to alarm her even before she's set foot in the schoolhouse?"

"I'm glad of the presence of the Bureau here," Miss Williamson said. "We were less fortunate in Bibb County."

"You had trouble, then," Hart said.

She gave each of them a searching look, a teacher making sure that all of her scholars had her attention. "The newly free welcomed us with open arms. Fed us, housed us, even though it was only in an old slave cabin. But their former masters—" She faltered and then recovered her composure. "They made it difficult for us."

"Did the Association know?" Adelaide asked.

"We wrote to them, my sister Mollie and I. By the time we left, they were well aware of the difficulties."

"I'm surprised that they would send you, even the two of you—young women, alone, with no one to protect them—"

Miss Williamson's face betrayed her weariness. "They sent us where the white teachers dared not go."

Adelaide sighed. "What a trial for you. It's as though you went into battle, even though the war is over."

"Oh, we do. The Association calls us 'soldiers of light and love'. All in service for Christ's poor."

Adelaide's eyebrows rose. "I don't believe I've ever heard that expression."

"Really? As the Association calls the former slaves?"

"Didn't Captain Hart tell you that I'm an Israelite?"

Embarrassment suffused Miss Williamson's face. "I didn't mean to offend."

"I know you didn't."

"I haven't known an Israelite before."

Rachel laughed. "Yes, you have. Captain Hart is an Israelite, too."

The teacher looked pained. "Please accept my apology, Captain Hart."

"Think nothing of it, Miss Williamson."

She took in all three of them. "In Bibb County—in fact, everywhere I've taught—I've always started the day with a hymn and never gave a thought to it. Would that bother an Israelite?"

Adelaide laughed. "What do you think, Captain Hart? Is the 'The Battle Hymn of the Republic' all right?"

Hart laughed, too. "You can sing that all you like."

Miss Williamson allowed herself a smile. "I think I can manage that," she said.

—⁓—

IN THE WEEKS since she arrived, Rachel had seen little of Miss Williamson, but she had thought about her a great deal. She had never imagined that the Association would send a black woman to teach in Adelaide's school, and she had never met a black woman who had gone to college.

Still, Rachel knew of Oberlin College. Before the war, as a rebellious, studious girl, Adelaide had provoked her parents with her desire to attend Oberlin, until her father decided that the Cassville Female College was good enough for her. The officer who spared their place in 1864, Captain Endicott, had been educated in Oberlin's abolitionist crucible.

Rachel knew that Oberlin was a place where young women studied alongside young men, but she hadn't known that the college admitted black scholars as well as white ones.

At the tap on the study door, she looked up from the ledger and rubbed her eyes, which burned when she worked in the low light of winter. It was Miss Williamson.

Miss Williamson's neat gray dress was covered by a gray shawl. Rachel wondered if she owned a dress in any other color. "I hope I don't intrude," she said.

"No, not at all."

"I find you at your work."

Rachel pushed the ledger away. "I keep the accounts for the place. Manage the business."

"I don't believe I've ever met a black woman who manages the business of a plantation."

"It ain't—excuse me, I know better—isn't usual. But Mrs. Kaltenbach and I aren't usual, either."

"I've seen that. Are all Israelites like her?"

"Don't forget Captain Hart," she said. "How do you get on with the school?"

"The school is a joy. The children are so eager to learn! And Mrs. Kaltenbach fusses over me like a mother hen."

Her Yankee accent and Northern turn of phrase were a continual astonishment to Rachel. She thought, *If I close my eyes, I don't hear a black woman.*

"I came to ask you a small favor," Miss Williamson said.

"I'll help if I can."

"At home I go to the Methodist church with my neighbors without any worry, but I've been in the South long enough to know where I'm welcome and where I am not. Tell me, is there a colored church nearby?"

Miss Williamson, like Captain Hart, spurred her to proper speech. "I don't have to tell you. I'll take you."

"Thank you!"

"I have to warn you, though, we're not Methodist. We're Baptist. Livelier than you may be used to."

"It's good to make a joyful noise unto the Lord," she said.

"Oh, we do, Miss Williamson."

The tension left her frame. When she smiled, Rachel could see the lonely young woman, far from home, under the missionary. "'Miss Williamson' sounds so stuffy," she said. "The little ones call me 'Miss Frankie.' Perhaps you would call me Frankie, as they do at home."

Warmed, surprised, Rachel said, "I can do that. Frankie, will you share Sunday dinner with us afterwards? Eliza and me?"

Her new friend broke into a bright smile. "Of course I will."

—⌇—

On the Sabbath day, Frankie enlivened her gray dress with a lace collar. In the churchyard, the waiting congregants swarmed around her, wanting to press her hands and welcome her whether they had children or not. She smiled and greeted all of them in return, telling every parent how well their child did in the schoolroom and how gladdened she was to see them there. Rachel trailed behind her, a little envious. No one had ever made such a fuss over her.

Before the service, once everyone was seated, the reverend announced their visitor. "We honored to have the new teacher with us. Miss Frankie Williamson, all the way from Ohio, who go to Oberlin College. Miss Frankie, will you say a few words?"

Another pang of envy, until Rachel saw the effort it took Frankie to square her shoulders and prepare herself before she strode to the pulpit. She stood before the crowd and waited for them to quiet. She swept her gaze through the room and spoke in a resounding voice. "Thank you, all of you, for such a welcome. I'm the one who has the honor of teaching your children. It's a joy to teach those who are so thirsty for knowledge. Bless you!" With a bright smile and a nod to the reverend Judah, she said, "Let us pray!"

When she sat down again, she breathed a sigh of relief. "I hope they'll allow me to pray in peace," she whispered to Rachel.

— ᴘᴘ —

RACHEL HAD SWEPT and tidied her house, but she hadn't worried about impressing a woman who, for all her ladylike ways, had grown up on a farm in Ohio and had spent the past year living in a slave cabin in Bibb County.

When they were seated at the table, Frankie bent her head. She murmured, "Thank the Lord for this bounty." She raised her head and looked at Rachel and Eliza with curiosity. "You don't say grace?"

"I talk to God sometimes," Rachel said. "Not all the time. I figure I shouldn't pester him."

"What a novel notion."

She smiled. "Grew up on a Jewish place. They weren't much for religion."

"Where was that?"

"Mr. Mordecai Mannheim's place, next door to this one."

"Have you always lived in Georgia?" Frankie asked, as she picked up her fork.

Rachel cut some chicken for Eliza. "Born and bred. I meant to ask you how your family came to Ohio."

"They were from Bern in North Carolina, but my father knew we could get a better education if we went north."

"You left? You were free before the war?"

"My father was a free man, and he cared so much for education that he ran a secret school for slaves."

Rachel raised her eyebrows in surprise. "How did he get free?"

"When he was eighteen. His master freed him." Frankie's face grew grave. "His father freed him."

So she had the memory of slavery in her family, passed down with the pigment that made her skin only a slightly paler brown than Rachel's. It must have whetted the edge of her abolitionist feeling.

"What did your granddaddy think of the school?" Rachel asked.

"He protected it. Protected all of us. When it got too dangerous for us to stay in North Carolina, he paid for our move to Ohio."

Rachel thought, *We're less different than I knew.* She asked, "How did you come to study at Oberlin College?"

"My brothers didn't care to get an education. They preferred to work the farm. But I was like my father, fierce for learning. He was glad to send me there and glad to pay the fees."

"What does he think of your teaching?"

106

"My mother and my father worry about me, but they're both proud of me, too."

"My mama knows how to read, too," Eliza said.

"I know that, dear heart." Frankie said to Rachel, "You're educated. As much as some who go to college. How did you learn?"

"Mrs. Kaltenbach taught me, when we were girls."

"She must have thought very highly of you," Frankie said.

"I'd hope so. We're sisters."

At Frankie's startled expression, Rachel said, "Didn't she tell you?"

"Goodness," Frankie said. "The two of you are full of surprises."

"It took us a war to get there. Even though we have our difficulties, we let the world know we're sisters."

"Is that why you stay here? For your sister?"

Rachel started. The question had been plaguing her since she received Henry's letter, with its plea to educate Eliza. "I don't know why I stay here," she said, surprising herself.

"You're a free woman. Free to go, and free to do as you desire."

Why was it possible to say this to Frankie, whom she barely knew? "When I was a slave I used to dream about being free. Free to get married. Free to make a living. Free to go to Atlanta. And now that I'm free, it's not so easy. I can't decide what to do with my freedom."

"But it's no longer a dream," Frankie said, her face alight. "It's all within reach." She let her eyes rest on Eliza. "What about your daughter? What do you dream for her?"

Rachel thought of the bank draft and its enormous sum of money. *Think of Eliza.* As Henry had pleaded with her, too. "Her education," she said.

"Think of the education she might have in Atlanta. She could go to college someday."

"To Oberlin?" Rachel asked, the words as sweet and unexpected as honey.

Frankie tucked in her chin, her defiant gesture. "Perhaps by the time she's grown, there will be a college for black girls right here in Georgia," she said.

— ᝰ —

WHEN ADELAIDE LEFT for the schoolhouse in the morning, it had become Frankie's habit to join her. As they walked through the February morning's darkness, Adelaide asked, "How many did we have yesterday?"

"Fewer. Once plowing starts we'll start to lose them." Frankie said, "We might have a Sunday school. We could teach them at least once a week."

"It's not a hardship for me," Adelaide said. "But wouldn't you miss your Sunday service?"

Frankie smiled. "Teaching them is a service, too."

Today, despite the winter dark, the children waited for both of them in the schoolyard. They flocked to their teacher, jostling each other to greet her, calling out "Miss Frankie!"

"Children! Children!" Frankie said, laughing as they crowded her in their pleasure to see her. A little girl sidled up to her. She kept her face downcast, and when she spoke, it was in a whisper. She wore the same dress every day. It was ragged and dirty at the hem, and her hair was in a tangle, as though she had no mother or older sister to brush it and braid it for her.

Today she tugged on Frankie's hand and said so softly that Frankie had to bend down to hear her. "Miss Frankie, I washed my dress last night." She put her hands to her hair. "And I neatened my hair with my fingers."

Adelaide thought of Rachel wincing as she brushed the tangles from her hair. This little girl must have bruised her scalp by using her fingers for a comb.

"Do I look all right, Miss Frankie?" the little girl asked anxiously.

Frankie put her hand on the girl's shoulder. "You look your best!" she said, smiling.

When the little girl was in the schoolhouse, out of earshot, Frankie dropped her voice to say to Adelaide, "The American Missionary Association doesn't realize that these children need everything. How hard they struggle! Not just to read. To wash and comb their hair. Soap and brushes. Is there money left at the Bureau for such things?"

Adelaide sighed as the children streamed into the schoolhouse. She thought, *Another duty*, but a second thought crowded out the first. It was an excuse to write to Captain Hart and to see him again. She dropped her voice to match Frankie's. "I'll find out," she said.

Frankie followed her scholars into the schoolroom and clapped her hands to get their attention. "I need a strong boy to chop wood for the stove," she said, and the boys all raised their hands and called to her, "Me! Pick me! I'll do it!" When she chose two,

109

from all the hands that reached out to her, voices resounded. "It ain't fair! I wanted to!"

She raised her voice, to keep the peace, and said, "And I need two more strong boys to fill the bucket at the well!" She admonished the sulkers, "And don't you fight over it!" but there was humor in her voice.

As the elect grabbed the bucket and ran to the well, Frankie said to Adelaide, laughing, "My brothers were never so eager to do their chores."

"They're eager to please you," Adelaide said.

That morning, she watched as Frankie taught. In the classroom, all her unease and worry fell away, as though her mission, in the most Christian sense of the word, was clear. Frankie knew when to encourage and when to press, when to praise and when to reprimand, when to help and when to let a scholar help himself or herself. She rewarded the ones who read and wrote better than the others by asking them to teach their fellows who were struggling.

The children sat according to their ability, not their age. Among a crowd of little ones on the front bench, just learning to stumble through their letters, was a boy of twelve. He was nearly grown, tall and lanky and very dark of skin. His family had come from one of the plantations ruined in General Sherman's wake and his shirt and pants were worn to rags. In the chill of a Georgia winter, he went barefoot. His name was Alonzo.

Frankie asked him gently, "Alonzo, young sir, can you read for us today?"

His hands were as big as a grown man's and already gnarled by heavy labor. He held the book in those hands as though it were an eggshell. He stared at the page. "Don't know where to start, Miss Frankie."

She continued in the same gentle tone. "At the top of the page."

When he hesitated, the little girl to his right pointed to show him. "Here," she whispered. "Right here."

He rose and tossed the book onto the bench with such force that the other children shied away. "Won't ever learn to read!" he shouted, and ran from the schoolhouse. The two little ones on either side of him began to cry.

Tears came easily in this room. Every child in Frankie's school-house had lost a family member to slavery and war, and every child grieved for someone sold away or gone away or dead. Many of the children had been abandoned or orphaned. Frankie, black like themselves, was sister and mother to all of them, from the littlest, who bawled in public without shame, to the oldest, who hid in the woods to weep.

Frankie knelt before the sobbing children and put an arm around each one. "It's all right. You sit quietly and read to yourselves for a moment." She rose and opened the door to let in the damp, chilly air. It also let in the words she addressed to her unhappiest scholar where he stood on the steps. "Of course you'll learn how to read," she said.

"Won't. Won't ever."

"Not at all. It just doesn't come easily to you."

"Too stupid to learn."

"Of course you aren't."

There was a sniff. In a littler boy, the sound would have been a sob.

"Do you recall what the Bible says, young Mr. Alonzo?"

"The Bible say a lot of things," he said, his voice morose.

"I know. But it says to be steadfast, for your labor is not in vain before the Lord."

"Work to pick cotton. Not to read."

"The Lord sees how hard you labor in learning to read. It's not in vain. You'll learn, soon, and the Lord will delight in it."

"Me? Delight the Lord?"

"Yes."

"Is you sure?"

Frankie's voice was very firm. "As sure as I've been of anything."

There was a long, thoughtful pause. "I try again, Miss Frankie."

"Come," Frankie said. She led gangling Alonzo back into the schoolhouse by the hand, and settled him gently on the bench. Adelaide marveled at her tenderness.

— ✎ —

A FEW DAYS later, Frankie stopped in the study, where Rachel bent over her ledger. She dispensed with all formality and walked around the desk to tap Rachel on the shoulder.

"What is it?" Rachel asked, but she wasn't bothered at all.

"Don't strain your eyes so. You'll need spectacles," Frankie teased.

Rachel blinked. It was a pleasure to be teased. "What is it, Frankie?"

"I want to go into town."

"To Cartersville?"

Frankie laughed and squeezed Rachel's shoulder. "Yes, since Atlanta's too far."

"Ain't much to see in Cartersville."

"Isn't. I know. I want to see it anyway."

"Are you sure?"

"Mrs. Kaltenbach has already admonished me. But what can be the harm, with the Bureau's eyes on us, just down the street?"

Rachel stood and said, "You're right. The war's over. We should be free enough to go into Cartersville, even though there isn't a thing to find."

She hitched up the horse and drove the carriage— Zeke was too busy with plowing to leave the field—and they drove to quiet, ramshackle, muddy Cartersville.

"I want to see the general store," Frankie said.

"He doesn't have much, either," Rachel said flatly.

"I want to see for myself."

Inside the store, the man behind the counter, who had never warmed to Rachel, didn't look up as they entered. Without raising his head, he said, "Don't put them elbows on my counter."

Frankie, who never leaned against anything, stood up very straight. "I'm Miss Frances Williamson, and I teach on the Kaltenbach place," she said.

The storekeeper looked up with a sneer. "You don't expect me to call you 'Miss,' do you?"

"Yes," Frankie said, holding her head very high. "Otherwise I'll take my custom to Atlanta, where the merchants treat me with courtesy."

The storekeeper shook his head. "You do that," he said, and he turned his back on both of them.

Rachel tugged on Frankie's sleeve. "Let's go," she said. "Told you he didn't have a thing for us."

In the street, as Frankie looked up and down, hoping for some other diversion, the Turner brothers emerged from the saloon. *Lord,* Rachel thought, *they must spend all their waking hours there.* They swaggered a bit, but they weren't unsteady on their feet yet.

They stopped before Rachel and stared at Frankie, who stared back at them as though they were bad boys in her schoolroom.

Ben said, "It's the other nigger teacher."

"Wasn't enough to have the ones we got already. The Bureau sent us another," Pierce added.

Ben moved closer, and Rachel pulled on Frankie's sleeve again. "Let's go," she said, but Frankie didn't move.

Ben dragged his boot through the mud and kicked a clump of it at Frankie. It spattered the hem of her dress. He said, "Jumped-up Yankee bitch. Still a nigger."

Rachel said nervously, "Frankie—"

Frankie didn't back down. She spoke to Ben in her ringing schoolroom voice. "I've seen people like you all over the South. I've been called what you called me and worse." She stood even taller, dignity expanding her small frame. "I'm not afraid of you."

Ben began to laugh, and Rachel pulled on Frankie's arm in earnest. She resisted, but Rachel dragged her towards the Bureau building, not letting go until they were inside.

It was only once they were inside that Frankie began to shake. Her face ashen, she said, "I believe I'll sit down."

Captain Hart, who had met them at the door, brought her a cup of water, which she held with trembling hands. She drank it in a gulp though it were whiskey.

"I see that you met our friends, the Turner brothers," he said.

Anger and fear transformed Frankie's pleasant face. "I was shot at, and my sister was shot at, in Bibb County," she said. "It ruined her nerves and she broke down. I swore I'd never be frightened like that." But when she reached for the cup again, her hand was still shaking.

As she set down the cup, some of her color came back. She said, "The Association calls us 'soldiers of light and love.' The people who hate us have pistols. Why doesn't the Association issue us pistols, too, the way the Army does? If I had a pistol, I'd use it on someone like that."

"I wouldn't fox with them, Miss Williamson. They're drunks, but they're hotheads, and they're good shots," Hart said.

A man's voice came from the office doorway. "Captain Hart, don't tell me there's another outrage to attend to." It was a weary voice, but tinged with humor.

Frankie said sharply, "Not unless muddying a lady's dress is an outrage!"

The man laughed as he stepped into the room. "If you knew what the Atlanta washwomen charge, you would think so." He was a shade darker than ivory, and he wore a black frock coat like a gentleman. His eyes were hazel and his hair had a European curl. His accent reminded Rachel of the speech of well-to-do Savannah that she had heard when she visited before the war.

He met Rachel's eyes and smiled at her.

Hart said, "This is the lawyer who works for the Bureau, Miss Mannheim. Mr. Daniel Pereira."

—⁓—

A FEW DAYS after she and Frankie visited Cartersville, Rachel looked up from the ledger to see Captain Hart standing before her desk. He must have come in while she was absorbed in her figuring. He sat in the chair opposite her, pulled an envelope from his pocket, and handed it across the desk. "This is for you."

It was unsealed, and inside were two crisp new greenbacks, ten dollars apiece, each with a portrait of President Lincoln's furrowed face. "What is this for?" she asked.

Hart smiled. "Your wages from last month, from Mrs. Kaltenbach. She wrote a draft, and the Bureau and the Army helped with the cash."

So Adelaide had decided to do it. Rachel stared at the notes. The paper was new and stiff under her fingers, not at all like the shameful weight of silver. She said, "I wasn't going to take it."

"Why not?"

"I didn't think it was right."

He grinned. "Take it. God knows you've earned it."

The great sum in the Bank of London, heavy on her conscience, was far away. This was her money, paid for work she had done in keeping the ledgers and maintaining correspondence. In running the business of the Kaltenbach place. Tears rose to her eyes and she turned away. What would Captain Hart think to see a black woman weep at the sight of her own money?

"Miss Mannheim," he said gently, "it's a small thing, but it's a triumph. A fair contract, fairly enforced. A deed for a piece of land. A month's wages."

"Free people get paid," she said, holding the envelope in her hand.

"Yes. Free people get paid."

—⌇—

ADELAIDE AND FRANKIE walked to the schoolhouse after their midday dinner. The yard was full of children who had finished their meal, at play until their lessons resumed. Sally bent over a little girl who had just learned to write, and who was so proud that she scratched the letters in the dirt with a stick. Frankie bent, too, and stroked the little girl's hair. "We have slates and slate pencils now, dear heart," she said.

The little girl said, "My name! I write it! Ain't it good, Miss Frankie?"

At the sound of horses' hooves digging into the grass, Adelaide was instantly alert. No visitor had ever ridden over the lawn.

They rode thin, spavined horses, and they drove their mounts too hard. The horses heaved, their ribs showing as they gasped for breath. The riders dismounted and strode toward the schoolhouse.

Ben and Pierce stared at the children. They stared at Sally, who put her arms protectively around the little girl. At Adelaide, who didn't move and didn't speak. At Frankie.

Her mouth was dry, but Adelaide found her voice. "Why have you come here?"

"So this is how you teach the little pickaninnies," Ben said.

She said, "If I want you here I'll invite you."

The Turner brothers ignored her. They circled the group of children, watching them as they'd watch for grouse to flush and shoot, hands touching the holsters where their pistols sat.

The little girl in Sally's arms began to cry.

The schoolhouse door creaked open. In the doorway stood Johnny Hardin, a rifle in his hands. He said, "What's this?"

"We're just making a call on the school," Pierce said.

Johnny took in the fright on his sister's face. The fear on the faces of all the children. The mask that was Frankie's expression. "Get away or I'll shoot you."

"Who said anything about shooting?"

Johnny raised the rifle. Naturally pale, he was now flushed like a drunken man. "My daddy was the best shot in the county. If I'm only half as good, I can shoot both of you dead."

Pierce pulled on Ben's sleeve. "Ben, it ain't sporting to hurt children. Even if they're niggers."

Ben laughed. "Not today," he said, as though he were refusing a day's hunting in the woods. He stared at Frankie, then at Adelaide. "Not today."

—❧—

A few hours later, as the children readied to leave for the day, they received a much more welcome visitor. Hart's face was flushed with exertion, and his eyes were bright with worry. Panting, he said, "I came as soon as I heard."

Matt lingered in the doorway at his mother's side. "I want to see Ben," he said in a thready voice.

Adelaide drew her son close. "I usually let him run off, but today I wanted him here," she said to Hart.

"Matt?" Hart asked as he crouched before the boy. "Are you all right?"

"They had guns," Matt said, and he began to cry like a much younger child.

Hart put his arm around Matt's shoulders. He took out his handkerchief and wiped the boy's face. "It's all right," he said. "You're safe, little soldier." He waited until Matt's tears subsided.

Hart rose and held out his hands to Adelaide. Without letting her refuse him, he clasped them in his own. "Are the rest of the children safe?"

"No one was hurt." It was a comfort to feel his hands over hers. "Johnny Hardin threatened them off with a rifle—did you hear that?"

From behind her, Johnny said darkly, "If they come here again I'll shoot."

Hart said gratefully, "You're a brave boy, Johnny Hardin. You take good care of Matt and all the rest." Still holding Adelaide's hands, he said, "I worry for you. All of you, and the children, too. I wish I could be here all the time to watch over you."

She should pull away. It was unseemly for him to touch her so and for her to take such pleasure in it. "Thank you, Captain Hart, but it would take you away from your duty at the Bureau."

"This is my duty at the Bureau."

There was too much passion in his eyes for a man talking about his work. She looked down at his hands, tanned and strong, their grasp so firm. She looked up. "And mine as well," she said.

"Ours together."

What had he said to her once? That he regretted being forward, but not being glad for her? That was before Henry had gone to Atlanta and made her all but a widow in Cass County. She stared at her hands, so coarsened by the life she had led since the war broke out. They were no longer a lady's hands. She couldn't accept the apology. With Henry in Atlanta, it was too hazardous to encourage Captain Hart.

Slowly, she drew her fingers away. "What do I owe the Bureau? For those slates and spellers? For Miss Williamson's presence here?"

"The Bureau is in your debt, Mrs. Kaltenbach. For your courage. And for your loyalty to what we do."

Slowly, she said, "I never thought about loyalty. Only to help. Do you recall the Passover service, Mr. Hart?"

The man who had brought news of freedom to slaves all over Georgia and Tennessee gazed at her. "All of it."

"How it begins? 'Let all who are hungry come and eat.' Is that a matter of loyalty, Captain Hart? Or merely kindness?"

With emotion, he said, "If you have any more trouble—with the Turners, or with anyone else—tell me, and I'll make provision to protect you." Before she could protest, he said, "As Sergeant Bailey protects me."

The day's fear swept through her. She felt faint. It would be good to sit in a soft chair, drink a glass of claret, and eat whatever Jenny, now the cook, had put together for her. She said, "Would you stay for supper, Captain Hart? It won't be anything special, but I hate to think of you riding back to Cartersville without anything to eat."

"With pleasure, Mrs. Kaltenbach."

He offered her his arm.

"I'm all right," she said.

He insisted. "Please lean on me a little." He held out his hand to Matt, calling to him, "You, too, young man."

"I'm a big boy," Matt said, now that his tears were dry, but his expression belied his words.

"Not today," Hart answered, and Matt slid his small hand into the grip of Hart's big one.

6 | SEDER FOR FREEDOM

RACHEL SEALED THE last envelope and entered the correspondent's name in the ledger. Her eyes burned from reading and writing for too long. Frankie was right. If she weren't careful she'd need spectacles soon.

The air that drifted through the opened window was sweet with new growth, and the midday sun made the day seem as warm as summer. She put down the pen and rose from the desk, rubbing her lower back where it ached, and left the study to open the front door and walk down the steps.

Henry's bank draft remained her secret, but getting paid meant that everyone, herself included, understood that she had money in her hands, earned by her own effort. And her confession to Frankie had honed her desire for something different. Frankie was right. The old dreams of slavery days might now be realized. What else might she do? How else might she get paid? How might she be able to reap for herself?

As the cotton season began, with its rhythm of plowing, planting, and chopping, an idea took root in her mind and started to grow. The new cotton plants gave her a notion, as Charlie called it, and as she pondered it, she decided to ask him for advice.

She followed the dirt path that ran between the fields. It led to Charlie's place, where Becky worked in the front yard, hoeing with vigor to plant a kitchen garden. Charlie boasted that he could manage the cotton crop by himself, and his wife was free to tend to the house and the garden.

Charlie walked slowly behind his big, black-coated mule as they turned the red dirt together. "Just wait until I finish this row," he called to Rachel.

Finally he halted, letting the mule rest. The mule gazed at her, and she asked, "Is he a good mule?"

"He a fine mule. Even temper. Smart. See how big and strong? Name of Jake." He rubbed his face along the mule's neck, and the mule nosed him hard. "Good boy, Jake!" he said, as proud of the mule as he was of his family and his farm.

She said, "He suit you."

Charlie laughed. "What bring you out here? Don't you have letters to write and figuring to put in that ledger?"

"Came to the end of the letters." She rubbed her back again. "Get weary of that ledger."

Charlie gestured toward his cotton field. "Hard work tire you, but it tire you less when you know you reap for yourself."

"No one reap anything from a pile of letters."

"Is you thinking about going to Atlanta?" Charlie asked.

She shook her head. "No." No matter how big Atlanta was, Henry lived there, and the place could not contain the pain she still felt. "Been pondering something. Thought I might stay here. Thinking of buying land, like you did."

"Odd thing for a woman to wish for."

. She narrowed her eyes. "Why shouldn't I?"

"Need someone to sell it to you."

She frowned, too. "I know."

"Marse Henry don't have it to spare. What don't belong to the house is rented out."

Rachel said slowly, "Is it true that Marse Mannheim planning to move to Atlanta?"

"I heard that."

"What's he going to do with the place?"

"Leave them renters to bring in the crop, I expect. Hire someone to oversee. Don't concern myself with it."

"Might pay him a visit to ask," she said.

"He ain't got any kinder since freedom come. You know that. Don't beg."

Charlie was right, but Charlie was a man who had been the beneficiary of Henry's kindness. Rachel thought, *I could manage a hundred acres, if I had it.* Stung, she said, "Just a visit."

Charlie said, "Heard you met Captain Hart's friend. That colored lawyer. Heard you got along fine with him, too."

Charlie would never stop judging any man who might interest her. "Good God, Charlie," Rachel said, irritated. "I said how do at the Bureau."

It had been a bit more than how do. She had learned that Mr. Pereira was born free in Charleston and proud of it. That he had attended college at Wilberforce University, where the scholars were young black men, some free and some fugitive, all hot against slavery. That he had wanted to be a minister until he grew too impatient and had gone to New York to clerk for a lawyer instead, to change the world in the here and now. And that he had rushed to muster into the New York 26th Infantry of the United States Colored Troops, which had brought him back to fight the war on his native soil in South Carolina.

She hadn't thought that anyone would care to overhear in the Bureau office and gossip about it.

Now Charlie chuckled as he said, "He ain't married, I hear."

"Well, you hear right, but that don't mean he want to marry me. He were grand before the war. Free. I believe he's half an Israelite. Educated. If he cast his eye here, he should cast it on Frankie."

"Half a Jew?"

She was still surprised by it. "Never met a Pereira who wasn't."

Charlie, who had named himself after his Jewish master, roared with laughter. "Then he suit you just fine, Miss Mannheim!"

"When he ask me, you the first person who get invited to the wedding," she said tartly.

She walked away. *What do you dream of?* Frankie's words rang like the refrain to a hymn. The dreams suddenly roiled in her. A life in Atlanta and an upbringing to ready Eliza for a college that didn't even exist yet. Marriage to a free black man, educated and half a Jew. A hundred acres of her daddy's land, an apology for slavery to start her own increase in freedom.

What did she want? She would start with the dream that seemed closest to her hand, real enough to be a hope and not an illusion.

— ᗱ —

MORDECAI'S HOUSE WAS in no better repair than before, but when Ezra met her at the door of the dilapidated porch, he was beaming. Rachel asked, "What cheer you so?"

The old man made a sweeping gesture, taking in the untended yard and the shabby house. "Leaving all this behind. Moving to Atlanta to live proper."

Mordecai looked cheerful, too. Cigars had reappeared in the Cartersville general store, and he was smoking again. Rachel waved away the smoke.

Mordecai laughed. "They sell better cigars in Atlanta," he said.

"Is it true that you're moving there?"

"Leaving in a couple of weeks. As soon as I finish up some business here."

"What are you doing with the place?"

Surprised, he asked, "Why would you care, missy?"

Before the war, he had called Adelaide "missy." It had never been a compliment. Rachel thought of the day Mordecai told her that the cotton they ran through the blockade sold for a million dollars. He had praised her head for business, as hard as his own. Now she leaned forward. "Henry sold Charlie a plot of land," she said. "Thought you might consider selling to me."

He shook his head. "You're too late," he said. "Already rented it."

"Tenants? Thought you already had tenants."

"Oh, they'll stay on. But I rented the whole place to a Yankee who thinks he'll make a fortune in cotton. Hah!" He snorted. "Paid me six months' rent in cash." He stared at Rachel. "What's wrong with you? You didn't think I'd consider selling it to you!"

Rachel clenched her hands so tightly that her knuckles ached. Without speaking, she shook her head and rose to go.

—⁓—

FRANKIE, WHO HAD maintained her refusal to buy anything in Cartersville, waited to visit Atlanta until the Missionary Association summoned her to make a report. When she asked Adelaide for a day free from teaching, explaining why, she said, "I hope it's all right to linger to buy a few necessaries."

"You should buy yourself a few luxuries, too," Adelaide said, with a smile.

Laughing like a schoolgirl, Frankie interrupted Rachel at her ledger and insisted that they go together. "I have business with the Reverend Ames at the school, but I want to buy ribbons and laces, too, she said. "How are the dry goods merchants in Atlanta?"

Rachel wished she could say, "We'll go anywhere you like, as long as it isn't Meyer's," since Henry worked there. But the words stuck in her throat. Frankie was religious and gently reared, but she had been in the South since 1863, and she wasn't a fool. She knew what had happened when a black woman had a child and called herself "Miss."

It was more than the shame. It was Rachel's own reluctance to show her grief, even to Frankie. Henry had written to her only once since he sent her the bank draft, and she couldn't bear to write back. The sight of his handwriting caused her pain and his words brought tears to her eyes. He asked wistfully after Eliza and sent his love to her. He begged her to give their child a kiss from Daddy, as he had wished during the war. Now he was gone again, and this time she had sent him away.

— ⌒ —

WHEN SHE AND Frankie got off the train, the smell of Atlanta assaulted them both. The air was thick with coal smoke and machine oil. Underneath it was the sewer smell of waste, animal and human, mixed with the smell of rotting mud. Frankie put her scented handkerchief to her nose, but Rachel coughed and said, "Lord, it do stink here."

The depot had just been rebuilt, and the smell of new wood mingled with the odor of char. As they got their bearings, the crowd streamed around them, men and women, black and white, people in every condition of dress and life. Next to them, a family of country folks, dressed in the clothes of their former servitude, gaped at the bustle. The man turned to Rachel and said, "Did you ever see such a commotion, sister?"

As Rachel turned to reply, a white gentleman in a frock coat and a beaver hat bumped into her.

Frankie said indignantly, "Sir!" but he rushed on without bothering to say "Excuse me."

Another black man, dressed in the nankeen trousers and wool cap of a laborer, smiled good-naturedly at the visitors as he passed. "We in a hurry in Atlanta! Got business to attend to!"

"Let's walk down Whitehall Street," Frankie said, pulling on Rachel's hand, as excited as a child. "We'll see the shops."

Whitehall Street was paved, the sidewalks covered with wooden planks against the raw red dirt beneath. On every block, a damaged building stood beside a new one, and nearby, a vacant lot piled with bricks and lumber awaited construction. Carts and wagons of all kinds, horse-drawn and mule-drawn, crowded the street, laden with bricks, boards, and bags of cement.

Whitehall Street thronged with women as well as men, moving just as swiftly. Frankie looked with appreciation at the white women dressed in postwar resplendence, silk and satin gleaming in the sun, hoops swaying under their skirts as they streamed down the streets, holding each other by the arm and chattering without a care of being overheard. Rachel heard clipped Northern speech like Frankie's as well as the familiar inflection of the Piedmont. Among the men were Union soldiers still dressed in their blue coats.

Frankie saw it before she did. "Meyer's Dry Goods" read the gilt lettering on the shining pane of glass, even brighter than on the old shop in Savannah. "This is fine!" Frankie said, her eyes shining. "Let's look inside."

Rachel felt sick to her stomach. "Don't you want to walk a little, to see what else there might be? Atlanta a big place. More than one dry goods merchant."

"Why? We're right here," Frankie said, pulling open the door, and there was nothing to do but follow her.

It smelled just like the shop in Savannah, the itchy smell of wool mingling with the pungency of lavender to keep the moths away. Behind the counter, the bolts had been arranged by color in a way that was pleasing to the eye. A well-dressed white woman stood at the counter, waiting for a parcel to be wrapped in brown paper. She turned her head to stare at the newcomers and said to the man who waited on her, "Do you really serve those people in here?"

Now Rachel was the one to tug on Frankie's hand. "They don't want us here, let's go."

But a very familiar voice said, "Mrs. Cohen, we serve whomever comes to us, and we're glad for the custom."

Mrs. Cohen sniffed and snatched her parcel from the counter. She left the shop in an indignant rustle of silk.

Henry looked weary, his face thinner, his eyes shadowed. Despite the cut of his suit, he had the air of a servant. Rachel knew that air, all too well. It bothered her to see him seem diminished by it. He met her eyes with the dark gaze so familiar that she had to lean against the counter to steady herself.

He had never been able to hide his feelings, and he couldn't now. He said, very softly, "Miss Mannheim."

She couldn't speak. All she could do was nod.

"Who is your friend? Will you introduce her?"

Frankie looked at Rachel in puzzlement.

Rachel stammered, "Frankie, this is Mr. Henry Kaltenbach. Miss Adelaide's husband."

Frankie's eyebrows rose. Rachel said, "Henry, this is Miss Frances Williamson. The Missionary Association sent her to teach in Adelaide's school."

Frankie glanced from Rachel to Henry—she was too polite to stare—and Rachel saw the understanding dawn in her face. Frankie struggled against her surprise and said nothing.

Henry said, "I'm glad to make your acquaintance, Miss Williamson. How can I help you?"

The question helped Frankie to recover her composure. "I'd like some trim for a dress," she said, shooting Rachel a sidelong glance.

As though this were the most ordinary moment, Henry began to ask Frankie about the dress. Was it for day? What was the material? The color? He pulled a tray of lace trims from the case. Frankie said, "Rachel, these are lovely, come look."

Rachel couldn't bear it. "I wait outside," she whispered. Without excusing herself, she fled from the store to stand in the street. Atlanta's bustle and Atlanta's reek flowed around her, but she was oblivious to both. When someone tapped her on the arm, she nearly cried out against the rudeness.

But it was Henry.

"How are you?" he asked wistfully.

"All right," she said, too full of emotion to say any more.

"How is Eliza?"

"She does well."

"Does she remember me?"

Tears rose to her eyes. She would not cry like this, in a crowd full of strangers. The old kitchen talk came back to her. "She ask for you every day." The words caught in her throat.

"Please, Rachel. Let me visit. Let me see her."

"No," she whispered. "Don't ask me."

He touched her arm again, the softest reminder of what had once been between them, and returned to the shop and the counter within it.

Rachel drew herself close to the storefront, where the crowd bothered her less, and waited until the door opened, the bell jangling. "Rachel." Frankie tugged on her sleeve. "What is it?"

"Eliza—"

"Is he her father?"

Rachel nodded.

"Oh, Rachel, why didn't you tell me?"

"How could I?" she said miserably.

—⁓—

FRANKIE LEFT TO call on the Storrs School, where the Association had sent the white teachers from Oberlin, but Rachel didn't accompany her. Outside Meyer's, full of distress, she let the crowd pull her along until she saw the gold lettering on a shop's window: *bookseller*.

Rachel drew a sharp breath. She blinked away the tears, straightened her shoulders, and crossed the street for the shop. Not even heartbreak would deter her. She would buy a book for herself, a token of her freedom, just as she had always yearned to.

She pushed open the door of the bookseller's and stepped inside. The shelves crowded every wall, the highest above her own height. She took in the smell of books: new paper, the tang of ink, the meaty odor of leather, the sourness of glue. *Like I dreamed*, she thought, and smiled as she gazed at the shelves, awed by their treasures.

"Hey! You!" The voice was sharp. "What are you doing in here?" The bookseller was a tall, weedy-looking man with a deep pallor. He was coatless and his vest had worn thin, as though he'd had nothing else to wear throughout the war.

"I came in to find a book," Rachel said.

"I don't believe you. I bet you came in here to steal a book and sell it somewhere else."

She said quietly, "No, sir. I came to buy a book."

"I don't believe you can read. I don't want a nigger in my shop."

Her desire for a book warred with her disgust for the man behind the counter. She said, "You can test me. Give me any book in your shop and I'll read it. Something brand new, so you can't say I learned it by heart."

He stared at her. Saw her for the first time. Shook his head. Finally he pulled a volume from the nearest shelf. He opened it at random and handed to her, saying, "You be careful with those cotton-picking hands of yours."

Her hands, scrubbed clean and smoothed with Frankie's sweet rosewater cream, were shaking as she held the book. She read carefully, glad of the practice that reading Shakespeare had given her. The book, about a war in Roman times, was full of long words, and dry.

The bookseller stared at her again. *I ain't a spectacle!* she thought. *Don't gawk so!*

He interrupted her. "That's enough." Sounding a little crafty, he asked, "Would you like to buy this book?"

He thinks I'm so ignorant I'll take his dull book, she thought. "I'm sure it's a fine book, sir," she said, handing it back to him, "but I hoped for something by Mr. Charles Dickens."

"Dickens? You like Dickens?"

"Yes, sir. I read the *The Old Curiosity Shop* and liked it."

"I'll be damned." He laid the dull book on the counter. "Wait a moment," he said, and he went in search of the shelf where

Dickens' books reposed. He returned with a book of satisfying thickness.

"What is it, sir?" she asked, reaching for it.

He laid it on the counter. "*David Copperfield.*"

"What is it about?"

"You'll find out when you read it."

"How much will it cost me?"

"Two dollars," he said. "It's cloth. Cheaper than leather."

"So I can buy more books for my money."

He looked startled that she might consider their mutual advantage. *He's fighting with himself,* she thought. *Dearly wants someone to buy more books and he's mad that it might be me.* As she opened her reticule, he said sharply, "None of that Confederate money."

She put two silver dollars on the counter. Lady Liberty's face gleamed bright on the coins. "Will that do, sir?"

He wrapped the book in brown paper, tied it with string, and handed it over without saying "thank you" or "please come again," courtesies offered to customers who were white.

As she left, she thought, *At least he didn't insult me again.* On the sidewalk, as Atlanta's crowd swirled around her, she clasped the book, her pleasure in it tainted by the way the bookseller had treated her.

Now she would find Frankie. She hailed a stout, dark-skinned woman in a faded calico dress. "Ma'am, which way to the Storrs School? Is it far?"

"No," the woman said, in the accent of the Georgia Piedmont. "In Sherman Town, not far. Whitehall turn into Wheat Street and it run into Houston, where the school is. Are your children scholars there?"

"No, I'm on a visit from Cass County."

"Sherman Town ain't paved, and the streets all over mud and full of holes. Watch where you step."

Rachel turned from Whitehall onto Wheat Street, where the houses were smaller and shabbier than the buildings at the center of town. Whatever had survived here had sustained worse damage, the walls burned, the roofs caved in, and the windows broken. Amidst the damaged houses were shacks and shanties quickly thrown together, built of whatever lumber people could find, with tin roofs salvaged from cotton sheds.

Wheat Street was full of black people dressed for hard labor, the men in nankeen trousers stretched out at the knees, the women in worn calico. A woman walked toward her, her face obscured by a huge bundle balanced atop her head. A brown hand kept the bundle in place but her feet were confident on the muddy street. Sherman Town's crowd bore her along. Wheat Street moved as quickly and as purposefully as downtown. Black Atlanta was going to work to make a dollar, and it was in a hurry, just like the rest of the city.

A pleasant voice called from behind her. "Miss Mannheim!"

She turned. It was Mr. Pereira, dressed in a good wool suit and snowy shirt, incongruous on the street in Sherman Town. Smiling, he asked, "What brings you to Atlanta?"

"Came to Atlanta with Miss Frankie. She calls on the teachers at the Storrs School. Going to meet her there."

"You look a little drawn," he said.

She steadied herself. "Too much bustle in Atlanta," she said, gripping her book tightly.

"My office is close by. Would you like to sit down and wait for your friend there? I can offer you a cup of water."

"Thank you," she said.

"May I escort you?" He held out his arm, the gesture a gentleman offered to a lady.

No black man had offered her this courtesy before, which Henry could not. She took Pereira's arm.

He smiled. "Come with me."

Pereira's law office was housed in a ramshackle wooden building that smelled of char despite the new paint. He pushed open the door to let Sherman Town's sewer odor into the room, where it mixed with the fragrance of tobacco.

The office, small and dark, was crowded with furniture: a large wooden desk, its legs scarred as though it had been in battle, and a chair, once fine, now marred by scorch. On the desk were neat piles of books with their bindings frayed and their titles rubbed away, and a packet of letters tied with string. He had cleared the middle of the desk for a makeshift table. On it sat a tin plate, smeared with the remains of a dinner of black-eyed peas, and beside it a chipped china pitcher and a tin cup.

He gestured to the rickety chair he kept for guests. "Please, sit down."

She sat heavily, not minding her skirt, and he poured her a cup of water.

She drank and set the cup on the desk. She was suddenly overcome by weariness, and she leaned back in the chair.

"Miss Mannheim, you look upset. What has happened to you?"

At his kindness, tears rose to her eyes for the second time that day. She struggled to keep her composure as she showed him the parcel and let the upset slip out without telling him the real reason. "Went to the bookseller and he was rude to me. Sold me a book but made me feel all wrong doing it."

"I'm sorry you were slighted. It's difficult to find a shop that is cordial to black customers." He brightened as he asked, "What book did you buy?"

"*David Copperfield* by Mr. Charles Dickens."

He smiled as though books pleased him. "That is his best story, about a poor boy who becomes a success through hard work. He took it from his own life."

It was easier to admit to her love for books than her hurt about Henry. She said huskily, "When I was a slave I used to dream about having a whole room full of books, all mine." It was strange to think that she had gone beyond that dream now.

"Have you other books?"

"Yes, I do," she said, thinking of the book of Shakespeare, Henry's first gift to her, and she blinked to keep the tears at bay.

"You're bothered, Miss Mannheim. Is it more than the bookseller's insult?" That speechifying voice could be beguiling, too.

"Thought they couldn't do such a thing to a free woman."

"What you can do in the law's eyes and what you can do for insult are two different things," Pereira said.

"Weren't much of an insult," she said, but she was horrified at the way her voice shook.

He said softly, "Miss Mannheim, do you need a handkerchief?" And before she could answer, he gave her his own.

She had seen Adelaide dab at her eyes to control herself. Now she made the same gesture. She said throatily, "Didn't come here to sob."

He regarded her with sympathy. "We lawyers hear all sorts of things, Miss Mannheim. We keep all kinds of secrets. Sometimes we offer advice and sometimes we offer handkerchiefs."

—⌇—

A FEW DAYS after Rachel and Frankie returned from Atlanta, Adelaide stood in the schoolyard, watching Captain Hart approach. He waved with his customary cheer, even though he was hampered by the crate he hauled. He was assisted by Sergeant Bailey, who lugged the other handle.

Adelaide stood in the doorway as they set down their burden. "Whatever have you got in there?" she asked.

"Miss Williamson's letter to the Missionary Association was very persuasive," Hart said, grinning. "They sent hairbrushes and combs, as you asked for, and bars of soap. For good measure, they sent you some toothbrushes, too, and tooth powder to use with them. And it didn't tap the Bureau's fund, not a cent of it. They took up a collection to buy everything."

This was Bureau business, so it was safe to laugh. "Oh, la, Captain Hart, I can't tell you how grateful we are. Hairbrushes and toothbrushes both! I can't wait to distribute them to the children."

Sergeant Bailey remarked darkly, "Never had a toothbrush when I was a young'un. Cleaned my teeth with a peeled twig."

"Don't be peevish, Bailey," said Hart.

Bailey shook his head. "Don't care for charity," he said. "Get tired of charity." He inclined his head toward Adelaide. "Excuse me, ma'am." And he was gone.

"Is he still mad about the freedom money?" Adelaide asked, sighing.

"I believe he's still mad about slavery," Hart reminded her.

"The Bureau calls them 'Christ's poor,'" she said, watching Bailey's resolute, retreating back.

Hart said, "I know. It sounds odd, doesn't it?" He sobered. "I was raised to think that we Israelites have an obligation to make the world a better place. I never knew it would be to read a contract and to insist on a living wage."

Adelaide felt a connection with him that made her shiver. She tried to make light of it by gesturing toward the crate. "And give out brushes, for the hair and the teeth."

"Passover is coming," Hart said. "Do you celebrate it here?"

She felt a deeper shiver, and it disturbed her. As little as she felt married to Henry, she was still married. She dropped her voice as though she were offering a confidence. "Yes. Since Emancipation, we have what we call 'the Seder for Freedom.' I invite all of the people who used to be on the place because they're so moved by the story of the Exodus."

"May I join you?" Hart asked.

No matter how drawn to him she felt, what could be the harm if he sat at her table with a dozen others? She smiled. "Yes, of course."

— ᔕ —

RACHEL LOOKED FORWARD to Passover as she anticipated no other holiday, not even Christmas. When she was a slave, she had served the meal during the Passover Seder, and had dreamed of the day when the words "We are free" might come true. After Emancipation, she had persuaded Adelaide to tell the story of the Exodus to everyone on the place who had been newly freed.

Just after Emancipation, it had been enough to say to herself, *Free. Forever free.* But three years later, freedom had shifted its shape. It could take any number of tangible forms. She had enough money to be free in any way she might desire. To set down roots in Cass County. To fly away to Atlanta. To make sure that Eliza would have the education to let her soar.

When Frankie poked her head into the study—she had trimmed her bonnet with the new ribbons from Meyer's—Rachel said, "Would you walk a bit with me?"

Frankie put out her arm. "Of course."

They left the Kaltenbach house by the front door. As they walked down the driveway, where the magnolias gave off a ghostly scent in the September air, Rachel said, "Still get a feeling of pleasure, coming and going out the front. It was forbidden to me in slavery days. Always the side door or the breezeway."

"I take so many things for granted as a free woman," Frankie said.

"Frankie! You still black! Just remembering." Rachel put her hand on her friend's arm. "And don't tuck in your chin like you're thinking about your sins."

Frankie laughed. "What happens at the Seder for Freedom? Ben and Matt have been talking of it for days."

"You eat a big meal. Drink a lot of wine. Tell the story of the Exodus."

"Do you tell the rest? The forty years in the desert?"

"That we don't need to tell. We trudge in the desert this very day."

"Every day a little closer to the promised land, I hope."

"Frankie, I've been thinking a lot about what you said to me. About Eliza's education. I want to make provision for it."

"It takes money," she said softly.

"I know," Rachel said. "I have money set by."

Frankie disengaged herself to search her friend's face. Very softly, she asked, "Was it Mr. Kaltenbach's doing?"

So Adelaide hadn't told her about the freedom money. The truth burned her tongue, and she couldn't bear to admit it to Frankie. "He gave all of us a sum to get started in freedom," she said. "Each of us."

Frankie's great-grandfather had helped his black son. She understood. She said, "It isn't the first time, and it won't be the last."

"I want to use it for Eliza, but I want to do it right. Thought you could advise me."

Frankie said, "When my father was still with us, he used to consult with a lawyer about his money. And after he left us, my mother talked to the lawyer, and he gave her good advice about what to do with the wherewithal."

"You had a lawyer?"

"Oh, yes. He was a good friend to the College, too." Frankie considered. "If you need advice, why don't you ask the lawyer who advises the Bureau?" She smiled. "Mr. Pereira, who seemed to be taken with you."

Rachel laughed. "Oh, he's much too grand for me. He'd suit you."

Frankie laughed, too. "I want to marry someday," she said, "but not yet. There are things I want to do first."

—⁓—

A FEW DAYS later, when Rachel opened the door to Pereira's office in Atlanta, he already had a visitor. She was a substantial woman, carefully corseted under her black silk dress, and when she turned, Rachel saw that she was still handsome, although she was no longer young. Her skin was a milky brown and her hair, carefully arranged atop her head, was smooth enough to take a curl. Her widow's dress was relieved only by a cameo at her throat. The scent of lavender water surrounded her and overpowered the room's odor of tobacco.

"Didn't mean to disturb you," Rachel said.

"You haven't," the woman said. "We were just passing the time of day."

Mr. Pereira introduced his guest as Mrs. Toussaint. She held out a hand gloved in kid and asked Rachel, "How do you do?" Her voice was musical, as though she were a fine singer.

"Very well," Rachel said.

Mrs. Toussaint rose. She nodded to Pereira and smiled at Rachel, a smile that recalled the beauty of her youth. "Take care," she said as she left. In her absence, the smell of lavender water lingered.

"Who is that? Or do you need to keep it secret?" Rachel asked as she sat.

Pereira said, "No, it's all right. She's a woman of substance in Atlanta. I advise her on some of her affairs of business."

"Is she a widow?"

"She owns some property. And she runs a business of her own."

"What business?" Rachel asked, intensely curious to know how a black woman had done so well for herself.

Pereira blushed. "She runs an eating house," he said. "Now, for the matter at hand. What brings you here to consult with me?"

"I just came into some money," she said. "I'd like to keep it safe to pass on to my daughter. To provide for her education, and her maintenance, too, once she's grown."

"How much money are we talking about?"

She thought of the promise of the freedom money, which would suffice. She had debated with herself about telling the truth until the moment he asked her, but he needed the truth. She took a deep breath. "This stays a secret?"

"Yes. I swear it."

She met his eyes, which glowed brown in the dim light of his cramped office. She told him, the words coming out slowly, still hard to believe, even as she heard herself speak.

"That's quite a sum," he said. "How did it come to you?"

If he weren't a lawyer, he'd be just like a Cass County busybody, poking into everything that people would rather keep to themselves. "After I got free, I factored the cotton crop for the man who used to be my master. We realized a good profit," she boasted, thinking of the pleasure in making so much money at the height of the wartime market. "He insisted on paying me for doing it. Said it was a commission. Wouldn't let me refuse it."

Pereira's face flickered with comprehension. "Ah, you must have run it through the blockade, to sell at such a price."

"War's over and done. Blockade's over and done. Don't tell me it's a crime to have the money now."

"It's not," he said. "Your former master must have had great confidence in you."

At the thought of Henry, tears rose to her eyes, but she blinked them away. "Yes, he did."

Gently, Pereira said, "Your daughter. Is she his daughter, too?"

Rachel pulled her handkerchief from her pocket. He had been right about the handkerchiefs. She balled hers up and willed the tears to go away. "Do it matter?"

His voice had gone very soft. "It usually does," he said.

Fair of skin. Name of Pereira. She asked, "Do you celebrate the Passover, Mr. Pereira?"

"That's an odd question, Miss Mannheim."

"My daddy was an Israelite, and I celebrate it."

His face suffused with sadness, Pereira said, "My father was an Israelite. But I am not."

— ᔕ —

ON PASSOVER EVE, Adelaide sat at the head of the Seder table, Rachel to her right, Frankie to her left. Captain Hart was at the foot, where she could see him smile at her, and where he presided over the youngsters—Matt and Eliza, Josey and Ben. She and Rachel had prepared for the holiday together, putting out the Seder plate and the cup for Elijah. They had set the silver candlesticks on the sideboard, added every leaf to the table, and covered it with the damask tablecloth. They laid the Passover china and a wineglass at every place.

The guests were now veterans of three Seders for Freedom, and they sat easily at the festive table, pleased to be welcome as guests. Full of feeling at seeing black and white together, Adelaide reached to take Rachel's hand, and she took Frankie's, too.

Her father was absent. She hadn't invited him. She knew he would have refused to sit down to a meal with black people, even if he hadn't left Cass County. She had yet to meet him in his new house in Atlanta.

Adelaide lit the candles and blessed the wine. She raised the dish of matzah and the Seder plate with its egg and shank bone—a turkey neck—and parsley and horseradish root. Adelaide asked, "Captain Hart, will you begin?"

He recited the familiar words, first in Hebrew, then he surprised everyone at the table. He translated them into English: "This is the bread of affliction that our ancestors ate in Egypt. Let all who are hungry come and eat. This year we are here; next year may we be in the land of Israel. This year we are slaves; next year may we be free."

Rachel pressed Adelaide's hand, her face glowing to hear the familiar words, her pleasure undiluted at being an honored guest at the Seder.

Captain Hart asked Adelaide, "Would you like me to read from the service?"

Adelaide said, "We don't read from the Passover book." She turned to Rachel. "We have our own version of the story. Rachel will tell it."

The story had come to her in the first year they had sat down to the Seder, and she had told it every year since. "A long time ago, in Bible times, the Jews were slaves to the Egyptians. The Egyptians made them work hard, in the hot sun, and their task-masters—their overseers—beat the people if they didn't work hard enough."

That first year the people around the table had murmured in a polite version of the way they called out in meeting. Tonight their voices rang out surely. "Tell it! Burdened and scorned. Tell it!"

Rachel lifted her eyes to look around the table. She said, "Pharaoh hated the Jews so much that he wanted to kill every boy baby that was born. But the Jews were too smart for him. They hid the babies, and one mother put her baby in a little ark of bulrushes, for Pharaoh's daughter to find and to take in."

Families torn asunder. Mothers and fathers, brothers and sisters sold away. It was too soon to forget, and they still remembered.

"Pharaoh's daughter called him Moses, and when he grew up he found out how the Egyptians oppressed their slaves. His people. He killed the overseer who was beating a slave, and ran away into the desert.

"But God had plans for him, and told him to go to Pharaoh and tell him to let the people go. Wasn't eager to do it. God had to prod him.

"Pharaoh was a hard man, harder than the worst massa you ever saw, and God made his heart even harder." Laughter around the table. Oh, they remembered. "He told Moses no, wouldn't let the slaves go free. So God sent plagues, one after another, every one worse than the last. Blood. Frogs. Lice. Beasts. Blight, like boll rot. Boils. Locusts to eat up the crop. Darkness in the middle of the day. And the last, the worst, striking every Egyptian firstborn son dead, from the poorest Egyptian right up to Pharaoh himself."

They could still laugh at the vengeance on the Egyptians, who had oppressed the slaves so badly.

"The slaves got ready to go, but they were in such a hurry they couldn't make proper bread. They made flat cakes, like johnny-cake, and they packed up to leave. Pharaoh wasn't done with them yet. He sent his army, all his horses and carts, right after them. But when they came to the Red Sea, the waters parted and they walked right through. Pharaoh's army came after them and the waters covered them. But the Jews, the slaves, they were saved. They were free."

There was silence around the table as all of them recalled the pain of slavery, and the joy of Emancipation, and the turmoil since of being free. Charlie reached for the Seder plate and held it high. He said, "This ain't the bread of affliction. It's the bread of freedom, and we eat it together."

Rachel raised the Kiddush cup. "We drink to that!" she said, and everyone sipped at the wine.

Charlie said, "Now we sing it, too." He began, his tenor voice sweet and sure, and the rest of them joined him. "Go Down Moses" had been a song in slavery, but it had taken on a new meaning during the war. They sang the plea to Pharaoh, reminding him of the oppression of the Israelites under their burden of hard labor, imploring with him to let the people go free. To Adelaide's surprise, Hart joined in, his face filling with emotion.

When they finished, Hart said, "We Union men called that 'The Song of the Contrabands' during the war."

"Not anymore," Charlie said, his eyes shining. "Song of freedom now." He raised his glass. "This year we free." And they drank again.

Hart asked, "Do you sing '*Dayenu*'?"

"Teach us," Adelaide said.

Hart began to sing, then he stopped to translate. At the refrain, he said, "Join me," and they sang with him, tentative at first, then with more vigor as they learned the tune. They began to clap to keep the tempo, as they would in Sunday meeting. And as the melody became theirs, they embellished it with the harmony they brought to their hymns, twining together Exodus and Emancipation.

A sharp knock on the door cut through the music. Adelaide rose, angry that alarm would cloud the jubilation she had just felt, and Hart was instantly at her side. "Don't go out alone," he said.

"Just to the porch to look."

They stood on the porch together, peering into the darkness. The air was very soft. They listened for the sound of footsteps or speech, but nothing disturbed the evening air.

"Let me look," Hart said.

Adelaide reached for his arm. "Not alone!"

"Just around the house."

He didn't go far, and he soon returned. "Nothing," he said. "It's as though we were visited by a ghost."

Adelaide laughed. "It wasn't the Turners," she said.

His face was grim. "That isn't a laughing matter."

"Elijah, then," she said. "It was the prophet Elijah. Doesn't he come to the Seder table for a sip from his glass?"

Hart's face brightened. "Adelaide! I never knew you to believe in miracles."

He must have been a little drunk to call her by her first name, but so was she. She reached for his hand and held it with affection. "Tonight I do," she said.

— ᥥ —

INSIDE, THE CHILDREN were asleep in their chairs from the late hour and the four sips of wine they'd been allowed. Charlie and Becky roused a sleepy Ben and Josey to take them home, and Rachel gathered up Eliza.

Hart bent over Matt, who was fast asleep. Adelaide said, "I'll wake him and get him upstairs."

Hart whispered, "Let me." He put the gentlest hand on Matt's shoulder. The boy stirred but didn't wake. The captain smiled and gathered him up to carry him to bed.

7 | FLY AWAY

Rachel took the familiar path that had been worn through the woods, from the Kaltenbach place to the Mannheim place, in slavery days. She wanted to see what Mordecai Mannheim's place looked like now that the tenants had plowed and planted the crop. Charlie would tell her not to torment herself by longing for something she could never have, but she would walk along the fields with Charlie's questions in her mind: Is it good land for cotton? How is the crop coming? And with Mordecai's: How many bales an acre?

Instead of taking the path to the side yard, she wandered along the edge of a field. It had been plowed once; she could see the upturned dirt. In it, a man guided a mule to plow again before planting the cottonseed.

He didn't have the look of prosperity. He wore ragged pants and a dirt-streaked shirt, and his mule moved with the slow gait of age. She knew him slightly. His name was Solomon Ballard, and he was a stranger to Cass County, part of the great wave of restless movement that had come with the end of slavery and the end of the war. He had a dark, lined face that made him look older than he was. This was Mordecai's tenant, who paid him in shares of the crop at the end of the year.

When he came close enough, she waved and greeted him. Solomon halted and so did the mule. He removed his battered hat and wiped his face with his sleeve. "Miss Rachel, what bring you here?"

"Grew up here. Wanted to see how it look now."

He shrugged, as though it was foolish for a former slave to have any feeling for the old place. "Ain't much to see. Got a late start. Haven't planted yet."

She regarded the furrowed red dirt. "They always made a good crop here, before the war."

"Hope so. If that Yankee who run it leave us alone to grow it." He spat. "The man don't know a thing about growing cotton. We lucky to have a crop at all."

Rachel said, "Yankees don't grow cotton. You have to school him."

"He don't act like a Yankee. He act like my old massa back in slavery. Tell me to do what he say, and tell me that I act insolent if I don't."

"Do he write you a contract?"

"Contract? He did not. He say he keep everything written down in his ledger book, everything he use to furnish me, and we settle when the crop come in."

"You should go to the Bureau."

Ballard regarded her with weary eyes. "The Bureau!" He spat once more.

From the distance, someone was driving a horse hard enough for the hooves to pound on the upturned dirt. The horse was a glossy, pretty mare, suited to pull a buggy along a paved road, not sturdy enough for a day in the fields. The rider was a chunky, swarthy man who had grown his hair long like a Confederate officer's. Without dismounting, he said to Ballard, "I don't employ you to dawdle. Get back to work, and get that mule moving." To Rachel, he said, "Who the hell are you? You get off my property." Without waiting for any obeisance from either of them, he spurred the horse and galloped away.

As Rachel turned to go, she took pleasure in a malicious thought. *It ain't your property. It's my daddy's property.*

— ✤ —

NOW THAT PLANTING season had begun, the ranks of Adelaide's scholars had thinned, and the school was home only to the littlest and the most delicate. Frankie said sadly, "I wish their mothers and fathers wouldn't take them away from school to work in the fields."

"They send the children they feel they can spare," Adelaide said.

"I miss young Mr. Alonzo. Tall and strong and old enough to do a man's work." She sighed. "He was just learning how to read and he took such joy in it."

"Where is he?"

"No one knows. He hasn't been to meeting either. I hope that he's all right. I hope his family is all right, too."

Adelaide said wearily, "We can't be mother and father to them. We do our best to teach them and give them midday dinner."

— ✑ —

LATER THAT NIGHT, Adelaide stepped onto the porch for a breath of air. She had already locked the kitchen and breezeway doors. In a moment she would throw the bolt on the front door to barricade her household for the night. Magnolias scented the air, crickets rasped in the night-damp grass, and the stars glimmered in a sky as soft and blue as a velvet gown. Swallows and bats, their flight similarly crooked and swooping, fluttered through the trees planted on either side of the driveway. An owl called. Owls were fierce predators, but the call was comforting. Adelaide thought of Minnie, who had loved owls so much.

Hart's worry for her, which had not left her, buzzed in her ear. Hart, who lived with threat all the time, had yet to lose the vigilance of his Army days, but tonight, the uneasy countryside of Cass County was momentarily peaceful.

Adelaide went inside and shot the bolt, tugging on it to make certain it was secure. She walked slowly through the darkened rooms, taking one last look to assure that every candle had been snuffed. She hesitated at the foot of the darkened stairs, not wanting to disturb anyone who was already asleep.

The sound of feet pounding on the driveway was such a surprise that her heart pounded along with it. All of her previous peace fled. Someone beat on the door, not bothering with the knocker, in a sound that reminded her of the wartime cannon fire that had come too close for comfort. *Why don't we keep a gun in the house?* she fretted.

She edged close to the door to hear the voice. "Miss Adelaide," he said, panting. "Help me, Miss Adelaide!"

It was Alonzo, the boy who worked on the Everett place.

She threw open the door to find him with his shirt bloodied and his face bruised. "Help me," he said again, leaning against the doorframe for support.

Behind her, footsteps sounded as Frankie ran down the stairs. Torn from sleep, she had had the presence of mind to put on her dressing gown. "What is it?" she cried in alarm.

"Alonzo." Adelaide felt dazed. "He's hurt. He came to us."

"Adelaide, help me," Frankie said. "Get a blanket, and anything you can use for rags. Do you have arnica for his bruises? Get some water from the kitchen, too. A basinful."

"Where will you put him?" she asked.

"Right here in the hallway, until we tend to him." Frankie ran to support Alonzo, who had now sagged against the doorframe. When she helped him to lie down on the floor, he left a bloody print on the wood. "Adelaide! Hurry!"

By the time Adelaide returned with the basin, the blanket, and the rags for bandages, Frankie had peeled off Alonzo's shirt. His back was bloody and welted. Frankie said matter-of-factly, "He's been whipped, too."

"What happened? Who did this to you?" Adelaide cried.

Alonzo shook his head.

"No," Frankie said sharply. "We'll tend to him first."

Adelaide watched as she washed the lacerations and the water in the basin turned bloody. "Draw more water," Frankie said, and Adelaide hurried to do her bidding. Frankie used another basinful before she had bound up Alonzo's back and washed the bruises on his face. She sent Adelaide for clean clothes—Henry had left an old nightshirt, and that would do for the night—and helped him tenderly into it. She arranged a blanket on the floor and knelt by him as she settled him there. "Have you any laudanum?" she asked Adelaide.

Adelaide brought the draught in a glass of water.

"What is that?" Alonzo murmured.

As she knelt to hand him the glass, she said, "It will ease the pain and help you sleep."

The boy drained the glass. As his eyes closed, Frankie picked up the soiled rags, the stained clothes, and the bloody water in the basin with a practiced hand. "Is he asleep?" she asked Adelaide.

Yes.

She rose, gesturing for Adelaide to follow her. From the kitchen, she tossed the basin's contents into the yard and put the rags and clothes into the hearth to burn them in the morning. Then she sat heavily in one of the kitchen chairs. She looked drained and ashen. Trying to keep her voice level, she said, "I'll sit with him tonight."

Adelaide touched her shoulder and felt the tremor of delayed fear. "Go back to bed, Frankie," she said. "You've already done your duty tonight."

Frankie shivered. "Our farm was a stop on the Underground Railroad," she said grimly as she stood. "We got used to helping runaways, Mother and I."

—⌇—

ADELAIDE KNEW THAT she should send word to Hart. The boy's mistreatment was a matter for the Bureau. But she hesitated. It was one thing to open the doors of her schoolhouse to allow anyone to enter, if they chose to. It was another to harbor a boy who had run away from his place in the field, even if he had reason to. Hart would call Alonzo wrongfully abused by his employer. She shook her head at how much of the Southerner remained in her.

She and Frankie moved Alonzo into the cabin that the Hardin brothers shared, and every hour, Frankie left the schoolhouse to tend to him. He slept a great deal, waking only to eat and to take more laudanum.

After one of her visits, Frankie returned to the schoolhouse with a grim, set expression. "Is he all right?" Adelaide asked, alarmed.

"He's no worse," Frankie said. "Adelaide, you have to tell Captain Hart about this. You have to let the Bureau redress it."

"Mr. Everett won't like me much if I keep his field hand and send the Bureau to chastise him," she said slowly.

Frankie grasped Adelaide's arm as if to make her point. "He doesn't like you now. Nor that woman he's married to, who talks against you so."

Adelaide laughed bitterly. "Miss Aggie used to be my best friend in the county before the war."

"Give it into Captain Hart's hands," Frankie pleaded. "Let it become a matter for the Bureau. Let the Everetts hate the Bureau."

"Don't press me, Frankie," Adelaide warned her.

But Frankie took her hand away. "If you don't send word, I will."

— ❦ —

HART ARRIVED A few hours later, his clothes dusty from the road and his face creased with worry. "How is the boy?" he asked.

"He was hurt, but we tended to him as best we could," Adelaide said.

His eyes gleamed with anger. "May I speak with him?"

"He's been in pain. We gave him laudanum. He's sleeping."

Frankie appeared behind her. Underneath her usual, pleasant scent of lavender soap and rosewater cream she smelled of the sweat of fear. "I talked to him this morning when I brought him breakfast. He told me what happened, Captain Hart."

"What happened, Miss Williamson?"

They stepped into the yard and stood underneath the live oak where the first school had been held. The air was warm and thick for spring. Copious rain had brought out the mosquitoes, and all three of them brushed the insects away as Frankie spoke.

"Alonzo's father fell ill a few months ago," she said. "He started to cough, and now he's bedridden, too weak to work in the fields. Alonzo is the oldest boy, and he's tall and strong for his age. He took his father's place behind the plow. It dismayed him terribly to stop coming to our school, but he felt obliged to help his mother. She hasn't been well either, since the last baby. The rest of the children are too young to do a man's work."

She slapped at a mosquito that had settled on her hand, and the dead insect left a smear of blood on her skin. "He was so proud of having learned how to read. He told me that Mr. Everett, who takes the Atlanta paper every week, threw it away when he was done with it. Alonzo figured no one would mind if he retrieved it from the trash. A few days ago Mr. Everett found him reading and called him lazy and insolent. He snatched the paper away and began to beat the boy until his back was raw and his face was bruised and bloody. The boy ran to us and begged for our help."

Frankie gestured at Hart with her blood-smeared hand. "Beaten bloody for reading!" Her voice was low and full of measured anger. "Treated like a slave!"

Hart rested his hand on his hip, where he wore the pistol under his coat. "I'll visit Mr. Everett," he said.

"I'll go with you," Adelaide said firmly.

His hand still resting on the pistol, Hart said, "It's too dangerous. I can't allow it."

"No, you misunderstand."

"I do not."

"I can speak to him as you can't," she insisted. She thought of going roundabout with Mr. Humphreys in the saloon, salving his anger at having to file a deed for her husband's sale of land to a former slave. She laid her hand on Hart's arm. "Before the war, my father was the biggest planter in the county. I'm still Mordecai Mannheim's daughter. Mr. Everett may hate me for running the school, but he wouldn't dare to hurt me. I'll go with you."

They took the buggy as though it were a social visit. Hart didn't speak, but he tugged angrily at the reins, even though she had always seen him kind to a horse.

The closer they came to the Everett place, the more troubled Adelaide felt. She thought of Frankie's shivering fit after she had tended to Alonzo. *Hart was right.* The thought chilled her in the hot spring air. *I should let this be a Bureau matter.*

The Everett place, the old Payne place, which had suffered badly when Sherman and Sheridan came through, had yet to recover. Without a gardener to keep it, the driveway was badly overgrown, and the gardens on either side had reverted to weeds. The house had been patched back together and had been recently whitewashed, but the charred and ruined wood showed through in a ghostly shadow. To the right of the house, the old slave cabins were in even worse repair, their steps caved in and their roofs crumbling. But they were inhabited. In the dirt outside the nearest ruined cabin, half a dozen young children played with a thin yellow hound. As they drove up, the dog ran after the buggy, barking wildly.

Hart jumped from the buggy and helped Adelaide out. As they approached the house, Everett opened the door. He was slender, with long, dark, disheveled hair. He had been handsome before the war etched deep lines of discontent into his face. He was coatless and his shirt, open at the neck, was badly wrinkled. His boots were crusted with red mud. The hound ran up to him, panting, but he kicked it away.

He stared at Hart. "You." And at Adelaide. "And you. I know why you're here. You're keeping the boy who ran away from me."

Adelaide saw Aggie creeping into the hallway. She stood behind her husband to listen.

"He's no longer your slave to command," Hart said coolly. "He's your employee, to be treated decently."

"He's a lazy, insolent nigger, and he deserves the beating I gave him."

Aggie's face hardened into malice.

Adelaide felt Hart's temper radiate from him like the day's heat. She grasped his sleeve and spoke sweetly, as though she had been properly invited into the parlor and given a cup of tea and a sesame cookie on a china plate. "Mr. Everett, I grew up on a place where we never beat anyone. And before the war, my husband showed kindness to all of his servants. He treated them with consideration. They stayed loyal to us and remained with us, even after they knew that they were free."

Everett snorted in derision. "I know how kind your husband was to his slaves. Didn't he have a bastard child by his servant?"

Hart started forward, and Adelaide yanked hard on his sleeve. She continued in the same sweet tone. "Mr. Everett, that's not exactly news, is it? I'm sure that Miss Aggie has told you all about it." She threw Aggie her own look, malice cloaked in sugar. *Bless your heart,* as Southern ladies said, when they meant, *I'd like to stick a knife through it.*

Everett pressed on. "What I hear is that it runs in the family! She's her master's daughter, ain't she? Miss Mannheim!" He laughed, the ugliest sound of mirth that Adelaide had ever heard.

She didn't change her tone. She continued to speak poison in the most honeyed way. "My daddy was the richest planter in Cass County before the war, and he still is, Mr. Everett. You may run a plantation in this county, but you aren't a gentleman and you'll never be one."

As Aggie watched, her husband said, "Don't you high-hat me. Everyone knows that you're the Bureau's whore."

Adelaide spoke over his shoulder to her old friend, her voice no longer honeyed. "Is that what you told him, Aggie?"

Everett didn't give his wife a chance to speak. He turned to Hart. "And you, you Yankee bastard, if I ever see your face again on my property, I'll shoot you."

Hart put his hand on the pistol at his hip, but Adelaide yanked again on his sleeve. "That's enough," she said, sounding like Frankie chastising a bad boy in the schoolroom. "Let's go."

Back in the buggy, on the untended gravel path that led to the road, Adelaide sat back and gave in to the shivers. Hart was too angry to ask after her or to offer to tuck a blanket around her. He drove her back to the Kaltenbach place at the brisk pace of a man who felt like taking out his anger on the horse. She was too upset to chide him for it.

When he pulled up to the house, she stormed up the stairs and through the door. He followed her, his boots clomping on the wooden floor. He shouted after her, "How can I protect you if you conduct yourself like this?"

She whirled around to shout back. "You can't! You aren't my husband, to compel me to do anything!"

"Someone should, since he's doing such a fine job of it. Running his business in Atlanta while you're in danger in Cass County. A man should have more care for his wife than that!"

"You stay out of it. My marriage is none of your business. Even if he abandoned me, it's not a matter for the Bureau!"

Hart moved close and grabbed for her hand. "It puts me into a fury to see how he treats you. He doesn't write, he doesn't visit. Doesn't he care for his son? What kind of a man is he?"

She tried to pull away. "You heard from our friend, Mr. Everett. In the words no lady should hear. Why shouldn't I hear them, since I know how true they are? He's an adulterer."

He grasped her free hand and beseeched her. "Why do you stay married to such a man?"

"Is a divorce such an easy thing in Ohio? Do husbands and wives go into court every day, to parade their shame for everyone to know about, so they can be free of each other?"

He said bitterly, "Of course not."

"Or perhaps they don't bother to go to the courthouse. Is that it? Is that how Yankees conduct themselves?"

"Can you really believe such a thing?"

"I don't know what to believe. What do people think when a man visits a married woman alone? Gives her gifts? Gives her money?"

He groaned. "You know as well as I do that it has always been the business of the Bureau."

"The county people don't put such a fine point on it. You heard what they call me."

"It's a lie, and you know it." "Is it?"

He pulled her closer. A closer embrace than the waltz, which had lit a fire in her when she had danced with William Pereira long ago. She recalled the heat she had felt as an unmarried girl, which had led her so badly astray. She was no longer a girl. She had made a bad marriage that was a shell of itself, as the old plantation houses were a shell of their former selves.

She thought of the destruction that fire could bring. Hart was much too close. Close enough to kiss her, if she let him.

What was dishonor? What was error? Her whole body seemed to burn.

She turned her head away. "Captain Hart, we can't talk about this, not anymore."

He let go her hands. He blushed and adjusted his collar, which needed no adjusting. "I understand," he said, raising himself into his soldier's stance. He softened his tone a little. "I will do my duty," he said, and he was gone.

— ∽ —

THE COUNTY BUZZED with the news of Alonzo's beating and the way he had taken refuge on the Kaltenbach place. Rachel didn't go into town, but she heard that Colonel Turner himself had gone to see Captain Hart at the Bureau to say sorrowfully, "How can we keep the people here to grow cotton?" Even mild Colonel Turner hadn't liked Hart's reply: "Treat them like free men and women."

That Sunday, before meeting, the churchyard hummed with opinions about Alonzo and Everett. Asa said angrily, "Everett treat the boy like he still a slave. No wonder he run away. All his tenants should run away!"

Zeke said, "It ain't running away if you're free. A free man free to quit if he ain't treated right."

Jenny stroked the head of her youngest, who clung to her skirt. She said hotly, "Just a boy! Think of a grown man, hurting a child so!"

"The man a brute," Rachel said. "He don't care who he abuse. Ask Adelaide."

After the service, Rachel sat on her front steps, hoping to catch a breeze. She wiped her face and wished she had a fan. She wondered if Frankie owned a fan, like a white lady.

Solomon Ballard emerged from the pine grove that bordered the Mannheim place, waving to her. As he sauntered toward the house, she asked him, "What bring you this way?"

"Sometimes I go to Miss Lucy and Miss Jenny in the kitchen, and they give me a little dinner. Pass the time of day, too," he said. "Lost my wife last year, and I enjoy their company."

"Sorry to hear it."

"May I set with you for a moment?" he asked.

She nodded.

Solomon took out his big, soiled handkerchief and wiped his face, and then he sat, sobered. "This business with young Alonzo has got me bothered. That fool of a Yankee already promised he'd give me a beating. Don't want to wait to get it."

"You said you don't have a contract. You could go."

"That's what I been thinking. I hear that a black man can get work in Atlanta. Work in a lumberyard or one of them mills. No one beat you or abuse you, and every week you get paid your money." He leaned closer and whispered, "Just might take myself to Atlanta."

She nodded again. "Don't tell anyone," he said.

"I won't."

—⸙—

A FEW DAYS later, as Rachel rose from her desk to go into the kitchen, hoping for a bite of fresh biscuit, she heard Jenny and Lucy laughing. She pushed open the kitchen door to ask, "What amuse you so?"

"You ain't heard yet?" Jenny asked.

"Ain't heard anything amusing. What is it?"

Jenny said, "Both of them tenants on the Mannheim place, they gone. Mr. Ballard, he act the gentleman with that Yankee and tell him that he leaving. And that Yankee lose his temper and strike Mr. Ballard. And guess what? Mr. Ballard strike him right back and go as swift as he can. The other tenant go with him."

"Still don't see why it amuse you."

Jenny laughed harder. "Oh, that Yankee, he hopping mad. He get on the train and go to Atlanta. Can't imagine what he think he do there. That he find them to bring them back?" Jenny laughed again and Lucy joined her. "Even I know how big a place Atlanta is. More people than you can imagine in Atlanta!"

Rachel had a very good idea who the Yankee sought in Atlanta. Tomorrow she would go there herself to talk to him with a plan of her own.

— ✍ —

RACHEL SLIPPED FROM the house early to drive herself to the depot in Cartersville. Mordecai had once written to Adelaide, and Rachel had committed the address on Peachtree Street to memory. Now she knew how to ask her way from the depot and to find her way in the maze of Atlanta's muddy streets.

The houses on Peachtree Street were brand new and belonged to people who had money enough for grandeur. They were three stories tall, faced with stone, and ornamented with bay windows and turrets in the newest fashion for houses that looked like castles. She stopped before the largest house on the block, its slate roof shimmering in the sun, its huge plate-glass windows blinding. The front yard was planted with magnolias that grew like a weed in the Atlanta spring, and the air was scented with them, as it had been on the old Mannheim place in Cass County.

The butler who answered was a stranger. She wondered if old Ezra, the only slave who hadn't left Mordecai for freedom, was still with him. The new butler said sharply, "You can't come in this way!"

"Yes, I can. Tell Mr. Mannheim that Miss Rachel Mannheim is here to see him." She let the name, and the relationship behind it, shimmer in the warm, fragrant air.

A woman's German-accented voice drifted from the interior of the house. "Amos, who is at the door?"

"Call herself Miss Mannheim, Missus."

"Does she? Let her in."

The voice belonged to a stout woman in an ornate silk dress, which was draped and ruched to hide her embonpoint, as the dressmakers called it. The fashionable curls of the day framed a strong, fleshy face. She regarded Rachel with a shrewd look. "What brings you here?"

"I came to see Mr. Mannheim."

"I'm afraid he isn't at home. He's at his place of business." A small smile played over her lips, which were full and rosy, like a much younger woman's.

"Where might I find him, ma'am?" Rachel asked.

"On Whitehall Street," she said. "He'll be there all day. Would you like to come in?"

"Begging your pardon, ma'am, but who are you?"

"You didn't know? He and I married as soon as he moved to Atlanta. You won't come in? I can't offer you anything?"

She said politely, "Thank you, ma'am, but I have business with him, and I'd best be on my way."

She looked at Rachel with interest. Her eyes sparkled like a mischievous girl's. She said, "Mr. Mannheim often speaks of you. He says you have a good head for business. Like his."

Miss Mannheim met the eyes of the second Mrs. Mannheim. "Does he," she said.

— ᘓ —

RACHEL WENT TO find Mordecai in his office. Even though white and black mingled in the crowd on Whitehall Street, few black people, and no women, entered the commercial building that housed the newly risen cotton brokers of postwar Atlanta. Her boots echoed on the marble floor. In the midst of the foyer, behind the splendid desk, sat a black man in a frock coat. He asked, "What do you want here?" Despite his smart appearance, he had the accent of a former slave from the Piedmont, just as she did.

Irritated, she said, "Looking for Mr. Mannheim."

"What's your business with him?"

She glared at him. "Didn't think I needed a pass to visit a man in his office. Where do he sit?"

Mordecai's office was paneled in dark wood and furnished with gentlemen's chairs upholstered in leather. The office smelled of cigars, like the study in his old house in Cass County. He had regained all the flesh he'd lost during the war, and his belly again strained against his waistcoat buttons. He sat behind a desk that was untidy with papers, in a big leather chair like the one he'd always had at in his old study.

"Rachel!" he said, surprised to see her. "What brings you here?"

"Called on you at home," she said. "Mrs. Mannheim sent me to see you."

He beamed. "You met Betty! Ain't she a treasure? Cheers me up. Not the least like Rosa."

Rachel gestured toward the big mahogany desk. "How much did she bring you?"

"Enough to get set up!" Mordecai roared with laughter. "Even though it ain't the least bit your business!"

She sat carefully on the edge of her chair and waited for him to compose himself. "I brought some news from your place in Cass County," she said.

"Oh, I already heard. My Yankee renter came to tell me that his hands ran off to Atlanta."

"He can't manage his tenants," she said. "He needs an overseer."

"I'll find someone. The county's full of men who need work, now that they're busted up. It ain't your worry."

She said, "Why don't you hire me?"

It took him a moment to catch up to her question. "To oversee?"

"I ran Henry's place during the war. And now I run the place for Adelaide."

"It ain't just writing in the ledger. An overseer needs to bring in the crop. Drive the hands. Make sure they keep working. Punish them if they don't. Can't see you whupping a grown man."

"If you treat people right, you don't need to whup. Learned that from Charlie."

Mordecai ignored her. "You ain't a fool," he said. "Don't act like one."

"Ain't foolishness to offer to do a job of work I can do."

"You can't," he said. "I won't hire you for it."

Stung, she said, "Why not? Is it because I'm black? Or because I'm a woman? Or because I'm your daughter?"

At this, he cooled. "You have a good head on your shoulders. Good head for business. Why don't you move to Atlanta and go into business for yourself?"

She wondered what he would suggest to her. She leaned forward. "To do what?"

He leaned back. "The washwomen do a good business. You could do well for yourself as a washwoman."

Full of fury, she rose, and brought her hand down hard on the surface of the mahogany desk. "Washwoman!" she said. "Is that the best you think I can do?"

"Go on," he said.

"Is that the best you can do for me?"

"Get out," he said.

She left the building in such a state that she didn't reply to the frock-coated man who watched over the foyer. She walked past Meyer's Dry Goods without seeing it. Washwoman! The insult resounded. She thought of Mr. Pereira and his lawyer's business in insult. Fueled by strong feeling, she strode down Whitehall, intending to veer onto Wheat Street to find his office in Sherman Town.

But she took a wrong turn and found herself on a back street, where a crazy quilt of hastily built houses ringed an open space that reminded her of the yard on a country plantation. Chickens roamed, pecking at the ground, and so did pigs. At one end, a group of black men leaned against a fence. They watched the activity in the yard, where a canvas canopy sheltered a group of women from the sun. There were about half a dozen, their arms in great tubs full of soapy water, and they called to each other and to the children who played in the dirt.

They were the washwomen.

One of them straightened up and said to Rachel, "Is you looking for someone, sister?" Her face was dark brown and lined, like someone who had worked in the field all her life. She had wide shoulders and big hands on a frame made bony by hard work and not enough to eat. Her knuckles were swollen from being often in hot water. She had a strong voice, the kind that led a holler to set the pace in the cotton field.

"Looking for Mr. Pereira, on Wheat Street. Took a wrong turn from downtown."

"The lawyer?" she asked. "Hope you ain't in any trouble."

"No," Rachel said, thinking that the place must not be so different from a plantation, where everyone knew your business.

"Is you new in Atlanta? Haven't seen you before in Sherman Town."

"Just visiting," she said.

"If you come to Atlanta and you need work, you can always take in wash."

Lord, no, Rachel thought.

The washwoman raised her wet arm to take in all of the women who worked in the courtyard. "We all make a good living," she said. "Help our families. Even if your man work, it's good to bring home some money." She gestured towards the men who leaned against the fence, talking in low tones. They were the only people Rachel had seen in Atlanta who weren't in a hurry. "And if your man lose his work, you keep on earning and helping."

I got free to do better than that, she thought.

The woman said, "Good steady work. Work for yourself, and say no if white folks insult you."

"Got an appointment to keep. How do I get to Wheat Street?" she asked, suddenly short of breath.

Once on Wheat Street, she hurried away, looking for Pereira's office. Before the door she hesitated. The building looked meaner than she remembered, the grayed boards smelling faintly of burned wood, the windows smeared with dirt. When she pushed open the door, the unoiled hinges whined. Pereira sat at his desk, holding a shirt in one hand and a needle in the other. What was he doing? Did black lawyers take in mending, like black women took in wash? He hastily hid the shirt in his lap, out of sight.

"Ain't there anyone who can do that for you?" she blurted out.

"If I pay for it," he said. "Why should I, if I can do it myself?"

"Thought you made a living from the lawyering business."

"When I was a boy, I was apprenticed to a tailor," he said. With some bitterness, he added, "I have a trade, in case the lawyering business disappoints me."

She was too angry to offer him sympathy. "You told me you do a brisk business in insult. I brought you some business."

He sat up straighter, interested. In a tone she hadn't heard before—cool and detached—he asked, "Who insulted you? What happened?"

She sat, too heavily for the rickety chair. "Is it illegal for a white man to refuse to sell land to a black woman?"

"Unfortunately not. A man can sell or refuse to sell to whomever he wants to."

"Is it illegal for a father to refuse to sell land to his daughter?"

"Not unless there's been a contractual promise made. Has he written you a note or a deed? Has he left you land in his will?"

"Don't know. Don't think he'd tell me, if I asked."

"In that, I can help you. I can make an inquiry for you." He reached for his pen. "What is your father's name?" he asked, the pen poised over a sheet of paper.

"Mordecai Mannheim." It gave her a tremor to say it so bluntly.

"Was he your former master?"

She lost her temper. "More of them busybody questions," she said, forgetting her good diction.

He flushed as he set down the pen. "This isn't a social call," he said. "If I'm to work as your lawyer, there are things I need to know. This may be a matter for the law, or it may not."

"If it's not?"

"Some insults are a matter of family feeling. For that, there's not much the law can do." He sighed, and poised the pen over the paper again. "Has he acknowledged you in any way?"

She thought of their last conversation. "I believe you already heard enough of my private shameful business," she said.

"I'm sworn to confidence, as I've told you. If it's a legal matter.""You're bound to keep it to yourself?" She knew it, but she wanted to needle him.

He said sharply, "Yes, as I keep reminding you. I'm obliged to."
She glared at him again. "When you call on him, you tell
me. We go together."

—⁓—

SINCE THEIR FIGHT, Adelaide had been haunted by the memory
of Captain Hart. She thought of his passion in defending her
and her own answering heat. It was forbidden and wrong, like
the pressure of a hand, a caress on the cheek, or a kiss. She ached
to write to him in apology, but every effort ended in a blot and
another ruined piece of paper in the wastebasket.

Hart finally sent a note in the formal language of acquaintance,
asking if he could call on her and Miss Williamson on the matter
of Alonzo. He brought Sergeant Bailey, as though he needed a
chaperon instead of a guard. They waited under the live oak
while Frankie brought Alonzo from his hiding place in the cabin.
Adelaide joined them, curious to know what Hart would say.

The boy looked at Hart with an expression of worry. Frankie
put a gentle arm around his shoulders—she had to reach upward,
he was so much taller than she—and said gently, "This is Captain
Hart, of the Freedmen's Bureau in Cartersville. He wants to look
into the matter of Mr. Everett's injustice toward you."

Hart asked, "How are you, young man?"

"Feeling better, captain, sir. Miss Frankie take good care of me."

"I'm glad to hear that," he said. "I'd like to bring you to the
Bureau office to tell your side of the story, and I'll insist that Mr.
Everett be there as well. I want to hear from both of you, and if

there's been wrong done, I want to make sure that Mr. Everett is punished and prevented from hurting you again."

Alonzo's eyes widened. "Captain, sir, you want me to speak against Marse Everett?"

"Just to tell the truth of what he did to you."

"Speak against him, while he stand and listen to me?"

"I need to hear from both of you."

"If I speak against him, he hurt me again," Alonzo said.

Hart shook his head. "I won't allow it. If he did wrong, he'll be punished, and he won't be able to hurt you again."

"Punished!" the boy cried. "Then he come after me, worse than he did before!"

Frankie, whose arm was still wrapped around Alonzo's shoulders, said, "He's right to worry." She glanced at Hart. "Can we take him somewhere safe?"

"He's safest here," Hart replied. He glanced at Adelaide. "I'll summon him to the Bureau office in a few days. Sergeant Bailey and I will assure that Mr. Everett will be there, too."

"Miss Williamson and I will bring him to Cartersville," Adelaide said.

"Don't come alone. Bring one of your tenants, or Mr. Charles Mannheim."

They fell silent. Alonzo, whose face had gone ashen, leaned against Frankie for support. Frankie asked, "Captain Hart, would you mind if I asked Sergeant Bailey to help me take Alonzo back to his bed?"

Bailey, a little puzzled by the request, asked Hart, "Do you mind, sir?"

"Don't linger," Adelaide said sharply to Frankie, as she left.

Hart always looked weary, but he looked worse than usual, with dark circles under his eyes. She wanted to soften her voice, but instead she asked, "Is this a matter of business?"

He shook his head. "No, it's plainer than that. I owe you an apology. I said some terrible things to you."

Her cheeks burned. "No, the fault was mine. I should apologize to you."

"You're more than my staunchest ally in this place," he said. "You're my dearest friend. I've put you in danger here, and if anything happened to you, I would never forgive myself."

She didn't dare. "You haven't put me in danger. I've brought it upon myself." She swallowed hard.

"All the more reason for me to defend you," he said. He took her hand and pressed it in his own.

—⌒—

Mr. Pereira wrote to Rachel to tell her that he was ready to call on Mordecai Mannheim, and Rachel took the train to Atlanta. It bothered her afresh to sit in the "colored car" behind the engine, the hottest and the dirtiest, where any man who felt like smoking could stretch out his legs, spit tobacco, and pester a black woman with the nastiest words he knew.

At the depot, she shook the fug of the train from her shawl and made her way to Wheat Street, where she met Pereira. On the street he held out his arm as though he expected her to take it. "May I escort you?"

"Thought we were doing business together."

"Allow me the courtesy," he said.

Blushing, she said, "I don't like it on a matter of business."

He offered his arm again. More gently, he said, "As your lawyer, I'm bound to help you. Please let me." When she hesitated, he gazed at her with those changeable eyes, hazel today. "Miss Mannheim," he coaxed her.

Matter of business. Legal business, she reminded herself. "All right." She took his arm, and they walked together until Wheat Street became Whitehall.

Pereira gazed at the imposing new building that housed Mordecai's office. "Mr. Mannheim does well for himself."

"Married some money."

Pereira nodded. "I know. I've made an inquiry."

It pleased her to think that Pereira had poked into Mordecai's private shameful business, too. "Just like a scout I knew, in the war," she said.

He smiled. "Not so different."

When they walked into the dark-paneled office, Mordecai looked up. "Rachel! Who have you brought with you?"

"I wrote to you, sir," Mr. Pereira said.

"I get a lot of letters," Mordecai replied, gesturing to the untidy heap of papers and torn envelopes on the desk. "Don't remember most of 'em. What was it about?"

"My name is Daniel Pereira. I'm a lawyer, and I'm representing Miss Mannheim in a legal matter."

"A legal matter?" He turned to Rachel. "What legal matter?"

"Miss Mannheim is curious as to what you might owe her, given the connection between the two of you."

"Pereira!" Mordecai said, hearing the familiar name. "Which of those scoundrels is your father?"

Pereira stood up straight, as though someone had stuck a tailor's pin into him.

Rachel thought, *Now he feel it, too. Now he understand.*

"Why do you ask, sir?" Pereira said, irritated.

"I'd ask anyone named Pereira. Don't trust them any farther than I can fling them. They're all scoundrels!"

"Mr. Mannheim, this really has no bearing on the matter at hand—"

Mordecai said to Rachel, "So you didn't tell him the whole story, did you, missy? How Adelaide nearly became Mrs. William Pereira, and cried off because he was such a rakehell?"

"The matter at hand," Rachel repeated. She was discomfited along with Pereira, but now she was embarrassed for him, too.

Mordecai addressed Pereira again, in a familiar tone. "Who was your father? If I'm to do business, I like to know who I'm dealing with."

"It really doesn't have any bearing" Pereira said again.

Rachel said impatiently, "We won't even get started unless you tell him. So tell him."

Pereira looked disgusted. "My father was Jacob Pereira of Charleston, a fine man."

"Now I recall," Mordecai said. "Your ma was a colored woman. The family kept it quiet, but they didn't like it, not a bit." He looked at both of them and laughed. "There ain't a thing you can hold against me in the law," he said.

Pereira gave Mordecai a withering look. "You might be moved by *family feeling*," he said.

Mordecai chortled. "Not unless it make me money. But it do not."

They didn't linger in the foyer under the eye of the disapproving majordomo in his frock coat. They stood on the sidewalk as the crowd jostled them in its hurry to get somewhere else. Pereira didn't stand as straight as he had striding into Mordecai's office. His hair was a little disheveled and his shirt collar a little wilted. Now she knew for sure. He was the child of a black woman and a rich Israelite who couldn't marry her. As she had with Frankie, Rachel thought, *We're more alike than I knew.*

"So that's how you're connected with the Pereiras," she said.

"Not that it has any bearing on the matter at hand," he repeated, but it was weak. "It do, if you trust me with it." She put her hand on his arm.

"Everyone in Charleston knew that my father loved my mother all his life," he said. "But when Jacob Pereira died, he was buried in the Jewish cemetery as a bachelor, and my cousin William said Kaddish for him." His voice turned bitter. "William Pereira, who wouldn't greet me if he saw me in the street. I was never a guest at his house, or at his table, and certainly not at his wedding. But he is my cousin."

—⁓—

IN THE DAYS before Alonzo was due in Cartersville, he became quieter and grayer by the hour. When he wasn't resting in his cabin he followed Frankie like a shadow. After midday dinner, when the rest of the children played together, he sat unmoving at the base of the live oak. He was stronger, but he was badly bothered.

Adelaide watched as Frankie knelt beside him to touch his forehead. "What is it, Alonzo?" Her voice was low, but it was resonant. Adelaide could hear her perfectly well.

"I'm a trouble to you," the boy said.

She rested her hand on his shoulder. "No, you're not."

"Can't go to Cartersville. Can't speak against Mr. Everett."

"I wish justice could be done," she said.

"I go away. Somewhere. Won't trouble you any longer."

"Oh, Alonzo," Frankie said, with profound sadness. She bent very close to him, and whispered in his ear so quietly that Adelaide couldn't hear, no matter how hard she strained to listen.

He nodded. Frankie touched his cheek and rose, her skirts rustling.

Adelaide caught up with Frankie at the schoolhouse door. "What was that about?" she asked.

Frankie shook her head.

That night, nothing disturbed the sleep of the people on the Kaltenbach place—not Adelaide or Sarah or Frankie in the big house, and not even the two Hardin boys in the cabin they temporarily shared with Alonzo. But in the morning, Johnny Hardin ran into the house and disrupted the three women at their breakfast. "Alonzo's gone," he said. "Crept off in the night without a sound."

—⌇—

THAT AFTERNOON, EVERETT rode up the drive and stomped up to the schoolroom. He pounded on the door, and Adelaide answered it. Frankie was beside her, and Johnny Hardin, who could fetch his rifle or run to ask Luke or Davey or Asa for help, was just behind.

Adelaide said sweetly, "Mr. Everett. What brings you to visit?"

"This ain't a social call," he snarled. "That boy ran off last night, and you let him go. Where is he?"

Some child in the school didn't keep it a secret, Adelaide thought. "We don't know," she said.

Frankie began to shiver, as she had the night they tended to Alonzo's cuts and bruises.

"Did you give him a fool notion to go to Atlanta, like every other nigger in this county?"

Frankie pulled her shawl tightly about her, trying to stop her shivering.

Everett stared at her. "What's wrong with you? Got the ague? Or do you know something?"

Frankie's voice was strong and assured, the schoolmarm's best voice. "No, sir, I do not, and when you address me, you will call me 'Miss Williamson.'"

"I'll call you nigger bitch if I want to." He moved closer to Adelaide. "Damn you, harboring a runaway, and giving him a notion to bolt the county!"

Adelaide said, "When I visited your place, sir, you told me you'd shoot at me if I came to see you again. Now that you're here, I won't return the courtesy. But I'll have to ask you to go."

"What will you do if I don't?"

"Mr. Everett, would you shoot at me? Would you dare?"

He spat, and the gob of spittle landed at Frankie's feet. "I wouldn't waste a bullet," he said. With a last contemptuous glare, he turned to stomp back to the house where he had tethered his horse.

Frankie shook uncontrollably as she watched him go.

— ᐱ —

THAT NIGHT, A scream tore Adelaide from sleep. *Frankie.* Adelaide threw back the covers, raced up the stairs, and threw open the door to the attic room.

Frankie sat up in bed, sobbing.

Adelaide rushed to her. "What is it?"

"A terrible dream," she sobbed. "I dreamed that I was back in Bibb County. They shot Mollie dead and then they came for me—to force me—"

Adelaide sank down on the bed and gathered Frankie in her arms. "Hush," she said, stroking her hair. "Hush, Frankie." As the sobs slowed, she said, "Mollie is safe, at home in Ohio. And you're with us." She tightened her embrace. She had never held a woman in her arms like this, not her sister Rachel, not even her dearest friend Sarah. Frankie's flesh was rounded and dense, and even in her sweat of fear, her skin had the scent of lavender. "Hush," Adelaide said, holding Frankie close. "Anyone who wants to hurt you will have to kill me first."

When the sobs stopped, Adelaide kissed Frankie's cheek. She said, "Lie back to rest."

"Will you stay with me?"

"Of course."

Frankie lay back on the pillows and gripped Adelaide's hand. Frankie closed her eyes and her lips moved in the whisper of prayer. "The Lord is my shepherd... he leadeth me beside the still waters... he restoreth my soul... even though I walk through the valley of the shadow of death, I fear no evil..."

Adelaide sat unmoving until Frankie's hand lost its grip and she was truly asleep. She bent down to kiss Frankie's brow as she slept.

8 | New Ventures

Rachel sifted through the day's mail. Since she had heard that Alonzo had fled, she felt restless again. She wondered if he had gone to Atlanta. Frankie knew, she was sure, because whenever anyone mentioned him, Frankie's expression closed up and she fell silent.

Rachel took up the newest edition of the weekly *Atlanta Intelligencer*. All over Georgia, the war was still felt. There was an unhappy article about the loyalty oath for Confederate soldiers. The trains were running again in fact, the Western and Atlantic Railroad was offering season tickets. In Covington, the Southern Masonic Female College was to hold exercises. She turned the page to learn that cotton was at twenty-five cents a pound, which gladdened the heart of no one in the cotton business. And at the bottom of the page, in a notice so small that anyone might miss it, was the announcement that $100,000 in Georgia state bonds were now available for sale, in denominations of $500 and $1,000, in the First National Bank of Macon.

So there was now a bank in Macon, several hours away by the now-reconstructed railroad lines.

Rachel let the paper fall to the desk. The matter of the freedom money had gone quiet during the rush of the planting season and the furor over Alonzo, but it hadn't gone away. If the bank in Macon could talk to their bank in London—or its counterpart in New York—the former slaves on the Kaltenbach place could finally feel their money in their hands.

Now she had good reason to write to Henry. As she dipped the pen in the inkwell, she felt a pang in her chest. For a moment she lost herself and let the ink drip on the paper, ruining it. "God in Heaven!" she said in irritation, Henry's favorite oath. It was a matter of business, with as much feeling as a letter to the cotton factor or the mule dealer, a venture familiar to them both. She crumpled up the paper and reached for another sheet.

When she finished, she was too impatient to sit at the desk. She slipped from the house to walk, and even though she knew better, she found herself on the path to the Mannheim place.

After Mordecai's tenants left for Atlanta, the Yankee had abandoned his plans to grow cotton and moved back north. The place was vacant. The cotton crop had never gone in, and Rachel walked past fields where the furrows were overgrown with weeds. She leaned on the fence of the field Solomon Ballard had plowed and itched with a planter's irritation to see good cotton land go to waste. "A bale an acre," she murmured, as though Mordecai were there to quiz her, as he had done throughout her childhood as his slave. "Twenty-five cents a pound, five hundred

pounds to a bale, that's a hundred twenty-five dollars a bale."
Twelve thousand and five hundred dollars, all foregone because
the Yankee had been a fool and Mordecai had been too stubborn
to rent or sell his land to her.

Charlie, who knew that she visited the unplanted field, had
chided her against it. "What good do it do? Don't grow any
cotton and make you feel miserable." But Charlie had twenty
acres planted in cotton, the plants vigorous and bushy in rows
free of weeds, and as much in corn, which popped and hissed
in its hurry to grow. Charlie didn't understand why she visited
Mordecai's place. It wasn't to cause herself pain. It was to remind
herself that she had a claim here, and she would find a way to
make her father honor it.

— ✑ —

"ADELAIDE?" RACHEL ASKED. Adelaide sat at the little table in
the parlor that she now used for a desk. Her fingers had become
ink-stained again, but she no longer wrote in her diary or to her
friends. Rachel knew that she wrote to the American Missionary Association, in Atlanta and in New York, to ask for help for
"Christ's poor" in Cass County.

She looked up and rubbed her wrist. "What is it, Rachel?"

Rachel told her about the *Atlanta Intelligencer's* mention of
the bank in Macon, and Adelaide swiftly replied, "The freedom
money." She gave Rachel a searching look. "So we can keep at
least one of the promises we made."

— ✍ —

HENRY'S REPLY TO her letter about the bank in Macon came swiftly, but the arrangements were slow. It took time to write to the Bank of England, it took time to explain the business to the bank in Macon, and it took even longer for one of the most imposing banks in the world to correspond with a weed of a bank in Georgia. Rachel began to worry that the bank in Macon would refuse to handle money for depositors who were black.

By the time that Henry wrote to her again, it was midsummer, the respite between chopping and cotton harvest. Tired of the study, Rachel sat in the parlor to read his news, opposite Frankie, who read a letter of her own.

The bank drafts had finally been arranged, he wrote. All of the accounts were ready in Macon. He couldn't leave Atlanta at the moment, but he would soon arrange a visit to let everyone know.

She thought of Sergeant Bailey's bitterness at Christmas and thought, *Henry should stay in Atlanta. I'll let them know.*

The rest of his letter was jovial. He told her that he had been to the opera, where he had listened to a troupe from New York singing *Il Trovatore*. He wrote that his nearest neighbor had eaten peanuts throughout the performance and thrown the shells on the floor, as though he were attending a variety show instead of an opera. It was an easy error to fall into, he said, since the hall was used for both.

Rachel let the letter flutter into her lap. Frankie said, "What is the news?"

"It's from Mr. Kaltenbach. About the freedom money."

"You look so uncertain, Rachel," Frankie said.

"Don't know whether it will come right or not."

"Of course it will." Her eyes sparkled. "It's money to help people live in freedom!"

Rachel shook her head. "No, I don't worry about that. They're all wise enough to use it well." She took a deep breath. "I do worry about seeing Mr. Kaltenbach again."

Frankie brushed her cheek. "But that's over and done, isn't it?"

"If you love someone, is it ever over and done?" Rachel said softly.

She meant that she would never be finished with Henry. But why, then, did she suddenly think of Daniel Pereira?

—⌒—

Rachel never expected to receive a letter from Betty Mannheim, but when it came a week after Henry's, she crumpled the envelope in her hand and went to tell Adelaide about it.

"That's odd," Adelaide said. "Why wouldn't she write to me?"

When Adelaide learned her father had remarried—no one in Cass County had been invited to the hasty wedding—she had asked Henry to send the new Mrs. Mannheim a fine set of table linens, along with a polite note. The two women, stepmother and stepdaughter, had never met.

"I visited him when I was in Atlanta last. I met her," Rachel explained.

Adelaide laid down her pen. "What does she say?"

"It's about"—she hesitated, not knowing how to say it—"your father. He's very sick."

"How bad?"

"Nigh dying."

The unloved daughter and the unacknowledged daughter looked at one another. Adelaide finally said, "Oh, Rachel. He always favored you. You go."

"It ain't seemly—" Rachel said.

"Nothing about our lives is seemly. I don't mind. Go."

"What if I mind?"

Adelaide met her eyes in surprise.

Rachel said, "What if I want you with me?"

—⌇—

THE SISTERS HAD difficulty at the depot. The stationmaster glanced at Rachel and said to Adelaide, "She can't sit with you. Third class, colored car."

Adelaide said firmly, "Then I'll take a third-class ticket."

"No ladies in the colored car."

Rachel fumed as she sat in the third-class car. When they arrived in Atlanta's depot, she found Adelaide, who said, "How can we find a carriage in this crowd?"

Rachel was still angry. "It ain't far. We walk, and we don't give a coachman the chance to refuse us."

Mordecai's house in Atlanta smelled of sickness, of sweat and stale bedsheets, an unemptied chamber pot, and the cloying sweetness of laudanum. Betty Mannheim had lost flesh, and her thinner face was newly lined. She wore black, as though anticipating her widowhood. She glanced from Rachel to her companion. "Adelaide," she said, grasping her stepdaughter's hands with an excess of emotion.

Rachel asked, "How is he?"

Betty shook her head.

"What does the doctor say?" Adelaide asked.

"The doctor can't figure it. All he'll say is that it's fever."

The smell of sickness was stronger in the room where Mordecai lay under the coverlet. He had lost all of his postwar girth—Rachel had never seen him so gaunt—and his skin was waxy and pale. His hands rested on the coverlet, the formerly fleshy fingers now bony, the skin spotted and gnarled, the nails yellow. He didn't stir at their entrance. Through his torpor, he grimaced in pain.

The three of them stood by the bedside. "Papa?" Adelaide said softly.

His eyes flickered open. "Eliza?" he asked.

"He's been asking for Eliza," Betty said, puzzled. "I thought his first wife was named Rosa. Who was Eliza?"

"My mother," Rachel said, and Betty's dark eyes glimmered with comprehension and jealousy.

Rachel stood beside Adelaide. Both of them watched the man in the bed, until Adelaide whispered, "I can't bear it. I can't stay." Betty followed her out to leave Rachel alone with Mordecai.

He's dying, she thought. *I should take his hand. I should say, 'Daddy, I'm here.' And I can't.*

She sat in the chair to watch him. She didn't know why, but she remained there, watching his suffering, feeling it echo within her, until, like Adelaide, she could bear it no longer.

Downstairs, she said to Betty and Adelaide, "He look like he don't have long." Kitchen talk, her own form of distress.

Betty said softly, "If there's news I'll write to you."

Rachel nodded.

At the door, Betty clasped Adelaide's hand, but she embraced Rachel. Clung to her. "Thank you for coming here," she said, her voice throaty.

Rachel thought, *Someone love him. She love him.*

On the train back to Atlanta, alone in the colored car, she sobbed into her handkerchief. *Has he made a promise to you?* Pereira had asked her. Daniel Pereira, the embittered, unacknowledged son.

No. Never. Only to ask me how many bales, and what we'd realize.

— ✍ —

HENRY WROTE TO fix his visit a few weeks hence, and Rachel went through the days before it with a feeling of increasing unease. She told Eliza that Daddy would see them soon, and after that every sentence from Eliza's lips began with the words, "When Daddy come."

When he arrived, Adelaide invited all of those who used to be held in bondage, save for prickly Sergeant Bailey as well as Micah and Lydia, who had left and could not be found, to came to hear about their money. They entered the house at their ease, now confident in their post-war freedom.

Zeke said to Henry, "So we can get our money now?"

"Yes, that's right," Henry replied.

"Go down to Macon and get it in our hands."

"If you want to."

"Or keep it there, in the bank," Charlie said. "Should be safer than under your bed!"

Everyone laughed, and the brandy decanter came out for a celebratory dram. They left together, laughing and talking, and it was a joyful noise unto the Lord.

After they'd gone, Henry said to Adelaide, "Would you talk to Captain Hart? Ask him to give the news to Sergeant Bailey? He won't take anything from me, even though it belongs to him. He thinks it's a master's largesse. Perhaps you can persuade him that it's justice."

Adelaide blushed. "Of course I will."

— ⌒ —

LATER THAT DAY, Henry rapped on Rachel's front door. He looked a little worse for wear; he must have taken another dram or two. The shadows under his eyes bothered her. She wanted to touch his cheek, but she forced herself not to. Instead she said, "Come in. I can brew some coffee, if you'd like."

"I still bless coffee every single day I drink it," he said. He carried a brown paper parcel under his arm. "Where is Eliza?"

Eliza ran into the room, shrieking, "Daddy! It's Daddy!"

Henry beamed and swept her up, kissing her face until she laughed and squirmed in his arms. "Liebchen!" he said.

"Missed you so much, Daddy."

He kissed her again. "I missed you, too," he murmured.

Rachel watched them, feeling the tug of Eliza's love for her father.

He let her down and held out the parcel.

"What is it?" she asked.

"Open it and see."

Eliza sat on the floor to tear off the paper. Inside was a doll in a gingham dress and a white apron, dressed just like Eliza herself on meeting day. Eliza caressed the dark wood of the doll's face and stroked the black yarn of her hair. She cried out in delight, "She's black, Daddy!"

He stroked Eliza's cheek. "Like my liebchen."

"And nothing for me," Rachel said, acerbic to hide her emotion.

"I didn't think you wanted anything from me," he said softly, and even though it was true, it made her heart ache. "I can't stay long."

"Sit for a minute."

He settled himself into the chair, as he had always done. It gave her a pang. "I've left Joe's employ. We had a disagreement. I was surprised at how bitter it was."

"What was it about?" She couldn't imagine easygoing Joe Meyer and amiable Henry angry with each other.

"He didn't like the way I treated the black customers. He thought it would drive away the white ones. So I left."

"What will you do now?"

"I'm planning a new venture," he said, his eyes twinkling. "It hasn't come to fruition yet."

New venture! Atlanta was growing like a cotton plant, and Atlantans had new ventures all the time. She wondered why he was secretive about it.

"What about you?" he asked.

"I'm planning a new venture, too."

"What is it?"

She thought of Mordecai in his sickbed in Atlanta. "Ain't come to fruition yet."

Eliza crawled into her father's lap and pulled on the lapels of his coat. "Daddy!" she asked. "Will you read me a story?"

"Eliza, honey," Rachel said. "Don't trouble—"

"It's no trouble. Of course I will, liebchen." He kissed his daughter's cheek with such tenderness that Rachel wanted to weep.

— ⌁ —

When the letter came to Rachel from Betty Mannheim, the envelope had no black border. It didn't mean much. Mrs. Mannheim might have been too busy to buy the envelopes or too distracted to find them. But the paper inside had no black border, either. Mrs. Mannheim wrote to tell her, Hes on the mend, and he's been asking for you. Please come if you can."

Rachel told Adelaide, who said, "Now it's right for you to go. He doesn't want to see me. He wants to see you."

Rachel pushed away Daniel Pereira's voice, whispering in her ear, and took the train to Atlanta.

She strode from the station to the house on Peachtree Street, elbowing her way through the crowd, and rapped on the front door with confidence. The butler Amos didn't question her, and Betty Mannheim, who had reclaimed her look of satisfaction in life, if not her fleshiness, asked after Adelaide and hugged Rachel in the hallway. "He's in the study," she said. "I can't keep him in bed. He insists on sitting up."

Rachel had been too upset to notice the interior of the house on her last visit, and now she gazed at it with interest. It was ostentatious in the new style, with dark, carved woodwork and heavily figured wallpaper. The carpet beneath her feet was thick and soft. She glanced upward. The ceilings were painted gold. So that was one way that Mordecai had spent his new wife's money.

The study was bigger and darker than the old one in Cass County, and the furniture was even larger, but otherwise it was the same, with the familiar smell of cigar smoke that she had always disliked. Mordecai sat in the biggest chair in the room, his still-frail body swathed in a blanket. His face was gaunt, but he now had the color of a living man.

"Betty treats me like a baby," he said. "Sits me before the fire, swaddles me like this, feeds me gruel, and won't let me have a cigar." But he smiled as he spoke. "She tells me you came to see me when I was so low. I don't remember."

"You were mighty sick," Rachel said.

"Betty told me that Adelaide came, too."

"We came together."

"Sit down," he said, and gestured to the big wing chair opposite his own.

She sat. She waited.

He said, "A man has some time to think about things when he nearly dies. I thought about what I'd do with anything I'd leave behind. Thought a lot about that land in Cass County."

Has he ever made a promise to you? the imagined voice of Daniel Pereira whispered.

"I don't want to leave it to Adelaide," Mordecai said. "She don't care for it. Wouldn't have a thought of what to do with it. But you do."

Has he ever acknowledged you? Pereira whispered.

"How many acres would you like?" he asked.

A fierce joy rushed through her. She knew what he would say next. She knew him better than either of them liked to admit.

"A hundred acres," he offered. "I'll sell it to you for fifty dollars an acre."

Has he left you anything in his will? Pereira whispered.

"For that land?" she said fiercely. "It's burned over and tumbledown and all over weeds. Take a season just to plow them under." She was Mordecai Mannheim's daughter, and she celebrated it. "Ten dollars an acre, and that's all it's worth."

He paused. She knew the dance he was leading her. She would follow him, step for step. "Well, I might see to forty dollars an acre," he said.

She laughed, nerves twined around the joy. "I'd come up to fifteen," she said. "That's what it's worth."

He grinned. He was dancing with her, too, and it gave him pleasure. He said, "You drive a hard bargain. But I could do thirty."

"Twenty," she said, grinning back at him.

"Meet in the middle?" He held out his hand. "Twenty-five dollars an acre?"

She reached out and their hands met in an awkward gesture, half business and half affection. "I say yes."

He didn't release his grasp. His hand was dry and bony over hers. "I'll have my lawyer draw up the deed and the note, and you bring that colored lawyer friend of yours here for a witness."

She nodded, too full of feeling to speak. As she left the house, she whispered back to Pereira: *A promise. A contract. An acknowledgement. Yes.*

—⤳—

AS SHE MADE her way back to Whitehall Street, she had to stop and hold her hand to her mouth in astonishment. People bumped into her and moved on impatiently. She didn't care.

A hundred acres of her father's land.

She should go to Pereira to make an arrangement with him, but she didn't feel right after his confession about his father. They had gotten the truth out of each other, and she wasn't easy with the recollection.

She wanted to talk to someone who would understand her triumph over Mordecai Mannheim. Suddenly she wanted to see Henry.

She didn't know where he had gone. She would ask at Meyer's.

Rachel hesitated before the handsome façade, where the gold lettering glowed in the morning sun. She resolutely pushed the door open, letting the cheerful bell announce her entry.

The clerk at the counter was a stranger, a young man with dark, curly hair, very nattily dressed. When he glanced at her and said, "Yes?" he meant, "What are you doing here?" and not "How may I help you?"

"I'm looking for Mr. Kaltenbach," she said politely.

Without looking at her, the young man said, "He's no longer with us."

"I know that. Where is he now?"

"I don't know," he said.

"Is Mr. Meyer here? May I speak to him?"

"Who are you?"

Stung, she said, "Tell him that Miss Mannheim is here. He knows me."

In a moment Joe Meyer emerged from the back room, frowning. He said, "Rachel, you shouldn't be here."

"Just want to know where Mr. Kaltenbach is now."

"You have to go—"

She had a fortune in the Bank of London and the promise of a hundred acres in Cass County. She was anyone's equal. She said fiercely, "Just tell me."

Joe Meyer shook his head. "He has his own shop now, in Sherman Town."

So that was the new venture he had been so secretive about. *Where can I find it?*

"Walk down Wheat Street. Rachel, if you don't leave, I'll have to—"

She pressed her hands on the counter and was glad to see the dapper young clerk wince at the sight. "I have as much right to be here as anyone, and you know it." She stepped back. "But I won't stay here to be slighted." As she left, it gave her satisfaction to let the door slam on its hinges.

She took the now-familiar route, Whitehall to Wheat Street, and as the crowd shifted from white to black, she found that she didn't mind being jostled by her own people.

Then she found it.

The building was more modest than Meyer's, but it was so new that it smelled of freshly sawn pine boards. The gold lettering on the window gleamed, *Kaltenbach's Dry Goods*. She pushed open the door and the bell jangled sweetly, just as at Meyer's. Inside, the fragrance of lavender sachets didn't mask the smell of fresh paint. Behind the handsome glass case, at the gleaming wooden counter, stood a clerk, a light-brown young man in a beautiful suit, and beside him stood Henry.

He had lost the stoop of servitude that he'd borne at Meyer's. He stood up straight, a man proud to have his own business. He looked pleased with himself and seemed years younger. "Miss Mannheim!" he said to her, smiling, because the clerk was listening.

She gestured to the rainbow of bolts on the shelves. "It's beautiful," she said. "When did you open?"

"We opened a few weeks ago. I knew there would be a living in selling to a black custom. What do black folks do, when they first come to Atlanta?"

"Buy new clothes for a new life!" the clerk said.

Henry laughed. "This is my clerk, Mr. Marcus Porter. Mr. Porter, Miss Mannheim, who is an old acquaintance of mine."

She didn't mind Henry's fib for his clerk. She smiled and said, "It's brand new. Did you build?"

"I did. I bought a plot of land and put up the building as fast as I could. Hired Peck's Construction, because they employ black men, and guess who they sent to be foreman on the job?"

His pleasure in the tale gave her pleasure, too. "Can't even try."

"Zeke's son, Luke Hutchens, who moved to Atlanta just after the war! He drove the crew and he built me a fine building."

"It's good that he does so well," she said, smiling. "I'll tell Zeke I had word of him." She glanced around again. "Where do you stay? Since you used to board at Meyer's, too."

"Let me show you. Mr. Porter, will you watch the counter?"

With dignity, the young man said, "I surely will, Mr. Kaltenbach."

Henry led her into the back room and up a back staircase. He unlocked the door, and they stepped into a big, welcoming parlor, prettily furnished with a new settee and a pair of chairs before the fireplace. Next to it was a dining room with a commodious table, covered with a linen tablecloth, and half a dozen chairs around it. He said, "There's a kitchen beyond, and two sleeping rooms."

"Who stays here?"

"I do, for now. But if I decide to build elsewhere, my clerks can live here."

It's a fine place.

He said softly, "I like to hope that you and Eliza might join me here someday."

The thought beguiled her. She imagined what it might be like to sit in that pleasant parlor, where the fire would burn in the grate in wintertime, with a cat to sleep before it, black and white like the kitchen cat of her childhood. To eat in the dining room, at the table to seat all of the friends who might visit. To sleep in one of those bedrooms, and to settle Eliza in the other.

She shook her head. What was she dreaming of? She said, "It ain't likely that I'd be coming to Atlanta."

"What keeps you?" he asked, sadly.

She swallowed hard against the pain in her throat. She said, "Best possible reason." She tried to recapture the joy she had felt in Mordecai's study. "Mr. Mordecai Mannheim just agreed to sell me a hundred acres of his place in Cass County."

He touched her arm. "Rachel, that is good news! You're a woman of property now." He teased her. "How many acres in cotton? How many in corn?"

She blinked back tears. "I'll get Charlie to walk it with me, school me."

He touched her cheek. "It's wonderful news. Why are you sad?"

"Thought I'd be joyful, but it's bittersweet." She fought back the sob.

"Oh, Rachel," he said, and he folded her into an embrace. He pressed his cheek to hers, as he'd do for Eliza, and he stroked her hair. He said softly, "Sometimes it is, when you get your heart's desire."

The sound that emerged was half a laugh and half a sob. "You're the first to know."

He released her and looked into her eyes. Brushing away the tear that lingered on her cheek, he said, "Will he write you a note?"

She nodded. "Yes, he will." Recalling all of the feeling—and the fear—of Henry's pre-war debt to Mordecai, she said, "At least I know I can pay off my note."

Henry laughed. "We both know full well what it's like to be in debt to Mordecai Mannheim."

—❧—

RACHEL WROTE TO Daniel Pereira to tell him that she needed his assistance as a lawyer, and even though he agreed, he wasn't pleased as they made their way to Mordecai's office on Whitehall Street. "Will he be rude to me again?" he asked, a tone too sulky for a man on an errand of business.

"What do you think?" Rachel answered.

They were uneasy with each other. They knew too much of each other to be lawyer and client, and not enough to truly be friends.

"If there's anything amiss with the deed or the note, I won't let you sign it," he said, with a little too much feeling.

"That's why you're along, ain't it?" Rachel said, feeling irritable.

Mordecai looked better than when she saw him last, fleshier and redder in the face. He was jovial, inviting them both to sit down, even offering Pereira a cigar, which he declined. He asked for a pen instead.

Pereira read the contract carefully, pen in hand, frowning as he turned the pages. Rachel wondered what might be wrong, but he said nothing. When he finished, he said to Mordecai, "It looks to be in order."

Mordecai said cheerfully, "It should be. My man's the best lawyer in Atlanta!"

Rachel said impatiently, "Let me read it, too." Pereira looked at her in surprise. She said, "Do you think I'd sign my name to anything without reading it first?"

Pereira was right. It was in order, a simple contract to transfer a hundred acres in Cass County from Mordecai Mannheim to Rachel Mannheim, for the sum of twenty-five hundred dollars, with five hundred in earnest money, and the rest in quarterly payments of a hundred dollars over the span of five years.

Rachel said, "I don't have the earnest money in hand today. I'll have to write to the bank for a draft. I have some money in the bank in Macon, it should be swifter than the Bank of London." She would leave the greater sum for another purpose.

Mordecai said indulgently, "That's all right. You can sign today, both of you. We'll seal it when the money gets here."

Rachel said, "Give me the pen." She bent over the contract. She had never signed a contract on her own account. Her hand shook with fear as well as joy. She took a deep breath, and in her best hand, she signed her name.

"Allow me," Pereira said, and she handed the pen to him. She watched as he added his signature as a witness, his hand very sure. He looked up and regarded her with a grave expression, then he gave the pen back to Mordecai. "It's done," he said.

Mordecai grinned. He extended his hand to Pereira and shook it. Embarrassed, Pereira said, "Sir, you should be congratulating your daughter. It's her transaction."

Mordecai laughed. "You're sweet on her, ain't you?"

Pereira said, "Sir, I don't believe that has any bearing on the matter at hand."

"You're an ambitious man. She'd make a fine wife for an ambitious man."

Rachel said sharply, "We'll let you know as soon as we hear from the bank in Macon about the draft." She rose to go, as did Pereira.

"You do that! You owe me money!" Mordecai said, still laughing.

They walked back to Pereira's office in a stiff silence. Once on Wheat Street, where he didn't care who overheard him, Pereira said, "My God, your father is a vulgar man."

"You already knew that," she said.

He unlocked the office door, which creaked on unoiled hinges. The room seemed closer than usual, the smell of tobacco and dinners of black-eyed peas mingling with the sewer smell of unpaved Wheat Street. He said stiffly, "Let me write the letter to the Macon bank before you go."

"It ain't necessary."

"Allow me." He picked up the pen and ground it into the paper, making a terrible blot. He crumpled the paper and threw it into the wastebasket.

She asked, "What are you so riled about? Are you sweet on me?"

He stared at the blotter on his desk as though it disgusted him. "It has no bearing—"

"Don't like it, do you, when I turn the tables and ask about your private business?"

"I'll be free with you in any legal matter," he said.

"Now you're lawyering me." She laughed. Fifty thousand dollars and a hundred acres. They sang in her blood like the "Battle Hymn of the Republic." "I believe you are!"

"Miss Mannheim, I am at your service as your lawyer, whenever you need me," he said, as stiffly as a man swearing an oath.

She left his office laughing.

—⌒—

Before she faced the indignity of the train, she strayed back to the courtyard where the washwomen labored. She felt safe in seeing them, since now she knew she would never join their ranks. The woman she had met last time, dark of skin, rawboned, and strong-voiced, stood over her tub, the water steaming in the summer air. "I recall you," she said. "Visiting from Cass County. What bring you back to Atlanta?"

"Went to see Mr. Pereira again. Came into a little money, and I buy some land in Cass County with it. He advise me." It was delicious to talk about, even though she kept most of her news a secret.

The woman nodded. "That's fine." She lifted her hands from the tub and wiped them on her apron. "I'm Hattie Tolliver." She gestured to the other women who worked over steaming tubs. "My daughter Keziah, and my friends and neighbors Miss Katie and Miss Amy." They nodded and smiled without interrupting their work.

A younger woman, carrying a basket full of cloth, came through the courtyard. Hattie called to her, "How are you today, Miss Annie?"

She frowned, wrinkling up her pretty face. "My mama named me Anna Victoria, Miss Hattie."

Hattie laughed. "Anna Victoria, that's a name like a good dress for meeting day. Miss Annie is for every other day of the week."

Anna Victoria said irritably, "Don't splash so. This is silk for Mrs. Cohen's new dress, the best from Meyer's. If you ruin it she'll carry on and I'll never make another dress for her."

Rachel started at the mention of Meyer's. "Did you know Mr. Kaltenbach at Meyer's?" she asked.

Anna Victoria threw her an odd look. "He used to wait on me for Mrs. Cohen's lengths, before he go into business for himself," she said. "Treat me better than Mr. Meyer. I don't think Mr. Meyer like colored folks. Why? Do you know him?"

"Went to Meyer's once to buy a ribbon. You right, he cordial to black folks."

Hattie said to Anna Victoria, "He always favor you because you flirt with him."

"I do not," Anna Victoria said, visibly irritated. "Act cordial. Seamstress need fine dry goods. Matter of business." She turned to walk away, her skirt swishing as she carried the basket full of Mrs. Cohen's silk.

Hattie Tolliver watched the motion of Anna Victoria's hips. She said, "If that girl don't watch herself she's going to end up at Madame Toussaint's."

"I met Mrs. Toussaint," Rachel said, puzzled. "You mean work at her eating house?"

"Eating house?" Hattie inclined her head. "Who tell you she run an eating house?"

"Mr. Pereira said so."

"Madame Toussaint run the bawdy house." Hattie pointed toward downtown. "She the richest black woman in Atlanta."

"Is she married?"

"Hah!" Hattie snorted.

— ⌐ —

THAT EVENING, RACHEL burst into the Kaltenbach parlor to find Adelaide and Frankie resting from their labors at the schoolhouse. "Went to Atlanta today," she announced.

From her place on the settee, Frankie teased, "Did you buy ribbons or laces?"

"No," Rachel said, and looked at Adelaide. "Something better." Without asking, she sat in the chair beside the settee, so that she could look her sister in the face. "Wanted to tell you that your daddy—our daddy—sold me a hundred acres of his land. Signed the papers yesterday."

"So that's what he wanted to see you about in Atlanta," Adelaide said.

"You ain't mad?"

Adelaide gave her a rueful smile. "Why would I be? I never wanted it."

"That's what he said. That you wouldn't know what to do with it."

"I don't." The smile broadened. "But you do."

"May we see it?" Frankie asked.

Rachel held out her hands to her sister and her friend. "Walk it with me."

They took the old path through the woods. Rachel stopped to look at the house that had once been the grandest in the county, where Adelaide had been a spoiled girl and she herself had been a slave. It had fallen into disrepair, the steps rotted, the roof caved in, the yard overgrown with weeds. The best house in the county, owned by the richest planter in the county, was now a ruin.

Adelaide tugged on her hand. "Where's your plot?" she asked.

"Behind the house." It was the one the Yankee's tenants had worked. She recalled coming here when Ballard plowed it, and after he left, returning to the weed-grown field with longing. It was heady and strange to think that it was now hers.

They wound their way behind the house, passing the old slave cabins that had been so badly burned in the war that they were charred wrecks. Brush grew over the remains, and birds and chipmunks had made their homes in them. They picked their way through the grass, hiking up their skirts against the nettles, trying to find their way on a path swallowed up by neglect.

Rachel stopped to shade her eyes. She took in the sweet, sappy odor of green things crushed underfoot, along with the fresh, loamy smell of damp earth. She gestured. "This is it. This field and the one beyond it, and the two behind the pine trees. A hundred acres."

"A hundred acres! A place of your own!" Frankie exclaimed. Her eyes were shining.

"You don't think it's strange for me to have my own place?"

Pleased and proud, Frankie said, "We fought a war to free black women, too. Why shouldn't a black woman buy a farm and make her living by it?"

"So you won't be going to Atlanta," Adelaide said, smiling.

"I guess not." She surveyed the overgrown fields that had once belonged to her father and now belonged to her. The Mannheim place. Rachel Mannheim's place now.

—⁓—

RACHEL HADN'T REALIZED that attaining her heart's desire would make her worry so much. She was a property owner, and she had the full burden of making a profit from it. Adelaide's support buoyed her, as did Frankie's good wishes, but neither the farmer's daughter nor the planter's wife had ever run a business of her own.

She decided to visit Atlanta again to consult the only black woman she had ever met who ran a business and made a profit by it without having a man by her side.

The house of ill fame stood on the edge of Sherman Town, within easy reach of the white men who worked in the central district. It was three stories tall and faced with red brick, and had either survived General Sherman's assault or had been refurbished since. The steps were swept very clean. Rachel walked up to the door, which was adorned with a large and shiny brass knocker. She rapped on the door, and a young woman answered. *Goodness,* Rachel thought, *in a place like this, even the maid is pretty.* She asked for Madame Toussaint.

"Madame is busy."

"It's a matter of business."

The maid asked for her name and ushered her into the front parlor, where the gentlemen came in the evening. There was an overpowering smell of rosewater in the place, even more noticeable after the stink of the street. The room had ornate furniture and new figured wallpaper, but it was no more vulgar than Mordecai's house. Rachel sat on the sofa, upholstered in red velvet, and waited for Madame Toussaint.

She swept into the room, a stately figure in black silk, her face remarkably smooth and her cheeks tinged with the slightest artificial color. She sat and regarded Rachel with the look of a dealer in flesh. Rachel hadn't been scrutinized like that since she was a slave.

"You know that I won't hire you to work for me."

She did, but it stung to admit it. "I know. I ain't pretty enough or bright enough."

"And in that other matter, I don't do that anymore. It's too dangerous."

"What other matter?"

"Aren't you in a delicate condition?"

Rachel's face burned. "No, it ain't like that. Not at all."

"Then what business could it possibly be?"

She said her piece. "You the only black woman I ever met who run a business without a man to order you. Or bother you. Wanted to ask for your advice."

Madame Toussaint laughed. It made her look like Betty Mannheim, fresh and cheerful. She said, "No Christian woman has ever asked for my advice."

"I'm half an Israelite."

Still laughing, she said, "Settle yourself, and I'll do my best to oblige you.

9 | A Hundred Acres
and a Mule

Rachel turned from the desk to stare out the window. Just beyond the pine trees, she knew, Adelaide's tenants worked their cotton fields. She imagined the cotton plants unfurling and bushing, the cornstalks forcing through the earth to reach a man's height, the kitchen garden abounding with peas and beans and potatoes and berries, the flower garden laden with bright, fragrant blooms.

Her mind was on her hundred acres. She wanted to be in her own fields, even if she couldn't plant a cotton crop so late in the season. She wanted to clear the fields. She wanted to plow.

She put down her pen and strode from the house to find Charlie.

He was in his field, bending to pick the ripened bolls, dragging the cotton sack behind him. She called to him and he straightened, rubbing his back where it ached.

"You drive yourself harder than you ever drove anyone else," she said.

"It's different when it's your own place."

She surveyed the field, where the bolls would continue to ripen until the frost. "I walked my new place the other day," she said.

"How do it look?"

"Overgrown. Trash and weeds. Believe it would be all right if I plowed it under."

He frowned. "Ain't worth bothering with it until the frost. Then you plow it all under, and start afresh."

"I want to start now. I need someone to work it for me," she said.

Charlie said, "Now? Everyone labor to get the crop in. Wait until after Christmas. People looking for new contracts then."

"Want to get a start now. Whatever I can do."

He sighed. "Rachel, wish I could spare the time to help you, but I can't. Have my own place to worry about. If you wait until harvest over, I can help you, and I'd be glad of it. Just not yet."

She thought, *I can't wait, and I won't.* "I go to Cartersville to buy a mule," she said.

"Marse Mannheim sell you the best land on the place," Charlie said. "He expect you to make something of it. Do it right. Don't act the fool because you impatient."

SHE WHEEDLED ZEKE, less driven than Charlie, into taking her to Cartersville to buy a mule. At the stock dealer's, Mr. Ray looked them both over—he had been a slave dealer, too, before the war—and asked Zeke, "Is Miss Adelaide planning to buy another mule?"

"I'm buying a mule!" Rachel said impatiently. "Just bought a hundred acres on the old Mannheim place."

Mr. Ray, whose fortunes had declined since his slave-trading days, stared at her. He said, "You Mannheim niggers are getting awfully jumped up. You and Charlie."

Zeke tugged nervously on Rachel's sleeve, but she said defiantly, "I have a place. I have cash. I need a mule."

Mr. Ray chewed a wad of tobacco as he thought, and when he spat, it was perilously close to the hem of her dress. "I have a mule that might do," he said. "Come on back, you can see her."

She was a pretty molly mule with big, dark eyes.

"What's her name?" Rachel asked.

"Haven't troubled much with a name. Just call her Mollie."

Rachel regarded the mule, and as soon as she was close enough, the mule began to nuzzle her. Rachel put her arm across the mule's neck and saw with satisfaction that her arm matched the color of the mule's coat. She thought of Brownie, the pony she had loved when she was a little girl, who was sold away to break her heart.

Mr. Ray said, "I can sell her cheap."

Zeke said softly to Rachel, "We look around a little. Make sure we find you a steady mule with a good temper."

Rachel rubbed Mollie's nose, and the mule gave out a deep snort of pleasure.

Mr. Ray said, "She likes you. Wants to go home with you," as though the animal were a pup instead of a mule.

In the same soft tone, not wanting to aggravate Mr. Ray, Zeke said, "If she cheap, she likely to be trouble. Balky or bad-tempered."

"Can't we school her not to balk?" Rachel asked.

Zeke looked sideways at Mr. Ray and said, "I hope so."

"I want Mollie," she said.

"Well, it up to you," Zeke said. And as he shook his head, Rachel agreed to buy her.

Mollie stood still as Zeke slipped the collar over her neck and the bit into her mouth. She was quiet as he yoked her to his own mule—big, steady Lou. Zeke hitched both mules to the wagon. He slapped the reins against their necks and called to them to get going. Lou picked up her feet, but Mollie didn't move. She turned to gaze at Rachel. Her eyes were as smart and wicked as a person's. Zeke slapped the reins again, and Mollie continued to stare at Rachel, not moving.

"See? Balkier than a month of Sundays," Zeke said glumly.

Lou nudged Mollie with her nose, but Mollie didn't turn her head. Lou, tired of being polite, nipped Mollie on the neck. Mollie let out an indignant snort, but she turned her head toward the road. Lou nipped her again as Zeke slapped the reins. Lou broke into a brisk trot, and Mollie, shamed into it, matched her pace to keep up.

Delighted, Rachel called, "Mollie! Good girl! Take us home, Mollie!"

On the way home, Lou paced Mollie, and Mollie had a good trot once she got going. When they arrived, Rachel said, "What do you think, Zeke?"

"I put her in the stable with Lou to keep her in order," he said.

Rachel followed Mollie into the stable, where the mule huffed and rubbed her face. Zeke said, "She loving you up because she behave so bad in Cartersville."

Rachel laughed as the mule rubbed a wet muzzle against her face. She wrapped her arm around the mule's neck. "We get on fine, don't we?" she crooned.

Later that day, Rachel dragged Frankie into the stable to introduce her to the mule. The mule decided to flirt with Frankie, too. She rubbed her nose against Frankie's cheek, a mule's version of a kiss.

Rachel asked Frankie shyly, "You don't mind that I call her Mollie? Like your sister?"

Laughing, Frankie stroked Mollie's nose. "Not a bit."

— ⌇ —

EAGER TO GET started on her field, Rachel asked Zeke to show her how to hitch her mule to a plow. Zeke obliged, and as she had in Cartersville, Mollie didn't fuss over the collar, the bit, or the bridle.

"How do we get out to the field?" Rachel asked.

"You set the plowshare on its side, so it don't dig into the dirt, and you walk the mule out to the field. Stay on a dirt road or grass, you all right."

"How do I get her going?"

Zeke said, "That up to you."

"You won't get her going?"

"She your mule. She like you," he said. "I got my own work today." He left her alone with the mule and the plow.

It was unseasonably hot for autumn. Rachel had covered her hair with a kerchief against the sun, and she began to sweat under it. She grasped the handles of the plow, which were set so low that she had to stoop for them. She gathered the reins in her hands, finding it hard to negotiate the handles and the reins at the same time, and she slapped the reins against Mollie's neck. "Go on!" she sang out, as Charlie had called his mule. "Get on moving!"

Mollie didn't budge.

Rachel tried again. Mollie turned her head to meet Rachel's eyes. Rachel began to feel foolish. It made her snap a little. "Let's go!" she called. "Get on moving!"

Mollie continued to gaze at Rachel with big, dark, wicked eyes.

Rachel slapped the reins again, but Mollie didn't even turn her head. Rachel's face began to burn. Any half-grown boy could drive a mule and guide a plow. She felt stupid and hot with impatience.

She dropped the handles and the reins and walked to stand alongside Mollie. She tried to remember how Charlie coaxed a mule. She rubbed the soft muzzle and softened her voice. "Mollie. We need to get going. Got a field to plow today. Can you do that, Miss Mollie? Pull this plow to the field, and help me plow it?"

Mollie blinked.

Rachel patted the mule's nose and resumed her spot behind the plow, twining the reins around her hands and grasping the handles again. She slapped the reins against the mule's sides. "Go on! Get moving!" she called.

Aside from flicking her ears, Mollie didn't move.

Panic rose in Rachel's chest. She had a hundred acres of weeds and trash that needed plowing under. She would never find someone to plow for her at this time of year. Every acre seemed to weigh on her shoulders. She was a fool who couldn't get a mule to take a single step.

Her voice rose. "Get moving! Get on! Get on with you!"

Mollie shook her head from side to side, just like a human being saying no.

Rachel quivered with shame and anger. "Don't you naysay me! Get on with you!"

Balkier than a month of Sundays.

"Don't you toy with me!" she shouted. She burst into tears. "Bought you to work for me, and you ain't worth the money I paid for you!"

The mule regarded her with eyes too knowing for a brute beast. Rachel was still sobbing. "I'll sell you! I swear I'll sell you!" In horror, she recalled the last time she had heard those words. Years ago, when she was a slave, Adelaide's mother, maddened with seeing the result of her husband's infidelity, had shrieked them at her as she beat Rachel with a belt that had left a scar over her eye.

Rachel leaned against the mule's neck and sobbed into the rough hide. "Mollie, sugar, didn't mean it. Mollie, help me. We get this done, Mollie. We do it together."

—≈—

BUT SHE DIDN'T know how. She visited her overgrown fields every day, brooding over her inability to get her mule going or to find anyone to drive and to plow. Charlie had been right. She should have waited until next season, when the weeds died and contracts were open again.

It was mid-November, close to the end of the cotton season, when he appeared on her front steps. He was a tall, light-skinned black man, whose eyes seemed to look at something else wherever they were focused. His skin peeled, and where it came off, he was even lighter than elsewhere. "Mr. Mannheim send me," he said.

The man gave her the shivers. She asked, "Mr. Mordecai Mannheim or Mr. Charles Mannheim?"

"Didn't know there was more than one. A black man, not far from here."

So Charlie had sent him. "What do he tell you?"

"That you just bought a piece of property, and that you need a job of work done on it."

"That is true," she said. She regarded him. "Where do you hail from?"

"Do it matter?" he asked.

She said, "I need to trust you."

"Mr. Mannheim said you'd be skittish. He said he'd come by to assure you. If you insist on it."

She thought of everything that weighed on Charlie these days and knew that her request would burden him. "I do have a job of work. We go to see the place and I show you."

"How do a black woman come to own a piece of property?" he asked.

"That ain't any of your business. What's your name?"

"John Shade."

"After your master? After your place?"

"Was a joke, when I was a slave. I favored the shade, whenever I could rest in it. So I call myself accordingly."

She took him in, tall and strange and near white where the skin peeled off. She thought, *Shade is a word for ghost, too.*

— ✍ —

SHADE WATCHED AS she harnessed Mollie, slapped the reins, and called her. He watched as the mule stood unmoving except to turn her head and blink her long-lashed eyes. "What did you pay for that mule?" he asked.

"Got her cheap," Rachel said, flushing. She reached to stroke Mollie's nose and Mollie nuzzled her.

"Got your money's worth. She ain't worth a dime as a mule." He stared at the mule and the woman who hugged her. "Did you buy her for a pet?"

Rachel let Mollie go. Shamed, she said, "Thought I might school her."

Shade glowered at her. "You? Not in a month of Sundays."

"Then you drive her," Rachel said, stung and hurt. "See if you can do any better."

"I will. Been skinning mules since I was a boy." He said to Rachel, "You go on. I *encourage* your mule to pull a plow."

"Don't you dare whup my mule!"

He glowered again. "Won't raise a hand to your princess. But I get her going."

—⁓—

LATER THAT DAY, Rachel left the house for Zeke's barn. She was sick of letters and the ledger, and she wanted to visit Mollie. But the mule wasn't in the barn. She was in the yard, and Shade was with her.

Rachel hung back in the barn to watch.

Shade was absorbed. He bent over Mollie. In a soft, pleasant voice—one he hadn't used for Rachel herself—he said, "Let me check your mouth, sugar. Is you sore anywhere? Do that bit bother you?"

With gentle hands, he felt around the mule's mouth, and Mollie allowed it. He said, "No, your mouth just fine. Now, you stay still, I check your feet, make sure you don't have a stone or a sore spot." He knelt and worked his hand down Mollie's leg to cup her hoof. "Let me feel under your hoof." The mule lifted her leg. "That's a good girl." He probed the hoof. "No, your foot just fine, too." He tested all Mollie's hooves, and when he rose, Mollie turned to press her nose against his face. He chuckled. "So you ain't hurting anywhere. Did someone tax you before you was ready? Give you a load too heavy for you to carry?"

Rachel stepped from the barn, and Shade saw her. He pulled away from Mollie and snarled at Rachel, "What are you looking at?" He sounded like a whipped dog who would never trust anyone again.

"Just come to see how you getting along."

"Ain't any of your business."

"I leave you be," Rachel said, and she stepped away quietly.

219

She wandered into Zeke's field and waved to him. Zeke walked his cotton field, Jenny with him, both of them looking to see if the last of the bolls were ready to harvest. Zeke waved back. She met him mid-row. "What do you make of Mr. John Shade?" she asked.

"Man, he an odd one," Zeke said. "Don't have a pleasant word for a single soul. And where his skin come off he turn white."

"Something hurt him so bad he don't care for anyone, even himself," Jenny added. "But he love up that mule of yours."

"I saw that," Rachel said.

—⁓—

A FEW DAYS later, she went to say good morning to Mollie in the barn, but the mule was gone. Rachel went looking for Zeke to ask him.

Zeke said, "Shade take her over to your place. Wanted to try her out in the field, he said."

Rachel never minded the distance to the Mannheim place— *Rachel Mannheim's place now*, she thought, still bright with pride. Taking her time, she picked her way past the ruined house and the burned-out cabins and the nettled path, finding the way to her own fields.

In her nearest cotton field, still overgrown with weeds, Shade had harnessed Mollie, but he hadn't hitched a plow to her. Rachel watched and listened from a distance. Shade said to the mule, "Now, we take it slow. Don't have to pull a heavy thing, not yet. We just walk the row. I guide you, and we walk the row." He pulled gently on the reins—for a mule, it was more a caress than a slap—and said, "Gee, Mollie! Get moving, Mollie!"

Mollie moved. She tried to trot, and Shade reined her in. "Slow, Mollie. Slow and steady, Mollie." When the mule slowed her pace, Shade called out, "Good girl, Mollie! Good girl!"

Rachel watched, fascinated, as the mule slowly walked to the end of the field, the length of a plowed row. Shade called out, "Haw, Mollie!" and she stopped. She turned toward him, snuffling and pushing his nose into his hand. He chuckled. "Good girl, Mollie," he said, and gave her a carrot to eat.

Rachel slipped away before Shade could snarl at her.

— ✑ —

THAT SATURDAY EVENING Rachel felt a need for company, and she decided to join the Benjamins at their impromptu frolic. She took Eliza to stay with Frankie, lingering in the Kaltenbach attic until her daughter was settled and asleep.

The moon had risen, and it silvered the familiar sight of the side yard and the old cabins beyond it. Shade sat alone on his cabin's steps. He had neither candle nor lantern. The moonlight dappled his face, adding to his piebald appearance. A whiskey jug sat at his elbow, and he held a tin cup in his hand.

He sang, "Sometimes I feel like a motherless child… a long way from home…" His voice was low, raw, and full of melancholy. He drank from the cup and said, in the same melancholy tone, "Sold away… sold away… all sold away…"

She turned to melt into the darkness.

—⌒—

EARLY IN THE morning, Rachel stopped at Zeke's barn. If Mollie was gone, she assumed that Shade had taken her to school her in plowing. But on the Monday morning after Shade's drinking bout, Mollie was still in the barn. She was glad to see Rachel, but Rachel was displeased. She went to look for Shade.

She found him lying on the floor in his cabin, smelling strongly of whiskey. "You ain't working," she said.

"I'm sick."

"You drunk."

"No, I'm sick," he insisted, drawing his knees to his chest.

Heartsick, she thought. Even though she knew what it was like to be heartsick, she lost her temper. "I ain't your mama or your wife or even your overseer. But I got a dollar a day for you, and if you don't want it, you can pick up and leave anytime. I'll clear and plow next season with a tenant who want the work."

He managed to sit up. His face looked like a piece of crumpled paper. "I need that dollar," he groaned.

Troubled, Rachel wished that she could talk to Charlie. But Charlie was still too busy. She found Zeke with a heavy bag on his shoulder, stooping for a low-growing boll.

"Zeke," she said.

He frowned as he straightened up. She could feel that pain, shoulder and spine, now that she had decided she wanted it for her own. "What is it? Better be quick."

"What should you do if a man who work for you drink?"

"Do he drink all the time?"

"No, just sometimes."

"You leave him alone." Zeke turned away and bent down for another boll.

— ∽ —

It tormented her to stay away from her place while Shade did whatever he did to educate her mule. She didn't seek him or bother him when he wasn't plowing, either. It made her agitated and snappish, but she waited for him to come to her.

On a sunny day, eerily like summer late in November, Shade knocked on her front door. He said, "Come along with me. Have something to show you."

Without taking off her apron, she joined him. He loped along the path through the pine grove with a determined step, and she hurried to keep up. On the Mannheim place, he strode past the tumbledown house and wrecked cabins on a path that he had tamped down. It was easy to follow him.

In her field stood Mollie, harnessed and hitched to the plow, waiting patiently. At the sight of Shade, she lifted her head and called to him, the mule's cry, half a whinny and half a bray. He called back, "Good girl, Mollie!"

Rachel followed. He slowed his pace until he was close enough to twine the reins around his hands. He grasped the plow handles. Mollie turned her head to gaze straight ahead.

He slapped the reins against her sides and said, in a level voice, "Get moving, Mollie. We get moving!"

Mollie moved. Shade angled the plowshare. Mollie stepped at a deliberate pace, making it easy for Shade to guide the plow.

He said, "Easy, easy. Steady, steady." The mule obeyed. She kept her gait slow and even, helping him use the plowshare to turn the earth.

A good smell rose from the fresh-turned dirt, loam and the decomposition that would enrich the soil for next year's crop, one that Rachel always associated with springtime. It was strange to smell it as the last bolls ripened a few miles away and the last cicadas screamed their metallic mating cry.

When Mollie reached the end of the row, Shade called, "Good girl, Mollie! Good girl! Now you turn!"

And to Rachel's astonishment, Mollie turned, her motion as slow and steady as her gait. Rachel watched as Shade guided the mule through the field to plow another neat furrow next to the first.

"Halt," Shade said, and Mollie stopped, perfectly still in the sunshine, moving only to flick her ears.

"What did you do?" Rachel asked, amazed.

Shade let go the handles and the reins. On his face was a look very close to happiness. "Now you try it. I school you, too," he said.

He guided her to take the reins—he showed her how to twine them, as he had—and how to place her hands on the plow handles. He said, "I walk alongside. Back and forth."

He waited, and she lightly slapped the reins, as she had watched him do. She said brightly, "Get moving, Mollie!"

And Mollie obeyed her.

As Mollie began to move, Shade walked alongside Rachel, speaking to her in the same low, even tone he had used for the mule. "Walk in the furrow, it easier," he said. "No, don't push on them handles. She pull. You guide. Easy, easy. Steady, steady."

Woman and mule moved together, with a slow, steady, even gait.

At the end of the field, Rachel looked back. Her row wasn't as neat as Shade's, but she and Mollie had plowed the length of the field. Mollie turned and together they plowed the next row, as Shade accompanied them and urged them both on. "Easy, easy. Steady, steady. Good! Good!"

When they returned to their starting point, Shade said, "You all right with her and she all right with you. She yours now." Before Rachel could protest, he touched his hand to his cap. Without another word, he walked away.

The sun beat down on her head. She tied her apron over it, a makeshift sunshade, and lightly slapped the reins. "Get moving!" she sang, and as Mollie pulled the plow, joy surged through her. "We keep plowing, Mollie! We make a bale and a half an acre next year, Mollie!"

Her shoulders began to ache, her hands began to blister, and she felt half dizzy with the sun. She had rarely been so happy. When she was too tired to plow any more, she stopped Mollie and hugged her around the neck. She pressed her face into her mule's hide and wept tears of joy.

—◡〜—

The next morning, she ran to the barn, ready to harness her mule and hitch her to the plow. She wanted to talk to Shade first. Boast a little. Figure what he might do for her next.

She knocked on Shade's door. There was no answer. She pushed the door open. The cabin was as empty as if no one had ever lived there.

She ran to the house, to the kitchen, where the Hardins, including the boys who stayed in the neighboring cabin, took their breakfast. She interrupted Johnny Hardin mid-chew. "Have you seen Mr. Shade?"

Robbie, who didn't mind talking and chewing at the same time, said, "Not since yesterday."

His sister Salley said, "Robbie, I've seen pigs with better manners than you."

Johnny swallowed before he spoke. "Is he gone?"

"Thought you'd know," Rachel said.

Johnny shook his head.

"I owe him money," she said. "If he's gone, and no one know where, won't be able to settle with him."

"Maybe he'll come back," Johnny said. "He needs the money."

Salley shook her head. "He appeared, and then he disappeared," she said. "I think he's gone for good."

10 | ACTS OF RECONSTRUCTION

AFTER CHRISTMAS, CHARLIE kept his promise to look over her fields. As they walked toward the place where they had both grown up, he said, "Heard you haven't found any tenants yet.

All of Cass County knew that she'd bought a hundred acres. White folks didn't like it, but black folks were proud of her. Yet no one was eager to work for her. "Don't have to remind me. Can't figure it. They make contracts with white men who torment them back in slavery days, but not with me."

Charlie scratched his head. "I believe they worried about you. Worried about how you'll do as a cotton planter."

"Could hardly do worse than that man Everett!"

"You been a house servant all your life, and now you lift a pen and not a hoe. Never planted a cotton seed or a picked a cotton boll. Puts them off."

"But that's why I want to hire someone. Because I need help."

Charlie laughed. "You and every other cotton planter in the state of Georgia," he said. "They ain't quite ready for you yet. Black woman who stand on her own." He shaded his eyes as they emerged from the path through the woods. "Make a crop this year, they feel different."

She grasped his hand, eager to show him the neatened fields. He let her lead him. He gazed at the cleared plot with its neat rows. "You do all this?" he asked in surprise.

"Mr. Shade school me. I do the rest." She grinned. "How many acres can I manage? Fifty?"

He turned and rested his hands on her shoulders, an old, tender habit. "Oh, no, Charlie," she said. "You about to disappoint me."

"You have a fine place. When you get it going, ten acres in cotton, maybe even twenty."

"Ten!"

"Rachel, I plant ten acres last year, and it were too much for me. I got it in, but I admit that I struggle. This year I do less. Five acres, maybe, and even though I hate the thought, I let Becky help me."

The pressure of his hands felt constricting rather than kind. "How many acres do you think I could manage?"

"A couple of acres in cotton. The rest in corn. Remember what I used to say to Marse Henry? We plant corn in case cotton disappoint us?"

She put her hands over his and gently removed their yoke from her shoulders. "I appreciate what you say," she said.

"I know you don't like it. But I hate to see you let ten acres of cotton go to waste in the field. That a worse disappointment than three solid bales and a hundred bushels of corn an acre."

At her unhappy expression, he said, "I ain't saying don't do it. I am saying do it slow. Do what you can, and rejoice in that."

She let herself sound sulky. "I didn't get free to be a corn farmer."

Charlie laughed. "Listen to you! As though you planned to get free to grown cotton."

They returned through the pine grove that had always been the shortcut. The pinewoods were fragrant with resin and quiet.

But they heard a sound.

Footsteps?

Rachel heard a noise that made her heart race. The sound of a safety coming off. The sound of a rifle being cocked.

Her heart began to hammer.

Charlie grabbed her hand. "Stay still," he whispered. They stood rooted to the spot. There was no sound in the woods, not a step or a breath or another noise from the gun.

She plucked at Charlie's sleeve. "They'll shoot," she whispered back.

"No, they won't," Charlie said.

The low sound of laughter floated from the woods. A voice. Ben Turner Junior's voice. "Are you afraid, you jumped-up Mannheim niggers?" he said.

Charlie swallowed hard. He answered, "I know who you are, and I ain't!"

She couldn't run fast enough to best a bullet, but she might confound whoever aimed the rifle at her. She let fear overwhelm her. She ran, her heart pounding, and she screamed when someone caught her by the arm.

It was Charlie. All of the cheer had drained from his face, and he held her fast. "We don't run. If they plan to shoot at us, we plan to fight back."

She recalled his reticence when the Turners had first threatened him. "Do we want to keep this from the Bureau?"

"Got a better weapon than the Bureau," he said.

— ✑ —

THAT SUNDAY, RACHEL joined Frankie to go to the meeting house, and when they arrived, they found Charlie in the midst of a group of men. He waved a folded newspaper in the air as he called to Rachel, "Did you read about the Reconstruction Act in the newspaper? The one that Congress passed up in Washington?"

Rachel read the *Atlanta Intelligencer*, which was biased on the subject of the government's depredations on the South, and it had never mentioned such a thing. "What newspaper is that?"

"*The Loyal Georgian*," Charlie said. "From Augusta."

"Haven't seen it," Rachel said, disturbed that Charlie knew something about the affairs of the world that she did not.

"Captain Hart have it sent and he give it to me. It's new, since the war. The paper say that Georgia divided up into districts. Every district pick men to register anyone who want to vote." He looked around the circle and began to grin. "To register us."

Rachel, still upset that that she hadn't heard the news first, said, "Tell us what that paper of yours say about registering black men."

"Congress put Georgia under military rule now. General Pope from the Union Army in charge, and he choose men who register everyone to vote. Not just black men. Any man who swear he loyal to the Union." As Charlie explained, he seemed to grow taller. "We in Cass, we in District 42, along with Floyd and Chattooga."

Rachel asked, "Once you all registered to vote, what do you vote for?"

Charlie's voice turned sonorous, like the reverend's when he preached. "Vote for delegates to send to a convention in Atlanta. They write a new constitution for the state of Georgia. Constitution to give black folks their due in freedom! That's what we vote for."

Rachel thought of her pride in owning a hundred acres and her exposure to the Turners' resentment. She had a stake in this new order of things. She said tartly to Frankie, "Why don't black women get to vote, too? Ain't we as free as black men?"

Frankie said, "My friends from Oberlin all say that it isn't fair and it isn't right, but it's a fight for another day."

Becky overheard them and chortled. "Maybe all you men can vote, but we women tell you and remind you how to vote! Stand right behind you to do it!"

—⁓—

IT WAS MARCH, but the heat was as thick as summer. At the sight of Captain Hart, Adelaide pulled the weight of her hair away from her neck and sighed. Not another runaway. Not another outrage. Not another difficulty that would increase the hostility that her neighbors, who had once been her friends, felt towards the school, Frankie, and herself.

She was uneasy with Captain Lewis Hart again. Since his apology—since his confession that he cared enough for her to do anything to protect her—his voice had echoed in her head. With it spoke another voice, her mother's, blaming and angry: *What did you do to encourage him?* As an innocent girl, she had been able to truthfully say, *Nothing, Mama.* As a grown woman, the list of her lapses rang in her ears like the Yom Kippur litany of sins. I invited him to my table. I sat alone with him in my schoolhouse. I accepted a gift. I let him give me money, never mind that it was the Bureau's money for the Bureau's purpose. I let him promise to care for me and protect me.

I let my husband go away.

Now Hart took off his hat in greeting and mopped his face with his handkerchief.

"Let me get you some water," she said. It would delay whatever he had come to tell her.

When he handed her back the cup, their fingers touched. She blushed and reminded herself, *It's Bureau business, as it always is, and always must be.*

"What's on fire?" she asked. Even in her embarrassment, it was easy to tease Hart. Any Southern girl could tease a man, even if she felt nothing for him.

He gestured toward the live oak. "Shall we sit?"

She welcomed the shade and followed him there. A breeze rustled the leaves at the great tree's crown, and it flowed over her heated skin, too.

"Oh, it's good news," he said. "News from Congress. Haven't you heard about the Reconstruction Act?"

"If it's news from the Republicans in Washington, the *Atlanta Intelligencer* will ignore it until Atlanta is on fire again."

"It's great news. A new constitution for the state of Georgia, written by delegates elected by all of the men of Georgia, black as well as white." She had rarely seen him look so pleased. "Black men will vote!"

She sighed. "More trouble in the county."

"Oh, it's bound to make the former Rebs unhappy. And it's more work for the Bureau, because we'll be making sure that no one keeps black men from registering to vote. But it's a great thing!" His eyes sparkled. "Black men, free men, voting for the first time!"

She frowned. "How will they register? Who will register them? Will it be the Bureau?"

"No. General Pope, who commands Georgia as a military district, will appoint the registrars. Three for every district in Georgia."

"Military rule," she said slowly. "The Army comes back, to compel us to do something we'd rather not."

He reached for her hands. His palms were dry and toughened, but his touch gave her pleasure. "It won't be easy, but it's only right. Like fair wages, or schooling."

The worry stirred by his news was nothing to the sudden shame stirred by his handclasp. She cried out, "You've seen what kind of trouble has come from fair wages and schooling!" and quickly walked away.

He ran after her. Once he was alongside, he rested his hand on her shoulder. "I won't leave it at that. Look at me." She looked. Let her eyes linger on his. He asked, "Will you listen to me? Let me persuade you?" He lowered his voice to nearly a whisper. "I can't bear to lose the good opinion of my best sub-agent."

Always the Bureau. She recovered the belle's tone. "I'm your only sub-agent," she said. The belle came back to protect the woman who would be an errant wife. "Captain Hart, this business of black men voting will be a trial. And so are you."

—⌒—

THE BUREAU'S BUSINESS kept Hart away for several weeks at a time. When he visited again, it was on a Friday in late April, a Sabbath eve when the air held such sweetness that Adelaide's house was perfumed with the scent of magnolia and honeysuckle blossoms. From her parlor window, she could see the white wisteria that grew with such vigor in the side yard. She thought of the day that Henry, courting her, had brought her a bouquet of the flowers and had blushed to hear that it was called "bride's bower." He had asked for her hand in a pergola covered with white wisteria.

She shook her head as she opened the door to Hart. He looked tired, more than the shadow of a few bad nights' sleep. He looked as gray and drawn as though he'd been in battle again. But he smiled to see her, forcing some liveliness into his face. He reached for her hands. "It's good to see you," he said, as though they had been separated for a long time, and she let his greeting and his fingers spread warmth through her.

She pulled him into the house. "I'm glad that you're here."

He sat in the wing chair intended for a gentleman, and he unbuttoned his frock coat. "You don't mind?" he asked.

"No. It's a warm night."

He took off the heavy wool garment and sighed. He sat in his shirtsleeves, as Henry had once done.

"Would you like a little whiskey, or would you like to wait until after the Kiddush?" she asked.

"Whiskey now, thank you." He sipped from the glass and leaned back in the chair.

"The usual injustices in the county?" she asked. "Or worse than usual?"

He sat up. "No worse than usual. But there was something odd today. It was the damnedest thing. I'd like your advice on it."

She was flattered. Henry had never asked for her advice on anything, much less taken it. "What is it?"

"I don't know if you heard, but Colonel Turner's been chosen as a registrar. It's a little irregular. He was a Confederate officer, and I thought he'd be prohibited from voting, let alone registering."

"I think he took the loyalty oath. I seem to recall that he wrote away for a pardon, too." She thought of Turner's kindly face. "Did you know he voted against seceding before the war?"

"That's to his credit," Hart said and took another sip of whiskey. "Well, he walked into the Bureau office today, in broad daylight, and made sure that every man, woman, and child, black as well as white, saw him open my door."

"And it weren't to say how do."

"No. It weren't," he said, teasing her Southern turn of phrase. "He told me that he and the other registrar had been charged with finding a third to serve with them. A black man. He asked me if I could help him in finding a good, solid colored man for the registrar's task."

"Did he say 'colored man'?"

"He did. He was very courteous. I was mighty surprised, but I told him that I'd be glad to put out the word and to ask the *colored* people of the county to recommend someone to him. "

"I can think of someone," Adelaide said.

"So can I. But I thought it would be best to let everyone have a say." He drank more deeply of the whiskey. "To let them have their first taste of democracy."

"Where were his boys?"

"On the steps of the saloon. Believe me, I was ready for trouble, but all they did was stand there and watch. Why would he do such a thing? Come to me, and ask for my help?"

"He wants peace," she said softly. "He'll go to the convention for the sake of peace." She spelled it out for herself. "He wants to be a delegate. And for that, he'll need the votes of black men. That's what he's up to." She met Hart's eyes, and she was unsettled by the feeling she saw there.

Smiling, he shook his head. "Such a cynical view."

Adelaide smiled back. "I've always taken a cynical view, Captain Hart. What makes you such an idealist?"

"A Republican majority in Congress, and hearing you tease me." The fatigue vanished from his face. "That gives me all the hope in the world."

"Are you flirting with me?" she teased. "Using an act of Congress to flirt with me?"

"And if I were?"

He had beguiled her before, but this plea, along with the deep, forthright glance, unsettled her. Was he teasing, too? Or not?

— ✒ —

THE FORMER SLAVES often gathered at Adam's place on Saturday night. The whiskey jug came out, and Asa joined his brother to play the fiddle. Women held out their arms to men to dance. After a hard week of labor in the fields, the music and dancing were as sweet on the tongue as the liquor. On a night in late April, Rachel left a sleepy Eliza in Frankie's care and slipped into the night to find the music.

In the soft, summery air, Asa and Adam made their fiddles sing as though crickets danced on the strings. Only Charlie and Becky were absent, at home with their children. Lucy listened to the music with gleaming eyes. She was still in love with her husband, and the sight still made Rachel envious. Less so now. She had her own reasons to feel proud.

The talk turned to Captain Hart's request and how to fulfill it. Since Hart had spread the word about needing a black registrar, and asked for a recommendation, black Cass County talked of little else.

Asa wiped his mouth and passed the whiskey jug to his brother. "I like to be asked. Don't know what I think, not yet, but I like to be asked!"

Adam was a little drunk. He said, "You always been a fool."

"No, I ain't," Asa said. "Just making up my mind."

"Ain't much to think about," Davey said. "Captain Hart ask us to tell him who's a good solid man. It's Charlie. Charlie Mannheim."

"Charlie!" Adam said. "Everyone go on and on about Charlie. Own a hundred acres. Learn how to read. All schooled from that newspaper about voting. Sick of Charlie."

"Known him since slavery days," Zeke said hotly. "Good man. Sober." He threw a pointed look at Adam. "He know how to handle men, black and white. Keep his temper."

Adam pulled again from the jug. "My daddy a fine man, too. Preacher. Good man all his life long. Know how to read and write. Tell Captain Hart about him." He spat. "Sick of Charlie. He ain't a saint. Just a man."

A low voice floated from the darkness, a voice with a chuckle in it. "Mr. Adam Benjamin, are you saying I ain't a good man?"

"Charlie!" Adam stammered, embarrassed. "Didn't say a word against you!"

"Heard every bit of it," Charlie said, still chuckling.

"Nothing against you!" Adam repeated. He turned to Lucy, beseeching her to help him.

Lucy laughed outright, a sound as musical as her husband's playing. "Just said he was tired of hearing about you, that's all!"

—⁓—

THE CHILDREN LISTENED to their parents' talk of voting, and the discussion became theirs, too. They brought it into the schoolyard, and one morning, as Adelaide and Frankie arrived to unlock the schoolroom door, they found a scuffle in progress. Charlie's son, Ben, had a headlock on Judah's grandson, Ezra, and he was panting, "My daddy the best man in the county and he going to register the voters."

Ezra's voice was muffled, but he said angrily, "My granddaddy a better man than your daddy, and he will! Let go of me!"

Matt ran to pull Ezra away. "You leave Ben alone!" he shouted.

Frankie ran to separate all the boys. She said sternly, "Children, this isn't the way that free people resolve their differences." She shook the two combatants and they let her, even though they were strong for seven. She glowered at the rest of the children, who had been enjoying the tussle and were now relishing the chastisement for it. "Free people talk to each other courteously. And then they take a fair vote, in everyone's sight."

Josey stuck out her tongue at her brother, and before Frankie could chastise her, too, she said sweetly, "How, Miss Frankie?"

"Don't make such a face, Miss Josey. All of you, go inside and settle down, and Miss Adelaide and I will teach you how to have a debate, as they do in Congress up in Washington, and how to take a proper vote."

That day in the schoolroom, the children debated the merits of Mr. Mannheim and Mr. Benjamin. Frankie allowed strong feeling, but she quelled any insult. After a lengthy discussion, she asked for a show of hands and carefully counted the votes.

"Mr. Mannheim is the winner, and the vote was fairly cast and fairly counted." She asked Ben and Ezra to shake hands. "Like gentlemen," she said, smiling.

As the children ran into the yard to play, Adelaide said softly to Frankie, "If only it were so easy."

—⁓—

Since Hart had asked for her counsel about Colonel Turner, Adelaide had worried about the business of choosing a registrar. She feared that Hart had made a promise that was bound to be broken. Black people favored Charlie, but the choice wasn't really theirs. Adelaide didn't know the other registrar, a well-to-do planter who lived in neighboring Floyd County, and she didn't think a call on him would do any good. But she was well acquainted with Colonel Turner.

She hadn't visited the Turner place for a long time, and she was appalled by how tumbledown it looked. Colonel Turner had never been a wealthy planter—before the war, he had owned just ten slaves—but they had all left him when they knew they were free. Now he had no one to take care of the place, whether to plant cotton or tend the front yard. The house had suffered during the war and been neglected since. The steps were badly weathered and creaked loudly when she set foot on them. She knocked on the door, which had not been painted since the war broke out, and wondered who would answer.

The servant was a stranger. Age had taken so many of her teeth that her words were undistinguishable. She gestured to Adelaide, and as she shuffled back into the house, Adelaide followed her.

Unlike her own place, spared by the Union Army, this house had suffered at the hands of General Sherman's men. The ripped upholstery remained, as did the tear in the carpet. On the mahogany mantel were someone's initials, deeply and roughly carved into the dulled wood.

Before the war, Mrs. Turner had done the heavy work in this house, plunging her hands into the laundry tub along with her slaves. She wondered how Mrs. Turner managed with only an age-lamed woman for a servant.

Colonel Turner sat in his study, which was tidier than the rest of the house, even though the leather furniture had been scored and the curtains scorched. He greeted Adelaide and said, "I can try to ask for refreshment."

"No, sir, it's all right." She gazed sadly around the room, recalling its prewar comfort. "How is Mrs. Turner? Is she at home?"

"She's not feeling very well, I'm afraid. She rests in the afternoons now."

"Is there anything to be done for her?"

"The new doctor prescribes rest and laudanum, if we can get it."

Adelaide thought of house-proud Mrs. Turner sleeping in a bedroom as ruined as her parlor. She must be sick with heartbreak. "I'm so sorry to hear it," she said. "If there's anything I can do—"

"No," he said sadly. "Don't trouble yourself."

The former planters were too proud to admit they needed help. Last year, when the farmers of Cass County suffered so badly, the poorest white families had accepted rations from the Union Army. The planter families had refused them.

She said gently, "It's good to see you again, Colonel Turner, but I've come here on a matter of business, too."

"I thought as much. People speak of you as the Bureau's deputy."

Startled, she said, "Not everyone says it so politely."

"I worry for you," he said. "Because of the feeling against the Bureau."

"But you're willing to ask for the Bureau's help."

"No one likes it, but black men will register to vote. And they will vote to send delegates to the convention. I hope that it can happen without bloodshed. We've had enough of that."

She nodded. "Now I want to enlist your help, too. It's not rightfully Bureau business. I've come of my own accord."

"How can I oblige you, Miss Adelaide?"

When she was a little girl, he had teased her by calling her "Miss Adelaide." The soft tone and the aristocratic accent were unchanged. She hardened herself against her pre-war memory. She said, "In the matter of the third registrar. The colored registrar."

"I've given it a great deal of thought, and I've talked it over with Mr. Shropshire, my fellow registrar."

"Do you have anyone in mind?"

"Yes, we do."

"Captain Hart has appealed to the colored people of the county, and they have someone in mind, too. I wonder if we've arrived at the same man."

"I've heard good reports of Charles Mannheim," Turner said. "Wasn't he on your father's place before the war?"

Roundabout, she thought. *Like Br'er Rabbit. As Rachel and Charlie taught me.* She said, "Yes, I know him well. Solid. Intelligent. I can't think of a finer man for the task. Will you tell Mr. Shropshire?"

He nodded. "I believe I can convince Mr. Shropshire," he said, his eyes twinkling as they did when he gave her a book as a birthday present.

She realized she'd been holding her breath, and she breathed out in relief. As she rose to go, she held out her hand and he clasped it with a gentle, fatherly touch.

—〰—

At midday Adelaide sat alone on the porch, hoping for a breeze in the breathless summer air. It was a sleepy hour, when the birds quieted and the bumblebees flew lazily from one bloom to another. She wished she had anything to fan herself—even this week's *Atlanta Intelligencer* would do—but she felt too languid to retrieve it.

Charlie approached through the side yard, waving to her in greeting. He strode up the stairs and doffed his hat, a confident, gentlemanly gesture just like Hart's, and stood before her, his face sunny.

"I heard that congratulations are in order," she said as she rose. "Mr. Charles Mannheim, registrar of the 42nd District of the state of Georgia!"

He didn't extend his hand—it wouldn't be seemly—but he said, "It's an honor, Miss Adelaide. And a burden."

"I've never seen you shirk a burden, Mr. Mannheim." How odd to call Charlie by the same name as her father's. "And you do honor to every task you take on."

"I owe you thanks, Miss Adelaide."

"Me? Whatever for?"

"I believe you put in a good word for me with Colonel Turner," he said.

"How do you know?" she asked.

He smiled. What a subtle smile he had. "Thought you might go roundabout."

—⁓—

THE FIRST DAY of voter registration came in June, high summer, and the air was sweet with every green and growing thing. When Rachel, Adelaide, and Frankie arrived in Cartersville, the Methodist Church, still doing its duty as a makeshift courthouse, was already full. Black families crammed themselves into the pews. The crowd waited with unusual quiet as the golden light streamed through the tall windows like God's grace. The three women squeezed into a pew at the back.

Between the pulpit and the first row of pews stretched the registrars' table. Mr. Shropshire, a fleshy man in a black suit, sat at the leftmost end, his registration book neatly opened, his inkwell carefully beside it, his pens lined up like soldiers. In the middle was courtly Colonel Turner, and to his right sat Charles Mannheim, his expression solemn, the image of dignity in his best suit.

Their Charlie, as official as a letter from the government.

A group of white men clustered at the back of the room. They were all hill country men, most of whom had deserted the Confederate Army or dodged the draft altogether. Today their disloyalty was an advantage. They could take the oath of allegiance without any trouble. They, too, were hushed by being in church.

A shout from the street disturbed the hush. "Niggers voting!" It was Ben Turner Junior's voice.

In response, Captain Hart raised his voice in warning. "This isn't a saloon. Be quiet, and show respect."

Colonel Turner rose. He turned to Charlie. "Will you begin by swearing the oath of loyalty?"

Charlie rose as well. "Yes, sir, I will." They faced each other.

Turner read from the oath book in a low, sonorous voice, like a church elder leading the Sunday prayer. Charlie raised his right hand for the oath to repeat the words, his voice carrying in the stillness.

Rachel listened. The dry words were like the dry bones at resurrection, given flesh by her longing for freedom. She thought, *A black man, a citizen.* A black man, swearing that he never gave aid of comfort to the country's enemies. A black man, promising to uphold the Constitution and its laws. A black man, pledging to encourage everyone he knew to do the same. In God's presence, and with God's help. She blinked back tears.

Charlie signed the oath, and when he lay down the pen, he asked, "Colonel Turner, sir, will you do me the honor of registering me as a voter?"

"Yes, I will." Turner opened the brand-new registration book and dipped his pen into the inkwell. When he finished, he said, "I've written here that you are the first man in Cass County to register to vote, and the first man to sign the oath book as well. Charles Mannheim, you are duly registered to vote in the County of Cass in the State of Georgia."

Rachel clapped her hands, and the crowd erupted in applause. The men cheered: "Charlie! Charlie!" The boys whistled, and even the littlest children stamped their feet.

"We're here today to do our duty as citizens. Let us do it as gentlemen, too."

The men rose, one row at a time, to form an orderly line down the aisle. One of their own sat in dignity as a representative of the state of Georgia—a free man, a citizen, and a voter. They would act in a way to make him proud.

Rachel let the tears roll down her face. Eliza touched her cheek. "Mama, why are you crying?"

"Proudest day of my life, sugar," she whispered. "Like getting free all over again."

When the crowd thinned, Rachel squeezed past Adelaide and Frankie, her sodden handkerchief clasped in her hand, to breathe the air outside. She found that the porch was tightly packed with women, most of them strangers.

She asked the nearest woman, "Where do you hail from, sister?"

She was gaunt and stood as though her back ached. Her dress had been washed so often that it had turned a dull gray. "Place near Adairsville."

"Your man register to vote today?"

She coughed. "My man run off in the war and left me with five babies to feed. None of them old enough to vote, either. Had to go scrabble to find a place to work, and it just like slavery, from can't see to can't see. Do voting put food in our mouths? Do it keep the overseer from bothering me? Do it keep the hoe out of my children's hands? Tell me that."

Rachel was still full of feeling—proud of Charlie and angry that his triumph was something that she had to celebrate second-hand. It welled up in her. She said, "It matter. It matter to all of us, man, woman, and child."

"You can't vote, either."

"I can't vote, but I can see it. If black men register, if black men vote, then whoever go to that convention and write that new constitution speak for us. Get us decent work. Get us paid for what we do. Make it wrong for anyone to interfere with us. Send our babies to school instead of into the field. Make all of that the law of Georgia."

The woman made a disparaging sound. "Still don't know what I can do."

"Talk to everyone you know. Women, not just men. Tell them, like I'm telling you." She thought of Becky's words. "Stand behind them and school them on voting. And stand with them when it come time to register and to vote. Walk down to the courthouse, all together, women and children, to cheer on the men."

The woman coughed again. "I ain't well. If we vote, can we vote for doctoring?"

Sobered, Rachel said, "Perhaps we should."

Rachel felt the gaze of Captain Hart, who stood on the steps. He had a thoughtful expression, like Charlie's when he was pondering, preparing to announce, "I have a notion."

In the street, the Turner boys stood to watch as a small group of white men trickled into the church to register. Disdaining Captain Hart, Ben said loudly, "It's a damn shame, when niggers can vote and white men can't."

Pierce shoved his brother. "You can vote if you take the damnesty oath," he said in a mocking tone.

Ben's voice rose. "Didn't fight a war to take the damnesty oath."

—✐—

247

AFTER THE REGISTRATION in Cass County, the registrars went far afield in the district to neighboring Chattooga County. When Charlie returned, he stopped at Rachel's house at midday, a farmer's moment of rest. "Set with me on the steps?" he asked.

She stood on the porch, wiping her hands on her apron, and said, "Come on inside and set proper."

"Steps more companionable."

She laughed. "You a man of dignity now. Set in the parlor."

As they sat in the chairs before the hearth, Eliza ran to him, crying, "Uncle Charlie!"

He scooped her up. "You getting so big," he said. "And a new doll-baby, too."

"Daddy give it to me," Eliza said proudly.

Charlie sighed as he glanced at Rachel.

"He's her father, ain't he?" she defended Henry. "Loves her. Gave her a gift at Christmas."

Charlie hugged Eliza and set her down. "Go on, sugar, and play quiet with your doll-baby while I talk to your mama."

"Should I send her to her room?"

"No, it ain't private. It about registering voters."

"Thought it went all right in Chattooga County."

Charlie sighed again. "Weren't like Cass, where everyone know me, and we have a celebration getting everyone registered. Black folks in Chattooga more skittish."

"Election ain't until November. Thought you'd go back more than once before then."

"We will. But it got me thinking about Floyd, where we ain't been yet, and Captain Hart and I talk it over."

"What do he say?"

"He think I might go on ahead to Floyd, talk to black folks there, school them a little, encourage them."

"Ain't a bad notion."

"He think you might go with me." That cajoling tone. And that coaxing look. Charlie was driving again.

"Me? Why?"

Charlie said, "I can talk to the men. But we think you could talk to the women, help them stand behind the men."

She recalled the moment outside the church, talking to the woman from Adairsville as Captain Hart watched her. She couldn't vote any more than the abandoned wife could. But she could persuade. She raised her head, feeling strong and defiant, and said, "If Becky watch after Eliza, I go."

"I tell Captain Hart," Charlie said, and he smiled at her with such a brotherly look that she was glad she had said yes.

—⁓—

THE NEXT SATURDAY, a day Charlie could spare from his fields, they traveled to Floyd County in his wagon, pulled by his even-tempered mule, Jake. They drove along the Etowah River, low in its banks since rain had been scarce that spring. Rachel stared at the brown, silty water. She asked Charlie, "Once we get there, what should we do?"

"Find black folks and talk to them."

The road took them past cotton fields—river bottoms were always good cotton land—and once they were in Floyd County,

Charlie stopped the wagon to hail a man with a hoe in his hands. "Big field," Charlie said companionably. "Your place?"

But the man shook his head and said curtly, "Leave me be."

Charlie slapped the reins, and Jake moved down the road. "We find someone else to talk to," Charlie said to Rachel. The road led them to a cluster of old slave cabins, where a flock of chickens pecked, a skinny hog rooted, and a woman knelt to weed a kitchen garden.

"Let me try," Rachel said. She hopped down from the wagon and called out, "How is you, sister?" Kitchen talk for country people.

The woman looked up. "Who is you?"

"Come from Cass County with my cousin, Mr. Charles Mannheim. He register black men to vote. I come along, help him."

She pushed her hat back from her forehead. She was expecting, about seven months along, and she looked hot and tired. "Vote?"

"The government say that black men vote this November. And they register, put their names on a list, so they ready to cast a vote. Mr. Mannheim, he from Cass County, but he register black men in Chattooga and Floyd, too."

She shook her head. "Don't want any trouble," she said.

"Ain't a trouble. The government say it's right. The Bureau help, too. Ain't you got a Bureau office here?"

At the sound of hoofbeats the woman raised her head. With fear in her voice, she said, "You go on before Marse sees you here."

Rachel said indignantly, "Marse? You free!"

The man who rode up was still a marse. He wore an unsullied white suit and a white hat, and he sat his horse with a pre-war grace. He said to the woman, "Who are these people?"

She dropped her eyes and mumbled, "Don't know, sir."

He stared at Rachel. "And who the hell are you?"

"Visiting from Cass County."

"Where did you run off from?" He took in Charlie, sitting quietly in the wagon, his hands on Jake's reins. "You and your husband. Who's your massa?"

Rachel said politely, "We're just passing through. We stopped to be sociable, say how do."

"I heard you. Voting! You've come to stir my people up, haven't you? Like in Cass County. Hear they nearly had a riot on the day niggers signed up to vote!"

"No, sir, we had a press, but it was all peaceable," Rachel said.

He said, "I won't have you stirring up my people. Get off my land."

"Yes, sir. We go now, sir," Charlie called. He gestured roughly to Rachel. "Now," he insisted, and she scrambled back into the wagon. She sat heavily on the hard wooden seat as Jake trotted away.

Charlie said, "Told you it weren't like Cass."

Cass, where they knew their enemies as well as their friends. "Find out the hard way." She was shaking.

"They go to meeting somewhere," he said thoughtfully. "Might be secret and private, like our meeting house."

She nodded and tried to let the sun warm her. "We sneak and creep a little and find out where."

At the next place, they fibbed to the man and woman at work in the cotton field, saying that they came from Cass County but planned on settling in Floyd, and hoped they might find a place to go to Sunday meeting. The man grinned and the woman

251

smiled shyly. "Have our own church now since the war, just for black folks," the man said. "We get married there!" At that, the woman's face shone.

"Where can we find it of a Sunday?" Charlie asked, and they told him. And since they had pretended they had nowhere else to go, the woman offered them a spot on the floor in their cabin until then, and a promise of dinner that night. Their names were Jim and Dell, and they had three children who helped in the fields. They were tenants paid in a share of the crop.

Over a meal of peas and pone, Jim and Dell talked in low tones, as though they were afraid that white people might overhear. They had heard about the Reconstruction Act and about registration in Cass County. "White folks here say it were a melee," Jim said.

"It were not," Charlie said. "And won't be a melee here if everyone come and act orderly."

"Can I be there?" Dell asked. "Want to see it happen."

Rachel said fiercely, "You stand with him. School and persuade him. Encourage and aid him. He represent you and the children when he vote, just like the delegate to the convention represent all of us."

—〜—

JIM AND DELL managed to spread the word throughout Floyd County like a fever. By the time Rachel and Charlie arrived at the church the next morning, a curious crowd awaited them. Jim and Dell's kin and neighbors and friends packed into the little whitewashed building to listen to Charlie preach, and afterwards, the women peppered Rachel with questions. Was she married to Charlie? Where did she hail from, and who were her people? Why was she traveling the countryside to talk about voting? They all wished they could vote, but since they could not, what could they do?

Rachel had her own sermon for them. "No, he's my cousin, and we grew up together on the Mannheim place in Cass County. Voting, it's about freedom. Do you want good work, and to be paid fair for it? Do you want to live in dignity? Do you want your young'uns to get schooling? We vote for a delegate to the convention to write us a constitution that give us a fair chance. An equal chance. We can't vote, but the man of your house represent you, like the delegate to the convention represent us."

As she repeated what she had said to Dell, the words bothered her. *Who represent me?* she thought. *And why can't I represent myself?*

— ∽ —

ON THE WAY home, Rachel slumped beside Charlie on the wagon's bench. She was tired, bone tired. She had never imagined that talking to strangers would be as exhausting as cooking a wedding dinner or doing a week's wash.

Charlie sat straight and slapped the reins against Jake's neck. "Go, boy!" he called brightly to the mule. "Go, Jake! Take us on home!"

Full of energy, the mule broke into an obliging trot. Charlie grinned. "Good boy, Jake! We register lots of voters now! Good boy!" Laughing, he said to Rachel, "We done good, even though you all worn out."

She tried to sit straighter. "Be all right after I set quiet. It suit you, though. You like it, driving all these strangers to register and vote."

"I do!" Charlie sang out, as though he were still encouraging Jake. "I do indeed!"

"Maybe you should put yourself forth as a delegate," she said.

He wasn't swift to reply. She wondered if she had bothered him somehow. He dropped his voice and said, "I been pondering it." This meant that he'd considered it, back and forth, yes and no, and he was now thinking of how to go roundabout to persuade some white man—in this case, Captain Hart—to help him get there.

They were still in Floyd County, where black folks always talked low in public, as though a white man were close by to hear.

She said, "Do Captain Hart know? That you ponder it?"

"He encourage it."

"Do he?"

He spoke slowly, as he had in his sermon to the uninitiated in Floyd County. "Them folks who write that paper, the *Loyal Georgian*, they have a society called the Union League, for people loyal to the Union. Help the Republicans. Register black men to vote."

Dear Lord, she thought. *He's ahead of me again. He's known about this for weeks.*

"Captain Hart start a League society in Cass County, and he ask me to help him," he said.

"To work with the Republicans. To register black men to vote."

"Yes."

"Could I join?" she asked.

He shook his head.

"Why not?"

"Don't want trouble," he said.

"We already have trouble," she said. "Both of us."

"All over Georgia, League men in trouble," he said. "Don't want you so close to it." Even though Jake needed no encouragement, he slapped the reins against the mule's neck and cried out, "Jake! Good boy, Jake! Hurry us on home!"

11 | THE ROAD TO ROME

RACHEL DROPPED THE last of the corn into the furrow. Corn was easy and would grow any old way, not like cotton, which needed to be drilled and planted and bedded like a newborn baby. She was abashed that Charlie had been right. She had managed only two acres in cotton, and it was as big a struggle as ten acres had been for him. She wiped her face with her sleeve and said to Mollie, "That's enough." She led the mule back to the Kaltenbach place.

Adelaide, on her midday break from the school, saw her come through the parlor. She teased, "You look like a field hand." Despite her words, her sister was proud of Rachel's place. She asked after its progress and had even come to see the cotton fields once they were planted.

"I'm not a field hand. I'm a cotton farmer," Rachel teased back.

"Wash those cotton-farming hands before you sit down to dinner with us." Adelaide laughed. "There's a letter for you. A Mr. Pereira, from Atlanta."

Rachel reached for the letter.

"Is he kin to—" Adelaide asked.

"Yes. A Charleston Pereira. His daddy was an Israelite and his mama was a free woman of color."

"How ever did you meet him?"

"He's the lawyer I talked to about my freedom money." She reached out her hand. "Let me see it. I don't mind if I get dirt on it." She opened it, scanned it, and smiled.

"Is it business?" Adelaide asked, knowing it wasn't.

"No, it ain't," she said, happiness sending her back to kitchen talk as grief had once done. "He invite me to dine with him in Atlanta two Sundays from now."

"Will you go?"

"Of course I will. Wear my good dress, too."

—⁘—

THE ADDRESS MR. Pereira had sent belonged to his boarding house on Houston Street, which had miraculously survived the war. The white clapboard was smoke-stained, probably during Sherman's incursion, and like many houses in Sherman Town, had yet to be repainted. The windows were intact, and someone had washed them to a sparkle. The front steps were swept and scrubbed clean, despite the stinking mud of the street.

The woman who answered the door was dark and dignified. Age had etched lines of weariness from her nose to the corners of her mouth. Her dress was a dark gray, and her apron was spotless. Her hands were older than her face, the veins prominent and the joints gnarled from a lifetime of hard labor. "I'm Mrs. Simpson, who keep this house," she said. "I been expecting you, Miss Mannheim. You come on in."

The house smelled of the beeswax Mrs. Simpson must use to freshen the furniture and the linseed oil she must use to scrub the pine floors. They mingled with the smell from the kitchen, a savory odor of roasting chicken. Chicken meant trouble and expense. Rachel wondered if it had been Mr. Pereira's idea or Mrs. Simpson's.

The house was small enough that Rachel could see the dining room if she turned her head to the left and the parlor if she turned her head to the right. Mrs. Simpson led Rachel to the parlor, which was crowded with a settee, covered in brown striped fabric that gaped with wear, and two large, mismatched wing chairs.

Mr. Pereira rose from one of the wing chairs and held out his hand to Rachel. "I'm glad to see you," he said softly.

"Glad to come here," she replied.

He led her to the dining room, as though they were in a much more elegant house, and pulled out her chair for her to sit.

The dining table could fit a dozen people, and the scarred chairs were solid and ornately carved. The only house in Atlanta Rachel had seen was Mordecai's, where money had bought everything brand new, but Atlanta must be full of lost things, half-destroyed things, things that had passed from hand to hand in the frenzy of the occupation and the war. Figured paper, which had never recovered from the fires of 1864, covered the walls. Over the sideboard hung a framed photograph of President Abraham Lincoln. The table was set with china, thick and plain, and dented, mismatched silverware. The tablecloth was good linen, but it had been badly scorched and inexpertly mended.

Once they were seated, they were joined by Mrs. Simpson's other boarder, Mr. Junius Haynes, who apologized for being late. "Lingered after the service at church."

"Talking to that young lady you like so much?" Pereira teased.

Haynes grinned. He had a countryman's face, even though he wore a citified suit. Rachel wondered if he had bought the cloth at Henry's shop. He glanced at Rachel. "What if I do?" he asked. "I could get married, if I please. Make a good living, enough for two."

Mrs. Simpson had gone to a lot of trouble. Besides the chicken, which had a wonderful smell, she had set out sweet potatoes, green beans cooked with bacon, and biscuits. Before she served, she said, "We bless this food first." She bowed her head and Mr. Haynes followed her example. Rachel glanced at Pereira. A skeptic's smile tugged at the corners of his mouth.

Once God had been satisfied and the food had been served, Rachel asked Mr. Haynes, "What do you work at?"

"Work as a messenger for the *Intelligencer*."

"The newspaper?" Rachel asked, interested. "Do you hear the news before the rest of us?"

"Oh, yes. See the pieces when I bring them in."

"You can read? When did you learn?" "Back in slavery days," he said between bites of a biscuit. "Had a secret school on my massa's place. Left for Atlanta when the Army came through in

1865. That was a time. Atlanta a wreck. Lived in a tent and dug holes for General Sherman's men."

"But you've done well since then."

He nodded. "Want to do better. Want to work as a printer at the paper, but they say no. They tell me that's a white man's job."

"Not forever, I hope," Rachel said.

Pereira flashed her a look of amusement. "Miss Mannheim is adamant about the progress of our race," he said. "She helps to register men to vote in Cass County, where she lives."

"How does registration go in Atlanta?" Rachel asked. "Are there many registered?"

"It goes well," Pereira said. "And peacefully, too. The Bureau has heard no complaints."

"Are you registered?" Rachel asked Haynes.

"Yes, ma'am, I am!" he sang out, as though he were in church.

Mrs. Simpson was surprised. "Why do you bother?" she asked Rachel. "You can't vote."

"Oh, but I can talk to people who do."

"And she does!" Pereira said, laughing. "She's very persuasive!"

She had never seen Pereira like this—jocose and at ease. She liked seeing the man underneath the lawyer.

After dinner Haynes excused himself—"I rest for a bit"—and Mrs. Simpson rose to clear the table. Rachel asked Mrs. Simpson if she needed any help, but the landlady said, "No, you a guest." She smiled indulgently at Pereira. "You let him entertain you."

Pereira rose and asked Rachel, "Would you like to promenade with me?"

"Where do we go?" Rachel asked.

He held out his arm. "Come with me."

Rachel had seen Wheat Street on a weekday, when its residents bustled about Atlanta's business, but she was unprepared for the different press of a Sunday afternoon. Wheat Street turned out in its finery for the Sabbath day. The sidewalks were so crowded that they made little progress, which didn't matter, since so many people wanted to stop to greet Pereira. She hadn't realized that he would be so well-known and so well-regarded in Atlanta. In the throng, she saw two familiar faces, the washwomen Hattie and Keziah. Hattie was dressed in a dark silk dress fine enough for a wedding, and Keziah was resplendent in plaid taffeta trimmed with lace. Both women wore hoops, which further crowded the narrow sidewalk.

Rachel praised Hattie's dress, and Hattie laughed. "I look like a pig in a poke. Keziah, she look fine."

"Miss Anna Victoria's work?"

"Yes, it is. You should see her! She look like the Queen of England! Hattie smiled. "Mr. Pereira, no one know that you so friendly with Miss Rachel, who come to see you on business."

Pereira blushed. He was fair-skinned enough to show it. "Well, now you do," he said.

Hattie asked Rachel, "How is your place in Cass County? How do it get on?"

"It get on fine! I finish planting corn a few days ago. Only have a few acres planted in cotton. More next year, when I get tenants to work for me."

"Do it suit you?"

The question stopped Rachel short. The answer came out less sunny than the previous one. "I believe it do."

"Wonder why you stay in the countryside," Hattie said. "Keziah and I, we couldn't bear to stay. It all felt like slavery. Came to Atlanta as fast as we could after the war."

"I buy a place, I work it, and I use it for my increase," Rachel said stubbornly. "I stay in Cass County."

Hattie nodded. "Wish you well," she said as she and her daughter moved on.

Pereira laughed softly and tapped her on the arm to lead her through the crowd.

Another familiar face appeared. It was Anna Victoria, dressed as beautifully as Hattie had said. She greeted Rachel with a sly smile. "Miss Mannheim! And Mr. Pereira!"

Pereira, who knew Anna Victoria, said to her in a mild tone, "Miss Mannheim has done some business with me, so I wanted to do her a favor and show her a bit of Atlanta."

Anna Victoria's smile broadened. She looked as though a promenade were as good as a proposal. "You do that," she said.

Rachel felt hot. "Is Atlanta always like this?" she asked Pereira, as they moved on.

"Hot? Crowded?"

"No, already knew that. Does everyone know and tell your business because you walk down the street?"

"That's not so different from Cass County." Pereira laughed. "Or Charleston!" He took her hand. "Let me buy you an ice."

Holding the paper dish in her hands, eating the lovely, creamy ice with a wooden spoon, she remembered the last time she had tasted the confection. It was in Savannah, before the war. She had been sixteen, and a handsome house slave named Octavian had bought it for her. Afterwards, he had taken her into an alley and had expected her to repay him.

She didn't think that Mr. Pereira would believe she owed him a favor for an ice.

"Do you like Atlanta any better?" Pereira asked her, smiling. "Now that you aren't hot and crowded and bothered by busybodies?"

"Yes, I do." She ate the last spoonful, savoring its sweetness. "Don't you start on me, though. Telling me to come to Atlanta."

"I wouldn't dream of it," he said. "I don't dare persuade you!"

He was flirting with her, and it felt as creamy as the ice. "Oh, no," she said, flirting back. "I've scared you off. My sister was brought up a belle, and she would be ashamed of me."

"I've never been afraid of a woman who knows her own mind," he said.

"That's in your favor."

He laughed hard. "I'm glad to hear it!"

"You're different," she said. "Not like you are in your office." She blushed and was glad it didn't show. "It pleases me to see it."

"It's a pleasure to be with you, too, Miss Mannheim."

"Did you grow up with a sister? Did you tease her?"

"She was the elder," he said. "I didn't dare. But I had a sweetheart, back in Charleston."

"A sweetheart? Why didn't you marry her?"

"No man should marry his first sweetheart," he said. "Besides, if I had, how would I have met you?"

"As my lawyer," she said, enjoying herself, "and you could have signed all the trusts and deeds I needed."

He reached for her hand, and she let him take it. "When is the train back to Cass County?"

"Too soon," she said.

He leaned forward and kissed her on the cheek. "I look forward to seeing you again," he said, his hazel eyes shining in the sunlight.

She could feel his lips on her cheek, the softest touch, all the way back to Cass County, and for days afterwards.

—⌒—

A FEW DAYS after she returned from Atlanta, Charlie came to visit her, sitting in her house with perfect ease now. "Did you tell Captain Hart about your notion?" she asked him.

"Not yet. Have other trouble first. Do you recall the place in Floyd County where the man on horseback insulted you?"

"Of course I do."

"A man called Mr. Hawkins. He won't let his tenants register. He's told them he'll shoot any man who tries to go to register at the courthouse in Rome, that's the county seat in Floyd, and that he'll hurt the women and children, too."

"Has he shot anyone yet?"

"Scared them so much they ain't tried," Charlie said. He made his hands into fists on the arms of the chair. "Can't have it. Talked to Captain Hart about. He'll go with me to talk to Hawkins. Plans to take Freddy along. Told me Mr. Pereira from Atlanta agreed to come with us."

Rachel thought of their conversation in Atlanta about her effort to register voters. "Why Mr. Pereira? Is he a good shot?

Or do he plan to lawyer those people down to the courthouse to register?"

"Said you convinced him, last you saw him. What did you say to him?"

"What I tell everyone. That it matter if black men vote."

"I hear he were a soldier in the war. He can stand with us to shoot if we need to."

Rachel nodded. "I go with you, too."

"No!" Charlie gasped.

"Oh, yes."

"It ain't safe. Don't want you getting shot at. Or worse."

She grabbed his arm. "Are any of us safe, those of us who stand up? Like that League of yours? I go with you."

∽

DESPITE HIS PROTESTS, Rachel traveled back to Floyd County with Charlie, in the wagon drawn by Jake. Charlie took his rifle with him. "Hope I don't need it," he said.

Rachel said, "I should have a rifle, too."

"Just the thing, so you can shoot yourself in the foot," he said irritably.

He's jumpier than he'd like to admit, Rachel thought.

They met Hart, Bailey, and Pereira, all on horseback, on the road outside the Hawkins place. Rachel was surprised to see how well Daniel Pereira sat a horse. He doffed his hat to her. "Miss Mannheim!" he said. "I hoped to call on you, but I'm surprised to see you here."

"I help with this, too."

His ivory skin was suffused with color, like a man preparing for battle. He said, "Mr. Mannheim, you shouldn't let her expose herself to such danger."

"Can't talk her out of it," Charlie said, but his face was full of pride. "She brave, and she stubborn."

Pereira shook his head, but he smiled, too.

"Any trouble?" Charlie asked Hart.

"No, it's quiet," Hart said. "Just like the war. Quiet until we had a battle on our hands."

The horsemen went ahead, a scouting party for the wagon. They trotted the horses up the driveway, and the wagon followed. The house and the grounds were in good repair, and the cotton fields had been planted and chopped. However Mr. Hawkins had done it, there were people to sweep his drive, prune his garden, and hoe his fields.

Mr. Hawkins, again dressed in a white suit and a white hat, stood on his front steps as they drove up. He stared at them and recognized Rachel. "I thought I told you to stay away from my people," he said.

Hart dismounted. "We're here to assure that your men register to vote."

"They were my people before the war, and they're still my people. I won't have anyone interfering with them," Hawkins said.

"These men are obliged to register, by the law of the state of Georgia and the order of the government of the United States."

Hawkins glared him. "Damn the federal government." He looked darkly at Bailey, dressed in his Union coat. "Damn bluebellies, all of them." He turned his ire on Pereira. "And who the hell is that? The jumped-up nigger in the frock coat?"

Pereira turned an angry red and started forward, but Hart grabbed him by the arm. "Steady, Mr. Pereira," he said. "Mr. Hawkins, we can do this the easy way, or we can do this the hard way. Let these people go to Rome to register."

"I told them that any man who ran off to vote would be punished when he came back," Hawkins said. "His wife and children punished, too. It wouldn't bother me to shoot you if you try to pull them along with you."

"I don't care to shoot a man who isn't a soldier, but I can if I have to," Hart said.

Hawkins reached inside his coat and pulled out his pistol. Both Hart and Bailey ran up the steps, Bailey to grab the pistol and Hart to hold Hawkins fast.

Hawkins struggled in their grasp. "I was a soldier!" he yelled. "Fought with honor for the Confederacy! God damn you!"

Bailey dropped Hawkins' pistol to the ground and kicked it away. Pereira ran to retrieve it. Hart said, "We'll hold you here while your people go to Rome to vote."

Pereira stuffed Hawkins' pistol into his coat pocket and mounted his horse. His color was even higher. He yelled to Charlie, "Follow me! I'll find some voters for you!" He spurred the horse, and Charlie encouraged Jake, who flattened his ears and broke into a gallop.

They sped down the driveway, letting the hooves and the wheels raise a cloud of dust. Once on the road, Pereira slowed his horse and let the wagon slow, too. As he rode alongside, Charlie shook his head and said, "Keep your temper, Mr. Pereira."

"Not when I'm insulted!" he said.

"Man, if you feel insulted every time a white man call you a nigger, your blood boil and it kill you," Charlie said.

The people of the Hawkins place were easy to find, because just down the road, they worked in a gang in the fields. *Like in slavery times,* Rachel thought.

Charlie waved his arms at them. "Hey! You free to register! Free to vote!"

A man dropped his hoe. "What happen?"

"Mr. Hawkins is under armed guard on his own porch," Pereira said.

The man asked, "The Army come?"

"The Freedmen's Bureau! Come with us! Free at last to register and vote!" Charlie said.

All of them, men, women, and children, dropped their hoes to whoop and laugh. They quickly piled into Charlie's wagon. "You lead us!" Charlie sang out to Pereira. "He scout you and we guard you, all the way to Rome!"

The exhilaration wore off, and Rachel felt a chill of fear. Would Hawkins' friends come to find them and ambush them on the road? She hoped that Pereira, for all his citified ways, really was a good shot.

But no one stopped them and no one challenged them, and in twenty minutes the town of Rome was in sight, the church spire tall, the courthouse tower to rival it, two red brick refuges for the black voters of Floyd County.

—❧—

By the time they returned to Cass County, it was nearly sunset, and the last train had left for Atlanta. Pereira said, "I'll ride to Cartersville. I can stay in the Bureau office." But even as he said it, he slumped in his saddle.

"Don't think of it," Charlie said. He glanced at Rachel, who had stepped from the wagon before her house. "Don't you have a spare room?"

"I need to collect Eliza." Her daughter had stayed with Becky, as she usually did when Rachel traveled to register voters.

"Becky and I keep Eliza tonight, it ain't any trouble for us," he said. He drove away smiling.

When he was gone, Pereira asked, "What was that about?"

"Charlie fuss too much over me," she said, blushing. Charlie was a busybody, just like everyone in Atlanta. She unlocked the door. "I can scrabble some supper, if you're hungry."

"Not much," he said. "I'd give a great deal for a shot of brandy."

"I have some. Good French brandy, from before the war."

"You do? God bless you."

Registration and its dangers had worn her out. "I could do with some myself," she said. She poured the brandy into tin cups, regretting that she hadn't used any of her freedom money for glasses. Her guest deserved better.

He took the cup from her hand, letting their fingers meet, and sipped. Sighed. Leaned back in the chair and closed his eyes. He raised the cup and took a draught this time. "That's good," he said. Henry's expression of pleasure, from the days when she gave him pleasure.

She thought of Henry as he had sat in that chair, as he had taken her hand to lead her to their room, as he had embraced her when they lay down together. The memory spoiled the taste of the brandy, and she set it down after a sip.

Pereira drained his cup. "Do you mind if I ask for more?"

"No." She filled it for him. "Saw today that you don't care for shooting."

"I did my duty in the war, but I never liked shooting, and I still don't." He sighed again. "I thought the pen could be mightier than the sword. Evidently not, in Floyd County, Georgia."

"What a miserable place, that Hawkins place. Those people back in slavery."

"And he insulted me, damn him." Despite his fatigue, his temperature rose a little.

"Can't be the first time you heard it."

"Of course not. But I won't stand for it any more than you would."

She smiled. "Stubborn about it."

"I won't persuade you differently." He smiled, too.

She felt a little light-headed. She sipped her brandy and asked, "You don't mind that I drink?"

"Not at all. My mother drinks claret every day with dinner, and I don't think any the less of her."

"What is she like?"

"Oh, she's very grand these days, but she wasn't always."

"How did she get free?"

His face changed. Saddened. "She was born a slave. Her father was Samuel Bennett, one of the richest planters in South Carolina. He freed her because he loved her mother."

She nodded. "How did she meet your daddy?"

"I never knew. She wouldn't say. But whatever she did, he was faithful to her, and took care of her like a wife. He bought her a house and some property so she had an income. And he took care of all of us. He paid for our education, for my sisters, my brothers, and myself, and if he'd lived, he would have sent me north to college."

She drank a little more and said, "So we're not so different, you and I. Jewish daddy who had to hide you away. Black mother, born in slavery, who he could never marry."

"We are, and we aren't." Sadness tinged his face, and he drank the rest of the cup down. A flush suffused his face. "I have something for you. I was hoping to give it to you under happier circumstances."

"What is it?"

He reached into his coat and pulled it out. "It's a little late," he said. "I know the holiday's over."

He handed her a slim volume, and at the sight of the title, stamped in gold and translated into English, she said in astonishment, "It's the Passover book! Wherever did you find it?"

Pereira looked impish. "I am half an Israelite," he said. "Like you."

She opened it. "One page in Hebrew, and the other in English, so I'll know everything it says! I wish I could hear the Hebrew."

"Perhaps I can help," Pereira said.

Surprised, she asked, "How could you?"

"We studied all of the ancient languages at Wilberforce—Latin, Greek, and Hebrew. I'm a little rusty, but I'll do my best."

She said, "Just that first part. The very first." She handed him the book, and their fingers touched. He blushed. She wanted to lay her hand on that warm, rosy cheek, to find out whether it was as smooth as his fingers.

He read the words, slowly and carefully, not stumbling, in his mellifluous voice. She closed her eyes to listen, remembering. When she opened them, she was in tears.

"What pains you so, Rachel?" he asked, very softly.

"When I was a slave I stood quiet in the dining room, all through the service, to hear that story. And to hear the words at the end." She knew those by heart. "This year we are slaves, next year we will be free…" The tears came.

He reached for her hands, his skin ivory against hers, his fingers soft. She let herself feel the pleasure of it. He smelled of sweat and brandy and very faintly of the soap he had used this morning before he left Atlanta. He looked at her with a sweetness she had never seen on his face before. She thought, *If I leaned forward he would kiss me,* and for a long moment she wanted to feel the tenderness of his lips on her own.

It had been a long time since she'd felt a man's arms around her. Longer still since she'd felt a man's naked skin pressed against hers in love. Suddenly she longed for it more than she had longed for freedom.

His eyes met hers, and she read the sadness and longing in them. If she leaned forward… If he did…

She took her hands away. "I'm wore out," she said, reverting to the kitchen talk she knew he disparaged in her. She rose. "I make up your bed for you, then I need to sleep."

He drew back. Softly, he said, "I believe I feel the same. Wore out."

Once she settled into bed she couldn't sleep. She felt his presence in the next room, a ghostly whisper in her ear, a ghostly touch of his fingers on her, a ghostly press of the lips.

Henry's first gift to her had been a book, Shakespeare's plays bound in leather with pages edged in gold. Pereira's gift of a book was as fraught with feeling as Henry's had been, and it touched her and troubled her the same way.

12 | INDEPENDENCE DAY

RACHEL JOINED ADELAIDE on the shaded porch after midday dinner, with Frankie between them, and all of them hoped for a cooling breeze.

Adelaide fanned herself with the latest copy of the *Intelligencer*. "La, it's hot for June," she said.

Rachel raised her arm to wipe the sweat from her face, since she figured that they were all familiar together. Frankie frowned. "Use my handkerchief," she admonished.

Rachel looked at Adelaide. "A free woman doesn't wipe her face with her sleeve!" they said in unison, and laughed at the same time.

As Rachel dabbed her face with the handkerchief, Charlie strode up the driveway. In his field clothes—sweaty shirt, dirt-streaked pants, muddy boots—he stood as tall as Sergeant Bailey in his Union coat.

He waved and doffed his hat. As he came up the steps, he greeted them. "Miss Adelaide. Miss Frankie."

Miffed, Rachel asked, "Don't I get a how do?"

He grinned. "Didn't give me a chance. How do, Miss Rachel."

"We do just fine, Mr. Mannheim," Adelaide said, letting all of them hear the way she honored the man who had been her slave. "Will you sit with us?"

"No, that's all right, Miss Adelaide. I can't linger. But I came to tell you something important. Wanted you to be the first to know about it."

Smiling, Adelaide asked, "Is there another baby on the way?"

"That would be a joyful thing," Charlie said, smiling, too, "but that ain't the news."

Without being told, Rachel knew. He had been readying himself in place after place in Cass and Floyd and Chattooga Counties, in meeting house after meeting house, in field after field, giving his sermon about registering to vote, so a man could vote for someone to speak for black folks at the constitutional convention. He had grown surer and easier with every sermon. "Miss Adelaide, I've pondered this for a long time, and I've spoken with Captain Hart about it," he said. "I'm going to run for election as a delegate to the convention in Atlanta."

"You don't need my permission for that."

"Glad to hear you say so, Miss Adelaide, but I thought it would be a courtesy to tell you. Since you helped me in the matter of becoming a registrar."

Adelaide blushed a little. Rachel thought, *He still play Br'er Rabbit. Let her think it were all her doing.*

"Mr. Mannheim," Adelaide asked, "is it true that Colonel Turner will be running as well?"

"I believe so, Miss Adelaide. That's all right. Our district send five delegates to Atlanta. There's room enough for both of us."

She set the newspaper in her lap. "Is there any way I can help you?"

"Yes, ma'am, there is. If you're planning to have a frolic this July, I wish I might invite people from Floyd and Chattooga and speak to them. Remind them to register, and let them know I'm hoping for their votes, when they do vote."

"I'd be glad to."

He stood quietly, tall and proud and at his ease. "Just one more thing."

"Yes, Mr. Mannheim?"

"Might we have our frolic on the Fourth of July? Day of Independence? It means a lot to us, who used to be the children of Moses."

Adelaide chuckled. "Yes, we'll remind old Pharaoh," she said. "We'll do it on Independence Day."

— ᔕ —

AFTER THE SUN had set, after Rachel had tucked Eliza into bed, she prepared to latch the front door. She had always locked the door, but in recent days, she had begun to think about adding a better bolt to it. As tension mounted in the county, she no longer felt easy about living alone. She was about to snuff her candle and go to bed herself when she heard the footsteps and muffled voices of men trying to pass quietly. She wished more than ever that she owned a rifle and knew how to use it.

But when she glanced out the window, the men who slipped past her house were all familiar. Charlie. Asa and Adam Benjamin. Zeke Hutchens and Davey Edgefield. She opened the window, holding the candle against the darkness, and called out, "Where are you bound?"

"Never you mind!" Charlie called back.

She unlocked the door and ran to stand on her front steps. She saw that they were all armed. "Hunting? Of a weekday night?" she asked, even though she knew they weren't.

Charlie said sharply, "Rachel, go inside and latch your door. This ain't for you."

Don't you order me like I'm Eliza's age, she thought. *I've been in peril all over the district, just like you.* But she waited until they disappeared into the trees. She woke Eliza. "Sugar, I need to run outside. Bolt the door after me, and don't open it until I come back."

Eliza's eyes went wide.

"Just to visit Miss Frankie," Rachel fibbed. "I'll be right back." As Eliza shut the bolt, Rachel ran down the steps to follow the men into the darkness.

They were on their way to the meeting house.

She followed them, trying to keep her tread soft on the path bedded with pine needles. She strained to see in the dark and started at a scrabbling sound. She felt for the path with her feet, but she blundered and a pine bough needled her cheek. She slapped it away and quickened her pace, not caring if she made a noise.

At the meeting house, light glowed through the oilpaper windows, and the sound of people settling into the pews—feet shuffling, coughs, a murmur of talk—came to her. She sidled closer and the voice of Captain Hart floated through the oilpaper. "It's so good to see so many loyal men gathered here," he said.

So the secret meeting was the Union League, the men loyal to the Union and the Republican Party.

She stepped onto the stairs, and the tread groaned under her feet. Inside, men rushed to rise. When the door flew open it was Charlie, rifle in hand, who stared at her with an anger she had never seen in him before. "It's you!" he said, lowering the rifle. "Told you to stay home!"

She tried to look past him into the meeting house, but he barred her way.

Captain Hart came to the door. "Mr. Mannheim, what is this?"

Charlie said, "It's Miss Rachel, who act the fool and wander here in the night."

"Weren't wandering," Rachel said sharply, appealing to Hart. "Wanted to know what you men were up to in your meeting."

Hart said sternly, "Miss Mannheim, it's dangerous for you to be out alone at night."

"It were dangerous in company in Floyd County in broad daylight. I think you try to frighten me to keep your Union League a secret."

Charlie glanced at Hart in exasperation. Hart said, "Miss Mannheim, let me escort you home."

"Charlie—" Rachel began.

Stern, Charlie said, "You go on with Captain Hart and don't you naysay me."

More gently, Hart said, "Please, Miss Mannheim. Let me take you home."

At least he's polite about it, she thought. She threw Charlie a sulky glance and followed Hart. Once on the path, in the dark, she inquired of Hart, "What happens in your meeting?"

"It's not so different from what happens when you and Mr. Mannheim go to persuade a group of people anywhere in the district. We talk about registering. We talk about voting. We talk about the convention. If a new man joins us, he takes the loyalty oath."

"I know all about that," she said, still sulky. "Why keep it such a secret?"

"Miss Mannheim, my father is a Freemason back in Cincinnati. Their meetings are secret, too, and underneath the mystery it is all a dull business, I can assure you."

"Why keep the women away? Tell them to stay at home?"

His voice changed, went stern again. "That's a different matter, and you know it. Our meetings may be dull, but the danger is very real. None of these men would forgive himself if his wife or daughter suffered any harm at a League meeting."

"But we're already in danger, we black women, whether we go to a meeting or not. Why do we get treated different?"

Hart sighed. "You and Miss Williamson. Ardent for equality."

Rachel said hotly, "It's not fair, and it's not right. Don't know if I want to wait, Captain Hart."

—✑—

A FEW DAYS later, Rachel opened her door to see Captain Hart standing on her steps. He started with an apology. "I'm sorry I had to strong-arm you home last week."

"You and Charlie." He didn't reply, so she said, "If we women could take care of ourselves, would it be different?"

"Take care? How?"

"Like Frankie said once. She called us women soldiers. We could use rifles, too."

He said ruefully, "Miss Mannheim, you press me whenever you see me."

"Like Miss Adelaide," she said, and she wasn't sorry that he blushed.

He insisted on coming inside, but he refused refreshment. "You and Miss Williamson shamed me into doing something I should have done a while ago," he said. "The Bureau is paying people to register voters. Mr. Mannheim shouldn't be paid, since he's running for office, but we should be paying you." He leaned forward. "I went to Atlanta to talk to the head of the Georgia Bureau. I had quite a time persuading him that we should pay a black woman for organizing black men to vote. But I got them to see reason."

He had surprised her. "Pay me? To tell the women to encourage the men to vote?"

"Miss Mannheim, why are you so surprised that what you do is useful in the world? And that you should be paid for it?"

She felt a surge of pride. She felt taller, like Charlie. Laughing, she said, "If I learn how to shoot a rifle, will you allow me at a Union League meeting?"

"One battle at a time," he said, and he touched his hand to his brow, very like a salute.

— 〜 —

ON THE DAY before the frolic, a mule-drawn wagon arrived, laden with a clan of ten people and a crate of unhappy chickens. They stopped before Adelaide's house and asked a surprised Frankie where they might stay the night. Adelaide came to the door, smiling at the sight of Charlie's voters and their families. "I believe you want Mr. Mannheim's place," she said and directed them to Charlie's house. As they drove, they joked and laughed, their voices carrying until they were down the road, out of sight.

After that, Charlie's voters came in a steady stream, some in wagons, laden with provisions, and some on foot, carrying whatever they could in a basket or wrapped in a blanket. They came until Charlie no longer had room for them. He asked Adelaide if they could stay in the old slave cabins, and she assented. By evening they had filled not only the cabins but the space around them. They spilled onto the school grounds, where they set up temporary camp on the grass.

Rachel and Frankie stood on the steps of Adelaide's house to survey the crowd. "Like a town," Rachel said.

It was a friendly town, remarkably orderly for so many strangers crowded together. Men gathered to share whiskey and talk. Women worked to scrape together dinner. Children ran underfoot, and those who knew the place guided their new friends to the delights of the pine grove and the little brook in the woods.

There were a few mishaps, though. Two of the men had brought a feud with them, and whiskey made them argumentative. One of the women yelled at another to leave her chickens alone, they were for dinner tomorrow. Several children came back from the brook crying that they had leeches on their legs, and they cried afresh when their mothers slapped them for being fool enough to wade in water full of leeches.

Rachel sat on the porch and watched Charlie as he walked through the encampment, lingering to chat with the men and bending down to tease the children. He beckoned to her. With a grin, he said, "Don't have to seek them out to remind them to register and vote. Today they come to us."

She thought of the money that came from the Bureau for her efforts. She nodded. "I go to talk to the women."

—⌒—

THE NEXT DAY, as the air filled with the smell of roasting shoat from the barbecue pit, Rachel slipped into the kitchen to find that it was full of women, neighbors and strangers, rolling out pie crust and cutting up chickens for frying. Adelaide sat at the great kitchen table, a paring knife in her hand, and beside her sat Sarah, peeling apples, not at all startled to be surrounded by the black women who encouraged the black men of Georgia's 42nd District to vote.

"Rachel, help us!" Frankie called from the corner of the room, rubbing flour from her nose. "And meet Miss Caroline, who

came all the way from a place near Summerville in Chattooga
County yesterday!"

Miss Caroline was round-faced and dark in complexion. Her
hair was neatly coiled at her neck and her calico dress was bright
and crisp. She smiled at Rachel. "My man register already. Want to
hear Mr. Mannheim speak. Think of it, a black man, in politics!"

"What do you think, sister?"

"When he went to register, I went with him. Just about busted
with pride to hear him take the oath. When he vote, I go with
him." Her smile was as bright as the midsummer sun. "Bust
with pride all over again!"

At noon, the Benjamin brothers began to play and the women
began to set out the food. To appease Frankie, Rachel helped,
but such a crowd meant that no one was taxed very much. It
was nothing like the frolics of her youth, when she sweated in
the kitchen and ran herself so hard she couldn't eat. This was a
celebration, as much hers as anyone's. She filled her plate and
joined Frankie on the grass, surrounded by cheerful, companionable strangers.

Charlie, dressed in his Sunday meeting suit, made his way
through the crowd, bending to talk, shaking hands, laughing at
jokes that Rachel was too far away to hear. It was slow progress.
They all wanted to talk to him, the black candidate for the convention, as much as he wanted to talk to them. Becky and the
children followed him, also smiling and clasping hands, looking
pleased and proud.

He finally made his way to the house, where he mounted the
steps to use the porch as a temporary platform. Becky stood to

his right, her arms around Josey and Ben, their faces quiet and expectant.

The crowd moved to see and hear him more easily. They filled the lawn before the house, spilling over onto the side yard and pouring into the driveway.

Adelaide stood at the foot of the steps, Hart by her side. Rachel and Frankie were not far away. Frankie said softly, "What a press, Rachel! There must be more than a hundred people!"

Charlie raised his arms, the preacher's gesture, and the crowd quieted.

Hart ascended the steps. He surveyed the throng. "Some of you are friends and neighbors," he said, "and some of you are strangers. But all of you are brethren to me, as an agent of the Freedmen's Bureau"—a cheer went up, and Hart raised his hand—"and as a member of the Union League and the Republican Party." Another cheer. "I'm very pleased to support a fine man, Mr. Charles Mannheim of Cass County, whom many of you know as the registrar for the 42nd District. And very pleased to introduce him as the district's candidate for next year's Constitutional Convention in Atlanta!"

Charlie let them cheer and applaud. When they were done, he spoke.

"I thank you, all of you, for coming here today. Chopping season over, and corn mind itself, but a farmer's work ain't ever done. Thank you for leaving your work to come here today. Hope that everyone had enough to eat, and the pleasure of visiting and listening to the music. We thank you, Asa Benjamin, Adam Benjamin, Judah Benjamin, for gladdening our hearts with your playing."

Asa played a refrain of "Turkey in the Straw," and Adam, not to be outdone, returned with "O, Susanna!" Their father Judah put his fiddle under his chin to play "John Brown's Body," and another cheer came from the crowd, followed by enthusiastic, if ragged, singing.

Charlie waited for the noise to subside before he spoke again. "Today Independence Day. July Fourth, the day our whole country got free. Now, until Emancipation, that weren't any of our concern. The men who wrote that paper about independence, they didn't consider us."

He held up a book in his right hand. "All of you know this book. It's the Good Book, and we tell the stories in it, and listen to our preachers preach from it, and now that we can learn to read, we read from it. It tell the story of Israel, how the people fell into bondage and how they got free from it. On our place, we sit down every year on the Passover the Israelites still keep, and we tell the story anew. From slavery to freedom."

He raised his left hand, where he held a smaller book, and held both books aloft. "Now this book, this ain't as familiar to us. This book has the paper that set our country free. The Declaration of Independence. Many of us don't know what it say, since it weren't for us. But we should know, because it belong to us now."

He raised the book in his left hand high. "This book say that all men are created equal." He surveyed the crowd. "White and black." His eyes lit on Rachel, and he said, "It say men, but it mean women, too. All equal." He scrutinized the book. "It say that God give us inalienable rights. Rights that belong to us, like they belong to everyone, and can't anyone take them away." People began to nod and to murmur. As he preached, they answered.

Charlie gestured with the book in his hand. He said, "The Declaration say what those rights are. It say life, liberty, and the pursuit of happiness."

"Tell us!" someone said, and the refrain echoed throughout the crowd.

Charlie set both books down. "What do that mean for us? Life. That mean a life that's safe. No insult, no interference, no outrage. Our women and our children safe. Good life. Long life." His gaze travelled across the crowd. He seemed to be able to look at every person as though he were speaking to them face to face. "Liberty. We know all about that. That mean freedom. Everything the Emancipation Proclamation give to us, and everything the Reconstruction Acts give to us. Freedom to work." His gaze rested on the men and women who worked the fields. "Freedom to own land." His eyes met Rachel's. "I been blessed that way. Everyone here deserve the same freedom."

Charlie said, "Freedom to do business, and make a profit. Get your due when harvest come, get fair weight and fair money for what you grow. And if you decide on any other kind of business, freedom to get it started, and build it up, and keep it for your increase and your children's increase." His gaze shifted to Adelaide, and then he took in Sarah and Frankie. "Freedom to get educated, and to see your children get educated. Learn to read, to write, to figure, and maybe even go on to college, like our teacher, Miss Frankie Williamson, done." His face lit up. "Imagine, our children, scholars at a college!"

"Tell us!" a woman cried, and the cry rippled throughout the crowd. "Tell us, Mr. Mannheim!"

Charlie said, "The Declaration talk about the right to happiness, too. We weren't considered when the Declaration was put down on paper. We was slaves, and our happiness didn't matter, any more than you'd care about happiness for a chicken or a mule. All that different now." His eyes swept over the crowd, but Rachel felt them linger on her face. "We the equal of anyone, free to think about what happiness might be. Could be the happiness of good work. Or wealth. Or family, gathered round us. Or schooling. Or something new that we never thought of before. We free to figure that, and pursue it, as we want to."

He waited, and then said, "Now, some of you look a little puzzled. Ask yourself, thought I was going to hear about registering and voting for the Republican Party. But it all of a piece. I don't want to be a delegate because fame beckon me. Want to be a delegate to lift up my voice. Speak for life, liberty, and the pursuit of happiness for us. For black folks, who never had a voice before. His gaze traveled again. "Lift my voice, and leave my mark on this Constitution, this new paper, to declare the freedom and the rights of black folks."

They broke into applause. They whistled. They cheered. "Charlie! Charlie! Charlie!"

Rachel blinked away tears, as she had in the courthouse when Charlie swore the oath, and she clapped until her hands ached. She joined the chant, a cry of affection for the man who would lift up his voice for them: "Charlie!"

As the tumult died down, they all heard the sound of a group of men on horseback. White men. They reined in the horses and halted, silent as ghosts, at the very back of the crowd. Adelaide, who had a better vantage point than Rachel did, frowned at the sight. She descended from the porch and began to pick her way through the crowd. Worried, Rachel followed her, and Frankie caught her hand and came along. As she drew closer, Rachel could see the Turner brothers, and half a dozen more with them.

Adelaide walked up to Ben Junior and put her hands on her hips. "You shouldn't be here," she said.

Ben slipped from the horse to stand too close to her. "Why shouldn't I?" he said. "Ain't this a free country, like your nigger just said?"

Adelaide didn't flinch, though he stood unpleasantly close. "You weren't invited," she said.

Ben laughed. "Invited! Didn't think I needed an invitation!" He grabbed her by the arm.

Frankie rushed forward. "You leave Mrs. Kaltenbach alone."

Ben stared at her, but he released Adelaide. "It's the little nigger teacher, telling me what to do." He called to his brother. "Help me out here, Pierce, she's a handful." Pierce dismounted and the two of them pushed against Frankie, who flinched.

Adelaide cried out, "Leave her alone!" and rushed the two men. Rachel ran to help her. Adelaide began to pummel Ben, and Rachel tried to wrench Pierce away.

The Turners' band dismounted. They surrounded the women, who disappeared inside their rough, jostling mass.

"Let us go!" Rachel shouted. A shoulder struck her cheek as rough hands pinioned her arms behind her.

Hart sprinted toward the disturbance. "You damned cowards! Interfering with women!" Bailey and Charlie, accompanied by a dozen men, all armed, followed him. Hart bellowed as though he were on the battlefield. "Let them go, you bastards!"

Hart and his men surrounded the intruders. Adam grabbed Ben and tore him away from Adelaide. Asa wrenched Rachel free. Bailey reached for Frankie, who was by now ashen and trembling. In a fury, Hart barked at the Turners, "Get away. Now! Or I'll command all of these men to shoot."

Adelaide, as pale as Frankie, put a restraining hand on his arm. She turned to Ben, held captive by Adam Benjamin, a man nearly twice his size. "Ben, don't you recall, that we were children together? How we used to climb trees, and wade in the brook?" She turned to Pierce, pinned by Asa. "Pierce, remember how you used to tug on my hair and tease me?"

Both men looked incredulous, but she continued, in a sweet, sad, caressing voice. "We used to be neighbors. We used to be friends. For memory's sake"—she hesitated—"for your father's sake, don't make this place into a battlefield." She gestured toward the crowd. "Not today."

Pierce seemed to choke. He said to Ben, "It's one thing to go after niggers who want to vote. It's another to go after a white woman. A planter's daughter."

Ben spat out his words. "You soft-hearted cowardly bastard."

Pierce sagged in Asa's grip. "I wouldn't shoot at Addie," he said. Ben glared at his brother.

"We know where the League meets," Pierce said. "We know when they gather to register. Not here, Ben."

"All right," Ben snarled. To Hart, he said, "Tell this nigger to let me go."

Hart glared at Ben, then nodded to Adam, who released Ben. He growled back, "You go quietly. And if you don't, I'll give the command, and we'll be glad to put a bullet into anyone who shoots at us."

The white troop, now outnumbered, made a show of not being cowed. They ambled back to their horses and rode away at a canter. The horses' hooves clopped on the dirt of the driveway, but the men were eerily silent.

—⁓—

AFTER THE INCIDENT at the frolic, Hart was convinced that women needed to learn how to shoot. He arranged for Bailey to teach Rachel and Frankie and told Adelaide that he would show her himself. When he came to the schoolhouse to fetch Adelaide, he carried a rifle, which was unusual for him. He was usually armed with a pistol.

Johnny looked with longing at Hart's rifle. "May I come along to watch?"

"If you're quiet and stand back," Hart said.

"I've known how to shoot since I was a little'un," Johnny boasted. "I could shoot a hole in your hat and you wouldn't know it hit you."

Hart shook his head. "Just stay out of the way."

He led Adelaide to a spot between the house and the fields where no one was likely to be hit by a stray bullet. He had set up a paper target like the Army used to train its men.

"What about the gun?" Adelaide asked. "Will I use yours?"

He grinned, unslung it, and handed it to her. The barrel gleamed in the sun. "This is yours now," he said. "A gift."

She blushed. "I can't take such a thing from you, Captain Hart."

"Yes, you can. It's a much more useful thing than any gewgaw. Please take it."

Johnny watched and grinned.

She picked up the gun, feeling its weight, not knowing what to do with it. She held it as though it were a broom. Hart said, "Let me show you," and stood behind her, using his hands to guide hers.

Johnny said, "When my daddy taught me to shoot he didn't wrap his arms around me."

Adelaide flushed bright red. "Don't you have chores at the school? Doesn't your mama need you?"

Johnny laughed. "Yes, ma'am," and he ran off, his pale cheeks pink with amusement.

Adelaide hefted the gun in her hands as Hart's arms encircled her. She thought of the damage a gun could do, and she felt dizzy. As Hart supported her, she said, "I don't think I can shoot a man."

Hart soothed her. "You aren't shooting a man, not today. You're shooting at a paper target. Now lift it," he said and settled his hands over hers. She was very much aware of his body pressed close to hers. The smell of his skin poured into her nose and flowed through her like the course of her own blood. He said, "Steady. Stand like a tree, rooted. Legs apart."

She tried to.

"Good. Now, steady, and look toward the target. Find the center. No, rest it on your shoulder. Not on your cheek! When it kicks, it will hurt you."

She moved the barrel.

"Good. That's good. Steady. Keep the barrel steady. Are you ready? Can you fire?"

She said, "Yes."

He took his hands away and stepped back. "Pull the trigger."

The report made her ears ring and the recoil bruised her shoulder even before she smelled the gunpowder. She felt faint. Hart walked toward the target to see where the bullet hit. He bent and smiled, then rested his hand on the paper to show her. "Look! A good shot!"

Weak in the knees, she nodded.

He said brightly, "Shall we try again?"

"Help me."

He returned to steady her. To embrace her. He let her go at the last minute. She was deafened. She was sore in the shoulder. It was another good shot. She was pleased because he was, but she was horrified to think that someday, she might shoot a man in the heart.

"Will you try again?"

"Steady me." She didn't need his embrace, and they both knew it. He stood even closer this time, his body radiating heat into hers.

"Are you ready?" he asked. He saw that she leaned against the barrel and reminded her, "Don't press your cheek to the gun. You'll get a bruise from the kick."

She changed her stance so that the gun rested on her shoulder. "I'm ready," she said, loath to let him release her.

"Aim," he reminded her, and she did, sighting on the middle of the paper target.

He let her go. "Now fire," he said.

She squeezed the trigger. The gun kicked against her shoulder and roared into her ear. *God help me,* she thought, closing her eyes.

Hart cried out with joy. "Look! Nearly a bull's-eye!"

On a living man, a bull's-eye was fatal. She let the gun fall from her shoulder and hang from her hand by its strap. Her arm trembled, and the trembling in her legs was even worse.

He saw her distress and ran to her. She felt the nausea heave through her and hoped that she wouldn't disgrace herself. She breathed deeply. *Steady,* she thought. *Steady yourself.*

"Let me bring you a drink of water," Hart said, and as he ran to find a bucket and a dipper, she sank to the ground, sick at her stomach.

I have the skill to kill a man, she thought, *and I am full of joy that Lewis Hart embraced me as I learned how to do it.*

— ⌒ —

HART CAME EVERY week on the pretext of giving Adelaide a shooting lesson, and Rachel knew where he set up the target for practice. She went looking for them one day, and when she was near enough, she saw how they stood so close together. She made a lot of noise getting closer, and by the time she was close enough to say, "Good afternoon, Captain Hart," they were far enough apart to look as though they were practicing marksmanship.

Adelaide's cheeks were pink. Rachel said, "I hope I don't intrude."

Also flushed, Hart said, "No, of course not."

Without acknowledging their embarrassment, Rachel went on. "Been worried, ever since the frolic. Been telling you so, Captain Hart." She looked pointedly at her sister's new rifle. "I know I'm not as good a riflewoman as Adelaide. But I'd feel better if I had a rifle I could carry with me."

Adelaide blushed as Rachel drew out her remarks to Captain Hart. "I don't dare buy a gun," she said. "Had enough trouble buying a mule. But no one would think anything of it, Captain Hart, if you bought yourself a rifle. You could say you needed it for hunting."

"Miss Mannheim, it isn't necessary to dance around it so. What do you call it, Adelaide? Acting Br'er Rabbit?"

Rachel wondered what other secrets Adelaide had shared with Captain Hart.

"I have reason to be in Atlanta soon, and no one would remark on it if I bought a rifle, or two, or a dozen boxes of bullets, Miss Mannheim," he said.

Adelaide was still flushed. Rachel smiled and said, "I'll pay for it, and I'd be obliged to you, Captain Hart."

— ✐ —

ADELAIDE KEPT THE rifle near the front door, like an umbrella or a walking stick. She saw it every time she left for the schoolhouse.

This morning, she picked it up and took it onto the porch. It was a beautiful thing. The wood of the stock felt silky under her hands, and the barrel gleamed brightly in the morning light. She lifted it, and even though she knew how to hold it properly and rest it on her shoulder, she felt reluctant. She raised it, set it on her shoulder, and tried to sight on something. She could not. The thought that this pretty thing could kill a man brought back the nausea, and she let the gun hang from its strap in her hand. Frankie found her sitting on the porch, the gun held loosely in her hand, her face as pale as a piece of paper.

—⌒—

WHEN HART ASKED her, "Are you practicing your shooting, Adelaide?" she replied, "I will if you help me."

The next time he visited, they walked together to the makeshift range at the side of the house. He had set up a paper target again. The afternoon air was hot and vibrant with the buzz of crickets. She had slung the gun over her shoulder but she made no move to unsling it so she could use it.

"You're bothered," he said.

"I don't want to kill anyone."

He said grimly, "The Turners have no fine feelings about shooting anyone around you. Believe me, they'll get around to conquering their unease about shooting you, too. You have to be able to defend yourself."

"I can bear it if you steady me," she said.

As before, he stood behind her, pressed close, his arms around her to guide her hands. A wave of passion washed through her, and she twisted around, wanting him to hold her while they were face to face.

"Be careful!" he yelled. "It's cocked! The safety's off!" Obviously upset, he added, "What are you doing?"

She was close enough that her lips could brush his cheek. At the thought, she blushed bright red, and he caught the reason for her embarrassment. He blushed, too. In a gentler tone, he said, "You could shoot us both and we'd bleed to death together. I don't think that's what you're after."

She didn't move, but she whispered, "No, it isn't." She raised her eyes to his, the pre-war belle reawakening, and asked, "Should I put the safety on?"

"No," he said. "Turn around and steady yourself."

— ✎ —

AT THE SIGHT of Mr. Pereira's handwriting, Rachel tore open the envelope.

Dear Miss Mannheim,

My mother will be visiting me in Atlanta next week, and I would be honored if you would join us for dinner. Please write to me to let me know if you are agreeable.

With regard,
Daniel Pereira

P.S. Whether next year is in Jerusalem or in Atlanta, I hope to hear you read from the Passover book.

Rachel felt a shiver at the thought of meeting Pereira's mother, whose father had been the richest planter in South Carolina.

—⧉—

RACHEL THOUGHT SHE had become accustomed to the smell of Atlanta, but today, when the weather was unseasonably warm, the smell of the street, manure and mud and machine oil mixed together, was worse than usual. As she strode down Whitehall Street, watching for the turn on Houston, her eyes watered anew. In unpaved Sherman Town, as always, the smell was ranker. She stopped before Mrs. Simpson's boarding house, and rued that the air was too foul for her to take a deep, fortifying breath.

Mrs. Simpson led Rachel into the parlor, where Pereira sat in the gentleman's chair. The settee was occupied by a woman who didn't rise. Despite her age, she was still striking. Her father's high cheekbones had served her well. Her dark blue satin dress showed off lovely shoulders that were a shade darker than Pereira's skin. She regarded Rachel with hazel eyes that were disconcertingly familiar. "So you're Miss Mannheim."

Pereira introduced the older woman. "This is my mother, Mrs. Maria Pereira."

"Pleased to make your acquaintance, ma'am," Rachel said, holding out her hand. Maria Pereira briefly clasped it with fingers even softer than her son's. Rachel looked down at her own hands, dark like Mrs. Simpson's.

"Please sit, Miss Mannheim," Pereira said, and Rachel perched on the remaining wing chair, where a loose spring dug into her backside.

There was a silence, as though it were proper etiquette to allow Maria to break it. She asked Rachel, "Who are your people?"

Rachel thought of the Bennetts and of the Pereiras, too. She told the truth about herself. "My daddy is Mordecai Mannheim, who lives in Atlanta now, but he owns a place in Cass County, where I live. My mama was his slave."

Maria Pereira frowned. "So you grew up in slavery."

As though it had been her fault. "Yes, ma'am, I did."

"But you're educated."

Had Pereira been boasting about her? "My master's daughter taught me to read and write when we were girls together."

"My son tells me that you manage the business affairs on your plantation."

So he had been boasting. "It started during the war, when I was the only one on the place who knew how to figure. I was capable, and now my former mistress pays me to do it."

Maria frowned again. "So you say you bought property up in Cass County. How did you manage to do that?"

Rachel smiled and replied sweetly, just as Adelaide would. "Came into some money after the war, ma'am." Then she delivered the venom. "It doesn't hurt when your daddy is the richest man in the county."

Maria Pereira coughed, a dry, dainty sound.

The kitchen door banged open, and Mrs. Simpson came into the parlor. Her face shone with sweat—it was a hot day to be cooking—and now a grease spot sullied her apron. She said, "Dinner all ready. We can set down to eat it."

Rachel saw that the table was set with the same scorched and mended cloth as on her last visit. When Maria sat, her skirt caught at the tablecloth's bad spot, and the cloth tore like a bandage ripping from a wound. Startled, Maria said, "What was that?"

"My tablecloth!" Mrs. Simpson said. "Tore in two!"

Maria shook her head. She handed the torn cloth to Mrs. Simpson. "You can mend it," she said.

Mrs. Simpson had put out everything at once, as Rachel was used to. But Maria said to Mrs. Simpson, "You don't serve it a course at a time?"

Mr. Pereira said gently, "We're very informal here, Mama. Like a family."

"A poor family," said Maria.

Injured, Mrs. Simpson said, "I do my best."

"Indeed you do, Mrs. Simpson," Pereira soothed. "What do we have for dinner?"

Mrs. Simpson said, "We have fish cakes with sauce, like she said she missed from Charleston. A nice roasted chicken. Some taters and carrots in butter, and a dish of greens, too."

"Is there claret?" Maria Pereira asked.

Mrs. Simpson said indignantly, "I am a good Christian woman and I don't keep any kind of spirits in my house."

Pereira reached for the nearest dish. "Mother, let me serve you."

Maria allowed her son to fill her plate. She poked at the greens. Mrs. Simpson said, "Perfectly good collard and mustard greens. Cooked with onion and a little bacon. You don't want any?"

Maria said, "I eat them on New Year's, like everyone does, for good fortune. But not every day, like slaves used to."

"Mother, please," said an embarrassed Pereira.

Maria took a tentative bite of the fish cake. Surprised, she said, "It's delicious." She asked Mrs. Simpson, "Did you cook all of this yourself?"

"Of course I did, ma'am," Mrs. Simpson said, with no pretense of politeness.

Maria put down her fork. "I suppose you learned how to cook when you were a slave," she said.

Mrs. Simpson's dark face went even darker with fury. "I got free before the war," she snapped.

After dessert—a peach pie that Maria poked with her fork and didn't eat—Mrs. Pereira said to her son, "We should retire to the parlor."

To leave the servants to clear the table, Rachel thought. Rachel rose and asked Mrs. Simpson, "Do you need any help to clean up?"

Mrs. Simpson watched as Maria folded her napkin, rose, and left the room. She shook her head. "I'd welcome it," she said to Rachel.

In the kitchen, where the banked stove still gave off an unpleasant heat, Mrs. Simpson leaned against the counter and pitched her voice low, the old habit of slavery, to speak ill of Missus so she wouldn't overhear. "Mr. Pereira a pleasant man and he always been cordial to me. But his mother! She complain about the street, she complain about the house, she complain about her room. And yesterday, she decide to put on a different dress for dinner than the one she wear when she get here."

"Ladies do that," Rachel said.

Mrs. Simpson snorted. "She call me upstairs and she don't ask. She command me to do up her buttons in back that she can't reach by herself. Told her I might run a boarding house, but I weren't a servant. Left her standing there with her dress undone. We don't get along after that."

Rachel smothered a laugh. "When do she go home to Charleston?"

"Not soon enough." She regarded Rachel with curiosity. "Mr. Pereira talk about you a lot. Look forward to seeing you, even more than last time. He think about more than just business, it sound like."

In the hot kitchen, Rachel felt her face grow hotter. "I get the dishes left on the table," she said.

In the dining room, as she reached for a serving dish, she heard the voice of Maria Pereira, who didn't seem to care who might overhear her.

"Why don't you come back to Charleston! Your old friends are doing well in the world, now that Reconstruction allows them into the schools and the government."

"I have business here." Pereira's voice was emphatic.

"As long as you live like the most wretched of the people you help! In Charleston, you could live like a gentleman."

"I'm a black man. No one in Atlanta would consider me a gentleman."

Sharply, Maria said, "You're a free man of color, and a gentleman of Charleston. Here, people treat you like—"

"Don't say it."

"A slave. What did you think I was going to say?"

Rachel thought of Pereira's fury at being insulted. "Do you think that white people make the distinction? We're all black to them."

"You know better. And so do I." Rachel heard her sigh. "You're making this hard for me," she said. "She's intelligent and ambitious. But she isn't the least bit suited to you."

"Why not?" Pereira replied, in an acid tone.

Maria's voice became caressing. "You're destined for great things," she said. "You can't have this woman by your side." He left a silence, and she filled it. "I let your brother choose his own bride. He found a free woman of color with hair so straight she has to curl it. And who have you found?"

A chair scraped loudly on the floor. Pereira snarled, "If you say it, I'll put you on the train back to Charleston tonight. And it will be a long time before I speak to you again."

There was a pause, and a surprised note in Maria's voice. "Danny, why are you so angry with me?" She laughed. "Don't tell me that you're in love with her!"

His silence gave all of them the answer.

Rachel fled into the kitchen. Mrs. Simpson spoke to her, but she was too stunned to hear. Through her daze, she was imagining Pereira as a boy called Danny.

13 | I Shall Not Be Moved

O N THE EVE of the election, the sound of gunfire seeped into Adelaide's sleep, and for a moment she wasn't sure whether she was awake or dreaming. She sat up, her heart pounding, and fumbled for her dressing gown and her shoes. She reached for the rifle that stood in the corner by the door, and then she ran down the stairs.

She had anticipated gunfire every day since black men began to register to vote, and as the black registrar for the district that included Cass County, Charlie was a particular target.

She tried not to think of her school or herself as a target for the men who rode at night and shot at the former slaves, whose only crime was to read, write, work, and vote.

But the gunfire had come from Charlie's place.

She was too wrought up to consider her own danger. Outside, she listened for the sound of further gunshots, cries, footfalls, or hoofbeats. She heard nothing but the sound of owls, the fiercest hunters of the night. Through the feathery branches of the pines, she saw bats, dark blots against the moonlit sky.

She inched her way through the pine grove that separated the Kaltenbach place from Charlie's fields. Her footfalls disturbed the mice that fed at night, and the skittering noise shivered along her nerves. She wouldn't let herself feel it, but she was afraid.

The sound of footsteps alerted her, and she cocked her rifle. She tensed, trying to see in the gloom.

Rachel whispered through the pines. "Adelaide, it's all right. It's me."

She could see the outline of her sister, who seemed to have a shawl pulled over her nightclothes. Like Adelaide, Rachel carried a rifle.

Adelaide whispered back, "Did you see anyone?"

"No."

"Why are you here?" she asked. "It's too dangerous!"

"Why are you?" Rachel answered back.

The air was too cool for a light dressing gown, and it was no defense against the scratch of pine needles. As the rush of fear wore off, Adelaide felt cold within as well as without. She thought, *If I've volunteered myself for a shootout, I have no stomach for it.*

When they emerged through the pines onto Charlie's place, they hesitated. "Are you ready?" Rachel asked.

"I'll never be."

They crept along the path through the cotton field to Charlie's house. She whispered to Rachel, "Safety off? Ready to shoot?"

Rachel whispered back, "Don't boast."

Adelaide stifled the impulse to laugh. It was fear, she knew.

Ahead, a lantern glowed in the darkness. As they came closer, Adelaide saw the men in a tight cluster, Charlie with Zeke and Asa, who insisted on guarding Charlie as the election neared and the threats worsened.

At the sight of the two women, Charlie scolded, "Miss Adelaide! Miss Rachel! You shouldn't be here!"

"As though we could stay away," Rachel said. "Are you all right?"

"They didn't come to hurt us," Charlie said. "Just to try to frighten us."

"Did you see them?" Adelaide asked.

"Saw some men on horseback, covered up with white sheets. Came up shooting into the air. Yelling. Asked us if we was afraid of ghosts." He snorted, unable to summon a laugh. "As though we fool enough to think a man in a white sheet is a ghost. I'd like to shoot at a ghost sometime, see if he bleed like a man."

"Could you tell who they were?" she asked.

"White sheet don't disguise a man's voice. I know the Turners when I hear them. Young Ben, for sure, and Pierce, since Pierce follow him like a whipped dog. And someone else, too. Tall man on a white horse. Didn't say a word."

"Pale horse," murmured Rachel.

"Don't say so," Charlie reproved her.

"What?" Adelaide asked.

Rachel said, "From the Bible. Death on a pale horse."

Adelaide felt worse than chilled. She felt sick to her stomach. "Are we all right for tomorrow?"

Charlie had done more than register the black men of the county. He had organized them for the Union League to vote for the Republican Party, risking the peril of men like the Turner brothers and the pale rider. Charlie knew that any man who traveled to the makeshift courthouse in Cartersville to vote would be in danger. "They all know, ma'am. They come down here from Resaca. We meet them and go on south to Cartersville together, ready to defend ourselves."

Adelaide pitched her voice low, not sure if she were talking to Charlie or God. "I hope it won't come to that."

"So do I, ma'am," said Charlie, his face showing the strain. "Hope and pray so."

—⁓—

ELECTION DAY DAWNED sunny, but the air was damp and cold. The smell of pine resin sharpened the air, and the birds, so noisy in the summer, now cheeped softly. Adelaide had buttoned a woolen coat over her dress. Rachel, who came with her, had put on her warmest shawl. Eliza stayed inside, peeking through the window, but Matt lingered on the porch, watching the crowd.

Both Rachel and Adelaide had argued with Hart and Charlie about joining the march to Cartersville. Hart had said no.

Rachel appealed to Charlie. "Becky tell me you allow her to go. And take the children with her."

"Didn't say I liked it."

Adelaide asked, "Are we any safer here?"

Now, on election day, Charlie's organizers and bodyguards—Zeke, Asa, and Davey, along with Sergeant Bailey—gathered in the front yard of the Kaltenbach house. Every man was armed. Bailey carried his Army-issue rifle, Charlie and Asa brought their new guns, and Zeke and Davey had the old muskets they used for hunting. They wore their Sunday best, the shirts lovingly ironed by their wives, the suits brushed, the hats proudly settled on their heads.

Bailey wore his Union coat, newly polished buttons gleaming in the rising sun. Hart, who represented the Union no matter how he dressed, had put on his wool frock coat, and beneath it, Adelaide knew, he had holstered his pistol.

Becky had been joined by Jenny, Harriet, and Salley, their children at their skirts and their infants in their arms.

"Everyone ready?" Charlie asked. Even today, Charlie was driving, a habit that had stood him in good stead as an organizer. "We wait for the people from Resaca, and we go together."

"Sergeant Bailey and I will escort you," Hart said.

Charlie hesitated. Finally, he said, "Surely you're needed in Cartersville today."

"This is the Bureau's task today," Hart said. "Making sure that black men vote."

Now, as they waited for the troop from Resaca, Becky put her hand on her husband's shoulder as Charlie made a sorrowful sound in his throat. "Still don't like it that you come along," he said.

Becky reached for her children's hands—Ben on her right, and Josey, just a little older, on her left. Stubbornly, she said, "We want to be there. See the glory of it! Black men free to vote."

Charlie said, "Hate that you put yourself in danger."

"No less than you."

Charlie embraced his wife and drew their children into his arms. "We do our best to protect you," he said.

Becky wiped her face. Bravely, she said to Ben, "In Cartersville we watch Daddy vote."

Ben squeezed her hand. "When I grow up I'll vote." His sister Josey, two years older, serious and thoughtful, said, "So will I."

From the road came the sound of a crowd—talk and laughter and snatches of song. It poured into the driveway, and Adelaide was astonished at how many people she saw. They filled the driveway and extended as far back as the road. The crowd was in the hundreds, women and children with the men, who were all armed. Not as disciplined as a troop, but pretty orderly for such a throng, even with so many little ones.

"Good God, man!" Hart exclaimed. "How many voters did you turn out?"

Charlie surveyed the crowd. "All of them!" he said, smiling. He called to them, "Where are we bound?"

They called back, "Going to Cartersville!"

"To do what?"

"To vote!"

Charlie tucked Adelaide and Rachel into the crowd, just behind himself and Hart, where they took the lead. Charlie called out, "Are we ready?"

The crowd shouted, "We ready!"

As the impromptu regiment turned around and made its way back to the road, Adelaide felt a chill independent of the weather. Beside her, Rachel held herself like a soldier. Adelaide wished she could take her sister's hand, as she had last night, but today she was ashamed to admit to fear.

Around them, people laughed and joked. It was like the frolics before the war, an island of pleasure in a life of work and worry about the crop. Before the war, Adelaide had wondered how slaves could sing with joy. After five years of war and two years of its aftermath, she heard the resistance that had always hidden beneath what sounded like happiness.

The sun rose and turned the sky to a thin, pale blue, kissed by clouds as soft as sprays of baby's breath. The air had warmed tenderly after the night's cold. The cotton fields on either side of the road were half-stripped, the highest and biggest bolls gone, the pickers temporarily idle, waiting for the smaller bolls to ripen.

The daytime hunters soared, watching for prey too foolish to hide. Rachel touched her sleeve. "Adelaide, look."

She was used to the sight of red-tailed hawks, but this bird's wingspan was easily three times theirs, and as it dipped to search the ground, its golden cap glittered. The eagle followed the crowd, rising and falling in a temporary escort, until it cried aloud, beat its great wings, and soared away.

As they marched southward to Cartersville, more people joined them, adding to the orderly throng. When Adelaide turned to look, the crowd stretched far behind her. There were hundreds of people, laughing and joking and singing. She heard snatches of "O Happy Day" and the strains of "John Brown's Body." *Charlie's doing,* she thought. *A multitude and a regiment!*

They were a few miles from Cartersville when they heard the sound of men on horseback. From afar it was impossible to tell how many. Their phalanx was too large to stop. Though Adelaide clutched Rachel's hand, they kept moving.

The sound of hooves came closer.

A man on a pale horse led them.

It was a beautiful horse, its coat shining white in the sunlight, its mane and tail white as well. The man sat very tall and straight upon it. He wore a white hat over his hair, which gleamed as it flowed over his shoulders, as bright in the sun as the eagle's feathers. Either he had preserved his Confederate uniform or he had ordered another from a postwar tailor. His coat was elegant against his slender frame, the braid golden on his sleeves.

He looked like General Lee before the war had aged and saddened him, down to the fair mustache and the groomed goatee. He differed from Lee in one thing. Over his left eye he wore a black patch. The war had left him half blind.

When he halted, the band behind him did, too, blocking the road ahead. They were a dozen, perhaps a few more. Behind the one-eyed man, Adelaide could see Ben Junior and, next to him, Pierce. The horses' coats steamed in the chill.

The riders, sheetless in broad daylight, stared at the sea of black people, and the voters' regiment stared back at the men who had come to interfere with their voting.

Captain Hart asked the one-eyed man, "Who are you?"

"A concerned citizen," he said calmly.

"Your name, sir," Hart demanded.

"It's no concern of yours."

"Whoever you are, let us pass."

The one-eyed man made no effort to move. Behind him, Ben Junior jerked on his horse's reins. The horse tossed its head and neighed in protest.

The one-eyed man asked, "Who are these people?"

"Citizens," Hart said acidly. "Free men. Every one of them loyal to the Union."

Ben Junior put his hand on his rifle. Hart and Sergeant Bailey did the same. The one-eyed man didn't move and didn't speak.

Charlie moved forward to stand between Hart and Bailey. Ben Junior said, "Didn't we frighten you last night?"

Rachel slipped forward to stand beside Charlie. Before he could send her back, Adelaide moved forward to join the front line. She stood beside her sister, and the two women linked arms. Adelaide's heart pounded. *Let them try it,* she thought. *Let them shoot us.*

Charlie took Rachel's arm, and Hart took Adelaide's, a human link at the head of the voters' regiment.

"Are you going to let these niggers vote?" Ben asked her.

The one-eyed man let his gaze sweep up and down the front line, a gaze as cruel as a raptor's. His eyes lingered on Charlie. He didn't speak. Ben Turner unslung his rifle, and throughout the crowd, all the way to the back, a murmur went up. As it spread, it grew louder.

The one-eyed man said, "Turn around. Go home."

The murmur increased. "Won't let no one turn us around." "Going to vote today." "Vote like free men."

Charlie turned his head and said, "Hush."

The hush rippled through the crowd, all the way through the hundreds gathered in the road.

In that hush, Charlie raised his rifle to his shoulder, and pulled back the bolt to cock the gun. Behind him, as if on command, the click of guns being cocked reverberated through the air. Hundreds of rifles, ready to fire.

Adelaide thought, *They'll fire on us. It will be a melee and a bloodbath.* She closed her eyes, too much the skeptic to be able to pray, and felt Hart tighten his arm around hers. *At least we'll die together,* she thought.

In the quiet, Charlie began to sing as though he were in church, his voice surprisingly sweet. "I shall not be moved," he sang.

Nothing disturbed the quiet: not a shout, not a shot.

Adelaide opened her eyes. "What is it? That song?"

Rachel was smiling. Wasn't she afraid? "Old song from slavery days."

Charlie sang, "Like a tree that's standing by the water, I shall not be moved."

The words, like the murmur and the hush before it, flowed through the crowd. The song rose and swelled: "I shall not be moved…"

Adelaide caught the melody, and she sang, too. As did Hart.

Hundreds of them, the women and children along with the men, added their voices to a song that was powerful enough to travel to Cartersville. Or to Heaven. She and Rachel, Charlie and Hart, stood linked together as the voters' regiment sang behind them: "I shall not, I shall not be moved… Like a tree standing by the water, I shall not be moved…"

Ben cried out, "God damn!" His voice was puny against a song in the throats of hundreds. He pulled on his horse's reins again. "Won't you do a damned thing?"

The one-eyed man asked, "How many men in that crowd?"

"Just niggers!" Ben protested.

"Hundreds," the man countered. "All armed."

The men pulled on their horses' reins and the horses shifted uneasily, not sure what the riders wanted them to do.

The one-eyed man put up his hand and his men fell silent. Charlie stopped singing, and the hush again moved through the crowd.

The one-eyed man let his gaze linger on each of them in turn: Charlie, Rachel, Adelaide, and Hart. The ice in the good eye made Adelaide feel colder than a night in the depths of winter. "That was a very pretty piece of theater," the man said. He turned to his men. "We're outgunned. Today isn't our day." And he turned back to look at the crowd that would not be moved. His good eye, blue and cold, rested on Adelaide. "Our day will come. Believe me, we'll be back, and our day will come."

He spurred his horse to gallop away, and the rest of his band followed him, cursing. "Damn! God damn!"

As their voices faded, voices in the crowd rose. "Singing!" someone said, laughing. "We whupped 'em by singing!"

Rachel gripped Adelaide's hand tightly. She bent close to murmur, "Sing a new song to the Lord. And carry a repeating rifle."

PART 3

—↜—

REDEMPTION, 1868

14 | Glass Windows

Rachel stooped over her cotton plants. Sweat ran down her neck as she reached to pluck the bolls from the branches. When she heard the footsteps, she pulled herself upright to see Charlie.

"Come to see how your harvest coming along," he said. He looked drawn and tired, as though he'd never rested from the effort of the campaign.

She'd been picking cotton for weeks now. Her hands were badly scratched, her shoulder ached, and at night, her spine tormented her. But as Charlie had said, it was different when you worked for yourself. "Already ginned a bale," she said.

He surveyed the field with a practiced eye. "Should have another on the stem. Just like I told you."

She laid the cotton sack on the ground. "Walk it with me," she said. "Help me figure what I can do once I hire a tenant."

Even though he knew the way—he had worked these fields for years—he let her lead him. When they reached an unplanted field, he bent down to feel the earth between his fingers. "This field always in cotton. The one beyond, that in cotton, too. Fine land. Bale and a half an acre." He stood. "How many tenants do you want?"

"As many as I can get."

He gazed over the field. "A man and his family, most likely. Ten acres in cotton, the rest in corn, like I planted." He smiled a little. "If he don't have politics to distract him."

"Oh, I make sure he vote, Charlie."

"You'll need someplace for them to live."

She gestured toward the spot she had picked out. "Build a house, right over there. A good house, like mine. Four rooms. Good iron woodstove. Glass in the windows."

He shook his head. "Glass? Not until you know they stay."

"Charlie, what's the matter? Ain't like you to be discouraging."

"I worry all the time, since the election," he said. "Worry about doing the right thing in Atlanta."

She reached for his hand. "You do fine in Atlanta."

"Worry about how everyone get on here while I'm gone."

"We manage."

A shadow passed over his face as he finally came to the point. "Worry about the Turner brothers. They ain't finished with us, now that the election over."

"Walk back with me," Rachel said. "I show you where I intend to build the house. Room for a kitchen garden, and a barn, too."

"Rachel, are you listening to me?"

She made her point, too. "I traveled into Floyd County with you. I marched to the voting place with you on election day. I stood with you to watch you vote. I didn't forget, Charlie. But now I think about my place, and I let myself feel the pleasure of it. Don't spoil it for me."

—⌇—

NOT LONG AFTER, Charlie knocked on her door. Behind him were a man and a woman, flanked by their three children. Rachel cried out, "Jim! Dell! What are you doing here?"

Jim said, "Come to ask Mr. Mannheim for help."

Dell's round face, so cheerful in Floyd County, was ashen and drawn.

"What happen?" Rachel asked.

"Got thrown off the place in Floyd County," Jim said.

"Thrown off?"

"Marse said we was agitating his people with all our talk about voting. Turned us out, never mind that we had a contract."

Dell shivered. "It were worse on the Hawkins place," she said. She stared behind Rachel's head at nothing in particular. "Strangers, men with white sheets over their heads, come at night to shoot at anyone who voted. Those folks run off."

"We left without a thing," Jim said. "Not a dollar, just what we stand up in." He added bitterly, "A whole year's work, and nothing to show for it."

Charlie said to Rachel, "I told them you might help."

"Do you need work?" she asked.

Dell said bleakly, "Who hire us?"

Rachel felt so excited that her skin tingled. "I will!" she sang out. "I have a place! I need folks to work it."

"You?" Jim asked. "A black woman with a place?"

"A hundred acres. Room for cotton and corn."

They stared at her with confused expressions. "Is it planted?" Jim asked.

"It will be, if someone work for me."

Jim and Dell stared at each other.

Rachel grinned. "It's close by. Would you like to see it?"

— ✒ —

ADELAIDE FOUND JIM and Dell and their children room on her place in one of the former slave cabins. Rachel assured them that it was only temporary. "Until I build a house for you," she said, delighted by the thought. The two of them were eager to get to work, but Rachel told them, "First we write up a contract. And then we take it to the Bureau, so Captain Hart can read it and let you know that it's fair."

Jim said softly, "We trust you, Miss Rachel."

"That's kindly of you. But we do this proper. If you ever work for someone else, you assure that everything is right, and that you get your due."

She wrote the contract and brought them into the study to explain it. Too awed to sit, Dell gazed at the wall of bookshelves behind Rachel's desk. "Can you read them books?" she asked.

Rachel smiled. "Yes." She read the contract aloud, which she had written to promise anyone who worked for her a dollar a day. "For you, too," she told Dell.

Dell demurred. "I can't be in the field like he can."

"What you do improve the place, too," Rachel said. "Shouldn't you be paid for it?"

Both Dell and Jim stared at her in astonishment.

"Jim, we go to Cartersville to buy you a mule."

"Thought you had a mule already," he said.

"I do. I work alongside you. You need your own mule," Rachel insisted.

Jim said, "It ain't right—"

"Don't say it ain't right for someone who own land to work it. I plow and plant and chop, just like you." She added, "And no fuss about it!"

Jim stared at the bright color of the Turkish carpet beneath his feet.

"One more thing," Rachel said, pretending to sound stern. "I don't want them children of yours in the field with you." Dell opened her mouth to protest. Rachel said, "I want them to go to school."

Dell wiped away tears with her sleeve. "Do you mean that?"

"Never meant anything more in my life."

— ✍ —

AFTER JIM AND Dell left, Adelaide put her head into the study. "So how do you like being a cotton planter?" she teased.

Rachel laughed. "Me, a planter!"

"In the best possible way. You're benevolent. As you learned from Henry."

"Learned about fairness, too. From the Bureau."

"There's a letter for you," Adelaide said, and handed it to her. "Mr. Pereira."

He hadn't written for months, and Rachel had a momentary stab of excitement, wondering what he had to say to her. But it was brief, written in a hasty scrawl unlike his usual copperplate, from a place called Thomaston in Upson County. She read it as Adelaide watched.

My dear Miss Mannheim,

The Bureau has been running me ragged in every county in western Georgia. I haven't been home to Atlanta for months. I see some very bad conditions in these small places, especially in the countryside. I hope that you are well.

Your friend,
Daniel Pereira, Esq.

"What does he say?" Adelaide asked.

She shook her head. "Just business. Bureau business."

"You haven't said a word about him since you came back from Atlanta," Adelaide said.

"Nothing to tell. He courteous to me, but his mama weren't." She took a deep breath. "No, he write to tell me he run all over Georgia for the Bureau. No time for anything else."

"When a man invites a woman to meet his mama, he's thinking of something," Adelaide said. "I thought he might ask for you."

"Hah!" Rachel said. "Where is Captain Hart? Haven't seen much of him lately either."

"Like your Mr. Pereira. He's busy with the Bureau."

"No time for shooting lessons?"

Adelaide blushed. "Now that's none of your business!"

It was a pleasure to tease Adelaide back, as sisters did. "More than shooting involved, if I guess right."

To her surprise, Adelaide turned away and covered her face with her hands.

"Adelaide?" Rachel touched her sister on the shoulder. "What's the matter?"

"Don't even speak of it," she whispered.

&⁊

SINCE CHARLIE'S ELECTION as a delegate, Adelaide had seen little of Captain Hart. He was consumed with the business of the Bureau. He wrote to her from Cartersville as though he were traveling the countryside like Mr. Pereira. "I am overwhelmed with the unfairness of contracts and with the injustices of preventing free men from voting," he wrote. "I think of you often and I miss our conversations over Sabbath dinner."

She thought of him more often than that, and she missed more than his conversation. She missed the shooting lessons, which gave him a reason to encircle her in his arms. She wanted to smooth the unruly lock of hair that fell over his forehead, a wifely gesture, and she allowed herself to whisper his name, a marital intimacy as tender as a caress.

He was so burdened this year that he declined her invitation to the Seder for Freedom. But he surprised her, finding her at the schoolhouse, telling her that he had just come from a confab with Charlie about his campaign for the Assembly.

He looked even more tired than usual, dark circles under his eyes, the unruly lock flopping over his forehead. He looked as though no one cared whether he had a clean shirt, or worried that he ate a decent meal. His frightened landlady, a former slave, was no substitute for a wife.

She let him speak his political piece, only half listening. "May we talk in private?" she asked, gesturing toward the pine grove where he had given her the good news about the Bureau's assistance for the school.

He looked askance at her, but in the shelter of the pine trees, he asked, "What is it, Adelaide?"

At the concern in his expression she began to stammer. "I shouldn't speak of it," she said, "but it torments me so. I can't bear to keep it to myself any longer."

"Can I help?"

"My marriage—" she stammered. "My marriage is a sham, but I am still married—"

"Your husband? Has he bothered you? Or hurt you?"

She shook her head. "I am so ashamed," she said, and she buried her face in her hands to hide the tears.

He put a hand on her shoulder as he'd touch Matt, in kindly reassurance. "You must tell me," he said.

She raised her head, and whispered, "Oh, Lewis, must I?"

He didn't move his hand. "Yes."

"I love you."

He didn't look surprised. "You know that it can never be," he said softly.

She met his eyes. "I know—but I wish that it could."

"Oh, Adelaide," he said, and she ignored the remonstrance in his voice to rejoice in the sweetness of her name on his lips.

She reached to touch his cheek. "Do you love me?"

He gently pulled away so they were at arms' length. He took her hands in his, a gesture that went back to their earliest meetings, and said, "I would give my life for you. But I can't dishonor you like this." He let go her hands. "I won't."

He looked at her with such longing that she cried out, "Lewis!" But he turned away, and he was gone.

⌐

ADELAIDE'S TENANTS OFFERED to help build the house for Jim and Dell. Zeke asked Rachel to write to his son Luke, the Atlanta builder, for help. She bought the lumber in Cartersville, but she sent Luke money to buy the best glass windows from his employer Peck's Mill and Lumberyard in Atlanta, and he wrote back to promise that he would cart them to Cass County swaddled like they were newborn babies.

The little house went up in a matter of days. Dell and the children watched as the frame took shape and the roof went on. When Luke unwrapped the windows, the panes of glass glittered in the wintry sun.

"Glass windows?" Dell asked. "For our house?"

Full of pride, Rachel said, "Only the best on my place, for anyone who work for me. Glass windows!"

Once the new tenants were installed in the new house, surrounded by Adelaide's generosity in the form of beds and linens, pots and pans, plates and cups, the whiskey jug came out and the Benjamin brothers began to play. That Saturday night, the new house on Rachel's place was the scene of the celebration, and Rachel took a cup of whiskey to toast Jim and Dell, the place, and the crop they would make together.

Her head was a little sore the next day, but she wasn't deterred from visiting to see how her tenants got on. "Don't come here to oversee," she said. "Just want to make sure you have everything you need."

Dell stood on the brand-new steps and took in the plot where she would plant her garden. "Never thought I'd have anything like this," she said.

Rachel surveyed the whole place, and her heart filled with joy. Her fields. Her mule. Her tenants. Her crop. Her place. Her profit and her increase.

— ᔍ —

THEY BEGAN TO plant cotton on a sunny day in early April. Rachel and Mollie drilled the row and Dell followed behind, dropping in the seeds. Dell had been reluctant to help. She was eager to plant her own garden. Jim persuaded her, saying, "We do whatever we can to help Miss Rachel. Make a good crop."

Jim followed behind his wife with his mule hitched to a harrow, covering the seeds that Dell planted.

Rachel was full of joy to be in the field behind Mollie, planting the seeds that would sprout and grow and flower into bolls.

As she and her tenants worked, three men rode up on horseback. It was the Turners, rifles slung over their shoulders, and with them, the one-eyed man, dressed again in white, the pale rider. They halted and watched as they had watched Charlie, acting like the overseers of slavery days.

She stopped plowing, and behind her, so did Jim and Dell.

Ben said loudly, "Look at that jumped-up nigger bitch. Thinks she can own a place."

Rachel straightened up. Charlie had warned her, but she was too proud to care. "I do own a place," she said.

"It ain't right, Ben," Pierce said. "A nigger with a hundred acres and tenants, and white men who go without."

Rachel said, "Nothing stop you from working your daddy's place."

"Us? Behind a plow?" Ben sneered. He rested his hand on the rifle barrel. "Maybe you'd like to work for us."

She knew she was was reckless to feel it, but she felt like anyone's equal. "Why would I?" she asked.

The one-eyed man gazed at the scene like a benevolent planter. When he spoke, his voice was mild. "We wouldn't want anything to happen to the place," he said. "Or to you."

Rachel turned her back on him. "I got work to do." She gripped the handles of the plow and called out, "Gee, Mollie!"

After the men left, Jim left the plow. He walked over to Rachel, and Dell followed. "Is you crazy?" he asked.

"No," she said.

"Slighting them men." He rebuked her.

Rachel waved her hand as though she were shooing away a mosquito. "I know them. Local men. Just ruffians."

"They give us trouble?" Dell asked, her voice shrill. It meant, "Have they?" and "Will they?" at once.

"No," Rachel said, thinking of election day. "It all talk."

Dell trembled. "Don't want trouble."

Jim put his hand around her shoulders. "It's all right, Dell. Miss Rachel wouldn't mislead us."

Now it was more than the Turners, Ben and Pierce, damn them both. It was that one-eyed man, gracious as Massa, until the moment he decided to sell you or kill you. Rachel thought of the lie that Charlie had told Hart, all those months ago, and the new lie she had just repeated to her tenants.

—⁊—

In Atlanta, Charlie had seen a wider world than a former slave was usually afforded. It had deepened his gravity and his worry. When he returned from the convention, he carried it with him, as though he were still dressed in his best suit.

He visited Rachel's place and checked the fields with a farmer's eye. "Should have room for a good crop. Jim and Dell working out?"

"Couldn't ask for better tenants," Rachel said, full of pride.

"Solid house. Nice garden."

"They all have comfort from it."

"I see you got them glass windows you boasted about."

"I did," she said, bristling a little. It still gave her pleasure to see the sun glint on the glass. She was ready to argue with him if he said that a black tenant didn't deserve it.

Afterwards, Charlie accepted her invitation to settle before her hearth. He even said yes to a glass of buttermilk, but he left it untouched at his elbow. His mind was still in Atlanta.

"I hear you plan to run for the Assembly," she said.

"I do."

Needled, she said, "It ain't like last time, where there's room for more than one. Colonel Turner's running as a Democrat."

"I know."

She wouldn't let him leave her behind. "Do you need me to travel the county with you? Talk to the women and help them stand behind the men?"

Charlie looked at her with a depth of worry to match his new gravity. "You lay low," he said.

"We need to vote, more than ever," she said.

"I hear about your trouble with the Turners."

"Just empty words."

"Armed men full of insult for a black woman with a place and a crop."

"They insulted us, all right. But they didn't shoot this time."

She insisted, "We know them, and we know how to handle the trouble they cause."

"Freddy find out about that one-eyed man," Charlie said. "He some kind of distant kin to the Turner family. A cousin. Colonel Benjamin Turner Loveless." Charlie rested his fists on his knees.

"Served under General Forrest. Freddy tell me what Forrest do, and why the black Union men hate him."

"Ain't secesh bad enough?"

"He were worse. Massacred black Union men at Fort Pillow." Charlie shook his head. "Took no prisoners. Shot men who surrendered. Shot their officers, too. It weren't war. It were murder." He leaned forward, a storyteller with the worst to tell. "Forrest run the Ku Klux Klan now. He call on this man Loveless to organize the Klan in Georgia." He added, "Rachel, it all of a piece. What the Klan do all over Georgia, and what the Turners do here, since they so besotted with the Klan."

She was silent.

"I know how much you want to make a success of your place,'" Charlie said. "But in Atlanta I hear what happen all over Georgia, and it chill me. You a black woman, and you own a hundred acres, and you aim to profit by your labor. And everyone in the county know how much you pride yourself on it. Believe me, Rachel, the Klan notice you."

"I get Jim a rifle. He already alarmed. Dell scared, and she rattle him."

Charlie shook his head. "Did you read about Mr. Ashburn? Even the *Intelligencer* write about it. White man, Republican, running for the Assembly, murdered in cold blood in Columbus. No one saw a thing. No one said a thing. Case thrown out. Whoever done it got away scot-free."

"Murder? And no one punished for it?"

"Yes. And he a white man. Don't like to think what might happen to a black woman. Don't be a fool, Rachel."

—〜—

MOST OF CHARLIE'S campaigning allowed him to lay low, too. He met his supporters at their churches, hidden in the woods away from white eyes, or at the Union League meetings, conducted in secrecy at night. But a man running for public office needed to show his face in public, and Hart persuaded him to speak to a crowd in Cartersville at the end of March.

In a county that had a courthouse, Charlie would address the crowd from it, but Cartersville was still without one. On a Saturday afternoon, when every man who worked a cotton farm laid down his work and came into town, Charlie stood on the steps of the Methodist Church, where he had been sworn in as a registrar and had registered black men to vote. The crowd gathered at the foot of the church steps and spilled into the street.

The atmosphere was festive. Women and children had accompanied the men into town, eager to hear what Charlie had to say, and even those former slaves who weren't sure yet about politics had joined the crowd for the sight of a black man who had made the law of Georgia in Atlanta and who wanted to return to finish the task.

As at every political gathering since voter registration began last year, a group of white men stood at the back of the crowd, the Turners and their gang, rifles slung over their shoulders and pistols holstered around their hips. Everett stood in their midst, indifferent to his task to keep the peace.

Down the street, a solitary figure, his shoulders bent, his face saddened, kept his eyes on the crowd. Colonel Turner.

Charlie stood quietly, dressed in the suit that he had worn to Atlanta, a man who now dressed for Sunday every day of the week. He took in the crowd, and Rachel was startled anew at his ability to seem to meet the eyes of every person in a multitude.

"It's good to see so many of you here today," he said. "We in the midst of cotton season, chopping season, and it's hard to lay down the hoe to leave the field and the garden." He smiled. "And not even the promise of barbecue or music today."

"Don't need any barbecue!" someone called out good-naturedly.

"Today we talk about a task that ain't finished. You sent me to the Constitutional Convention to speak for black folks. We did good work at that Convention, we Republicans, white men as well as black. We made it law that black men can vote."

A cheer went up from the crowd, so loud and prolonged that Charlie waited for it to subside.

"We help the white folks of Georgia, too. A man who sit in the Assembly have to speak for everyone. We ask to help out anyone who have a debt from the war. A debt can crush a man. It ain't right not to help. And we make it the law that women can own property, so any woman left a widow can support herself, and not be at the mercy of her father or brother."

The black crowd listened politely, but they didn't care about the troubles of white folks. They wanted to hear about a remedy for their own.

"We make a good start at the Convention," Charlie said, "but there's more to do. We talk about schools, public schools that the government pay for, for black children as well as white. Think of it, schooling for your children, paid for by the state of Georgia! We talk about public accommodation. Anyone who ride that train to Atlanta know what I mean. Third class! Anyone who buy a ticket should sit in comfort, without the smoke of the train or the rudeness of any man for a bother. Especially the ladies."

Nodding and sounds of agreement.

"But those things ain't the law of Georgia yet. That kind of fairness and dignity ain't the law of Georgia yet. Send me back to Atlanta, and I keep on speaking for you. I raise my voice for what's fair and right. I keep on raising my voice until justice written into the law of the state of Georgia."

The air filled with the sound of applause. With whistles of appreciation. With cries of "Tell it!" and "Fair and right!"

Rachel felt the excitement sweep through her. "Charlie!" she yelled. "Charlie!" She clapped until her hands burned.

From the rear, white men pushed through the crowd. Someone, angry at being jostled, shouted, "Don't you push me!"

A slow, venomous voice answered, "Get out of my way, nigger."

"Don't call me a nigger!"

Alarm flashed through Rachel. *Not a melee,* she thought. *Not today.*

Charlie ran down the steps.

Are you crazy? she thought. *Into the midst of it!*

He called out, "Order! Order!" Plowing through the crowd, he raised his voice: "Calm, people! Easy, easy!"

From the street rang a voice that had carried in the heat of battle at Gettysburg. "Ben! Pierce!" he shouted. "For God's sake! Keep the peace today!"

Ben Junior turned. In a tone of contempt, he said, "What's wrong with you? Did you forget that you're a white man?"

"The war's over," his father said. "We live by the law, not the rule of the mob."

Everett, who stood in their midst, said to Colonel Turner, "It ain't against the law to listen to a speech. Even if a nigger gives it."

"It's against the law to start a riot."

From the corner of her eye, Rachel saw the one-eyed man, Colonel Loveless, friend to General Forrest, officer in Forrest's new army, as he watched and waited.

— ✍ —

RACHEL WAS TORN from sleep by the heavy pounding on the door. As she came fully awake, she heard the screaming, too. "Miss Rachel! The windows! Miss Rachel! Broken glass!"

Eliza ran into her room, eyes wide. "Mama, what is it?"

The screaming continued, Dell's voice: "Miss Rachel! Broken glass!" Horrified, Rachel ordered Eliza, "You stay here. I go to see."

Rachel threw open the door to find Dell in her nightdress, her three children clustered around her in terror. Rachel dragged her inside, slamming the door shut and bolting it behind them. "What happen?" she demanded.

Dell sobbed so hard that she couldn't speak.

Rachel wanted to slap her. "Stop it! Stop crying and tell me what happen!"

The oldest boy's eyes were wide with fear. "Someone shoot through the windows in our house," he said. "We wake up with glass all over. Mama grab us and we run here."

Rachel gripped Dell tightly. "Jim? Is Jim all right?"

Dell gasped, "He all right. He stay behind to watch the place. Glass! Broken glass!"

"You stay here." She ran into her room to stuff her feet into her boots, tying them just enough to keep them on her feet, and to fling her shawl over her nightdress. She said sharply to the oldest boy, "Bolt the door after me!"

She snatched up her rifle, which rested by the door, and without slinging it properly over her shoulder, ran down the steps and into the pine grove. She was in such a state of fear and rage that she was most of the way there before she thought, *The Turners might still be in the woods.*

Still she ran.

As she came close to the house she yelled, "Jim! It's Rachel!"

Both front windows were shattered. A rifle barrel protruded through one of the ruined panes. Rachel gasped, "Jim. It's me, Rachel. Are you all right?"

Her tenant lowered the rifle. "Miss Rachel," he said weakly. "Don't come inside, it's all over glass. They shoot out every window."

"Come outside and tell me what happen."

He opened the door and limped onto the steps, leaving a trail of bloody footprints.

"You're bleeding!" she said.

He looked down. "Didn't even notice. Too wrought up to notice."

"Tell me what happen."

"We was all fast asleep, Dell and me in our room, the children in theirs, and we hear the shots. Then the glass fall. Fall on my babies while they was sleeping!" He sparked with anger. "Could have cut them bad. Could have killed them!"

"How many men?"

"More than one. Heard them talking and laughing. Asked we was afraid. Said they'd find you next."

Rachel stared out the broken window. "Did you see them?"

"No. By the time I made sure the children was safe and Dell was safe, they was gone."

"Are they really gone? Not lurking somewhere?"

Jim seemed to wake from a daze. "Miss Rachel, did you come here by yourself?"

"Ran through the woods as soon as Dell tell me. Didn't take the time to find an escort."

"Did you see them?"

"No."

Jim said bleakly, "Then they is probably gone."

She said, "You stay in my place tonight. How bad is your foot?"

"Don't know."

"I bind it up so you can walk." She pulled her shawl from her shoulders.

He protested, "Miss Rachel, not your good shawl."

"I won't worry about a shawl," she said, and she wrapped his foot so they could make their way to the illusion of safety at her house.

— ⤨ —

JIM'S CUT WASN'T serious. Dell washed it, smeared it with comfrey paste, and bound it properly with a clean rag. The children piled into Eliza's bed, and Rachel gave up her own for Jim and Dell.

She slept on the floor before the hearth and woke with pain in her shoulders and a pounding ache in her head.

At breakfast, her tenants sat at the table, their faces haggard with fatigue and ashen with fear. No one ate much. When the meal was over, Dell rose and without thinking, stood before the window to stare down the driveway.

The oldest boy cried out, "Mama! Don't stand by a window! If they come back the glass kill you!"

Badly shaken, Dell said to her husband, "We can't stay here. It ain't safe. It's like Floyd County. Worse than Floyd County!"

Jim rose from the table to pull his wife away from the window. Dell's voice rose, her fear disguised as anger. "We go somewhere else. Somewhere safe!"

"And where is that?" he asked.

"Don't know. Not here."

"We run off from Floyd County because it weren't safe," he said. "We can run from here, too. What kind of life do we lead if we run off whenever we don't feel safe?" He reached to hold her, but she squirmed out of his embrace. "We as safe here as anywhere. We stay, Dell."

—⌒—

JIM, STILL LIMPING, insisted on accompanying Rachel to look at the damage to the house. Every pane had been shot out, the jagged edges like broken teeth. Rachel shuddered to think of the damage the splinters might have done to the children who slept inside.

In their haste last night, they had left the door ajar. Jim swung it open and picked his way inside. Rachel followed. There was glass everywhere, in fragments as dangerous as knives. It would take a day of shaking everything out and sweeping everything clean, and not even that precaution would remove all the glass from the children's beds.

Every pane had been shattered, but the window frames seemed to be intact. "Miss Rachel?" Jim asked. "Can they be mended?"

"I don't know."

Jim said, "It cost trouble and money to do it."

"It ain't about the money," she said.

"What if they come back and shoot out the glass again?"

Rachel couldn't reply. She thought of a child hurt by shattering glass.

"Miss Rachel, we can get by with oilpaper for a while. Until this trouble is over."

When would that be? Rachel thought. She stared at the ruined panes. "I wanted for you to have glass windows."

Jim said, "We safer with oilpaper. For now." Taking her silence for assent, he said, "I help you take out the windows. We put them away for safekeeping, mend them later."

Jim couldn't do the task alone. He asked Zeke for help, and Rachel watched as they removed the windows. The sight of the ruined windows, leaning against the house, hurt her as though her own flesh had been torn.

Zeke neatly cut the oilpaper and attached it to the window frames. The sun hit the oilpaper and gave it a pleasant yellow glow. It was nothing like the sparkle of glass, and Rachel felt as though the house, like her hopes, had been cast into darkness.

15 | MOLLIE

As in a dream, Rachel heard the pounding on the door. She woke, her heart racing, thinking, *Lord, not again.* She threw off the covers and grabbed the rifle, unlocking the safety as she ran to the door. Disregarding the danger, she looked out the window. She opened the door to Jim and Dell's oldest boy.

He could barely catch his breath. Shaking, he said, "Fire. The fields on fire."

"Where your mama and daddy?"

"They stay to put it out. Sent me for help."

No time to dress. She pulled on her shoes, like last time, and said to the boy, "You watch Eliza."

As she ran for the Kaltenbach house, it sank in. Her fields on fire. Her crop on fire. How long to pump the water into buckets and carry it to the blaze? She had seen lightning hit a cotton field and burn it to a cinder so swiftly the buckets had been useless.

Now she understood Dell's frenzy. She pounded on her sister's front door, screaming, "Fire! Help! Fire!"

The door opened with a resounding thud. Adelaide stood in the doorway, her hair loose around her shoulders, her dressing gown hastily pulled over her nightdress, her rifle over her shoulder. She gasped. "Fire? Where is it?"

"My fields! Hurry! Get help, and everyone bring a bucket!"

"I'll wake the others, and we'll wake the tenants, too. There's a bucket in the kitchen. Take it!"

Rachel retrieved the bucket and ran. Her rifle banged against her back, and the bucket clattered against her leg. She ran, oblivious to the scratch of the pine boughs, to the annoyance of the gnats and mosquitoes, and to the danger that might lurk in the trees.

She ran. Was the barn on fire, too? Mollie was tethered there. She thought of Mollie, burned, hurt, dying, and she ran faster.

She smelled it first. The cotton was close to harvest, the bushes dry and woody, the bolls full and fluffed, the worst possible moment for a blaze. The air smelled of burning lint. As she ran, she saw the glow, a great low-slung bonfire. Ash and lint filled her nose and made her cough.

"Jim! Dell!" she called.

"Over here!" Jim called back.

Behind her, footsteps pounded on the dirt, and buckets rattled. Behind Adelaide was the fire brigade: Frankie, Sarah and Johnny from the Kaltenbach house, and all of Adelaide's tenants. The men were doubly armed, with guns and buckets, and the women carried anything that would hold water. Becky had lugged the washbasin.

They stopped at the sight of the blaze, which girdled the field and the one adjacent to it. Zeke stepped forward, taking a leader's place in Charlie's absence. He said, "We find a place to fight it," and he ran, looking for a break in the fire. Adelaide and the others followed. Rachel did, too.

They ran toward the cornfields, but the cornfields were as solid a bonfire as the cotton. The cornstalks, green and full of sap, produced a thicker and ranker smoke than the tinder-dry cotton plants. The air smelled of smoldering stalks and scorched ears. As the fire crackled, it popped the kernels from the ears, and just before the kernels burned, they gave off the pleasant odor of popped corn. Popped corn had always been the odor of a December frolic, when the last of the corn was shucked. Rachel thought that she would never be able to eat popped corn again.

The brigade halted, still looking for the break. Zeke asked Rachel, "What lie beyond this field?"

"Fallow. Just dirt."

Zeke hesitated.

Rachel shouted, "Why do you linger? Look for someplace we can stand to fight it!"

Zeke asked, "Is it fallow all around?"

Rachel stared at the fire's glow and listened to its hiss and crackle. "Yes! Why?"

"We let it burn out," Zeke said.

Rachel shrieked. "My crop on fire! A year's work for nothing if it burn over! Must be something we can do!"

"Too far gone," Zeke said. "We bring a hundred buckets and it don't do a bit of good. It burn out in an hour, and it don't spread."

"How in God's name do you know?"

"Used to burn over the fields, corn and cotton, many a year."

"After the harvest! Not before!"

"We can't save it."

The house. The barn. She screamed at Jim, "Is the house on fire? Did we leave the house to burn?"

Jim said, "They leave the house alone."

"The barn?"

"Didn't have time to check."

The image of her mule, her mane and tail on fire, dying in agony, rose before her eyes. Rachel raced back to the barn, screaming, "Mollie! Mollie!"

The barn was intact and untouched. But it was empty. Someone had undone the traces and let both mules loose.

She ran across the Mannheim land, still screaming, "Mollie!"

Someone grabbed her from behind, too fast for her to unsling her rifle. It was Zeke. She cried, "Let me go!"

"No! Won't let you run into another fire."

"My mule!"

"What if they still here?"

She struggled and wept. "Mollie! Mollie!"

"Quiet!" Zeke had never spoken so roughly to her.

"No! Let me go!"

"To run into danger?"

"You tell me the fire burn itself out!"

"Who do you think set it?" Zeke demanded.

She sagged in his grasp.

The rest of the brigade straggled back from the fields. They huddled together, a tired, frightened, disconsolate gathering.

They watched the orange glow, listening to the crackle, smelling the popped corn, and choking on air full of smoke and lint.

— ᔰ —

IT LOOKED EVEN worse in daylight. The crop had been close to harvest, and now it was gone. The corn, food for man and beast, was gone. The untouched house, the oilpaper glowing in the morning sun, mocked her. What good was a house for tenants without a crop?

Now that the fields had cooled, and the danger of further fire was past, she plunged into the woods to look for Mollie. She found nothing, not even the print of a shoe. Perhaps Mollie had fled and she was safe somewhere.

Likely she was dead.

Rachel sat heavily on the steps of Jim and Dell's house. She was done as a cotton planter for this year. She thought of Jim's bitterness. A year's work, and nothing to show for it.

Whoever had shot out the windows had also done this. She had no proof, but she had no doubt.

The sound of footsteps brought her to her feet. It was Captain Hart, his hat askew, and his hair wild beneath it in the hot, damp air.

"Miss Mannheim," he said, extending his hand.

She shook it. "Captain Hart."

"I heard about the fire and I came as soon as I could. Have you surveyed it?"

"Yes," she said. "Ruined. Burned to the ground." She tried to keep her voice level. "A season's work, and all for naught."

"I am so sorry, Miss Mannheim." As though he had come to a funeral.

"Sorry don't begin to help."

He said, "This wasn't an accident."

"I know."

"Miss Mannheim, it's a Bureau matter. Please let the Bureau help you."

"Let me ponder it," she said.

He nodded. "All right. But not too long."

She turned to look at the fields, barely visible from the steps of the house. The smell of burned things, cotton lint, cornstalk, corn ear, was so thick in the air that she could taste it, and the smell of popped corn came back to her.

—⟨∽⟩—

DELL WAS TOO badly shaken to remain in Rachel's house. The next morning, she insisted that her family move back into the old slave cabin where they had waited for the house with glass windows. Jim visited the field, but Dell refused to leave the cabin.

"Don't you want to see your garden?" Rachel asked, her tone soothing, as to a child.

Dell flared. "Won't go back there, not for nothing."

Jim tried to persuade Dell that there was work to be had on the Kaltenbach place. Rachel offered to pay them to pick cotton alongside Zeke or Davey or Asa, to no avail. Jim spoke for Dell when he said, "Can't stay, Miss Rachel."

"Thought you didn't want to run away."

Dell rose from the rough pine chair she sat in. She shrieked at Rachel, "We stay here, they burn our house, and they burn us, too! Won't wait to find out how or when." She glowered at Jim. "We go to Atlanta. If you decide otherwise I go without you."

Jim said softly, "Dell, wherever we go, we go together."

She burst into tears. "We go to Atlanta," she said. "If we have to run off."

Rachel said, "No, don't do that." She thought of Jim's bitterness about leaving Floyd County with nothing.

"We go," Jim said, his arm protectively around Dell, who was still sobbing. "Hate to break the contract, Miss Rachel."

"You didn't sign a contract to get shot at," Rachel said. Her heart sank, even as she felt pity for these people, caught up in her trouble.

"I know you saved your wages," she said. "I know how careful you were." She could see the crisp bills that she had handed Jim every week, eleven dollars for their labor.

Jim said, "Never did get to that bank down in Macon."

"Where did you keep it?"

"In a little wooden box in my house. It's gone."

Stolen. Whoever had ruined the crop had stolen Jim's money. Rachel buried her face in her hands at the loss. When she recovered, she said, "I give you some money to get you started in Atlanta. Would a hundred dollars cover it?"

A few days later she pressed the money into Jim's hands. Dell tied it into a handkerchief and buried the handkerchief deep in her pocket.

— ✍ —

WHEN RACHEL TOLD Adelaide that she would drive her tenants to the depot in Cartersville, Adelaide said, "You aren't going by yourself." Johnny Hardin, tired of teaching, volunteered to accompany her.

"It's not safe for you either," Adelaide said.

Johnny picked up the rifle that he kept in the schoolroom. "I can shoot straight."

"Be careful, and don't shoot for the pleasure of it."

Rachel didn't stand beside the tracks to wait for them to board the train. She couldn't bear to watch them go. She waved to her tenants and slapped the reins to get Zeke's mule, big, patient Lou, going back to the Kaltenbach place.

They weren't far from Cartersville when the sound of hooves followed them. It was the Turners, who paced her to ride along-side the wagon.

She knew better than to taunt them, but she couldn't keep her temper. "What do you want?" she snapped.

"Listen to her, sassing us," Ben said to Pierce.

Rachel slapped the reins, trying to encourage Lou into a trot. When Lou sped up, so did Ben and Pierce.

Ben said, "I reckon that now you know what it's like to be burned out. Like Sherman did to us during the war."

Rachel said, "God will damn you for what you did to me."

Ben said, "What does a nigger gal need with a cotton farm, anyhow? You can find some big buck to marry you and keep you where you belong."

Pierce sniggered. "She don't seem to mind if she's married or not," he said.

"Maybe she'd say yes to me," Ben said, laughing in an ugly way. "Since Adelaide won't have either of us."

Pierce said, "Don't see why you'd bother to ask. She's there for the taking."

Johnny Hardin spoke up. "Leave Miss Rachel alone or I'll put a hole through your heart."

"Will you? You'd better watch yourself, too."

Johnny's hands tightened on the rifle barrel. "I'm not fooling," he said.

Ben laughed again, another ugly sound. "Miss Rachel," he said, making the courtesy sound like an insult. "We'll see you again." And they galloped away.

—❧—

RACHEL HAD SUSPECTED who set the fire, and now she knew. She thought about it until it her anger burned, as though the Turners had lit something inside her that could never be properly quenched. It engulfed the despair of losing her crop and everything that would come from it, this year's profit and the year's beyond. When she thought of Mollie she was overwhelmed with grief. As a little girl, Aunt Susie, who raised her, had told her bitterly, "As a slave, don't nothing belong to you." It was no different being free. If you were black, anything that was yours could be taken away.

—⟡—

SHORTLY AFTER JIM and Dell left, Adelaide came to see her. She came in and sat down without invitation. Familiar. Family.

"Rachel, please think about coming to stay with us. Let us keep an eye on you. Let us make sure that you and Eliza are safe."

"No," Rachel said.

"Think of going to Atlanta, then, like Jim and Dell did."

Atlanta shimmered before her eyes, a haven and a seduction. She snorted. "Just what they want me to do. Run away."

"Then go to the Bureau," Adelaide said, her face full of concern.

"Bureau don't do either of us any good," she said, and her laugh was bitter.

"I worry about you and Eliza all the time," Adelaide said. "As does Captain Hart."

She let her anger surge. "I won't let your worry sway me, any more than whatever the Klan plan to do to me."

Adelaide lost her temper. "Don't wait to find out. Do you think I want to bury you?" Her sister grasped her hand so hard that it hurt.

Rachel blinked in surprise. "Don't need to break my hand to show you love me," she said.

"You'll go to the Bureau?"

"Let go my hand. I will."

—⁓—

THE NEXT TIME that Zeke went into Cartersville, Rachel accompanied him and marched into the Bureau office. Without preliminaries, she told Hart, "I know who done it." She told him about the exchange on the road back from Cartersville.

"They said so?" Hart asked.

Rachel's temper rose. "I'll give them what they deserve," she said. "I'll take my rifle and go after them, both of them. I'll shoot them dead."

"I know how you feel," Hart said, "but as a Bureau agent, I can't condone your doing it."

She leaned forward in the chair, which creaked under her weight. "Have to do something."

"I know. We'll ask for justice."

"Ask who? The sheriff?" Rachel cried, too upset for good grammar. "He in league with them. He belong to the Klan. He boast about it. Justice!"

Hart said, "I wish with all my heart that the Bureau could call upon a military tribunal. But I can't. We'll do it properly. We'll appeal to the county court and to the sheriff."

—⁓—

A FEW DAYS later, Rachel met Hart at the Bureau office in Cartersville. He was slowed by the black people who stood outside the store. One man greeted him pleasantly, but another said, "Is you the Bureau man? I have trouble, need the Bureau's help."

Hart said, "I have some other business to attend to first. Wait for me in the Bureau office." He asked the man, "Have you seen Mr. Everett?"

The man nodded. "He go into the saloon."

Rachel followed Hart up the steps and entered behind him as he opened the door, blinking at the darkness inside. The smell of whiskey and sawdust were strong. Against the bar leaned half a dozen white men in threadbare suits, all of them strangers. In the corner, at a rickety table, sat the Turner brothers, and with them, Everett.

She felt the eyes of every man in the place on her. She thought of the words of the pale rider on the election day: "We're out-gunned here."

Hart strode to the table, and she trailed behind him. "Sheriff Everett?" he said crisply.

Everett drank and set his glass down hard on the table. "What do you want?"

"There's a matter I'd like to discuss with you."

Without offering Hart a seat, Everett said, "Well, speak your piece."

Hart gestured to Rachel. "This woman owns property in Cass County. She had a crop on it, cotton and corn. Last week it was destroyed by fire."

Everett said, "Can't help if she was careless with a match."

"There's reason to think that it wasn't an accident."

Ben Junior turned to stare at Hart, and Pierce sat up straighter. "Really?" Everett asked. "What reason?"

Hart's voice rose. "When a fire starts at night—a clear night, no lightning strike anywhere, all the candles and lamps extinguished in the house—I'd look elsewhere for the cause."

Everett drank a long draught of whiskey. "What do you want from me?"

"To look into it."

Everett began to laugh, and both of the Turners joined him. Rachel pushed Hart aside and shouted at Everett, "I know who done it! Burned my crop to the ground!" Hart grabbed her arm, but she ignored him. "They done wrong in the eyes of the law! You supposed to enforce the law! Arrest them and put them in jail and try them for the wrong they done me!"

Unmoved, Everett said, "Shut up, you nigger bitch." To Hart, he said, "And you. You get out of here, you bastard, or I'll put both of you in jail for disturbing the peace."

Hart dragged Rachel from the saloon into the street. "I told you!" she said, panting with rage. "Just like I told you!"

Hart pitched his voice low, but it was the voice of command. "Miss Mannheim, calm yourself."

"Done me wrong, and no one want to put it right!"

The Turners emerged from the saloon to watch the struggle between the furious Rachel and her Yankee escort.

"What's wrong, Hart?" Ben jeered. "Is the nigger too much woman for you?"

Rachel stopped struggling and tore herself from Hart's grasp. She fired out the words. "What happen to my mule?"

Ben grinned. "Little brown molly mule? Pretty little thing?"

"Did you shoot her?"

Ben shook his head. "Sold her. Got a good price for her, didn't we, Pierce?"

Stolen and sold away. Rachel spat in the dirt, as close to Ben's boots as she dared. "I hope you burn in hell!" she said.

— ༄ —

RACHEL WROTE TO Mr. Pereira in Atlanta, knowing that he wouldn't see the letter. Then she got on the train to see someone who might be able to do something for her.

She couldn't bear the thought of Betty Mannheim's sympathy, so she announced herself at Mordecai's building, where the man at the desk asked her, "Where's the colored lawyer you brought along last time?"

In response she merely sniffed. "Do they pay you good money to be a busybody?"

Mordecai had recovered—his color was ruddy, even if he would never be as stout as he had once been—and he smoked a cigar, which filled his office with a noxious odor. He waved the cigar and the smoke plumed through the air. "Betty doesn't worry about my health anymore," he said with a grin. "I can eat and drink and smoke just as I like."

"Don't have time for chitchat," Rachel said. "Did you hear what happen in Cass County?" In her distress, her good diction slipped from her.

"You lost your crop."

"Lost!" she said bleakly. "Someone put a match to it and steal it from me."

"Did you go to that Bureau fellow? Couldn't he help you?"

"Went to Captain Hart. We both went to Sheriff Everett."

"Everett? Miss Aggie's new husband? Don't know him well."

"He don't do a thing. He threaten to arrest us for bothering him."

Mordecai puffed on the cigar. "Well, that's too bad," he said.

"Bad? It an outrage!"

"What do you want me to do about it?"

"Help me."

He said, "I don't know any of these new fellows in the county, like this man Everett. I don't carry any water with them."

"Colonel Turner still there. He remember you."

"Turner! He's a fool. Thinks he can keep the place quiet. Can't even keep his own boys in check."

At the mention of the Turners, her chest ached with anger. "They burn my place."

"Did they? It don't surprise me."

"Thought you'd be mad," she said, feeling despair wash over her. "Thought you'd want to set it right."

"Rachel, I'm not about to ride into the countryside to take on the Klan. You're a fool to stay there and let them take potshots at you. Why don't you come to try your luck in Atlanta?"

She said bitterly, "To make a living as a washwoman?"

He looked abashed. "I reckon you can do better than that. Or you could marry that Pereira fellow, who seems to like you."

She was so upset, despair and anger roiling around inside her, that she couldn't reply.

A little more gently, he said, "Maybe you don't care so much for him." At her silence, he said, "Well, I learned the hard way not to force a gal when she doesn't want to marry a man."

"Is that all you can offer me?" she said, tasting bile on her tongue.

"You've been set back," he said. "Happens to all of us. Just set back."

She raised her head and regarded him with fury. "How can you say such a thing? You, whose people were slaves to Pharaoh in Egypt? These folks don't want me set back. They want me dead."

—⁊—

Mordecai couldn't help her, and Daniel Pereira was in some godforsaken corner of rural Georgia, as he had once chided her for being, on the unending and heartrending business of the Bureau. She didn't know whether he was her lover or her lawyer, and there was no way to find out.

She would go to see the man who had been happiest for her success in buying her own place and who would grieve the hardest for her loss. She left the grand office on Whitehall Street for Henry's dry goods shop on Wheat.

He led her upstairs and settled her in his best chair before the hearth. He offered her refreshment but she shook her head, so he sat close by and reached for her hand. "It's trouble," he said.

"How did you know? Did Adelaide write to you?"

"I can see it in your face." He knelt before her and put his arms around her, stroking her back as he'd touch Eliza.

She had forgotten how much kindness was in his touch. She sobbed against his shoulder, and he let her tears wet his shirt. When her sobs slowed, he gently lifted her chin with his finger. "Oh, beloved," he said, and he kissed her cheek.

She turned her face so that he could kiss her mouth. She had forgotten the tenderness in his lips, too.

As they kissed, he pulled her from the chair, and she pressed close, letting him feel her desire as she could feel his.

He led her into his bedroom and shut the door. The old passion returned, and for a moment, it kept the terror and the sorrow at bay.

—🖎—

FULL OF ANGER at the way that Everett had treated Rachel, Adelaide decided to make an appeal of her own. Accompanied by Johnny Hardin, who did guard duty during the day, she drove to the Turner place to call on the colonel.

She and Johnny walked up the half-rotted stairs, and when the old, toothless servant let them in, they entered the parlor together.

Colonel Turner said, "I see you come escorted."

"Sir, I believe you know young Mr. Hardin, who teaches in my school."

"How do, sir," Johnny said. "Don't mind me."

"He has my trust," Adelaide said.

Colonel Turner sighed. "Miss Adelaide, I hope I can be of assistance to you."

"So do I," she said. "My sister has been badly wronged."

He hesitated to hear Rachel called a sister. Unlike his sons, who made it into an insult, Colonel Turner was too well bred to admit to it. "I heard about the business with her crop."

"It's a bad business. I wish that Sheriff Everett would look into it. Perhaps you could persuade him in the name of fairness, sir."

He said, "People are very stirred up about this."

"The colored people are, too." She reached for his hand, which was mottled with age. "It isn't right, sir."

"I have to speak for the farmers and the planters, too. We can't risk the kind of trouble they've had elsewhere."

Adelaide said, "We know full well who causes the trouble." She thought before she spoke, but she spoke. "Men like your sons, and the company they keep."

He shook his head. "I want to keep the peace, Adelaide."

"There is no peace. The Klan has broken the peace. Do you know how angry the black people of this county are?"

"Don't ask me to start an insurrection here."

"Insurrection!" Adelaide said angrily. "A cry for justice!"

He stared at her, once again the Confederate commander. "Do you want the land drenched in blood?"

She forced herself to talk more softly. "Please, Colonel Turner. Help Rachel. Help me."

"I can't," he said, and the effort of refusing her aged him a decade.

She let go his hand. "May I see Mrs. Turner?"

"She's not well. Don't trouble her."

"Just to say good day."

The colonel relented. He himself led her upstairs. He knocked on the half-opened door and asked his wife tenderly, "Miss Adelaide has come to see you. Will you greet her?"

A faint voice said, "Ben, I'm so ashamed."

Mrs. Turner's room was hot and close. It smelled of unwashed sheets and sweat. She lay back on a ragged pillow, her gray hair straggling around her face. Before the war she had worn lace mitts to hide her work-worn hands, but now her hands were bare, coarsened and gnarled on the coverlet.

Adelaide said softly, "Mrs. Turner." Her eyes fluttered open. Adelaide asked, "Did you hear what happened to my servant Rachel?" She forced herself to say, "My sister Rachel?"

Mrs. Turner made no reply.

Adelaide lowered her voice. "Do you speak to your sons? Will they listen to you?"

The sick woman closed her eyes, and tears leaked from her lids. She whispered, "My boys. My poor lost boys.

—✍—

ON SUNDAY, A crowd gathered outside the little meeting house. Word of the Klan's effort at intimidation had already made its way through the county, to white and black alike, but word of the injustice had stirred the souls of Cass County's black folk. More than a hundred of them had journeyed to show their support for Rachel, and their fury at her treatment. All of the men had come armed.

Charlie, who had emerged the victor of November's elections and was in the thick of Assembly business, had rushed home to attend the Sunday service today. Hart, who had refrained from bothering black Cass County at its devotions, was in attendance, too.

As Rachel passed through the crowd, people reached for her, some murmuring words of comfort. "We so sorry to hear about the fire." Others muttered in anger. "Wouldn't do a thing! Bastard of a Klansman!" She walked with her head high, ignoring both. In her hand she carried a folded sheet of paper.

The reverend Judah, who stood before the door to greet the worshipers, clasped her hand. "This a terrible business, Miss Rachel," he said.

She raised the paper. "I have a few words to say," she said.

"After the sermon, you're welcome to, Miss Rachel."

"I need to preach today," she said.

She walked slowly to the pulpit, where she unfolded her paper and waited as the church filled. Judah waited with her. People crowded into the pews and overflowed to fill the aisle and the space by the door. Someone propped the door open to let the words of the service and the sermon reach those who stood on the steps and in the yard.

The oilpaper over the windows held in the heat, and the crowd made the room feel hotter. The room was quiet save for the small movements of many people together, feet shuffling, skirts rustling, a cough, a yawn.

"Today Miss Rachel speak to us," Judah said.

Rachel surveyed the crowd as it accepted this news. She let her eyes rest on one person after another. She caught Charlie's eye. He looked back at her, unblinking, staunch.

"I reckon that all of you know what happen to me," she said. "That someone shoot out the windows on my tenants' house. That someone come onto my place and shoot at all of us and frighten my tenants away. Burn my crop and spoil our hard work, my tenants and mine, and ruin any chance to make a crop and a profit this year. All of you hear about that."

"Tell us!"

"And you hear about what happen when I go to ask for justice. Go to the sheriff of this county, the man charged with seeing justice done, to demand that he do what's right. He laugh. He insult me. He say he arrest me for disturbing the peace. That ain't justice."

"No, it ain't."

I turn to the Good Book, because I hear it can be a comfort. I read that book, and I don't find comfort in it. I read the book of the prophet Isaiah. And I find this."

She read, "Their works are works of iniquity, and the act of violence is in their hands." She looked up. "We know a man like that. A man in white on a white horse. A pale rider."

She continued to read. "Their feet run to evil, and they make haste to shed innocent blood: their thoughts are thoughts of iniquity; wasting and destruction are in their paths." She said, "The Turner brothers."

She read again, "None calleth for justice, nor any pleadeth for truth." She looked up. "Sheriff Everett." She returned to the page. "And judgment is turned away backward, and justice standeth afar off: for truth is fallen in the street, and equity cannot enter." She said, "As long as we live in the Klan's shadow, we'll never see justice.

"How do we get justice? Do we ask? Do we beg? Do we demand? Or do we fight for it?" Rachel said.

"Justice!" someone shouted, and the congregation took up the cry. They rose to their feet, shouting, "Justice!"

Charlie strode to the pulpit and held up his hand. "Silence!" he thundered. "All of you!"

They quieted. "It feel good to get mad, don't it?" he said. "It feel good to talk about fighting, don't it? It feel good to put a hand on the rifle barrel and think about using it, don't it?"

He glared at them, as impassioned as a prophet. "If we arm ourselves, if we band together, if we talk about vengeance, you know what happen. Our enemies say we planning to murder them in cold blood, and they come after us. They murder the innocents, women and children along with the men. Won't be a fight. It will be a massacre."

He cried out, "How can we fight for justice if we all dead?"

— ᔆ —

PERHAPS FRANKIE WAS right, Rachel thought, as she buttoned Eliza into her dress to get her ready for school. Perhaps she should leave for Atlanta and call it "a fresh start" rather than "running away." She ran her hands over Eliza's shoulders and kissed the top of her daughter's head. "Now you ready," she said. She held out her hand and Eliza took it.

Eliza had been fearful all the time since the Klan's visit. Rachel now walked her daughter to school every morning, worried about letting her traverse the short distance to the Kaltenbach place by herself.

Eliza asked, "Mama, will you take your rifle?"

She had weighed the idea, back and forth. Eliza had reason to be frightened, but carrying a rifle all the time, like moving to Atlanta, was a way to admit that she lived in fear, just as the Klan wanted her to. "It's all right, sugar. Just a little way to go. We all right without it."

But Eliza's fear had sparked her own, and as soon as they set foot on the sheltered path that ran from her house to the Kaltenbach place, she was as alert as a Union scout. All of the sounds of the pine grove—the cheeping of the nestlings, the scrabbling noise that squirrels made—increased her wariness.

Did she hear hoofbeats?

She grasped Eliza's hand more firmly and quickened her step.

Did she hear footsteps?

She clenched Eliza's hand so hard that Eliza said, "Mama, you're hurting me."

She could see the opening at the end of the path, where it gave onto the Kaltenbach land. Just a few feet. Open ground, and safety. "Hurry, sugar," she said.

She heard the sound of running, booted feet, and before she could tell Eliza to run, someone grabbed her from behind, his arm choking her as he pressed the pistol to her temple. He said, "If you scream, I'll shoot."

It was Ben Turner Junior.

And as she watched, Pierce grabbed Eliza, holding her tight enough that she gasped for breath. She cried, "Mama!" and Pierce hit her on the face. "Shut up," he said, and he pressed his pistol to her temple to assure it.

Anger surged through her. She wanted to hurt Ben. To kill Pierce. Anything, to save Eliza. But death was down that road, for both of them.

"Hush, sugar," she called to her daughter.

Ben pressed the pistol harder against her temple. "You shut up, too," he said.

Rachel closed her eyes. They had warned her, over and over. And now she stood captive in Ben Turner's chokehold as Pierce Turner choked the breath out of her daughter.

Ben tightened his grip. "If you go back into that cotton field, if you hire anyone to work that place of yours, we'll come back for you." He looked at Pierce. "We'll shoot this little nigger dead, while you watch, and then we'll shoot you, too." He pressed the gun deeper into her temple, bruising the skin. "Do you understand?"

She nodded.

"You call me 'sir.'"

"Yes, sir," she whispered.

"No. Like back in slavery."

The word burned her tongue, but she whispered, "Yassuh."

He relaxed his grip. "Good. I'm glad we understand each other." He let her go and Pierce released his hold on Eliza.

The two men holstered their pistols, pleased with themselves, and they sauntered away to mount their horses.

Eliza came to her and clung to her skirt, too terrified to cry. Rachel put her arms around her daughter, too stunned to move, as the sound of hoofbeats faded away.

16 | ON FIRE

THE FOUR OF them sat awkwardly in the parlor, which had been pressed into service as a meeting room—Frankie and Rachel close together on the settee, Adelaide in the ladies chair that faced the hearth, and in the gentleman's chair, opposite her, Captain Hart, who shifted in his seat with discomfort.

Rachel had moved back into the Kaltenbach house. She had resisted Adelaide's pleas and tears. It was Frankie who convinced her. "Do it for Eliza," Frankie said, more fact than plea. Rachel had burst into tears and agreed. Now she and Eliza slept in the attic, close to Frankie.

Frankie balled her hands into fists and buried them in her skirt. "Adelaide," she said, "I've bitten my tongue over this for weeks. But after what happened to Rachel and Eliza, I can't stay silent any longer."

"What is it, Miss Williamson?" Captain Hart asked.

Frankie let her teacher's gaze rest on Captain Hart and Adelaide. "It's about the Turner brothers," she said. "We know that they're firebugs, and now we know that they wouldn't hesitate to murder a child." She reached for Rachel's hand and held it tightly in her own. "I think that the school is in danger, Adelaide, and so are you."

"They've threatened me. But they wouldn't dare to hurt me."

Frankie implored her. "I don't speak lightly."

"I know you don't."

"Adelaide, I've never spoken of this to anyone, and it costs me dear to tell you. But I want you to know what happened to Mollie and me in Bibb County." She took a deep breath, bracing herself. "Those who hated us—there was no Klan yet, but they were the same as the Turners—set the school on fire."

She turned to Rachel. "It was at night, like your farm. We lived close by, Mollie and I. We could see the blaze from our cabin." She faltered. "And no one came to help. No one dared."

She raised her head and gazed at Adelaide, looking somewhere beyond her into the past. "We always knew we were in danger, every moment that we breathed. And when the school burned, we were sure we would burn along with it."

Adelaide was stunned into silence. She remembered Frankie's nightmare and thought, *There's something still worse that she can't even talk about.* "No," she whispered. "Not here."

Hart broke the silence. "I'm inclined to agree with Miss Williamson," he said, struggling to keep his tone matter-of-fact, as though this were ordinary Bureau business.

"Surely you don't think—" Adelaide said.

"I do, and you'd be well advised to keep a watch, as Mr. Mannheim does."

"How can we do that?"

"Let me talk to Sergeant Bailey, and we can arrange it."

"Frankie, Rachel, will you excuse us?" Adelaide said. "I'd like to talk to Captain Hart in private."

Frankie's face was as gray as ash. She nodded. Hand in hand, she and Rachel, equally stricken, rose and stumbled from the room.

Hart looked drawn, as though he didn't sleep well. "We're already on guard here," Adelaide began. "If you worry, don't worry about me. They won't harm me. Not a white woman who's a planter's daughter. I've lived here all my life, and I know."

"You're wrong," he said. "Adelaide, I'm worried sick about you—all of you, and the school. I want to do more than post a guard. I want to stay with you."

Her marriage and her desire shimmered in the air between them, as did his pledge of honor. His promise to her—that he would die for her—hung in the air between them. "You can't."

"As your guard," he said. "Nothing more."

She met his eyes and asked, "Do you really think it's that bad?"

He drew a ragged breath. "I do."

"As my guard," she repeated.

"Yes."

She stared at her hands, knotted in her lap. She looked up and met his eyes, even though it caused her pain. "Then I'll allow it."

—❧—

THAT NIGHT, INSTEAD of riding the perilous ten miles back to Cartersville, Hart followed her up the stairs to the second floor, and when she bid him good night, she watched as he shut the door of the room that had always been Henry's. After she put on her nightdress and brushed her hair, after she blew out the candle and got into bed, she lay awake.

The threat of the men who roamed the countryside at night, their rifles at the ready, had never kept her from sleep. Tonight, she imagined Lewis Hart, dressed in the nightshirt that had been her husband's, laying in the bed that had been her husband's. Her mind raced as her flesh itched and burned, and sleep escaped her.

—☙—

AT THE SOUND of the explosion, Adelaide woke, threw off the covers, and ran to the window.

The school was on fire.

The roof blazed, a great and terrifying torch, a mesmerizing, dancing burst of red and orange and yellow. The smoke rose in a great billow, gray at its base and white against the night sky. For a moment the fire crackled, no different from the sound a log made on the hearth, but at the sound of another explosion, the crackle turned to a roar. The flames burst through one of the window frames and the fire bellowed as it fed on itself. The smell of charring wood overpowered the resinous tang of burning pine and the sweet smell of last year's whitewash. Even at this distance, the smoke was harsh enough to make Adelaide cough.

Hart threw his door open. He had dressed so hurriedly that he had stuffed his nightshirt raggedly into his trousers. "Get everyone out of bed," he said. "I'll find buckets."

She stood at the window, awestruck by the power and the terror of the flames. He raised his voice. "Adelaide! Hurry!"

This time, she was prepared, and so were her tenants. Rachel handed Adelaide a bucket and they both ran towards the fire. Frankie followed. Hart passed them, shouting, "We're forming a line from the pump. Get in line and be quick about it."

Asa worked the pump, the handle complaining as he filled a bucket. In her haste to move the bucket from pump to fire, Adelaide let the water slosh on her shoes. Asa snapped, "Be careful! Want the water for the fire!" Now was no time to be polite or roundabout.

She breathed in the smoke that made her throat raw and blinked away the ash that made her eyes hurt. She could feel the fire's heat from twenty feet away.

Asa pumped and Adelaide handed the buckets down the line. Hart and Bailey struggled to douse the fire. They couldn't reach the roof, where the flames were at their worst, and they couldn't get close enough to wet the walls. They flung bucket after bucket through the burning door and the burning window frames, without even the consolation of a hiss of steam.

We might as well be spitting on it for all the good it does, Adelaide thought bleakly. But she continued to send bucket after bucket down the line.

The smell of charred wood grew stronger and the smoke became more acrid. Suddenly the roof caved in and the whole building collapsed as though it were made of toothpicks. As the sparks flew, Hart and Bailey retreated. "Get back!" Hart yelled, pushing the bucket brigade to safety. "Get away!" The line broke apart as everyone ran from the building that was now a heap of char and ash.

The fire leapt and roared, but as it consumed the charred wood, it weakened. "Line up again!" Hart shouted. "We'll try to douse the roof!"

They reassembled and worked in a rhythm that reminded Adelaide of chopping cotton. The groan of the pump. The grunts as they handed over the buckets. The slosh as the water flew through the air. The water soaked the burning roof and the flames began to die down. Groan. Grunt. Slosh. Adelaide's eyes burned and her throat ached. The fire turned to steam, then slowed to a smolder.

Hart set down his bucket and wiped his face with his sleeve. Ash had settled into the lines of his face and powdered his hair to give him the look of an old man. "It's done for," he said in a hoarse voice.

Adelaide ran to him. "Lewis!" she cried. "Are you all right?"

He slumped, admitting fatigue and failure. "I'm so sorry, Adelaide," he said.

"Rachel? Where are you?" she asked frantically.

"I'm here. I'm all right," Rachel said, putting her hand on Adelaide's shoulder. "Nothing more we can do. We look at it tomorrow."

Adelaide stared at the maw of the fire. She asked, "Where's Frankie?"

Frankie stood beside the great live oak, where sparks floated through the air to settle on the leaves. They gave off an incongruous smell of sap. Her face was coated with ash.

"Burned to the ground," Adelaide said.

Frankie nodded. She put her arm around her shoulders and consoled Adelaide in her embrace.

—✍—

THE NEXT MORNING, when Adelaide woke, the smell of charred wood seeped into her room. The memory was worse than the smell. She pulled on her dressing gown and her shoes and slipped outside to look at the still-smoldering remains of the schoolhouse.

The wooden frame had charred to splinters. Fragments of the roof covered them like a ragged blanket. Even though the flames had died out, the residue was still warm. Only the iron stove, badly blackened and covered with ash, had survived. At her feet was the remnant of a speller, the spine twisted, the cover blackened, the pages scorched.

She thought of the power of the fire as it torched into the night sky, and shivered at the power of the hatred that had set it.

She started at the sound of footsteps.

"It's me," Rachel said. They stared together at the wreckage, then picked their way carefully toward the live oak, the tree that had been their first school.

Adelaide rested her hand against the bark. The lowest leaves had shriveled and blackened, and the trunk was covered with burn scars. "They burned the tree, too," she said, and she was flooded with despair.

Rachel steadied her with a hand on her shoulder, and Adelaide covered it with her own. As they stood together in silence, Frankie ran across the lawn to join them.

A group of children marched up the driveway. The tallest, a slender thirteen-year-old named Emma, waved and called out, "Miss Adelaide!" She was surrounded by half a dozen younger children. "We all come to attend school today," Emma said. "I know we early."

"Did you hear?" Adelaide asked.

Emma nodded. "We hear about the fire. After we smell it."

Adelaide was startled anew at how well the human telegraph worked. She said, "Someone set that fire last night."

"The Klan done it," Emma said, matter-of-factly.

"How do you know?"

"Everyone know."

Adelaide said, "It's dangerous for you to come here."

"It were dangerous for my daddy to vote, but he was brave and marched to Cartersville on election day. It were dangerous for my mama to go with him, but she was brave, too. I reckon I can be brave enough to come to school."

Frankie knelt and held out her arms to the littlest children, who ran to her and broke into tears.

"Miss Frankie?" Emma asked. "Will we have school today?"

Frankie rose, letting the children cling to her skirt. "We certainly will."

—〜—

LATER THAT MORNING, a solemn group gathered under the live oak—Adelaide and Rachel, shoulder to shoulder; Hart and Frankie, their posture ramrod straight; and all three Hardins. Hart had sent all the children, Eliza and Matt as well as Emma and her charges, to play quietly in the yard, telling them, "You stay in our sight."

They stared at the wreckage in silence, until Frankie put a hand on Adelaide's arm. "We don't need a schoolhouse to have a school."

When Adelaide didn't reply, Frankie said in her best schoolroom voice, "Miss Adelaide, are there books in the house we can use for the children?"

Adelaide nodded. Rachel said, "I'll fetch them."

"Sally, will you gather some sticks so the children can practice writing their letters?"

"Yes, ma'am," Sally said.

In her sweet, quiet voice, Mrs. Sarah Hardin said, "The children will need something to eat for midday dinner. I'll see to it." Sarah Hardin was used to catastrophe. Her husband had tried to murder her. Since then, very little ruffled her.

Through her daze, Adelaide said to Frankie, "I should never have doubted you. What a fool I've been!"

"Don't speak of it," Frankie replied.

As the others dispersed, Adelaide remained under the tree, her hand on its damaged bark. Johnny Hardin lingered, too. "Miss Adelaide," he said gently.

She shook her head, and he addressed himself to Hart. "Captain Hart, I reckon they'll be back. Don't know how, but they'll be back."

Hart glanced at Adelaide, who didn't move or change her expression. "I believe you're right."

"I've been guarding Miss Rachel when she goes into town. I can help Miss Adelaide, too, if you say so." Hart hesitated. Johnny said, "I'm a good shot."

"You're too modest. I hear you're a fine shot," Hart said. "It's a good idea, young Mr. Hardin."

"But you ain't easy in your mind about it."

"Now I don't know what they'll stoop to," Hart said. "It was bad enough that they burned out Miss Rachel. I didn't think they'd burn down the school. And I hoped that Miss Adelaide was right, and they wouldn't hurt a white woman. But now I doubt all of that."

Johnny Hardin looked up from the wreckage. "Begging your pardon, Captain Hart, but you're thinking like a soldier. It won't help you. You need to think like a bushwhacker. Did you ever trail the bushwhackers in the war?"

"Some," Hart said.

"My daddy was a bushwhacker," Johnny said. "Angry all his life, and crazy after he came back from the war. Didn't care what he did. Didn't care who he harmed. Didn't care if he lived or died. The Turners are like that."

"How do you think like a bushwhacker, young Mr. Hardin?"

"You think like a man who don't care that he's going to hell."

—⁓—

THEY ALWAYS HAD fewer children during harvest, but a surprising number, another dozen, straggled into the schoolyard later that day. All of them were jittery and determined. Some of them burst into tears at the sight of the burned-out school, and others sat defiantly on the ground, reading from the makeshift primers and using the dirt as a makeshift slate.

Hart, who usually rode into Cartersville, remained on the Kaltenbach place. When Rachel asked him, "Don't you need to attend to the Bureau's business today?" he replied, "This is the Bureau's business today."

Adelaide sat heavily at the desk in the parlor. She should write to the Missionary Association, at the very least, to ask for more slates and spellers. She should ask her tenants to help her rebuild the school. She should help Frankie, who was in no condition to carry the school alone, no matter how resolute she sounded.

The Turners hated what Adelaide did enough to destroy it. They hated her for doing it. Did they hate her enough to kill her, too?

I don't know if I'm as brave as Emma, she thought.

Her head ached. She thought of the spoiled girl she had once been, who could crawl into bed and insist that someone bring her a dose of laudanum. Now she was a grown woman who had shouldered a burden that made her former friends stand aside as the Ku Klux Klan plotted to murder her.

"Adelaide," Hart said, startling her, even though the hand he laid on her shoulder was gentle. "We have to take this to Everett."

"We won't get any satisfaction," she said. "Not from Sheriff Everett and not from Colonel Turner. And now we know that they strike back when we do."

"I know that as well. But we can't let this go by."

"I've been hearing the stories for months," she said. "The Klan's doing, all over Georgia. The threats and the gunshots for the Union League. The insults and the beatings for the Bureau men. Mr. Ashburn's murder in Columbus. I always thought I'd be spared."

"Adelaide—"

"The Turners are Klansmen, and they're madmen, too. They don't care what they do. It isn't enough to insult and threaten and intimidate. They won't be satisfied until I'm dead."

"You don't have to stay. You could go to Atlanta, where you'd be safe."

"And what about the people here? Would they be safe? Can you guarantee that?"

He was silent. She rose. "This is my home. This is my work. I shall not be moved." She said, "We'll go to Everett, as we went to Cartersville to vote. We shall not be moved."

—⌇—

A FEW DAYS later, after the word had spread, Adelaide's black neighbors and friends assembled at the Kaltenbach place. They were joined by every man or woman who had ever sent a child to Adelaide's school, fifty strong. They clambered into their mule-drawn wagons. Hart and Bailey preceded them on horseback, and they drove in a slow, wary train to Cartersville.

When Adelaide alit from the wagon, she linked arms with Rachel and Hart. Frankie joined them, her arm around Rachel's. Adelaide's supporters massed behind her. They marched down the street in silence, and after Adelaide and her companions entered the saloon, they crowded into it, too, filling it, outnumbering the white men who leaned against the bar.

The black mothers and fathers of Cass County stood in silence. Not even in church were they so quiet. Under their calm, Adelaide could feel their fury burning like the embers of the school.

Everett sat at the table in the corner with the Turner brothers. He pushed aside his glass and demanded, "Who the hell are these people?"

"People whose children go to my school."

"What are they doing here?"

"They're here to protest what happened." She gazed at Everett, taking in all the marks that war and defeat and hatred had carved on his face.

Everett said to Adelaide, "What did you expect, running a school for niggers?" His eyes rested on Frankie.

The silence behind her strengthened her. Is that what you'll say to me after they burn my house to the ground? Is that what you'll say to my son after they shoot me dead?"

She turned her gaze toward Pierce. Pierce turned his face away. She searched Ben's face. The once-familiar blue eyes had become as cold as the pale rider's. They both stared at Frankie, singling her out.

Not a word from the crowd behind her. Their silent resistance was as powerful as a fire's blaze. As powerful as a gun's report.

"I can't help what a man might do if he gets drunk," Everett said.

Very quietly, Adelaide said, "Or punish him after he does it." She turned to look at the immobile faces of the people at her back. She spoke to Everett. "Our day will come, too."

—⌇—

Several days later, when Emma arrived with her charges in tow, she told Adelaide in her matter-of-fact tone, "Someone shoot at us when we come through the woods."

Adelaide asked, "Did you see who it was?"

"No. Don't think they meant to hit us. Just to frighten us."

"Emma!"

"The little'uns cried." She said defiantly, "I wanted to. But I had to stay brave."

"You can't walk through the woods again," Adelaide said. "I'll have young Mr. Hardin drive you home this evening."

Very badly shaken, Adelaide told Hart about the incident. "It's too dangerous for them to come here," she said. "And I don't know how to refuse Emma."

"I do," Hart said.

—⌇—

At midday, he took Emma aside. She was tall enough to look him in the eye. He said, "Miss Emma, you've a very brave young lady. You'd be a fine soldier."

She smiled, just a little.

"A good soldier is brave, but a good soldier is wise, too. He doesn't go heedlessly into danger. He doesn't run into a fight he knows he can't win. Sometimes a good soldier knows to retreat and to lie low. To gather strength to fight again."

She nodded.

"If I were your commander, that's what I'd insist that you do. Retreat for the moment. Lie low and take care of those little ones. And wait."

She considered this.

"Will you do that for me, soldier?" he asked.

"Will I come back to school again, when the fight is over?"

"I'll do my damnedest to assure it," Hart said.

After Emma turned to go, Adelaide said to Hart, "I'm just as worried about Frankie. The Turners wouldn't blink an eye to shoot at her."

"I know."

"This isn't her battle. I want to send her home. I couldn't bear to see her come to harm."

"You love her," Hart said.

Adelaide's eyes misted. "I do." She took out her handkerchief and sighed. "I can just hear the lecture she'll give me. About her duty to the Missionary Association and to Christ's poor. She'll know I'm sending her away."

"You are. You just have to find the right way to say it."

—⁓—

THE NEXT MORNING, after breakfast, Adelaide put her hand on Frankie's arm. "Sit with me on the porch," she said.

The sun rose late enough to take the edge from the summer's heat. The last of the cicadas buzzed, and the crickets, which had a longer life, sang in their silences. The cotton was in full bloom, Adelaide knew. It gave her a pang to think of Rachel's crop, stillborn on the stem.

Adelaide reached for Frankie's hand. "Since the fire we're all in danger."

"I've never shrunk from danger," she said.

"Everyone knows that. But it's one thing for Rachel and me. This is our home. We'll stay here and we'll do whatever we have to. It's another thing for you."

"It's my duty," she said. "As a soldier of light and love."

"It isn't your duty to stay to get shot dead by Ben Turner Junior. I won't have that on my conscience."

"It isn't on your conscience, Adelaide!"

Adelaide said, "I'll say to you what I've said to Rachel. That I'm sick with worry every day. That it haunts my dreams that you might come to harm. That I'd never forgive myself if the men who hate us made a martyr out of you."

"His truth goes marching on," Frankie said bitterly.

"Oh, it does. For us Israelites, too. But I'd rather have it march on while you're safe in a parlor in Ohio than in peril in Cass County."

Frankie said bleakly, "The Association will think that I've failed you."

"Not if I write to the Reverend Ames and tell him that I want you safe."

"Soldiers don't run away."

"Soldiers get sent away all the time. He'll understand, Frankie. I hope the Association sends you home to see your mother and your sister. Before they send you somewhere else you aren't welcome."

"I hate to leave you. And Rachel."

She's wavering, Adelaide thought. "I hate to see you leave," she said.

Frankie stuck out her chin in her old way. "Let me say goodbye to everyone."

"Of course! I'm not pushing you away! Don't linger too long. I want you to get away soon, that's all."

Frankie stared at her hands. "You won't think less of me for agreeing to go?"

"Frankie, you've taught me more about light and love than anyone I know. It breaks my heart to say goodbye to you."

Frankie raised her head and let her eyes rest on Adelaide's face. "All right," she said. "Write to the Reverend Ames in Atlanta."

—◦—

HART SUGGESTED THAT Frankie might want to get off the train quietly, or even travel to Atlanta in secrecy by wagon as Charlie had done. But Frankie, who looked much better now that the Reverend Ames had excused her, told him, "I won't slink away. Let everyone come to the depot to see me off."

They came, the parents of Frankie's scholars, the mothers and fathers who had backed Adelaide in protesting the fire. They lined up outside the depot, waiting their turns to hug Frankie, press her hands, offer their prayers, and wish her well. When the children threw their arms around her, the tears came.

Adelaide and Rachel were the last in line to say goodbye. Adelaide hugged Frankie and said, "God bless you."

When Adelaide released her, Frankie said to Rachel, "What about you?"

Rachel grinned. "You know how I feel about bothering God. Don't have to fuss to show it."

Frankie pulled her handkerchief from her pocket. "Soldiers of light and love," she reminded them, her eyes glistening.

Rachel hugged Frankie hard. "Pistols ready," she whispered in Frankie's ear. Frankie laughed.

Rachel and Adelaide stood together to wave as Frankie boarded the train. Together they watched until she was out of sight.

— Ᵹ —

THAT NIGHT, AFTER Matt was settled and Rachel had gone upstairs to the attic with Eliza, Adelaide sat in the parlor, alone with Hart. She had poured him a glass of brandy, and she had taken a glass for herself, too. She hadn't lit the candles. The fire in the hearth, burning low, was the only light in the room.

"I can't stop thinking about what might happen," she said.

He nodded. "I used to feel that way before every battle."

"Do you feel that way now?"

"Yes."

She could barely see him in the dark. "Do you think about dying?"

He sighed. "I try not to."

"But you do."

"Yes, I do."

"Lewis, do you believe in heaven?"

"I'm an unbeliever, Adelaide. You know that."

"You believe in justice. You believe in the Union. Why not believe in heaven?"

"I believe in making the world a better place than I found it," he said. "Not in a heavenly reward."

"But there's no comfort in that," she said. "Lewis, I am afraid. I am so afraid."

He came to her and took her hands, the only touch he'd allow himself. She wasn't fooled, and a wave of desire washed through her, as destructive as fire.

"Lewis," she whispered, tasting the sweetness of his name. "Your promise to me—"

"I intend to keep it."

"Before I die, I want to lie in your arms." As soldiers said.

He sighed. "That's a cheap thing, and you know it."

"Does it matter, now?"

"Yes," he said.

She put her hand on his cheek and he didn't draw away. She leaned forward and kissed him, the feel of his lips against hers like a burning coal. She tightened her embrace, but he reached for her arms, his touch careful as though he was afraid he would hurt her.

"Adelaide, no."

"You love me."

He pulled back, his hands gently encircling her wrists. "Not like this," he said, and he left her. She listened to his tread on the steps up to his room, and waited until she heard the door close shut.

—⌇—

AFTER FRANKIE LEFT, Rachel missed her. She yearned to go back to her own house, despite the danger. She yearned to walk her fields and try to salvage the cotton crop. At her worst moments, she yearned to leave it all behind for Atlanta. But it was all far away, as distant as Frankie's safety in Ohio.

When the letter came from Daniel Pereira, she felt too weary to open it.

> *Dearest Miss Mannheim,*
>
> *Now that I've returned to Atlanta, and had the leisure to read all my correspondence, I am sick with worry about you in the countryside. I castigate myself that I didn't know.*
> *Write to me immediately to let me know that you're all right. As soon as I hear from you I will rush to see you.*
>
> *Fondest regards,*
> *Daniel Pereira*

Speechifying, she thought. *He had to say "castigate," as though he was much too good just to be ashamed of himself.* She wasn't sure she wanted to see him, even though she enjoyed the notion of his rushing to her, whatever the reason.

He was welcome to visit, she wrote, but it was ticklish for a black man to ride alone through the countryside. She told him that she'd come escorted to meet him at the depot.

The man who got off the train was disheveled. His good frock coat was worn, as though it had seen hard use in the small, troubled places of rural Georgia. He looked tired, not just the pasty look of a bad night's sleep, but the deep weariness of a man taxed too hard for months. *Like a slave at cotton harvest,* she thought, startled. Peril could wear you out, even if you never lifted anything heavier than a pen.

He clasped her hands. "Rachel," he said softly. "You look so sad."

Her eyes stung and she blinked against it. "Been a sad time. You read my letters."

"Your place. And the school."

"Come meet my bodyguard," she said, and led him to the carriage, where Sergeant Bailey sat in the driver's seat, his rifle slung over his shoulder. She had asked Hart, "Why not Johnny? Adelaide can spare Johnny."

"Johnny's a good shot, but he isn't a soldier."

So they were at war again.

Now Sergeant Bailey greeted Pereira. "I hear you've had a bad time in western Georgia," he said.

"I hear you've had a bad time in Cass, too," Pereira said.

Bailey opened the carriage door. "I'll let Miss Rachel tell you."

She had never minded sitting near Adelaide on the narrow carriage seat. She felt differently about being pressed into Pereira. She had never been so close to him before.

As the carriage rattled along the road, he asked her, "How much did you sugarcoat for me?"

"Didn't want you to worry."

The carriage hit a bad spot in the road and threw him against her. He tried to right himself. "Now that I know I'm worried sick. How bad is it?"

"It's very bad in these small places," Rachel said, mocking him.

"Don't fox with me," he said, clearly angry. "Just tell me."

She repeated what she had told him in the letters. The broken windows. The gunshots. The fire. The sheriff's disdain. Jim and Dell's decision to leave, and Frankie's departure for the safety of Atlanta. She had never written about the Turners and the moment at gunpoint.

He listened carefully, never interrupting, encouraging her with a nod or a brief word. She talked as though she were starved for someone to listen.

"How do you remember without writing it down?" she asked as she paused for breath.

"I remember," he said somberly.

It was a physical relief to talk to him, to feel his attention and his well-controlled anger on her behalf. She talked until they neared the Kaltenbach place.

She leaned forward to speak to Bailey. "Don't take us to the main place," she said. "Take us to my house."

"You know it ain't safe to be there," Bailey said.

"What?" Pereira asked.

Rachel shouted at Bailey, "It should be safe enough if you set on the steps to guard us!"

"I promised Captain Hart—"

"Let me talk to Mr. Pereira in private!"

They alit from the carriage, and she pushed open the door. The place smelled close, and dust swirled when she walked across the floor. She turned to yell out the door, "Sergeant Bailey! You set to guard! Not to eavesdrop!" She slammed the door shut.

Pereira asked, "Don't you live in your own house anymore?"

"Adelaide worried so much I decided to stay with her."

"You haven't told me all of it," he chided.

She wondered how he knew. She swallowed. "It were worse than that." The memory made her feel sick, but she told him.

He stared at the neglected room. "You can't stay here!"

"I won't run off."

"Don't be a fool. To risk your life—to risk Eliza's—"

She said stubbornly, "My farm here. My family here. My life here."

"Good God! Come to Atlanta, where I know you'll be safe."

"To Atlanta? What would I do in Atlanta?"

"At least I could take care of you there!"

Surprised, she said, "Take care of me? Why would you want to do such a thing?"

The words came out in a rush. "Because I love you with all my heart."

Plain words, for once. Any fool could understand them. She met his eyes, those changeable hazel eyes that were so odd in a black man's face. She was silent.

He reached to touch her cheek. His fingers were soft. In a tone of tenderness she had never heard from him, he asked, "Rachel, dare I hope that you might love me?"

She couldn't say a word, and she couldn't look into those pleading eyes, either. He leaned forward and kissed her. His lips were very soft against hers, and despite all her doubt, she felt the pleasure of his kiss. If she leaned forward—if she parted her lips—if she tangled her hands in his hair, which would also feel soft—

If she let the spark of desire in her body warm, grow, and flame, would she look at him afterward to regret the ruin she had made?

She pulled away, more abruptly than she intended. He drew back, his expression hurt and ashamed. He released her and said, "I'm sorry."

She wished that she could find the words to explain to him. How could she, when she was unable to explain it to herself?

He rose. "I'll see myself out," he said, and she watched as he left her, closing the door quietly behind him.

17 | READY TO RISE UP

ADELAIDE SAT WITH Rachel on the porch after midday dinner. Even though it was September, cotton harvest was far from over. Their scholars were kept at home, some because of their parents' need for their work in the fields, and others because of their parents' fear. The school was left with only its very first scholars: Matt, Eliza, Charlie's children Josey and Ben, and the littler Hardins, Robbie and Mary.

In the first weeks of panic after the fire, Adelaide had kept all the children indoors. She had been afraid to venture into the yard. She had paced the parlor and stood anxiously by the windows, listening for the sound of men on horseback. But no one could live at that level of alarm, and she had learned to push it toward the back of her mind. There were moments when she forgot to be wary.

But the sound of a man running toward the house brought her to her feet.

It was Charlie. "Good Lord," he said. "Come to see you and you point a rifle at me."

Abashed, both Adelaide and Rachel set the guns down. Rachel said, "The rifle ain't meant for you."

He was still, but anger crackled around him like lightning. Without his customary courtesy, he demanded of Adelaide, "Did you hear what happen? Why I'm here, while the Assembly still sit?"

"Read about it in the *Atlanta Intelligencer* and couldn't believe it," Rachel said.

Charlie's anger boiled over. "Threw us out! All us black men. Said we weren't elected proper." He shouted, as he had never done before in Adelaide's presence. "Said that black men weren't proper voters. All of us! Every black senator, stripped of his seat and sent away!"

"It's a disgrace," Adelaide said quietly.

"More than a disgrace. It's an outrage!" It was the word that Republicans used for the Klan's worst offenses, especially murder.

"Will you be reinstated?" she asked, still quiet.

He glared at her. "All my life I lay low. Try to go roundabout. It get me this. Thrown out! Don't care to go roundabout anymore. I stand up and I raise my voice like a tocsin." He glared at Rachel, too. "Free at last!" He flung his arms wide. "Great God Almighty, free at last, and I don't care who hear it and who know it!"

Her voice heavy with sarcasm, Rachel said, "I believe that black men can still vote for General Grant come this November."

Charlie replied with equal sarcasm, "I do hope so. If the Klan don't burn, shoot, threaten, and frighten every man into staying home. Make him think that if he cower and lay low, he'll be all right."

Adelaide said thoughtfully, "Captain Hart will want the League to remind the local men to vote in November."

"He do better to organize them into a battalion to fight the Turners, and that man Everett!" Charlie balled his hand into a fist. "A disgrace to the office of sheriff, and that crony of Forrest's."

Adelaide had never heard Charlie talk so bitterly.

"You know how bad it is here," Rachel said. "We on the edge of bad trouble, Charlie. I lost my place and we lost the school. Sent Miss Frankie home to keep her out of danger." She wiped her face with her sleeve. "I'd dearly love to give them what they deserve. But none of us would live to tell about it afterwards."

"I won't run and hide from it," Charlie said.

"I shall not be moved," Adelaide said softly, and she met Charlie's eyes, a sister's glance to soften a brother's rage and hurt. "I'd be glad to host a political meeting, if you'd like to address the Republican voters of the county." She glanced at Rachel. "We can have a barbecue. Music. A bit of a frolic, as we missed in July."

Charlie forced himself to calm. "A gathering. A speech. A call to the League men, to the Republican men, to march to the polls on election day. To raise my voice. To stand up."

"Don't make a speech to us about how you'll die trying," Rachel warned him. "Plenty of folks around here glad to oblige you."

— ✍ —

CAPTAIN HART STILL traveled to Cartersville every morning to attend to the Bureau's business. Adelaide worried about him whenever he was out of her sight, and Rachel didn't blame her.

The Turners and the Klan had had no compunction at all about shooting him.

He preferred to ride back to the Kaltenbach place in daylight, and now that the days had begun to shorten, he usually returned before six in the evening. But the hour of six came and went, and there was no reassuring sight of Hart on horseback, or of his greeting as he knocked on the door.

"Do you want supper?" Rachel asked Adelaide.

"You eat, if you want to. I can't."

She paced the parlor and the hallway. She stood at the front windows. Rachel thought of Jim and Dell's boy, warning his mother away from the glass panes. She didn't sit down to her supper. She had caught Adelaide's dread and she couldn't eat, either.

Darkness fell, and still Hart hadn't returned. Adelaide was white with fear. Rachel knew what she feared, and it made her sick to her stomach, too.

They both heard the sound of hooves on the driveway. Adelaide sprang to the window and Rachel reached for her rifle.

The tread of boots sounded on the steps. Adelaide was as pale as paper. Not caring about the danger, Adelaide stared out the window, and when she saw who stood outside, she wept. She pushed Rachel's rifle aside as she reached to unbolt the door.

It was Hart, with a bullet hole in his left coat sleeve. He winced as he pulled off the coat. His shirtsleeve was soaked with blood. Behind him stood Sergeant Bailey.

Adelaide began to scream. "Who was it? Who shot you?"

"Who do you think?" Bailey said.

Hart said, "It looks bad, but it isn't serious. Bailey's all right."

"Captain Hart, set down," Rachel commanded. "Adelaide, make yourself useful. Get a rag and a basin."

Bailey, who suddenly looked a little ashen, began to laugh. "The world turned upside down! Black commanding white."

"You hush and set down, too," Rachel told him. "I'll bring all of us some brandy."

— ✎ —

THE NEXT MORNING, a bandaged Hart rose from the breakfast table. "I'm going to Cartersville."

"You're still hurt," Adelaide said.

"I've been hurt worse."

Now she pleaded, "Don't go."

"I need to see to the Bureau's business."

"See to it from here. Send word that you're here."

He frowned and she said, "I dread that next time their aim may be better."

He sighed. "All right. I need to talk to Mr. Mannheim about this meeting he's planning. I can do that from here. Will that satisfy you?"

That morning, he and Charlie made the front porch into their office. They planned and organized and drafted a notice about the meeting for anyone who might be able to read it. Adelaide listened as she and Sarah helped the children with their lessons. Johnny Hardin lounged nearby, his rifle within reach.

At the sound of hoofbeats in the driveway, Adelaide rose. She said to Sarah, "Get the children into the house. Quickly!"

Rachel stood in the doorway, her gun in hand. Adelaide picked up her own rifle, too. "We have visitors."

"How many?"

"We'll find out."

It was the Turners, accompanied by Everett, and not a man more. All three dismounted to stand at the foot of the steps and stare at the men and women on the porch.

"Why are you here?" Adelaide said, instead of a greeting.

"I've come to arrest that boy Charlie," Everett said. "I hear he's planning to incite a riot."

Charlie stepped forward. "My name is Charles Mannheim. Mr. Charles Mannheim. I ain't inciting a thing. I'm planning on giving a speech."

"Stirring up the niggers in the county," Everett said.

"Talking to men about casting their votes."

Everett spat. "I hear that niggers are coming from all over the county. Armed. Ready to rise up and start a riot."

Charlie said, "We live in a troubled time. Most men go about armed. You're here with your guns. Are you planning on starting a riot?"

Everett advanced onto the steps. "If you come with us, there won't be any trouble."

Adelaide said, "With you? To go where?"

"We'll take him to Cartersville. Lock him up." Everett sneered. "For his own protection."

Rachel snorted. "You take him to Cartersville to let a mob shoot him along the way."

"Damn you, Everett," Hart said. "Do you want to start a massacre here? Do you think the black people of Cass County would let you get away with such a thing?"

Adelaide came forward, spreading her arms wide to act as a barrier between her allies on the porch and her enemies on the steps. In her gracious lady's voice, she said, "Mr. Everett, do you remember when Captain Hart and I called on you? You told us that if we ever set foot on your property again, you'd shoot us."

"What of it?" Everett snarled.

"I'd like to return the favor." Adelaide smiled. "We're all armed here. We can all shoot. If you and your friends step on my property again, if you and your friends bother any of my neighbors, we'll shoot you dead." She was still smiling.

Pierce plucked at Ben's sleeve. "I believe she means it."

"I do mean it," she said, in a voice that belonged at a cotillion. "Why would you doubt me?"

Ben shook his head. "She's crazy," he said to Pierce and to Everett. "Whether she means it or not, she's crazy."

"You don't want to test me," she said sweetly, and she raised her rifle to point it at Everett, then Ben, and finally Pierce, who recoiled at the sight.

"Remember what Loveless told us?" Pierce said. "Don't just pick a fight. Pick one you can win."

Ben stared down the rifle barrel. He said, "Next time we'll be better prepared." But when Pierce tugged on his arm again, he turned, and all three men mounted their horses to ride away.

As the sound of hooves faded, Adelaide said weakly, "I believe I need to sit down." She fell into the nearest chair with the rifle in her lap. "Well, now they've warned us, Charlie. I don't know how they'll do it—whether they'll shoot out your windows or set your house on fire—but they want you to know they're after you."

"They been after me since the day I signed that deed to my land," he said.

"This is different," Hart said. "I'll ask Sergeant Bailey to guard your family and your house. And your neighbors would do well to be on watch at night."

—✺—

ADELAIDE WAS TOO restless to stay in the house. She longed for her old days of rambling, when she put on stout shoes and a ragged dress and let her mind wander along with her feet. For a moment she missed the days before the war, when it was safe for a lone woman to walk in the woods and to enjoy the peace of the countryside.

She couldn't bear it. The house felt like a prison. She would go into the pine grove, where the house was still in sight. She would lean against the rough, scaly bark of a pine tree and take in the sharp smell of its sap. Just for a moment. Then she would go back to the waiting, the fear, and the rifle within arm's reach.

As soon as she slipped into the grove she heard the soft sound of hooves on pine needles and saw the gleam of the white hat. The pale rider reined in his horse, and even though he was armed, he left his hands on the reins. He was a handsome man, despite the patch over the ruined eye.

"Who are you?" she asked, even though she knew.

He said, "A friend to the South."

"A friend to General Forrest," she said.

"Who told you that?"

"The Union Army men know."

"The Bureau man? Your lover?" He spoke softly, without derision.

"My friend, Captain Hart," she said defiantly.

He dismounted. "You're a disgrace," he said. "You demean all Southern womanhood by what you do."

"Do I? Am I the first woman in the South to marry the wrong man, and to fall in love with another?"

"The Turners call you the Bureau's whore," he said, his good eye flickering.

"Which is the betrayal? My marriage, or the Confederacy?"

He said, "I believe you know."

"I hear that you serve a man who murdered black Union soldiers. Is that honor?"

"They weren't soldiers," he said. "They were slaves. They had betrayed their masters. If they lived, we wanted to carry them back into slavery."

"I had slaves. One of them was my own sister. It was a bitter struggle to let her go free. The bitterest struggle was in my own heart."

"You're a traitor," he said softly. "To everything that I hold dear. That you're a lady makes me sick at heart."

She opened her arms wide, palms out. "Will you shoot me? A white woman, who was born a planter's daughter?"

"I should," he said.

She kept her arms spread wide, Christ's pose on the cross. "Will you?"

He stared at her with his good eye. He remounted the horse and sat easily in the saddle. "I will not," he said. The sun shone brightly through a gap in the trees and turned his hair to gold. "But I know men who will." He pulled on the horse's reins and disappeared into the thicket.

—◡—

WHEN SHE TOLD Hart, he was furious that she had exposed herself to danger. He was doubly worried for Charlie, and he joined Bailey as a guard on Charlie's place. If Charlie visited anyone, he never went alone, and even as he worked in his cotton fields, his bodyguards shadowed him. Charlie joked to Adelaide, "Got two new overseers. One from the Freedmen's Bureau and the other from the U. S. Army."

Hart wanted Charlie someplace safe, where he and his family could be easily defended. He tried to persuade Charlie to stay in Adelaide's house. Adelaide sat on the porch while they argued. Charlie said, "If I live like a prisoner, they already beat me. I won't do it."

Adelaide was too edgy to help much with the school, and Rachel couldn't settle to business at the ledger. They sat on the porch together, their nerves torn up, their rifles close at hand.

Adelaide asked Rachel, "Have you heard from Mr. Pereira lately? Or is he still chasing injustice in the countryside?"

"I don't know," Rachel said. "He don't write since his visit."

"Visit?" Adelaide raised an eyebrow. "He came here and you kept it a secret?"

"Not a secret. Just private."

"So it wasn't legal business."

"No," Rachel said. "It were not." She took a deep breath. "He said he was in love with me. Asked me if I love him, too."

"Do you think he'll ask for you?"

Rachel was silent, her expression somber.

Adelaide laughed ruefully. "Do you recall, when William Pereira asked for me, how my mother told me that he would set me up very well?"

"I remember that."

"I learned the hard way that being set up isn't the same thing as being happy. Would you be happy? Or would you be swayed by being set up?"

Rachel's eyes flickered. "I'm not sure."

Adelaide shook her head. "We haven't had much luck with the Pereira men," she said. "Do you know if he's in debt?"

Rachel laughed. "He won't set me up. I know he ain't got a dime." She turned to her sister. "You're in love with Captain Hart, ain't you?"

"Yes, I am."

"He's in love with you. I can see it."

"It doesn't help either of us, as long as I'm still married," Adelaide said.

"I believe Henry would give you a divorce. If you wanted him to."

"I'd have to live with the scandal," Adelaide said ruefully.

Rachel stared at her. Then she began to laugh. She gestured to the rifle that leaned against the leg of Adelaide's chair. "Scandal? Will it matter?"

Adelaide began to laugh and couldn't stop. Tears came to her eyes and she brushed them away with her hand. "I believe I'll find out," she said.

—◦—

A FEW DAYS later, as Adelaide and Rachel and Hart sat at the breakfast table, they were startled by the footsteps in the hall. It was Charlie, who had never come into the house without being invited, or sat at the dining room table without being asked.

At his grim expression the sunlight seemed to dim and the air to grow chill. "What is it?" Adelaide asked.

Charlie's face was set as stone. "A massacre."

Adelaide grabbed Hart's sleeve. "Here?"

"No. In Mitchell County. Place called Camilla."

"What happened?"

Charlie said, "The man who run for Congress as a Republican, a white man, call a political meeting. They plan to meet in Camilla." His gaze rested on Adelaide. He pressed his hands against the edge of the table. "The Democratic Club in the county—we all know they the Klan without a sheet over its head—they buy five cases of repeaters so they can be ready."

Hart's expression, like Charlie's, was flinty. Rachel had turned ashen.

"A crowd make its way to Camilla. Women and children in that crowd. And as they march toward Camilla, the white men gather, too. And when they reach the town, to hear the speech, fifty white men, armed with them repeaters, lie in wait for them."

He regarded his audience. "They fire into the crowd. They shoot to kill, and when the people flee—the women and children along with the men—they pursue them and shoot them, too. They ain't done yet. When the local people appeal to the Bureau, the white men keep on looking for black people. They keep shooting."

Adelaide clutched Hart's hand and Rachel put her hand to her mouth, as if to stifle a cry. Hart was silent.

Adelaide was the first to find her voice. She said, "Mr. Mannheim, perhaps we should postpone our political meeting—"

Charlie said, "That's what they want. To cow us. To keep us so afraid that we act like slaves and not free men."

Hart struggled to speak. "What did you say once, Mr. Mannheim? That it's hard to act free if you're dead?"

"Do it matter? Whether we lay low or speak out? Death down either road. I'd like to die standing up. Die like a man."

Hart said, "Mr. Mannheim, we can stand up to the Turners and Itch gang, a dozen men. But if they bring together enough men to start a massacre, I don't like our chances."

"Outnumbered and outgunned," Adelaide murmured.

"We do different," Charlie said to Hart.

Hart sat up straighter. She could see the soldier waking. "Twenty? Fifty?" he asked.

"Say fifty," Charlie said.

"Then we need more than fifty. Better to have more than a hundred. How many did we gather on the road to Cartersville?"

"Didn't count, but it was in the hundreds."

Hart's expression was stern. He was a commander again. "When we send the word out, tell them it's like election day. Remind them to come armed, and not to travel alone."

Charlie said, "We can do that."

Hart surveyed the lawn, still lush and green in September, and the late-blooming magnolias that lined the driveway. "They'll bring a mob," he said. "We'll meet them with an army."

—◦—

ON THE DAY before Charlie's speech, Rachel watched as the wagons began to arrive. They came in convoys, the women and children bunched together in the middle of the wagon beds, the men alert and armed around them. There were fewer children than there had been at the Independence Day frolic, or even on election day. Frightened parents had kept their children at home. Rachel saw familiar faces from Cass, Floyd, and Chattooga among the strangers.

As they alit, Charlie greeted the newcomers. "Where do you hail from?" he asked a wagonload full of men.

A broad man, dark of skin, met Charlie's welcoming hand. "Come from Mitchell County."

"Mitchell? Anywhere near Camilla?"

The man said derisively, "Anywhere in Mitchell too close to Camilla."

The crowd that had come for last year's Independence Day frolic had been merry. The crowd that had assembled to march to vote in Cartersville had been resolute. This crowd was ashen and grim. They settled quietly on the grassy expanse between the big house and the ruin of the schoolhouse. Even though the wreckage had been cleared away, the smell of char, so like the war, lingered where the foundation had been.

Charlie walked through the temporary encampment, stopping every few steps to talk to people he knew, people who remembered him from his days as a registrar and a candidate. Rachel watched as he greeted the men, pressed the hands of the women, and knelt down to tease the children. Hart and Bailey followed after him, scouting for men who were good shots and who could keep their heads. They were looking for soldiers.

On Independence Day she had moved through the crowd herself, inspiring the women to stand with the men. Today she had no stomach for persuasion and no gift for cheer. She sat on the steps, her chin in her hands, to watch the politician and the soldiers do their work.

When Charlie had answered the last plea for reassurance and let go the last pair of entreating hands, he made his way to the house to sit beside her on the steps, as he had when they were children and slaves together. He looked tired, as he had not when he preached to them about voting and persuaded them to vote for him.

She raised her head. "They all upset. Are you?"

"Don't let myself think about it. Why are you setting here? Lots of people here remember you and would dearly love to talk to you."

She said bitterly, "What can I say to them? That the Klan drove off my tenants and burned me out? Fine thing to tell people who wait in fear, since what happen in Camilla."

He said quietly, "Never had a chance to tell you how sorry I was about your place."

401

"Don't make a bit of difference now."

He rested his hand on her shoulder, as though she were another soul who needed encouragement. "What happen to your place was an outrage," he said. "What happen with Everett, that were an outrage, too. But I never figured you for a cotton farmer."

She shifted, as though the pressure of his hand bothered her. "Don't try to sugarcoat it."

"I don't. I always thought your happiness was in something else. Something you ain't tried yet."

She thought of Daniel Pereira's words and his kiss, and tears rose to her eyes. Was that the happiness she pursued? She still didn't know. She shrugged off Charlie's hand and rose. She walked away swiftly before he could try to hearten her.

— ⌒ —

ADELAIDE HADN'T INTENDED to fall asleep. She wanted to keep watch. But Hart had ordered her upstairs, and she had stretched out on the bed, fully dressed, and had closed her eyes.

She had fallen into a shallow sleep when she heard the first scream, a trickle of fear. Then another. Then the rest, the screaming like a river of fear, and the gunshots.

They were here, and she was ready.

She jumped from the bed and grabbed her rifle. There was more screaming close by, on the landing. Matt ran from his bedroom, crying. "Are the bad men here? Will they kill us?"

Rachel ran down the stairs from the attic, a sobbing Eliza behind her.

Adelaide put her arms around her son and tried to calm him as Rachel tried to soothe Eliza.

Sarah threw open her door. "Let me take the children," she said.

Eliza clutched Rachel's skirt. "Mama!" she screamed.

"Matt, will you be a brave boy and stay with Miss Sarah?" Adelaide asked. She did her best to keep her voice level.

"The bad men," Matt sobbed.

Sarah held out her arms and gathered Matt into them, smoothing his hair, whispering to him. Eliza refused to let go of her mother's dress. "Don't go, Mama," she pleaded.

All of them could hear the cry of anguish from outside, Zeke's voice. "Captain Hart! They're on Charlie's place."

Eliza cried, "They shoot out the windows!" Rachel scooped her daughter into her arms and joined Sarah as they herded the children to safety in Sarah's room.

Adelaide hesitated. She heard Hart's voice in her head: *Don't put yourself in danger. And her own. They won't shoot a white woman who's a planter's daughter.*

I won't, the voice of the one-eyed man whispered inside her head. *But I know men who will.*

Outside, a volley of gunshots rang out, and someone screamed, "Lord, help us! They're killing us!"

Adelaide ran down the steps and out the door. Without waiting for Hart to stop her, or for Rachel to follow her, she ran.

She took the shortcut to Charlie's place, the one that threaded through the woods. The moon was new and cast no light. Behind her, the shots and the screams were like a thunderstorm, loud and indistinct.

Lord, help us, she thought, *unbelievers that we are.*

They had all been fools. They had prepared for a massacre like Camilla. They had forgotten that these men sowed terror at night. She had been a fool, too, thinking that hitting a paper target had prepared her to shoot a living man.

She ran wildly through the trees, too wrought up to listen or watch. She didn't hear the footsteps and she didn't see anyone until she came face to face with Ben Turner.

She raised her rifle, but Ben lunged at her and seized the barrel. She tried to jerk it away from him, but he whacked her left wrist hard with his pistol. In pain, her left hand useless, she couldn't keep her grip on the gun. He wrested it from her and threw it on the ground, out of reach. With a practiced hand, he grabbed her, putting his arm across her neck in a choking hold, and he pressed his pistol to her temple. He whistled, as to a dog, and footsteps responded.

"Look what I found," he said. "Where's the other one? Did you see her?"

Pierce shook his head.

"Do we find her so we can shoot her first, while Miss Adelaide watches? Or should we just shoot Miss Adelaide?" He prodded her with the pistol barrel, as though he expected a reply.

Pierce said nothing. His eyes were fixed on her, and on the contact of the pistol with her temple.

"Sister to a nigger," Ben said. "Wife to a traitor. Bureau whore."

She thought, *Why doesn't he just shoot me?*

"You're a traitor, Adelaide. Do you know what a traitor deserves?" Ben said. He pulled harder on her neck, and she thought she would choke before he shot her. It wasn't enough to terrify. It wasn't even enough to kill. He wanted to torment, too.

She met his brother's eyes. "Pierce," she choked out.

"Ben," he said, his voice also sounding choked.

"Shut up," Ben said.

She continued to gaze at Pierce. Underneath the Klansman and the Confederate, she tried to find the poor lost boy.

"Damn you, Pierce, what's wrong with you?" Ben said.

Pierce hesitated.

Ben said to Adelaide, "Don't say a word about how we used to be children together."

Pierce raised his pistol and walked deliberately towards Ben.

"What in God's name—" Ben said.

Pierce kept coming.

"What are you doing?" Ben asked.

Pierce put his pistol to Ben's temple. "Let her go."

Ben didn't release his grip. "You damn coward," he said.

"Let her go."

"You fool."

"Let Addie go."

Ben dug the gun into Adelaide's temple.

Pierce fired. The sound of the shot reverberated in Adelaide's ears and she screamed, full throat, because Ben slumped and his arms went slack as he fell to the ground. Pierce bent down and shot him again.

Pierce looked up. He fell to his knees and dropped the pistol. In a broken voice, he said, "Addie. He's dead."

There was a commotion in the trees. Pierce didn't look up, but Adelaide started at the sight of Rachel, with her rifle drawn. She took in the scene—the dead man, the stricken man, her sister—and gasped, "Adelaide!"

405

"Ben Turner is dead," Adelaide said.

Pierce didn't move. Rachel trained her rifle on him. "Why didn't you shoot him?"

Adelaide lifted her eyes to her sister's. "I can't."

"I can," Rachel said, her finger on the trigger.

"Would you?"

Rachel didn't move. Adelaide knew that she was thinking of the way Pierce had threatened Eliza.

"Let it go to justice," Adelaide said softly.

"Justice? In this county?"

They could hear rifle fire. "Let him walk into it."

Rachel raised the gun to her shoulder and put her finger on the trigger. It woke Pierce from his stupor. He bolted past her through the trees, toward Charlie's place.

Rachel fired after him, but he didn't stop and didn't fall. The shot must have gone wild. "Let's go after him," Rachel said.

Adelaide grabbed her sister's arm. "No. Wait."

They heard someone shout, "Nigger, are you afraid of ghosts now?" Everett's voice.

There was no sound in response. Adelaide hoped that Charlie and his family were laying low on the floor and not dead.

Everett catcalled. "Come on out, you coward! Show your face, you black bastard! Or I'll set fire to your house with your children inside it."

Adelaide felt Rachel start beside her.

The sound of the melee on the Kaltenbach place drifted toward them like smoke, and a burst of rifle fire came from close by, from the trees behind Charlie's place.

Bullets whistled, cracked, exploded. A voice rose above the sound of rifle fire. "Come to fight us fair, you cowards!" The returning shots rang out, aimed at the raised voice. There was a scream of pain, and a further storm of rifle fire.

The screaming stopped, and so did the shooting.

Adelaide and Rachel waited until they heard the rustle of footsteps, and Rachel pulled her rifle to her shoulder again.

But it was Johnny Hardin. He looked at the dead man and the dropped rifle. He asked, "Are you two all right?"

Rachel nodded.

"Miss Adelaide?"

Adelaide felt dizzy. "Is it over?" she asked Johnny.

"Wait."

They heard one more shot, and then silence.

"It is now," Johnny said. He edged out of the grove. "Follow me," he said, and all of them walked gingerly toward Charlie's house. When they emerged from the trees, they saw Bailey bending over a crumpled form. They came close as he rolled the man over, and all of them bent to look.

It was Pierce Turner.

Bailey rose. "Who else?" he asked Asa and Davey. Davey gestured, and Bailey bent over another crumpled form, this one in a white sheet and a hood stained with blood. He pulled off the hood.

It was Everett. Bailey flung the hood on the ground, leaving it where anyone who passed would trample on it. They found three more men, strangers under their white hoods.

The sounds from her place had begun to fade, like a thunderstorm as it spent itself and traveled away.

Zeke yelled, "Charlie! Becky! It's safe! Come out!"

Charlie staggered from the house. He saw Bailey first and grabbed him in a crushing embrace. "Freddy," he said. "Is you all right?"

Adelaide had never seen Sergeant Frederick Bailey lose his composure, apart from his anger over slavery. Now he fell on his cousin's neck and said in a voice thick with tears, "I am. Are you?"

Rachel dropped her rifle and hugged Charlie. Although she longed to, Adelaide did not. She knelt to gather Charlie's children into her arms, and wept into their soft, dark hair as they clung to her, and she to them.

Bailey said, "Let's go back." Adelaide rose. She felt dizzy and sick. Rachel held out her arm. Suddenly she looked sick, too. They braced each other as they stumbled behind Bailey.

As they approached the house, her fog began to lift. She thought, *Lewis. Oh, Lewis. Lord, help us.*

No gunfire, no screaming, only the lingering whiff of gunpowder. She coughed at the smell of smoke. But the storm had subsided. As they limped through the side yard, a stranger greeted them, grinning widely, holding his rifle high in the air in triumph. "Ran them off! Shot them to pieces and the rest ran off!"

Lewis came running through the crowd, which cheered him and parted as he ran. He held out his arms for her and grabbed her so hard that he nearly knocked the wind out of her. "Adelaide," he said, his breath coming like a sob. She broke into tears as he kissed her with such passion that it would last her until she got to heaven. She thought, *Dear God, let that be a long time from now.*

—⌒—

408

THE MORNING AFTER the battle, the sun was slow to come out. A fine fog settled over the fields. On the grounds outside, a subdued crowd had quietly woken to make coffee and breakfast. Charlie walked through it, his family with him. His neighbors, friends, supporters, and voters let him pass by in silence.

Charlie's face was lined and gray as he surveyed the crowd. He said, "Thought we'd talk about voting today. About supporting the Republicans who stand for our freedom. Always knew we'd have a fight. Didn't think it would be like this."

"Tell us," the murmur rose from the crowd.

"There were men who scourged us. Men who threatened Miss Rachel, because she wanted to work for her increase. Men who threatened Miss Adelaide, because she taught our children to read and write. Men who threatened Captain Hart, because he worked for justice for us. Men who tried to kill me and my family, because I went to Atlanta to speak for all of you."

"Tell us," the crowd murmured, louder this time.

"We have a battle last night. We triumph over them, the men of this county who beset us, and the Ku Klux Klan that aided them."

"Triumphed like Israel over Egypt!" Judah Benjamin called out.

"But men are dead today. Our hearts are heavy." A woman raised her apron to her face and sobbed. Charlie said, "We all grieve with you."

Adelaide saw the lone figure as he hobbled up the driveway. She tugged on Charlie's sleeve. He raised his voice. "Who come here?" he asked.

The figure was bent and walked with the pain of old age. He held out his hands, showing everyone that he was unarmed.

Adelaide nodded. "Let him pass," she called to the men and women who waited for Charlie's words.

He approached the stairs. He removed his hat. Under the unkempt gray hair his eyes were swollen with weeping. "I've come for my sons," Colonel Turner said.

Charlie rose. "They died like they deserved."

"I know," Colonel Turner said.

"They were evil men."

The colonel bowed his head.

A man yelled, "We glad they dead!"

Charlie hesitated. He rested his gaze on Colonel Turner and returned to the crowd. He took a long breath, and the crowd waited to hear what he had to say. "We bury our dead, and we let him bury his." He spoke to Colonel Turner. "I show you where they lie."

He descended the steps to stand beside Colonel Turner. In silence, the crowd parted for them. The two men walked slowly, accommodating the Colonel's gait, until they were out of sight.

— ᔓ —

THE PERIL WAS over, but the fear remained. Since the encampment broke up and the crowd went home, Rachel had slept badly, starting awake every hour, thinking that she smelled gunpowder and heard rifle fire. She should return to her own house to air it and sweep the floor. She should walk her place to see if she could plant another crop of corn. She should decide whether to stay in Cass County or to leave for Atlanta.

She fell heavily onto the striped settee in the parlor in such a haze of fatigue and indecision that she could do nothing at all.

At the rap on the door, she shot from the chair. *It's not done yet,* she thought, her heart still pounding. *Where did I leave my rifle?*

"Rachel!" he called. "Open the door!"

It was Daniel Pereira.

She unlocked the bolt and opened the door. He was travel-stained and haggard as though he'd ridden all night. He gasped, "I heard about your melee. I came as soon as I could. Are you all right?"

She leaned against the doorframe. "I'm in one piece."

The sound of feet running down the stairs startled her. Adelaide called, "Rachel? Who is it?"

She turned. "It's Mr. Pereira. Come to ask after me."

Adelaide's wary expression melted into a smile. "Perhaps you and Mr. Pereira would like to talk in private."

"I believe we would," Rachel answered.

He held out his arm. She remembered leaning on him after her disappointments in Atlanta, the bookseller's snub, Mordecai's refusals to help her. How insignificant they seemed now.

She said, "We talk private in my house."

As they walked, Pereira took in the trampled grass and the ruined magnolias. He turned pale and asked her, "How bad was it?"

She shook her head.

When they were settled in her neglected, dusty front room, before the cold hearth, he took her hands. "You're safe. That's all that matters," he said, his eyes moist with emotion.

She felt curiously detached. Soldier's heart, she thought, remembering Henry's troubled months after the war ended.

"If anything had happened to you—if any harm had come to you—"

She said, "It's over. I'm all right."

He knelt at her feet. "I never want to be parted from you again. I want to be with you, every day, for the rest of my life."

Until death do us part.

He had never looked at her so tenderly or spoken to her so sweetly. "Let me cherish you. Protect you."

He reached to caress her face. He looked into her eyes, his expression full of emotion. He said, "Rachel, dearest Rachel, will you do me the honor of becoming my wife?"

She thought of Lucy's wedding to Adam, recalling how she had yearned for the white dress, the church ceremony, the well-wishers in the pews, smiling and dabbing their eyes in their joy for her. She thought of every hope she had cherished about being free to marry. She thought of every doubt that had haunted her since she knew that Daniel Pereira was in love with her.

She met his eyes and saw the feeling in them. She said slowly, "I'm not sure."

He cupped her face in his hands. She felt his need and desire in the press of his fingers. She gently took his hands away, but she held them in her own as she said, "Once it's done, it can't be undone. It has to be right."

Because it might not be.

"How will you know?" he asked, his voice low.

"I'll have to ponder it."

He said, "Don't wait too long."

"I won't."

He pressed her hands again before he rose to go.

18 | PURSUIT OF HAPPINESS

IT WAS SUNDAY, a day for Israelites and half-Israelites alike to join together for midday dinner. In Henry's dining room, the December light was so low that Rachel had lit candles. Adelaide had joined them in Atlanta, bringing both her son and Captain Hart. The three of them had come from their rooms at the National Hotel, recommended to Hart by the Bureau men in Atlanta.

Henry raised his glass. "I never thought I'd be thanking a man for dishonoring me," he said to Hart. "But I'm grateful you've made it easy for us to divorce."

Across the table from Henry, Hart laughed as he squeezed Adelaide's hand. "To divorce, you should go to Indiana," he said. "It's swift and it's discreet. You go to court, but it doesn't get into the papers."

"How do you know?" Adelaide asked. Her smile was full of indulgence.

Hart laughed. "We freethinkers know these things." His mood had lightened a great deal since he had resigned from the Bureau.

Henry asked, "What are you planning to do, Adelaide? After the wedding in Cincinnati?"

"We're going west," she said. "To California."

Henry was tipsy on the few glasses of wine he'd drunk. He couldn't keep up with Hart, who outweighed him. "I hope you aren't planning to pan for gold," he said.

"No, Mr. Kaltenbach," Hart said, good-humored, also tipsy. "Mr. Levi Strauss has shown the way. An Israelite should make his fortune in commerce."

"Adelaide, what shall you do in California?"

Hart said affectionately, "I'm sure there are unfortunates to help. And injustices to put right. You'll find some, won't you, Adelaide?"

Her cheeks were flushed. She was tipsy too. "Yes, I'm sure I will."

"Have you visited your father, Adelaide?" Henry asked.

"As though he'll miss me!" she said. She sighed. "I'll see him before I go."

Henry spoke to Matt, who was listlessly poking at his food with his fork. "What about you, my boy? What will you do in your new home?"

Matt dropped his eyes to stare at his plate.

Adelaide said, "We'll get you settled, won't we?" She addressed Henry. "You've been good to agree to let him come with us after the divorce."

Henry looked a little sad. "He belongs with you." *He's seen so little of his father, between the war and the move to Atlanta,* Rachel thought. *They scarcely know each other.*

Matt, who had been quiet until now, began to fidget in his chair. Adelaide said, "Matt, honey, be still."

"I want to go home," the boy said.

"We'll be going back to the hotel soon. Why don't you and Eliza play together?"

Matt slid down in his chair until all that showed above the table was his head. He wailed, "No, home! Back home!"

Adelaide rested her hand on her son's head. "Matt, please don't throw a fit at the table. You know it isn't seemly."

Matt slid off his chair and fell to the floor. His sobs floated from beneath the table. "Home," he wailed. "Josey and Ben. Uncle Charlie. Aunt Becky. Home!" His sobs seemed to go through Rachel. Her bones ached in sympathy.

Adelaide apologized. "He's been like this since we left Cass County."

Rachel thought, *We all have.*

"Let me," Hart said. He crawled under the table. "Matt," his voice came softly from the floor. "Matt, it's all right. You're safe now. You're home, with your mother, and with me."

Softer sobs. "Home," Hart said, very softly. "With us."

Hiccups. "Can I visit Josey and Ben?"

"Your friends? Of course. You can write to them, wherever you go, and come back to visit."

Snuffles. Hart said, "Will you come out? Sit with all of us, just for a moment?"

Matt's head emerged and Hart followed him, crawling on his hands and knees. Matt clambered into his chair. "Mama, can we visit?"

Hart tousled Matt's dark, curly hair. He said to Adelaide, "Don't fib to him."

Adelaide put her arms around her tear-stained son. "We'll visit."

"When?"

"Don't press your luck, my boy," said the captain, smiling at Matt, and Matt wiped his face with his sleeve.

Rachel glanced at Henry, wondering how he felt that Hart was more of a father to his son than he was.

"Miss Mannheim," Hart asked her, "what will you do, now that things are settled in Cass County?"

She hadn't drunk as much as the rest, but she felt heavy-lidded and heavy-hearted. Part of her soul was still in Cass County, buried in the ashes of her place, lost with her mule, burdened with the fear of peril and death. Cass County would never be home for her again. She tried to smile and sound interested. "I'll stay in Atlanta," she said, her refrain these days. "I haven't decided what to do yet."

Henry asked Hart, "What is the news from Cass County, now that the local ruffians are laid to rest?"

"The Bureau is closing its office," Hart said. He snorted. "Not that the work is done, even though Mr. Mannheim won the legislative seat."

"Did I hear right?" Henry asked. "That Charlie Mannheim struck a deal with Colonel Turner?"

"More than that. Mr. Mannheim supported Colonel Turner in the special election for sheriff. Turner won that election with the votes of black men. And Turner persuaded the Board of Supervisors to appoint a superintendent for black schools in Cass County. They chose the Reverend Judah Benjamin."

"With Mr. Mannheim's help, no doubt."

"No doubt at all," Hart said.

"Will it keep the peace, do you think?"

"So much blood was spilled before we came to that," Hart said. "I'm not a praying man, but I like what Mr. Mannheim says. That I hope and pray so."

—⁓—

AFTER THEY LEFT, Rachel felt weary. The accumulated weeks of worry and confusion weighed on her; all she wanted was to lie on her bed and sleep.

Like Adelaide, she was still dazed to have left Cass County. She had accepted Henry's offer of the spare bedroom. She would have preferred to lodge elsewhere, but it reassured Eliza to stay with her father. Rachel could deny herself, but she didn't have the heart to deny her daughter, who had nightmares of her own.

It was strange and comfortable at once to sleep in that pretty room with Eliza and to eat her meals in Henry's company. It was strange and not at all comfortable to think that Daniel Pereira worked and lived just down the street.

Since she had come to Atlanta, Henry hadn't pressed her for any further intimacy than sleeping in his guest room and eating at his table. He knew that she had come to him in despair, and he thought too highly of her to presume on her lowest moment.

He was still the kindest man she knew.

Eliza sat at the table, trying to stay awake. Her father said, "Do you want to lie down to rest?"

"No."

"I'll read to you first."

"All right."

"What should I read to you?"

"The big bad wolf!"

Henry said to Rachel, "I'd think she had enough of violence back in Cass County."

"She likes to hear the part where the huntsman shoots the wolf," she said.

"A bad wolf, and the hunter fight him like we fight the Klan, and the hunter win!" Eliza crowed.

Henry sighed. He lifted Eliza onto his lap and took the book from Rachel's hands. He opened the book and began to read. At the sound of her father's voice, Eliza's eyes fluttered shut, and her head fell against his chest.

"Let me lay you down to rest," Henry said softly to his daughter.

Half awake, Eliza put her arms around her father's neck. "Daddy," she said sleepily.

He kissed the top of her head as he picked her up. "Liebchen," he murmured.

Rachel followed him as he carried Eliza to bed, and watched from the doorway as he tucked her in. He kissed Eliza again and came to stand beside Rachel. She moved close enough to touch him with her hip. He curled his arm around her waist, and she laid her head on his shoulder. Twined together, they watched their sleeping child.

This was the bond that would hold them forever. This was the only vow they could swear. Not money. Not marriage. Eliza.

—◡—

SHE COULDN'T PUT off her visit to Pereira any longer, and a few days later, she left Henry's rooms on a cool, cloudy morning. She dawdled in walking the short distance to Pereira's office. She slipped behind Wheat Street where she would find the washwomen.

Hattie and Keziah labored at their washtubs and Anna Victoria stood by, a basketful of lengths over her arm, reminding them not to splash.

Hattie waved a dripping arm and said to Rachel, "Heard you come to Atlanta to settle."

Rachel thought irritably, once again, that Sherman Town was too much like the countryside, where everyone knew your business. "Who tell you?" she said.

Anna Victoria said, "I did. Saw you in Mr. Kaltenbach's shop. Wondered if you had gone to work for him."

Embarrassed, Rachel fumbled for an answer. "I served the family before the war. They always been kind to me."

Hattie said gently, "Some people—not us, we ain't like that, but some people—might think it weren't seemly for you to stay alone in the house with him."

Now that ain't your business! Rachel thought. She managed a little heat. "Just for a little while. Once I determine what I plan to do, I find a place for myself."

Hattie said, "If you want a place with a good Christian family, or a spot in a boarding house—"

Rachel thought of Mrs. Simpson and her house full of Atlanta's scorched, scarred, lost, and mended things. "When I do, I ask you," she said firmly.

Keziah said cheerfully, "Will we see you in church this Sunday? Bethel, down the street? The Reverend Peck preach a fine sermon against sin."

"I'll consider it," she said, trying to stay polite, but she fumed. Busybodies! Tell me not to live in Henry's house and insist I go to their church to hear the minister talk about sinners! "Excuse me, I have some business on Wheat Street," she said, and she turned, unable to postpone her task any longer.

She stood before the damaged door, still hesitating, until she was ashamed of herself. She was acting more the child than Eliza. She pushed open the door.

Pereira was at his desk, pen in hand, his eyes a little unfocused from staring at the page too long. She wished she felt light enough to tease him about needing spectacles.

He stood when he noticed her. "Miss Mannheim."

"Mr. Pereira," she said, as though he had never spoken words of love to her.

"What brings you to Atlanta?"

"I stay here now."

Softly, regretfully, he said, "You didn't write to me to tell me."

She felt a stab of shame. "Didn't write to anyone, not even my own father. Just came."

"Are you well?"

"I think so," she said.

He reached for her hand and she was struck anew by the contrast between his soft, light brown skin and her own. "May I call on you?"

To give him his answer, he meant. She didn't press his hand, but she didn't pull away, either. "Not just yet," she said. "Soon."

—⁓—

RACHEL LEFT ELIZA in the shop under the watchful eyes of Henry and Marcus Porter, telling Henry that she planned to make a call. He waved from the shop door as she walked down Wheat Street in the direction of Whitehall.

The pretty housemaid showed Rachel into the red velvet parlor, where Madame Toussaint awaited her and invited her to sit. "How bad were it in the countryside?" she asked.

"Did you hear?"

"Don't have to hear. Atlanta full of people who have a rough time in the countryside."

"Yes," Rachel said, and she left it at that.

"What bring you to me? Is it buying property? That lot on Houston Street?"

"No. Private business."

Madame Toussaint's eyes gleamed. "Who asked to marry you?"

She wondered if Madame Toussaint knew and was too discreet to say so. "Mr. Pereira."

Her eyes flickered. So she probably did know. "Sound like something a woman would welcome."

She hadn't realized she'd been keeping in such anger. "He have such an idea of the life he want! For me to stand by his side while he do great things."

Madame Toussaint nodded.

Rachel said, "Back in Charleston, where his mama hate me, and where his bright-skinned friends whisper that I used to be a slave." She took a deep breath. "Not sure I got free to do that."

Madame Toussaint said, "You free in ways most black folks aren't."

"How? Free is free."

"You got money. That makes for a different kind of free."

Rachel let herself feel her confusion. She shook her head. In Cass County she had stood up for freedom. Nearly died for freedom. It was all of a piece, as Charlie had said. Free to work. Free to marry. Free to fight. Free to love. Free to pursue her happiness, in a way she hadn't thought of yet. Freedom was more than being free to marry.

"Something else bother you," Madame Toussaint said.

Rachel retorted, "Don't you know? Since everyone in Atlanta know all about me without my say-so?"

"What I know, I don't tell," Madame Toussaint said. "But I'd guess there's someone else you care for."

It was a relief to admit to it. "He ain't suited, either."

"Is he married?"

"Wouldn't matter if he were. He's a white man," she said.

"Wouldn't be the first time."

"What should I do? Between 'don't-want-to' and 'can't.'"

Madame Toussaint met her eyes. Rachel couldn't hold that gaze. She dropped her eyes to her boots, caked with Atlanta's mud, the red diluted with the city's dirt. Madame Toussaint said softly, "Believe me, I know."

Rachel didn't ask why. Instead, she raised her head to ask, "What's your given name?"

She was quick to answer. "Madame Toussaint. The name I give myself."

"That weren't the name you begin your life with."

A little vinegar crept into Madame Toussaint's voice. "My slave name? My whore's name?" she asked. "That ain't my name anymore."

Rachel insisted. "What were it? Who were you?"

After a long pause, Madame Toussaint gave Rachel a piercing look. "If you tell anyone—"

"I won't."

"You can't tell a soul."

She could keep a secret. "I promise I won't."

"I was called Bessie Truitt."

Rachel squinted. She said, "I can see it."

Madame Toussaint said, "Don't you have some business to attend to? A marriage proposal to say no to?"

Rachel rose. She felt a peculiar lightness, as though she had laid a burden down, as the old slavery song had it. "I do, Miss Bessie. I do."

When the door closed behind her, Rachel paused, taking in the smell of Atlanta, mud and manure and machine oil, thickly twined with the fragrance of magnolias.

A different kind of free. A house of her own. A living of her own. A life of her own.

A new name. Coldbrook. It was English for "Kaltenbach," a way to acknowledge her tie to Henry without being bound by it. She tasted it on her tongue. Rachel Coldbrook.

She ran easily down the steps. On the sidewalk she turned toward Wheat Street. She belonged to Atlanta now. She had business to attend to, and she was in a hurry.

BEFORE YOU GO...

IF YOU ENJOYED this book, please let other readers know by leaving a brief review at Amazon, Amazon UK, or Goodreads. Just a few lines will help other readers find the book and make an informed decision about it. It's the electronic version of telling your friends or your book club (although that's great too). Thank you so much!

If you enjoyed this novel, you may like my other books as well. Visit my website for more information about me and my books.

WWW.SABRAWALDFOGEL.COM/BOOKS/

Want to stay in touch? Sign up to hear about new books and to get special glimpses at the "history behind the story." And as a thank you, you'll receive a link to my free story, "Yemaya". When a slaving ship meets an avenging African mermaid, what happens? Find out.

WWW.SABRAWALDFOGEL.COM/CONTACT/

Historical Note

THE CIVIL RIGHTS movement of the 1960s has often been called the Second Reconstruction. It would be equally true to say that Reconstruction was the first Civil Rights movement. In the 1860s, as in the 1960s, the act of standing up for freedom gave many people—black as well as white, women as well as men—a new perspective on the meaning of freedom in every aspect of their lives.

In the public realms of work, education, and politics, three institutions shaped the experience of former slaves, in Georgia as well as across the post-Civil War South. They were the agencies of the Freedmen's Bureau, the schools of the American Missionary Association, and the Republican Party, both in its official capacity and through its allied social organization, the secret society of the Union League.

Work and the Freedmen's Bureau

THE FREEDMEN'S BUREAU came to Georgia immediately after the war ended, and by the summer of 1865, offices had been established both in Georgia's larger cities and in its smaller rural places. The Bureau was broadly charged with helping former slaves, but one of its most important tasks was to address the problem of labor in a non-slave society. Bureau agents spent much of their time either drafting or enforcing labor contracts between cash-poor white farmers and free black laborers. As in this novel, the employer-worker relationship was greatly complicated by the lack of capital in the South. The tenancy and sharecropping system, so rife with abuse after the end of Reconstruction, was a way to pay workers in an economy that had neither capital nor cash.

In Georgia, some of the agents were natives, but many were Union officers who had just mustered out. The agents had a difficult relationship with the white communities where they lived and worked. Most white planters and farmers despised the Bureau. The Bureau agents were socially isolated, and in the worst cases, they were met with hostility and threat, just like the former slaves whose lives they struggled to improve. While it was rare for a Bureau agent to be allowed the opportunity to fall in love with a local woman, a friendly reception from the locals, scalawags or Republicans, must have gladdened a Bureau agent's heart.

Education and the American Missionary Association

WHILE THE BUREAU did establish some schools, the majority of schools for former slaves were the work of religious missionary groups. By far the largest and best organized was run by the Congregationalists, whose American Missionary Association (AMA) already had a conversion network in Asia, Africa, and on the American frontier. Starting in 1863, the AMA began to recruit and send teachers into the war-torn South.

The AMA had a stronger presence in Virginia, Mississippi, and Louisiana than in Georgia, but by the end of the war, they had established a school in Atlanta. The Atlanta teachers were white, but black teachers went all over the South under the AMA's auspices. Black teachers were often sent to the smallest, most isolated, and most dangerous places, where they set up schools and ran them in the face of local hostility, intimidation, and violence. They were "soldiers of light and love, armed only with slates and spellers and zeal for helping "Christ's poor." Their courage was all the more admirable for it. Like the Bureau agents, they overworked themselves under conditions of social ostracism and daily fear.

Frankie Williamson, the black AMA teacher in this book, is a composite of four remarkable women, all born free before the Civil War, all staunch abolitionists in the 1850s, all graduates of Oberlin College, and all "soldiers of light and love" for the AMA between 1864 and 1870. Sara Stanley, who was born a free woman in North Carolina, provided Frankie's background. Her classmates Blanche and Frankie Harris, Michigan natives, provided the strong bond between sisters (not to mention Miss

Williamson's first name!). Clara Duncan, another dedicated AMA teacher, provided Mollie Williamson's reaction to the strain of life in Bibb County: she had a nervous collapse and had to be escorted home to Ohio to recover.

The Republican Party and the Union League

THE ACTS OF Reconstruction, which offered black men their first chance to vote as free men, were passed by a Republican Congress in 1867, and on the grassroots level, ensuring political participation became the charge of the party of Lincoln. Its daily activities received strong support from the Union League.

The Union League, also called the Loyal League, had its start during the Civil War as a fraternal organization to support the Union. After the war, it spread to the South, where it rapidly became associated with the Republican Party and its platform of equality for former slaves; its membership became predominantly black. In Georgia, as elsewhere, the League was concerned with grassroots organization, voter registration, and fair participation in elections. In the most conflicted parts of Georgia, like Augusta, just over the border from South Carolina, or in southwest Georgia, the river delta that was home to large cotton plantations, League members banded together to fight intimidation and violence.

Black men voted for the first time in 1867 in Georgia, as in other parts of the South, and voter registration was conducted under the dual auspices of the Army and the Freedmen's Bureau. The black registrars, who were chosen by the Army's white appointees, tended to be men of substance, either as successful artisans or farmers, and men of good reputation—a number of them were ministers. For the registrars, as for the registrants, their involvement in voter registration was the first time that these black men had ventured into public life, and the first time that most white people had seen them conduct themselves with official dignity.

While black men were the only ones to cast ballots, black women were deeply involved in the political process. They had strong opinions about assuring black equality and dignity, and they lobbied their male relatives into casting a vote that represented the entire household. They attended rallies, listened to speeches, and accompanied men to the polls. When violence threatened black voters, women were in danger, too.

The seeds of Reconstruction's demise in Georgia—of the Democratic Party's "redemption" of Georgia's government—were sown early. In 1867, the Ku Klux Klan was organized in Atlanta, and by the election of 1868, the Klan had captured the hearts and minds of disgruntled and violent whites in the countryside. Angry Confederates were glad to support the local "regulators" and "Democratic Young Men's Clubs" that rode at night to terrorize black voters and their families. In some parts of Georgia, the elections of 1868—for the state legislature in April, and for the presidency in November—were battles between the Union League and the Klan.

By 1872, Georgia had been "redeemed," and the social experiment of Reconstruction was over. The experience of continuing the struggle for freedom was a heady one for all of the men and women who stood up for equality and justice. Even though the society they hoped to build took a century to realize—and a fight that continues to the present day—they were forever changed by their efforts to achieve it.

Sources

ON THE FREEDMEN'S Bureau in Georgia, one of the best sources is Paul Cimbala, *Under the Guardianship of the Nation: The Freedmen's Bureau and the Reconstruction of Georgia,* 1865-1870 (Athens, Georgia: University of Georgia Press, 2003).

On the black teachers in Georgia, see Jacqueline Jones, *Soldiers of Light and Love: Northern Teachers and Georgia Blacks,* 1865-1873 (Athens, Georgia: University of Georgia Press, 2004).

The best source on Georgia's black politicians is Edmund Drago's *Black Politicians and Reconstruction in Georgia: A Splendid Failure* (Athens, Georgia: University of Georgia Press, 1992).

On the post-Civil War Ku Klux Klan, see Allen Trelease, *White Terror: The Ku Klux Klan Conspiracy and Southern Reconstruction* (Baton Rouge, Louisiana: Louisiana State University Press, 1995).

Author Biography

S ABRA WALDFOGEL GREW up far from the South in Minneapolis, Minnesota. She studied history at Harvard University
and got a Ph.D. in American History from the University of
Minnesota. Since then, she has been fascinated by the drama of
slavery and freedom in the decades before and after the Civil War.

Her first novel, *Sister of Mine*, published by Lake Union, was
named the winner of the 2017 Audiobook Publisher's Association
Audie Award for fiction.